FINDING
— THE —
BUDDHA

To Mark Wladika,
wherever he may be.

I would like to thank those who helped me with this book and read the manuscript in its various forms: Bernadette Almanzar, Margaret Bertels, Jeffrey Candelaria, Deb Crosby, Rebecca Eagle Ferguson, Elke Zinnert, Kimberly and Duke Pennell, Meg Dendler, and, most especially, Kate Boulton for her time, patience, and wisdom.

FINDING
— THE —
BUDDHA

A DARK STORY OF GENIUS, FRIENDSHIP, AND STAND-UP COMEDY

EDDIE TAFOYA

P
Pen-L Publishing
Fayetteville, Arkansas
Pen-L.com

"If you meet the Buddha on the road, kill him."
ZEN MASTER LINJI

"The kingdom of God is in the midst of you."
LUKE 17:21

PROLOGUE

Miriam Torreon caught her breath and pressed her fingers to her sternum, as if trying to slow her heart rate with her hand. She slid a key card through the electronic lock and pushed on the steel panel too quickly. When it didn't open, the psychiatric nurse repeated the process. This time the door swung wide, its doorknob ramming into the cinder block wall. What she found in that room that Sunday morning continues to confound her. The pink linen was folded and laid at the edge of the mattress, as if the last person in there were a house guest wanting to leave the place impeccable for his hosts. Two vinyl restraints were pulled taut and tied in a square knot. All wrinkles in the bottom sheet and pillow cases had been smoothed away. An IV hose hung around its stand, the loops held in place by a graying strip of medical tape. Hints of isopropyl alcohol, rose water, and patchouli lingered in the air. She drew up the shade, inspected the window frame for evidence of force, and scanned the grounds of the Northern New Mexico Behavioral Health Center. Everything remained in order: enamel-painted chairs resting against a metal table, ready to be sprayed off with a garden hose, a newspaper broadsheet flapping against the chain-link, the gardener raking mulch in the lily beds.

Some thirty minutes earlier, Torreon, the graveyard supervisor, had stepped into that room where, for two days, Mark Wladika lay sedated. She had felt his forehead with her hand, instinctively checking his temperature as though he were her own sick child. She slid a blood pressure cuff around his bicep, punched a button on a monitor mounted near the bedside, and waited for the sleeve to inflate. She checked his body temperature and blood oxygen level. She noted on his chart that the patient was stable, that there had been little change in three hours, and as ordered by the attending physician, she administered another 70 milligrams of Librium and 30 milligrams of Abilify, a partial dopamine agonist. She gave the room one last glance, made sure the door latched, chatted with an orderly in the hallway, and returned to her work station downstairs.

Now, as she stood before the empty bed, she took a long insuck of breath. She imagined events that could have lead to this moment. She feared for her job and, thereby, the well-being of her six-year-old son, who had eleven days prior been diagnosed with a learning disability. She wondered what would happen if she were blamed for Wladika's disappearance. She turned, shut off the light, and let the cell door close behind her. She made her way through the hallway and down the stairs, as if unaware of the emergency. Back at her desk, she jotted the time down on her calendar blotter, telephoned the San Miguel County Sheriff's Office, and reported the missing patient before calling her boss at home.

Three months earlier, Wladika was considered the nation's fastest-rising comedian and on the brink of superstardom, a surefire heir to

Richard Pryor and George Carlin, and a showman whose skills, genius, and refinements left the top names in the business both awed and exhausted. Today, Wladika's whereabouts and disappearance remain a mystery.

The following, compiled between February 2010 and April 2011, is drawn from a series of interviews with those best acquainted with Wladika and his contributions. They have been edited for grammar, style, fluidity, and clarity. Some of the names have been changed.

JACK

Stephen Paulson—jackass that he was—pressed the fingers of his free hand together like a fin. He pointed his whole damned arm into the onrush of air, allowing the appendage to rise and dip, as though imagining it were a dolphin racing through choppy water. Just a few minutes earlier, the twenty-eight-year-old psychology student had climbed onto the back bumper of a seafood delivery truck to hitch a ride.

What a dope.

The goon crooked his arm through the steel handle bolted onto the sidewall and braced himself as the sixteen-footer lurched up the onramp. Once on the freeway, Paulson waved at the driver of a vintage Ford Mustang coming up behind him. The motorist tapped his horn, downshifted, cut to the next lane, and raced up Interstate 25, going north toward Santa Fe.

The young man repositioned his feet on the textured metal and swung his body out to look at the road up ahead. He seemed to enjoy both the thrill of the ride and the way the wind pressed his curls against his scalp. As he readjusted his stance, his right foot slipped. He caught himself, held the grip with both hands, and leaned out again, invigorated by the excitement. Maybe he was just having fun. Maybe he was late getting home. Or maybe, just maybe, he was pretending to fly.

That night—or, really, that morning—I drove behind him, returning home from my job at a greasy burrito stand on Central Avenue in a part of Albuquerque called EDo, short for East Downtown. My ditzy boss was slow counting the cash register money and zipping it up in a canvas bank bag, so when I dropped my apron in the laundry barrel, waved goodbye to her and the airheaded cashier, and climbed into my mother's Corolla, I was tapped out. Who wouldn't be after six hours of high school and eight hours of slogging over-seasoned, high-fat beef into deep-fried taco shells for the street slugs trolling along Albuquerque's main drag? Tell me that won't take the wind out of your sails. I double dare you.

My T-shirt was splattered with chile and reeked of taco spices and trans fat-laced grease, and I felt about as sharp as a bowling ball. Still, once I stuck the key in that ignition, I did everything by the book, just like that anal-retentive driving instructor had told me to a few months before. I checked my mirrors and looked over the space behind me twice before releasing the emergency brake and easing out the clutch. I drove out of the parking lot, turned up Central, and down toward the highway. At the one-way, I looked in both directions, making doubly sure some drunk wasn't coming against traffic. With all the psychos out, you never know. At the Martin Luther King Avenue stop sign, I counted to three, just like Mom always insisted. I followed the rules to the letter.

On the interstate, vehicles sped by: an eighteen-wheeler, a station wagon, a motorcycle, and some sports car. Then the Seattle Fish Company truck with plenty of room behind it and that idiot riding its bumper, holding on with one hand, leaning out, and smiling into the wind. I zoomed up the incline and shifted into fifth gear. That's when Paulson, in his beatnik glasses and denim jacket, stuck his arm out like a wing, that imbecile acting like a twelve-year-old going for a joyride on the back of his grandpa's camper.

Like I said, what a dope.

As the rider played airfoil with his hand and reset his feet, I tried to change lanes. Just then, the truck driver swerved to avoid a corrugated carton in the middle of his lane. Paulson's foot must have slipped again because he lost his grip. I turned back from checking my blind spot just as the man's arm shot out and his hand clutched at empty air, all desperate-like. His head crashed into my windshield. It didn't bounce. It slammed into the glass, splattered like a cantaloupe on concrete, and slid down, leaving a pie-sized contusion of shattered glass, streaks of blood, and grated skin.

The car behind me swerved to the other lane, and the refrigerated transport full of oysters and salmon or whatever continued northward, maybe to Taos, Walsenburg, Colorado Springs, or Denver, the driver oblivious to the destruction he just played a major role in. Paulson clawed at the hood of the car, his mouth open, blood gushing from his nose and ear, and one green eye turned up, asking how I could be so cruel. Like I planned all this. Like you don't take a major risk when you do something so damned boneheaded. By the time I got the car to the shoulder, red and blue lights flashed behind me. Within thirty seconds, another squad car arrived, and a minute after that, another. In the distance, a siren wailed.

The first officer, the witness, was a sergeant named Roman—this guy with a lantern jaw and blond crew cut, who two hours before ordered diet sodas at my drive-up window. He stepped over, asked if I was all right, and I said I wasn't the one who just got plowed into. He asked my name, and I said John David Marison, and then he asked if my car was drivable. Before I answered, he stepped out to the roadway and motioned for a Buick to slow down. He checked over his shoulder, directed the ambulance to the body, and sent the sedan on its way.

While the rescue team worked, I planted myself on the concrete safety pylon. Drunk drivers whizzed by at about a hundred thousand miles an hour, and this gibbous moon dangled over the West Mesa. The Russian olives and honeysuckle were in bloom, lending a fairy tale fragrance to the Albuquerque night. Downtown, the Wells Fargo building was alive with green lights that shot from its lawn up the length of its twenty-one stories. Lights sparkled along the western hills. The night held this certain tranquil beauty—if you could ignore the labored breathing of the dying man in the middle of the road.

Just after three a.m., the EMTs inserted Paulson into the ambulance, the legs of the gurney collapsing easily and automatically, the bed sliding smoothly into its slot. One of the medics, a short and stout woman, slammed the door, tested the latch, and pounded twice just below the window with the flat of her hand. With emergency lights still flickering, the GMC rolled toward Lomas Boulevard in no particular hurry.

Roman and another cop exchanged a few words before the sergeant nodded, glanced up the Interstate, and then over to downtown—at the glowing pyramid atop the Albuquerque Plaza Tower, at the illuminated windows across the eighth floor of the Lovelace Medical Center. He let a car pass, stepped over to me, and tucked his cap under his arm. All his initial hardness was gone. He asked my age, and I said I'd be seventeen in a month and that I worked the late shift at the Pup 'n Taco most weekend nights. He said oh, that's where he'd seen me. An old Ford pickup rattled by, some geezer at the wheel. After he took my statement, Roman clicked his pen, closed his metal binder, coughed into a fist, and said Paulson was apparently high on something and had two marijuana cigarettes—I guess cops aren't allowed to say "joints"—in his jacket pocket. That his nose bone shot up into his brain. That he never had a chance.

I covered my face and stepped back, all dramatic-like. Roman said something like "We know it wasn't your fault" before giving a one-pump nod, replacing his cap, tugging it into place, and quickstepping back to his slick top. I turned, braced myself against the concrete barrier, and held my body steady with both arms. I didn't want him to see me laughing.

Once back in my bedroom, I couldn't sleep. Diffused morning light turned the curtains blue-gray. I pulled the bedspread under my chin and turned on my side as the room brightened. I smiled, thinking of Paulson's last minutes. The events reassembled themselves in my head until they became something like a film loop. The frayed sleeve of his Levi jacket flapping as a car passed him and his seafood truck. The blue stars on the heels of his basketball shoes shifting as he reset himself on the dimpled chrome. The rocking and fishtailing of that clumsy diesel-powered transport. The squeak and wisp of smoke from the back tire as it lost and regained traction while avoiding a harmless piece of litter. The horror on Paulson's face as he flew toward me. The way he clutched, squeezed, and bent the windshield wiper, digging his bleeding fingernails into the white paint of the Corolla's hood. How he summoned his last particles of strength up from his gut just to stay alive a few extra seconds.

The events replayed themselves again, and I giggled. Soon, the images became more vibrant. The paramedics lifting the body on the stretcher. The hinges and swivels of the gurney clanking, clicking, and humming as the ambulance cavity swallowed that shattered body. The medic pounding the back door, telling the driver to go.

A chuckle rose through my chest. Then another and another. I stuck my pillow to my face to muffle the guffaws so I wouldn't wake Mom.

Before that, I never considered what it would be like to extinguish a life, to participate so fully in catapulting another person into oblivion. I knew right then, while lying in that bed after a sleepless night, that I could do it again. Although I was just a kid, there was already one person I was sure the world would be better without. I knew I could get rid of her, even if it meant spending the rest of my life in prison. I wasn't sure I would, but at that moment, I knew I was capable. That made me laugh. So I switched on the radio next to my bed and lay there, listening to the blending voices and harmonized electric guitar licks that rose like smoke through the thinning darkness. The singer crooned, going on about African dogs barking in the night, about how he looks up at Mount Kilimanjaro and gets all freaked because visiting the Dark Continent has unleashed some demon from deep in his gut.

And I wondered what it would be like to spend my life trying to get away with murder.

Today, the memory of killing Stephen Paulson remains as fresh as it was that morning during the first month of my junior year of high school, and whenever I think about it, I have to choke back giggles. Today, there is only one person I am sure I want to kill.

His name is Mark Wladika.

FIRECRACKER

I absolutely adore the *David*. You know, by Michelangelo? Absolutely adore it. Even you breeders do, don't you? If that stud ever decided to stride out of that marble into full flesh—my, my, my, what this sissy boy could teach him. Just give me a little wine, a little olive oil, and a little fairy dust, and he'll be whipping that slingshot and flinging those rocks in a way that would make mean ol' Goliath want to rise from the dead and come over and play. With or without his head. That little shepherd is the total package, you know? Big hands, big feet, abdominals that are literally rock-hard. With just that whisper of worry on that precious Greek face so that you just want to kiss the sweat off his skin—then make him sweat more.

That boy David is fine as desert sand, but that's not the only thing about him that spears me straight through to my gut. Certainly not. That particular block of granite is the crème de la crème, the top of the heap, the star on the tree, the Mount Everest of Western art. Just tell me it's not. I saw him once, you know. We were in Florence, Jonnie and me. It's already been four full years. Once my eyes fell on that statue, I actually wept. Right there in the Accademia di Belle Arti, in front of God and everybody. I didn't care. Really, I didn't. I sauntered right up, not six feet from the Pride of Bethlehem himself, and before I could think, I covered my mouth with my hands and bawled like the bride's drunken mother. Some oversized, sixty-year-old, ginger-headed Fraulein held out a Kleenex, and I took it, and I dabbed my eyes and wept some more. Then she handed me another. I didn't care if my sniffles destroyed her moment. I really didn't. If you've never seen that seventeen-foot-tall statue up close, you don't know. You simply don't. Although your eyes tell you it is made of stone, your soul tells you something different. You can actually feel the blood coursing through those meticulously carved veins in his feet and arms—even his temples. The very memory gets me all misty, I swear it does. The way that little queer Michelangelo took so much care, so much tenderness, with every curl in the future king's hair. Every line on his face. You look long enough at David's skin and you see the pores. I swear to the Buddha, you believe with all your being Michelangelo gave that most perfect specimen actual pores.

He loved that statue, absolutely loved it, every millisecond he was coaxing it out of that stone. He absolutely had to. Stand right next to it, bask it its glow, and tell me I'm wrong.

I couldn't, I absolutely could not, rip myself away. Jonnie wanted to leave after five minutes. But what do you expect from a day laborer from the west side of Española, New Mexico? Jonnie's the guy who stands quiet by the door when we go to parties and I teach all the viejitas the Macarena or the fox trot or something. That really happened—more than once. Jonnie's an excellent contractor. You gotta give the big lug that much. The man lays the best radiant flooring in the Southwest. He absolutely does. But when it comes to art, he's a boor. A monstrous boor. I admit it. But he's my cuddle bunny boor, and I love him.

Anyway, we're there in Florence, and I touch my fingertips to my chest, just paralyzed, absolutely rigid, for a good twenty minutes. Maybe longer. Absolutely arrested by the majesty of that Renaissance masterpiece. *The* Renaissance masterpiece. I wasn't just studying every square centimeter of that he-man. Rather, I was in its spell. Something held me there. Some magical force kept me from moving, no matter how many times Jonnie said we were late meeting Todd and Thelma for drinks.

That moment never really went away. It throbs deep in my chest to this very day. Not a month ago I lay in bed thinking of it. That Jonnie, you know, he snores like an eighteen-wheeler groaning up a hill. He really does. Especially those nights when he drinks too much, which is just too often these days. That night, I pushed him on his side, and he stopped the grinding for a while but then started all over again. I lay there with my eyes open, soaking up the darkness, and it was as if the memory fell from the sky and covered me—heart, body, and soul. I swear to Yahweh, it was like a flat sheet floating down from the heavens and settling over me. I practically saw it. There before me was that moment that I stood cradled in the glow of that boy David. I reached to the nightstand and grabbed a tissue and knew it wouldn't be enough. So I grabbed another and blew my nose. Then another. I actually had a revelation while lying there with a wad of wet tissues in my hand. An honest-to-goodness, full-blown, soul-shattering, spine-tingling epiphany.

You've seen the Sistine Chapel? At least pictures of it? You know where God's reaching out to Adam, just pointing casually, as if passing that invisible spark that animates the empty flesh? I guess everyone knows that one. What slapped me right across my pretty little face that night was how that is what it is like. Some moments of time, some works of art, just transmit that tiny spark from God so fully, the grace that comes through them is so unfiltered, that you feel that electric pulse that passed from God's finger to the artist, then to the masterpiece, and straight into your heart. Think of Beethoven's *Ninth* or Bach's *Saint Matthew's Passion*. Think of works like *Sense and Sensibility*, *A Streetcar Named Desire*, or Anaïs Nin's *Delta of Venus*. Think of Elaine Paige singing the lead in *Evita*, or even the costumes in *Gone with the Wind*. If you let yourself, you can experience those things and feel the electric current of the universe—the power that created the stars, black holes, and billions of suns. You absolutely feel it. But you have to trust enough to let go.

There are some moments, some works of art, that are simply special. Beyond human comprehension, really. Just get near them, and you feel the power of life radiating like heat. You absolutely do.

I felt that when I shuddered before the *David*.

And the first time I saw Mark.

I was there that first night at Laffs—the comedy club right up there on San Mateo Boulevard, here in Albuquerque—the summer before it went under. Jonnie and I got there half an hour before the open-mic show started, and the room was a dungeon. Absolute desolation. We were the only ones there. You could hear the busboy chopping lemons in the back, that's how empty it was. The hostess put us right up front, at the table butting up against the stage. Jonnie ordered me an appletini and a Miller Lite for himself, and just then the girl walked over these two breeders to have them sit with us. One look at that girl and I thought, *Where did this drum majorette get her fake I.D.? Hellooooo?* She looked no older than fourteen. Not a day older. And her man: your garden-variety South Valley homeboy, with his stiff-brim cap sideways and the shorts down to his ankles. I thought, he either works at his uncle's auto body shop or his grandmother's meth lab. I said to myself, *Let's play fashion faux pas, shall we?* I mean, if you are going wear to Bermudas down to your ankles, why not just wear ugly golf pants? I mean, hello? But she turned out to be the sweetest little thing in the world. So cute with her thick lip lines and her baby bump and everything. When their nachos came, that little darling—it turns out her name was Bethany—scooted the plate right in front of me with her skinny, tattooed finger and said, "Go ahead. Help yourself." Just like that. Then she beamed. A cute little chola smile. So nice. It was obvious we were faggots. They didn't care. They simply did not.

I don't know if you've ever been to an open-mic show at a comedy club, but the way it works is that about ten minutes before the show starts the manager calls all performers to the back and gives them the line-up for the night. About ninety percent of the acts are just God-awful, so horrendous they make you want to call your mother and cry. Mostly kids who go up on stage and drop F-bombs because that's all their tender little minds pick up when they watch comedy on HBO or BET. They don't understand that there is actually an art to this and it takes hard work. Usually, everyone getting on stage gets between three and five minutes, depending on how bad they are and how many comedians are on the bill. When you have thirty seconds left, the house manager shines a light from the control booth in the back, letting you know you have to wrap it up. If you're not off in sixty seconds, they shut the mic off altogether and don't let you go back on for two months. I swear they do. It's happened to this little Firecracker. I learned my lesson the second time.

The headliner that night was Patrick Candelaria, out of El Paso. He always packs the room. Albuquerque simply adores him. The whole city. So by the time I got on stage, the room was filling up.

I did four minutes. Not a great four minutes, but a solid 245 seconds. Black Tom was the emcee, and I just went up to polish my bit about how I like to sip my coffee in the morning wearing nothing but bikini underwear, and each time I do, the people at Starbucks get so bent out of shape. The routine wasn't so good back then, but you have to work and rework every line, every word—every syllable, really—until the bit just shines. That's the game: you compose, you try, you evaluate, you refine, and you try again. When you bomb, you shake it off. You figure out what's not working. You re-evaluate and make changes. After a year or two or three or four, you have a decent routine.

So my set was okay. Three big laughs. I came off and went back to sit with Jonnie, Bethany, and Lazo. Once I was there, I could relax, get tipsy, and enjoy the rest of the show. Next up on stage was this guy who, I swear, brought no juice. None whatsoever. He started out saying "I need to get something straight" and adjusted his cock through his jeans. My God. But that's what it's like at these shows. So Jana Boan, this cute little dyke with a six-inch Mohawk haircut followed him, then another newbie nobody ever saw. Then Mark. After Mark was supposed to be Jamie Jupiter, Jana's girlfriend. That's the line-up the manager gave us when we signed up.

Well, Mark walked up the three steps to the stage looking scared out of his mind. Totally mortified. Really, he looked like nothing. Like absolutely nothing. Not the least smidgen memorable about him. He was short, bald, and very white. I swear the child looked like somebody yanked him out of the oven an hour too soon. Like he should be hawking insurance, designing software, or selling used Chevrolets. Like he only had sex by default. I mean total Downtown Geeksville. I picked up a nacho, dipped it in cheese sauce, balanced a jalapeño on it, and told Jonnie—but loud enough so Bethany and Lazo can hear: "Oh, yikes. If you want to step out for a cigarette, this is the time." I absolutely did. Jonnie doesn't even smoke. Two minutes later, I swear to Allah Himself, I was holding my ribs, keeping my hand over my mouth, and trying to keep from spraying flavored vodka all over that nice little hetero Latino couple sitting across the table. Mark opened up talking about how he was adopted, about how each year he sends out four million Father's Day cards, just to cover all his bases. That pasta-colored white boy had me rocking with laughter. Absolutely convulsing.

I didn't see him get the light. Maybe my eyes were closed. Maybe I was working too hard trying to keep my chair balanced. Mark ended his set by saying, I swear: "I'll be here all week. Tip your waitstaff. Try the veal. Two shows on Saturday." A cliché. Even that got a major laugh. He put the microphone back, waved, and disappeared down the steps. Absolutely disappeared. And it's Jonnie, my panda bear, of all people—the guy who can spend four hours at a party and not have anyone remember he was there—who slammed down his beer bottle and stood up so fast his chair tipped over. It absolutely did. He cupped his hands at his mouth and yelled, "Bring him back. Bring that gringo back." He clapped and yelled some more. Bethany stuck her forefingers in her mouth. Her whistle so shrill, I swear it could shatter glass. Fraternity boys at the next table were cawing, cheering, and howling. Everybody in that room was yelling and clapping and stomping their feet. Absolutely everybody. Black Tom stood on stage, the microphone in his hand, the mic stand behind him, and people screamed, clapped, hooted, pounded beer bottles, and yelled for Mark. I thought the roof was going to cave in. I absolutely did. Prison riots have been quieter.

So Mark came back, and this wave of cheers tore through the house. He did another hour and seven minutes, so the club had to push back Candelaria's show by eighty-five minutes. I later found out it was Mark's first time out.

His first time. I thought, this little white boy will be headlining at major venues, A-level clubs like The Comedy Store, the L.A. Improv, the Ice Palace in Pasadena, or Pancho Pilot's there in downtown Denver in no time. No time whatsoever.

That kind of a show your first time out—that's like painting the *Guernica* the first time you pick up a paint brush. That's when I knew that the same spirit that anointed Mozart and Michelangelo had touched that man. The spirit burst out of him and washed over you. It absolutely washed over you. I so thought that this is what the Albuquerque comedy scene had been waiting for—for oh, so very long.

HELEN DENISE

This breezy October night, I swear, I got my whole face just about smashed up against that front picture window, my hands braced around my eyes to block out the glare of the yellow bug light. Through the parted curtains, I get a good look into the front room of that big ol' apartment. I am not sure what I see or what I am supposed to see. Against the far wall, you got this bookshelf about chest high just stuffed with books. I recognize a few of the titles: *Being and Time, The Critique of Pure Logic, The Attack upon Christendom, Einstein's Universe, The Biography of Saint Teresa, Against Interpretation,* Descartes' *Meditations.* What gets me, though, what really gets me, is that on top of the red varnished wood you got all these candles. I swear, there must be about twenty-five or thirty sticks of white wax in two rows, all arranged tallest to shortest, like pipes of a pipe organ, each with a thumbnail-sized flame flickering at the tippy-top. I'm thinking the whole darned place will go up in smoke, if someone's not careful.

On the console behind the couch are another ten or fifteen votives, all these glass tubes—you know, they sell them at the grocery store with all those depictions of the Sacred Heart, Saint Jude, Saint Michael, and the Virgin of Guadalupe—all shoved together on the polished walnut and under this Nigerian textile hanging there as a wall decoration. Most of those transparent tops are streaked with soot, and inside of each jar is a tongue of fire, floating on an inch or so of liquid wax. Smack dab in the center of a braided rug sits this glass coffee table, and on top of that is a cobalt-blue bowl about the size of a split watermelon, and inside of that are seven little wax floaters, all of their wicks aflame. Six of those itty-bitty candles are scooted up against the edge, and one actually appears to be making its way across the ripples, as if it's carrying a message or something. Swear to God. On the other side, you got a row of dime store tapers, stuck in these tiny little glass holders, all lined up on the breakfast counter. Three box-shaped candles of different heights sit on this wrought-iron plant stand right beside the couch. There is not a single electrified bulb anywhere in that whole darned place, and yet the room is awash in light. I tell myself I wouldn't be a bit surprised if all that fire sets off the smoke alarm and scares the daylights out of the whole darned neighborhood.

I open my purse and reach under the bottle of Syrah in there and find that little scrap of paper torn from a spiral notebook. I uncrumple it and check the address: J-146. It matches, all right. I mean, those are the tin figures right in front of me, nailed to that post, so, naturally, I assume I wrote something down wrong, or that maybe I have the wrong street or wrong side of Central Avenue. I raise my hand to tap on the door, but then I stop myself—for a few reasons, really. I feel that if I make any noise, some plug-ugly old crone will walk out of a back room, shove open the window, and cuss me through the screen for interrupting her exorcism or spell casting or whatever she's fixin' to do back there.

That's just an excuse, really. So I sit down on the steps there with my Ropers planted on the mulch of the tiny flowerbed, reach down, and pick up a maple leaf. I look over the veins and the way the orange and red stretch into the green. I wonder why I always let my feathers get so darned ruffled.

The breeze scatters these yellow-brown cottonwood, elm, and poplar leaves all across the porch slab, and I pull my sweater tighter around my shoulders, and suddenly the weight of all the changes I'm going through comes screaming down on me like nobody's business. It was like I got swept up in a whirlwind of change back then. Those first months away from home, I felt like the planks holding up the roof of my life were strained and rotted, and that, piece by piece, it was all dropping down right on top of my head.

So even though I figured I could be standing in front of the right place, I really didn't want to be there anyway, just getting myself all aggravated. On those nights when I wasn't working, I swear, I was happy as a cat in the sunshine, just sitting on the futon with my legs curled under me and Marti's afghan around my shoulders—me, alone there, squeezing lemon into a cup of tea and reading my commentary on dialectical materialism or whatever. So I lick my thumb and wipe a smudge off my boot, swipe the leaves and dirt off my sweater, and light off back down that slate brick path to my car.

You see, just the middle of that summer—not five months before—when I was working at the Piggly Wiggly, I came home for lunch just as Daddy drove in from the hospital and visiting with Dr. Lukes. Standing there in the driveway, he told me there wasn't a doubt about it. Mama had pancreatic cancer and real bad. Not four weeks later, we were all fighting back tears and waiting for Father Nico to get there. I sat there on that fluffy comforter, massaging myrrh oil into Mama's palm with my thumbs—just like I did practically the whole three days leading up to that. And we all knew full well what was coming, so I drew close to the sweet woman, and I whispered so that Daddy and Marti could just hear.

"Go ahead," I said. "Close your pretty brown eyes, and let yourself go, if that makes you happy. You can go now, Mama."

I said it just like that, too.

She shook her head just so slightly that Daddy and Marti couldn't see it. For a whole second she was once more that pretty Texas cowgirl, who every day tied a ribbon in my hair, packed my lunch, and patted me on the rump as I lit out the back door headed for school.

Then, right there under her picture of Saint Rita, Mama's eyes fluttered and closed.

And she drifted off.

It was right about that time that Mace—he was my boyfriend since junior year—informed me he's got a daughter on the way, and yet he still has the nerve to call over and over again, practically begging me to move into the single-wide his granddaddy left him. I am not sure exactly when he told me all that. Every trauma of that summer gets kind of bunched together in my head when I try to remember what happened first, especially all these years later.

Not three days after the funeral, then comes another wrinkle. Marti and I were still sorting through Mama's hope chest when the postman walks up the porch steps bringing a letter from the University of New Mexico telling me that they would indeed accept my thirty-three junior college credits, and that they wanted to give me an academic scholarship besides. So a month later, to the day, I load my Honda with two Hefty bags stuffed with sheets and winter clothes, two suitcases, one of them Marti's, and eight boxes, six of them filled with toiletries, kitchen supplies, denim jeans, and whatnot, and the other two with my essential oils. I pack that car so full I practically got to jump up and down on the hatchback to get it shut.

Then came the part that still gets me all teary-eyed.

I go back into the house and tell Daddy not to bother getting out of his chair. I roll his little table aside, sit there on the ottoman, and take his hand.

"Come Christmas break," I say as I rub his spotted knuckles, "I'll be right back here, whipping you up another batch of that eggplant Parmesan with black olives and those teeny-tiny caper berries you like so much. You mark my words, you lovely man."

And Daddy, he stands right up and takes my head with both those big old hands and plants a kiss right in the middle of my forehead. He squeezes me and says how proud he is. He didn't do that stuff too often.

I give him a peck on the cheek, wipe my eyes, and I gather up my purse, cassette boxes, and book bag, and back my way out the door. Daddy steps out on the porch, shoving his handkerchief into his back pocket, and no sooner does the screen door slam shut than Marti comes crunching across the gravel. She runs up and opens the passenger door for me. I lay my stuff on the seat and tell her not to forget that she is Daddy's favorite, like there's a chance of that. I call to Daddy that I'll phone from the road if I stop, but for sure when I make it to Albuquerque. Then Marti hands me a paper bag full of cut celery, baby carrots, apple slices, Fig Newtons, and Hershey's Kisses, all sorted neatly in their own baggies.

"We don't want you passing out from starvation out on that lonesome road," she says.

I tell her it's not but a seven-and-a-half-hour drive, if I stop for lunch.

She draws back, picks a piece of lint off my tank top, and smooths out the wrinkle. I actually break right out laughing. There is, indeed, a tear rolling down that little stinker's cheek. Swear to God. My kid sister already missing me when I'm not even out of the driveway. I saw it with my own eyes.

Once I do get to town, the apartment I thought I reserved, well, it turns out that got rented out, and so I'm in a fix. The property manager didn't have the good grace to phone me or anything. So I stayed in this Motel 6 way up on East Central Avenue, this creepy part of town. Two days later, though, I answer an ad for the cutest little casita down just the other side of the Rio Grande. Then, the week before classes, I bounce around like a bee-stung horse. I apply for jobs cashiering and answering phones at a call center and have to run down to the campus and get my schedule squared away. The lady at the registrar's office, she tells me my forms need a stamp from the Arts and Sciences Advising. So for six hours on one day and three hours the next, those university bureaucrats, they just got me carrying papers from office to office to office and advisor to advisor, taking the wrong documents to the wrong people, feeling like a blind dog looking for home. To make matters even worse, on my first two days of school I get to classes late because I get so lost on this campus that's ten times bigger than I'm used to. I mean, Midland College was just a dinky little place that didn't have but three buildings, four with the Industrial Arts Center.

And then here I am, just a couple of months after that, standing on this porch with a bottle of expensive French wine weighing down my purse, looking at all those candles, and getting all worked up wondering if I am lost or, if I'm not, if I should have dinner with this man I barely know. It is like I am standing right under that big ol' avalanche of change, I tell you. Just when I thought things were normalizing a little.

All this is pretty overwhelming for a simple girl from a dirtwater ranching town like Fort Stockton, Texas.

Since I find myself pretty much incapable of something as simple as knocking on a door, I light off back down the walk and climb back in my Civic and grip the steering wheel with my keys still dangling in my gloved hand. I fight real hard with myself. I got to town two months before and only went out with other people twice. I had lunch once with some girl from my existentialism class, who I turned out not to like so much, and then I went to a wine bar with the girls from work before it came time to check in.

So I just waited there in my car, looking at the top of the bottle poking out my purse, and wondering what to do. I stuck the key in the ignition but then told myself that lack of socializing isn't real healthy for a girl like me. After a good long heart-to-heart with myself, I got out and headed back up the sidewalk, ready to ask whoever answered to help me figure out just where the heck I am supposed to be. So seconds later, I shiver again out there under the glow of that yellow porch light. I am about to tap on the door and take that leap of faith. But I just can't do it.

The whole thing didn't feel right. The way Mark had asked me over was just so odd that I really didn't know what to think. He did it all so casual-like.

That happened when he and I sat in the back room of this diner right across Central Avenue from main campus, a place where a whole bunch of kids go to read, and all these study groups like to meet—even the Bible thumpers. A big ol' restaurant with tasty chile, buttery sweet rolls, and cheap coffee. Well, Mark and I, we're sitting at this little table in the last room, over by the back exit, and Mark, he takes a compass and draws a circle on a sheet of typing paper, then measures the distance from the pinprick to the edge. He scrawls figures, calculating the circumference and the area on a legal pad, and I ask him to show me what he did once more. He repeats the process, and this time, as he draws a line across the arc, he says, without so much as lifting his eyes, "I'm whipping up some buffalo Florentine on Friday night. Wanna drop by?"

Just like that. Like he's telling me a receipt slipped out of my purse. There's not so much as a speck of fear or self-consciousness in any of it, like he didn't care if I showed up or not. The way he said it, I just assumed a bunch of people were headed over anyway, and he was asking just to be nice because he sensed that not only was I kind of shy, but that I was so busy with work and school that I didn't have much of a chance to make friends. Then he jots down his address on the corner of a sheet of notebook paper, tears it off, and slides it across the table.

You see, the reason I met Mark in the first place was that I couldn't handle geometry. That started everything. One afternoon I'm sitting there in Professor Simon's office, scraping fingernail polish off my thumbnail and looking at that pile of tests on his desk. On one side of the stack of folders is this twenty-ounce root beer mug just jam-packed with gel pens, sticks of chalk, paper clips, and Post-it pads. Even a little Israeli flag sticking out the top. On the other side he's got this crystal dish full of snack-size Hershey bars—the kind you give out for Halloween.

So the professor reaches over and takes the top off the candy dish, lifts his bushy ol' eyebrows, and peeks over his cheater readers, asking me, without saying anything, to have a couple of candies. I take a Mr. Goodbar, and he shakes the dish and tells me to have some more. I do, and I keep one of them on top of my closed binder and fold back the paper. I tell him the woman in advising said that sophomore geometry would be the easy route to fulfilling my math requirement. I certainly didn't tell Dr. Simon—just like I didn't tell that little girl at Arts and

Sciences—that if I'd stayed in algebra back at Midland, why, my grade point average wouldn't be near as good as it was right then. And I wouldn't have a scholarship. And I wouldn't be in Albuquerque, just about pulling my hair out.

He rolls back on his chair, pats his big ol' tummy, sticks his finger in the opening between two buttons, and scratches his hairy belly. He swivels around to his computer and fidgets with buttons.

"Help, help, help," he says, like he's talking to the screen. "Where we can get Miss Helen Denise help?"

He turns and gives me this little smile, like he just saw something he's waited decades for.

"Ahhh . . ." he says, "I might just have ticket. I might just have answer for you, my friend."

I don't have the teeniest clue what he's talking about.

He digs into the mug with two fingers and pulls out this little green pad, looks over at the document he just called up, writes something down, tears off the slip, and hands it over.

"This boy here," he says, pointing with the eraser end of his mechanical pencil at the name I can hardly make out. "Our acer. He will work with you, break everything down. Everything. Make simple. Everything. A good man. Very, very, good boy."

I must have turned white as a tuna fish's belly. I never took a tutor before in my whole darned life. Not through fifteen years of schooling. So I peel back the wrapper on the candy bar, exposing the blond peanut flecks poking through the milk chocolate.

"You're telling me I need special ed?" I say as I spread out the wrapper on the hard plastic cover and snap the little mud-colored rectangle in half.

"You learn math," says Simon, and he jiggles one of the candies in his hands like he's about to roll dice. "You learn math by stick to it. By not give up. By stick to it. You stick to it, you get it. Skill level— doesn't matter. Not in lower-level classes. Persistence, persistence. That matters. That simple. Really that simple. Besides, Mark, he's a good man. A very, very good boy."

Just a few minutes later, I walk through the student union on my way to my aesthetics class, and I plant my backpack there at the information desk so I can take another look at Simon's note. I can't even figure out how to pronounce the last name he wrote down. A "W" followed by an "L." What kind of a dumb ol' name is that? So I stop, balance my math book on my knee, slip the scrap somewhere in the back pages, shove the text behind my three-ring notebook, and zip up the bag.

At first, I really thought there wasn't much use in calling. I figured I could just work out my mathematics problems myself, like I do everything. I mean, after all, Dr. Simon himself said all I had to do was to keep at it, didn't he? That's what I tell myself, anyway. Besides, here I am, almost twenty-six years old with no babies. An independent woman, working her way through college. I even started selling essential oils way back when I was at Midland, just to pull in extra money. I tell myself all this as I hurry across the big brick courtyard there in front of Zimmerman Library. I actually say "independent woman" right out loud, as I convince myself that ol' Ralph Emerson himself would surely compliment my self-reliance. I mean, I was a bona fide success compared to all the girls I grew up with. At the grocery store, I made it to head cashier in just over two years. And wasn't nobody helping me get through school, unless you count the folks who gave me the scholarship money. But I earned that. What in the world did I need a Mark Wladika for?

Well, two assignments later, and I'm sitting there at the kitchen table, and I'm going over all this stuff about the radius and the circumferences, and I'm trying to calculate the volume of a dodecahedron, and the whole thing has me feeling about as settled as a dog in a corral full of broncos. My kettle whistles, and I pick it up, but once again, I had the flame too high, so I have to grab the handle with a pot holder. I shut off the stove, tear open a little pouch of chamomile, lay the bag in the cup, and pour in the water. I lift the string and agitate. When my tea gets good and strong, I lean against the sink and hold my mug with both hands, breathing in the steam. Meanwhile, all that stuff about circumferences and radii and multiply this by that and then calculate it against pi and so on and so on is just ricocheting around inside my skull. I spend a good minute thinking about packing up my car and hightailing it back to Pecos County. I squeeze some honey on a spoon and try to get my mind to just simmer down. I lean against the sink. Outside my window, there's that serrated edge of the Sandia Mountains, and just under that you got all those aspens and cottonwoods looking downright electrified with all those pumpkin-colored leaves. A sparrow circles over the meadow, flutters down, and lights on the telephone wire. I remove the tea bag and drop it in the trash, wondering what life has in store for me. I take another sip and look outside and see that a whole bunch of birds came to join their little friend during the eight seconds I had my head turned away. They're all standing at attention on that black line, looking like beads of a rosary.

Finally, I flip through my geometry book, find that little green square Simon scribbled on, go to the telephone, punch in Mark's number, and let the phone on the other end ring once before I hang up. Doesn't take me but an hour after that, and two more false starts, to work up the nerve to actually talk to him. He sounds nice enough, though. That makes things easier.

Now here I am, standing here on this porch, looking through the window, and agonizing whether to rap on that darned door. I bite my finger and raise my hand, and I am just about to do it, but again, I just can't. I turn around, tug my purse strap up my shoulder, and set out across that lawn, hurrying out to the street corner. A gust blows my hair across my cheek, and I pull a strand out of my mouth. A quarter moon shines through gauzy clouds, and the only other heavenly body I can make out is Jupiter, which hangs just so pretty, like a pearl in the northern sky. I figure, what the hell. So I retrace my steps across the grass and step over the flowerbed, onto the porch. I pull off my glove with my teeth and lift my hand, when the deadbolt clacks and the door swings wide. Mark stands, smiling, right in front of me, as if he appeared out of the vapors. He wipes his hands on a blue kitchen towel that he flops over his shoulder. He asks if I was out there long, and I say I just walked up not two seconds before.

After all those changes, Mark slips into my life. Talk about getting slammed upside the head with a sledge hammer.

BLACK TOM

Mark Wladika? The mac daddy of Albuquerque comedy. A white boy so dope he was illegal in five states. Thirty seconds on that stage and the homeboy was slapping us around. The material? Sometimes off-the-charts, total fireworks. Sometimes mediocre. Like he talked about working a gig up in Española, this town thirty miles north of Santa Fe. He says it's not a town—it's Mayberry with a meth problem. Talks about seeing a head-on collision between two low-rider cars, and all sixty-seven people inside get sent to the hospital. We've all heard jokes like that. Hell, we've all done jokes like that. But Mark—the guy had stage presence. The dude understood timing. He knew how to pull it all together. The guy brought the sweet stuff. I'm talking pound, pound, pound, pound, every damned second he was on stage. My first thought was that he was one of those headliners from Pancho Pilot's, that hot spot up in Denver that brings in all the top-notch national acts. I thought he just stopped in Albuquerque on his way to The Comedy Store or the Dallas Improv or something.

The white boy takes on everything: drugs, sex, suicide, poisoning babies, bestiality. I mean, that ofay was fearless, and he could take just about any topic and wrangle a joke out of it. And so damned vivid. With just his face and voice, the dude paints pictures. He talks about his messed up family, and you can practically see the Cheetos under the couch cushions.

That next Monday, I'm on my knees, there at the hardware store, lining up boxes of fluorescent light bulbs on the bottom shelf, when I catch something out the corner of my eye. My first thought is that body coming my way looks like it's made of animated clothes hanger wires, just like my homeboy Thad Powell's. But I think it can't be him because the dude never rolls out of bed before it's time for *Judge Judy* reruns. Meanwhile, I'm working double shifts and taking night classes, working my ass off trying to produce comedy shows so I can bring in a little more scratch, the whole time worried that my old lady is pregnant again.

Turns out Thad borrowed his mother's car and drove clear across town to ask me about this guy in his forties who lit up the Laffs open-mic stage the night before. He's already heard so much about it. I tell him the whole story while standing on the concrete floor with an empty corrugated carton in my hand. Tell him how Mark whips out line after line, laying it all on so thick we don't even have time to breathe before he belts us with another one.

I go on about how this homeboy has pinpoint timing, that I never seen nothing like it. I tell him that this comedian that nobody ever saw before knows exactly when to take a beat—or even half a beat, or an eighth, or a thirty-second of a beat—to lay out a punchline or to punch up a tag. I never seen nobody take that kind of control. Not Pryor. Not Carlin. Not Cosby. I seen George Lopez at the casino just a month before, and the superstar had nothing on this cracker.

I go on about how Mark climbs up on stage and doesn't even introduce himself. Just shakes my hand after I introduce him, lays out two one-liners, and starts riffing into the audience. Getting big-time laughs. We think that he and the folks he's talking to planned the whole thing out. That we're being punked. I tell Thad about how Mark asked some jock sitting up front what he did for a living, and the guy says he's a weight trainer. Mark hits back with, "You train people to wait? Most people know how to do that. We practice it in the check-out line at Walmart." He says it with major attitude. The jock says back to him that he means "Weights that you work out with," and Mark says, "What do you train weights to do?" He says it instantly. The homeboy is right on top of it. Like he knew what the guy was going to say when he was back in his bedroom, rehearsing his act in front of his mirror.

Then Mark turns to someone sitting at the side of the stage and says, "This guy talks to dumbbells. I thought only televangelists did that." Everything the personal trainer says, Mark has something for. He doesn't dig for the jokes, like other comics do. Two words come out of the meat boy's mouth, and Mark blasts him again.

I tell Thad all this, and I get laughing all over again.

The funniest thing Mark did that night, I say, comes right in the middle of his act. He goes stiff, like he was zapped with a bolt of electricity, and moves like a robot. His eyes go wide, and he makes that grinding sound, you know, like motors are turning in his arms and hips? He reaches down, picks up a boneless chicken wing off a customer's plate, pivots at the hip, and feeds it to some chick sitting at the next table. He's making all the buzzing, grinding, and popping noises as he does it. People were rolling.

I'm still laughing, still bent over with my hands on my knees, still holding the carton, still in the spell of the night before, and once I catch my breath, I tell Thad I got shelves to stock. Then I got to get home to feed the kid and then get to class. I tell him to hit the open-mic on Sunday and that we need to put together another show sometime soon. I wipe my eyes with my shirttail and go back for more light bulbs. Before I get to the storage room door, I call over my shoulder, telling Thad how we need to watch this guy because when he becomes a national sensation some of the attention has got to spill over on the rest of us. It's just got to.

NICHOLS

What am I thinking? I'm thinking you can always pick the winners at the starting gate.

This one night this blond kid whips aside the curtain under the exit light as he emerges from the green room right behind the stage. He saunters up the steps, adjusts the microphone, stands in one spot, and doesn't move from it his whole time in the spotlight. Looks so much younger than the rest—high schooler or something. Total rookie. But he impresses. He's Barry Bonds at the home run derby, cranking meatball after meatball over the left field fence. Loaded with material, attitude, and energy.

He goes on about how he got excommunicated from the Unitarian Church. They burned a question mark on his lawn. About how a priest once told him that the Virgin Mary was taken bodily into heaven, and he said, "Aw, that's just an assumption." About how no other country is hung up on sex like we are in the United States. How you don't have Australian bushmen walking around saying, "I think I am a gatherer— in a hunter's body." How he walked into a university classroom and some sorority girl is breastfeeding. The professor says to her, "You can

31

stay, but your mother has to cover your face with a blanket." About how Zeno and Pythagoras walk halfway into a bar, then halfway into a bar, then halfway into a bar, then halfway into a bar.

Intelligent, original, inventive stuff.

One-liner after one-liner. You never knew where he was going to take you.

Was he perfect? No. But everybody in the comedy club that night knew the kid had major league mojo. The whole package: boyish good looks, brains, creativity, sparkling imagination, killer stage presence. You couldn't peel your eyes off of him. The girls dug him. Hell, the guys dug him. The best thing he had going? Something people don't see at first: this hint of anger that leaked out from behind his prep-school cynicism. Like the time he asked the crowd, "Anybody here work for the state of New Mexico?" Someone in the back clapped, and he hit back with, "What do you do there? Do you have any idea at all?"

Did the kid need coaching? Absolutely. Did some of his jokes cross the line? Sure. Too much of that peepee/ca-ca stuff.

Could I sell him? You bet your sweet ass. His charisma alone was enough.

So after his set, I step into the cold to puff on a butt. When I reenter with that February chill still radiating off my topcoat, there in the lobby you got the club manager standing behind the cash register, counting the till. I drum my fingertips on the counter, waiting for her break in concentration so I can collect the youngster's vital stats: name, experience, where he comes from, where he works, and so on. After about six minutes, she finally points at me with her chin. Whatever happened to saying "Can I help you?"

I ask about the straw-haired kid who just got off stage, and she says he's Jack Marison. That he was some photography prodigy at the university before he dropped out and moved to Denver the year before. She says that I need to catch him now because pretty soon he'll be working some big-time club up there called Pancho Pilot's, this highbrow spot that's supposed to be top tier. Once he breaks in, she says, he'll be a national touring headliner and will come through town once a year, if that much. She says how, for the next two months until he turns twenty-one, he can't even stay in the barroom once he finishes his set. As she talks, Marison himself comes through the office door, looking all droopy, vulnerable, and innocent. I introduce myself, tell him he has the gift, and slip him my card. Was I willing to bet he'd call? Of course. Come on. These comics? They dream of these moments. I figure I can get him booked at twenty or thirty gigs the first year, even get him on TV. Get him some real money.

After twenty-seven years in business, I know that nothing motivates like the moola, 'nero, and frogskins.

Besides, I know the business. I've worked trucker bars, biker bars, downtown dives, and upscale hotel bars—every kind of place you can think of—and I spent thirteen years slogging beer in comedy clubs. One thing I've learned? You want to build a team that wins the World Series? You start working the minor leaguers. No two ways about it. I'm thinking this kid could really take us places. All of us. Just when we need it.

That Thursday, I get to my bar, Nichols' Silver Dollar, around ten a.m. The lock sticks again, and so I have to jam the paper bag I got under my arm so that I can work the door knob and dead bolt with both hands. Once inside, I plop the sack on the counter, fish in my pocket for a nickel, slap it on the hardwood, and go punch in the burglar alarm code. I find my coffee mug in the glass rack and pour myself a double shot of Old Crow, neat. I climb on a barstool, light a cigarette, dump the tickets out on the counter, take the coin, and go at working the gray, waxy covering off four hundred dollars' worth of Lottery Scratchers. After twenty minutes or so, my mug is empty, and I have two hits: one for five dollars and one for twenty. Those go directly in my wallet.

I score the edge of another rectangle, scratch away just enough to know that the imprint is the ace of hearts and not a winner. It hits me that at any second Cyn, my bar chief, will swing open that back door, flip on the house lights, and come over with the vacuum and give the carpeted section the once-over. Doing her job. Meanwhile, I got all these little iron-filing-sized, gray-black granules all over the wood that needs revarnishing, so I sweep the debris into a pile at the edge and brush the stuff into my palm. I clap it off my hands, right there on the floor. The tickets I have yet to look at? I shove all of those back in the paper sack and take it back to my office and drop it on a stack of Miller Lite cases next to my desk. The losing Scratchers? They sit there like a pile of red, black, and yellow potato chips under the Guinness tap. I need a quick, efficient—and surreptitious—way to dispose of them. Just then bottles clank in the back, so I yank out the front of my polo shirt and stretch it out like a net in front of me and use my whole arm to sweep the useless cards into the makeshift pouch. What do I look like? Grandma carrying apricots in from the yard.

There in the back office, I grab a few more Scratchers and work off the coating. I down some more rotgut, brush the flecks off my pants, and I get to thinking that any second Cyn might come in hollering about something, so I roll back, reach over, twist the lock in the door knob, and make sure it won't budge. I know that girl. She'll bug me about how she can't find the Auto-Chlor, the chemical we add to the rinse water to keep spots off glasses, and then I'll have to practically take her by the hand to the pile of supplies that came in late the day before. Stuff the bartender left stacked by the back door. Besides, no need for her to catch me doing what I'm doing. I don't care if you're in the seventh game of the World Series, and it's bottom of the ninth with two men down, two men on, and a full count. I don't care if you're a businessman, a musician, an actor, a comic, or a cocksman on the make. I don't care if you're down by three in the championship game, and your shooting guard just sprained his ankle. Success Rule Number One? Never let 'em see you sweat.

After all this? I still got half the stack of tickets to go through when my nerves catch up with me, and I know a gut ache's coming on. I tear open a carton of Black Velvet, extract a bottle, crack the plastic seal, and pour two fingers' worth into my coffee mug, something I should wash out one of these days. I pat my shirt for my Bic, find it in my front pants pocket, click up a flame, puff on a Marlboro, and spread the cards out smooth—like I'm performing a magic trick with a poker deck. I wave my hand over the string of lottery cards and choose one from the middle. I find a penny in my desk, close the drawer, and score off the coating. Nothing. I do another and another, keeping at it until my hand cramps. Twenty minutes and a pile of spent cards later, my prayers are answered: one thousand dollars. I sigh. I have one last drag off the cigarette before snuffing it out in my ashtray. I pour more firewater.

Timothy calls in sick, so before happy hour begins I have to go dump three buckets of ice into the bins of the back bar. Still, I have enough time to go through every one of those tickets, fire up the computer, call up the Excel spreadsheet, twiddle some figures on my desk calculator, and clear my head. For a four-hundred-and-twenty-dollar investment?

I got one thousand and twenty-five dollars. No need for a payday loan to cover the electric bill this month.

Did I know I was acting crazy? Absolutely. But sometimes you got no choice but to put your money on the long ball.

The next month? I couldn't count on being so lucky. Did I have a plan? Not really.

Then Black Tom invites me to Laffs to catch his set. What do I see? I see Marison charging out of that gate, and deep in my gut, I know he's a godsend. I think that, while the rest of Albuquerque goes all apeshit over that guy Wladika's supposed brilliance, I am ready to plunk down my chips on Marison. Not to place or show. I bet Jack Marison will cross the finish line first. By four or five lengths.

What did I see on that stage? Raw—but real—star potential. I knew right then that the greenhorn was the golden boy, the all-star, the phenom, the kind of franchise player who could put Albuquerque on the comedy map. Make the Duke City a national sensation—what Chicago is to the blues, New Orleans to jazz, Saint Louis to beer.

Like I said, sometimes you can spot the winners at the starting gate.

EDDIE

Those Albuquerque comedians—Mica Pierson, Jana Boan, Firecracker Rael, Black Tom, all ten or eleven of them—they talk about Mark like he picked up a microphone and jokes just flowed. Like he was just some Amadeus of stand-up comedy, channeling bits of genius from some other realm. As if Thalia constantly whispered in his ear. It wasn't like that. I was there. Every step of the way. Mark did comedy because of me.

At every club I visit, every time I step into a new classroom, comics and students talk about working with Mark—about seeing him in some obscure venue or some long-cancelled television show, going on about how they wrote jokes together. All lies. Lies or fantasies. It's like the way three million people claim they were at Woodstock the morning Jimi Hendrix cranked out "The Star-Spangled Banner." Ninety-nine percent of them remember something that never happened. Not to them.

I met Mark my sophomore year at Saint Pius X High School here in Albuquerque. I didn't think much of him the first month. Nobody did. He was just this quiet, bespectacled kid with all the personality of a throw rug, hanging lifeless in the back of the class, like one of those outpatient types who puts his books away five minutes before the bell rings so he can grab his backpack and skitter out of the room, not to be heard from until the next day.

Then one Wednesday, Judy Scribner comes to school all whipped up and squawking about the speed of light. Maybe she saw an installment of *NOVA* on public television, and that got her engine revving. Perhaps she was reading Heisenberg or Planck or someone like that for a class project. You never knew with Judy. She was always onto something. She served as student body president as a junior and then half her senior year before graduating a semester early. She turned down a presidential scholarship to Columbia because she was so hell-bent on getting an appointment to the Naval Academy, serving at sea for two years, attending Villanova Law School, and emerging as this hotshot corporate shyster. She planned it all out. She was always getting those wild hairs and going all-out on some issue that she suddenly determined held the fate of the world in balance. One week she ranted about stopping abortions, the next about getting recycling bins set up in the cafeteria. This was the 1970s.

This one day, I come through the double doors holding books in one hand and two pens in the other. Even though Judy's down at the other end of the hallway, her squeals rise over the sound of shuffling feet, the slamming of lockers, and the din of students changing rooms, and they just about suck the air out of the place. She stands between the bulletin board and the water fountain, gesticulating and spouting something about Einstein and Special Relativity, holding court with two of her sycophants. Students file into the classroom, and she continues with her mini seminar, repositioning her front row desk so that it faces her protégés. None of those three girls notice when Father

Farris—the guy we called the Designer Priest—struts in and writes the next assignment on the chalkboard. Judy prattles on, pounding her desk with the tip of her finger.

Farris takes attendance, and you still can't hear anything over Judy's polemics. Finally, that priest, with his Brylcreemed hair, shiny black sports coat, and trimmed salt-and-pepper mustache, jots down the names of absent students, stands dead center of the room, right under the clock and crucifix, and clears his throat. Judy waves him off, as if telling him to be patient, that he'll get his turn, and keeps at it. After another "ahem," she stops, glances over her shoulder, and then gets all over him. She says that if you are traveling in a rocket ship at 185,999.99999 miles per second, just a tad below the speed of light, and you switch on your headlights, the beams supposedly shoot away at 186,000 miles per second.

"How can that happen?" she asks as she straightens her chair. "Those beams should be going almost twice the speed of light, and you said nothing can go faster than the speed of light. How can this happen?" At that, she slaps both palms on the desk, demanding an answer.

Farris clips his pen to the inside flap of the attendance roll and sets the book on his desk. He strokes his mustache, unbuttons his jacket, and presses his fingertips together, as if he's starting a sermon. He speaks precisely. He knew how to command the stage. I'll give him that.

"First of all," he says and clears his throat, "if your craft went that fast, it would be squeezed into a speck smaller than a hydrogen molecule."

Judy leans forward, plants her elbows on her notebook, pushes up her glasses, and says, "But theoretically. What would happen *in theory*?"

Farris opens his hands, as if he is invoking the congregation to pray, as though he didn't hear her and merely needs to finish his point.

"So," he says, "the question is purely hypothetical."

Judy slaps her desk again and stomps on the tile.

"So?" Judy says, "I'm not hearing an answer."

Farris makes another church steeple with his fingertips, as if taking his time to prepare us for another piece of the puzzle. He tugs on his collar and takes a deep breath.

A voice rings out from the back of the room: "Time will slow and space will contract."

Farris's eyes flare. Judy's head whips around. One of Judy's underlings titters, and Ron Montoya rolls his eyes and muffles a laugh. But you can practically hear the clicking of necks as heads turn, and all that energy redirects itself to the back corner. In the crabapple tree just the other side of the window, a magpie flutters her wings, rattling the leaves.

There, under the stylized retablos—those two-dimensional depictions of the Father, Son, and Holy Spirit, of Saint Francis Xavier with his halo, surplice, stole, and crucifix—under a collection of Ojos de Dios fashioned out of colored yarn and wooden dowels, in a pool of morning light spilling in from the eastern windows, sits Mark Wladika, staring over an open Superman comic book. His permanently-tinted, photo-gray eyeglass lenses hide any emotion or vulnerability. Thin locks of blond-brown hair curl up at his neck.

He speaks softly, almost meekly, as if discomfited by the sudden attention. "The speed of light must stay constant," he says, "so time and space have to compensate."

He adjusts his glasses and looks around.

The clock ticks.

"What I mean," he says, and his voice trails off before more words come out bold and forceful. "What I mean is that time and space are illusions of consciousness. Only light is real."

He surveys the room. Judy grips the front of her desk, her mouth agape. Farris seems frozen in shock. A fluorescent light hums.

"Just saying," Mark says. He puts down his head and goes on reading.

Those words—"the space will contract"—came out with such authority it felt like it took a good ten minutes for them to finish ringing out of the air.

Three weeks later, I come out of art history into the afternoon light, and I catch Farris crossing the grass, on his way to hear confessions. I walk alongside him and ask about what Mark said. At the entrance to the chapel, he pauses, removes his sunglasses, and says that it took him three weeks of research, but every account he read, every conversation he had, indicated Mark was spot-on.

"That young man," Farris said as he tugged on his belt, "that young man condensed one of the secrets of the universe into what? Three sentences, eh?"

Farris was six hours and half a dissertation away from a Ph.D. in physics. Judy Scribner was the pride of St. Pius. That morning both were put in their places by a fifteen-year-old nobody noticed before.

That's when I knew we were dealing with a superior intellect.

JACK

This one February night during my last year of college, I came home from waiting tables at the Red Lobster feeling lower than whale dung. I kicked the door behind me and didn't even notice whether it clicked shut. I found my last can of Pabst Blue Ribbon in the fridge, popped it open, and slurped off the foam. I flopped onto the couch with my legs cantilevered over the arm. I didn't touch the beer again. Within a few minutes, I got all hung up thinking and lost myself in the charcoal air. Difficult work nights always leave me feeling limp as a lettuce leaf in a sauna.

When I woke the next morning, my arms were crossed over my chest. The television was on low volume, and a talking head blathered on about something that was supposed to be paramount to the fate of humanity. I checked my watch. Still three hours before class. I closed my eyes and saw once again those events that haunted me for weeks but were, for whatever reason, especially vivid that night. It's funny how, when you get tired and angry enough, past events and ongoing fantasies jumble all together in your head.

I saw myself ease my Toyota up the slope of the driveway and let it roll along the sidewalk, into the shadows under a line of junipers, a few feet away from a black mailbox. When it comes to a stop, the car sits at a slant—the driver's side wheels on the tarmac, the passenger's side tires resting on the concrete. I cut the engine and turn down the radio. I shiver, rub my bare hands together, ball them up, and huff steam into my fingers. Even with the heater blasting, the morning cold is almost unbearable. I wait, listening to the last of a story on NPR about how some father from Texas will not be executed for strapping his two sons into car booster seats in the back of his Ford and pushing the car into an icy lake.

Next to me, on my passenger seat, sit a pair of binoculars and a six-inch boning knife, the best Chicago Cutlery has to offer.

Minutes later, Nina Totenberg's report on a Supreme Court ruling fades into a musical segue. Then Frank Deford discusses the ridiculousness of the World Cup, how Brazil and Sweden spent three hours running around the grass, and with zillions of fans watching all over the world, ended their match in a zero/zero tie.

Before very long, a light goes on in the house across the street, and so I lift the binoculars and twist the diopter wheel until the shadow behind the curtain sheers comes into sharp focus. At first, it is impossible to tell if it is Gustavo or his wife. Certainly, not one of his children. The large fluorescent comes on, and the harsh light displays the fullness of the silhouette. It is a male with big, goofy eyeglasses, like he hasn't updated his wardrobe since the 1980s. It is Gustavo Kaiser. He walks—actually, he takes two bounding steps—toward the refrigerator to where the parted drapes allow me a full, unobstructed view. His starched shirt collar, turned up, points at his jowls. An unknotted necktie hangs like a stole around his shoulders. Then he leans over the kitchen sink, letting water run as he scrapes the crust of microwaved oatmeal from the side of the bowl with his thumbnail. He dries his hands on a towel, which he redrapes over the handle of the built-in oven.

Once he disappears toward the back door, I pick up the knife, get out, shut the car door as quietly as I can, slink across the street, and hide in the shadows behind a line of spruces.

Clicks and clanks come from the back fence as Gustavo works the frozen latch. He shoves the slatted gate with his shoulder, and it pops open. He turns up the collar of his thigh-length coat and tucks his muffler under it. He fumbles with a car key before opening his Volvo Sport, steps into the compartment, and sets his briefcase on the passenger seat. With one heel resting in the driveway and the rest of his body deep in the cavity, he sticks the key in the ignition. The engine cranks, coughs, and gives up. Gustavo gives it another go, and the motor gasps and then goes silent. He pumps the accelerator, waits, and turns the key again. This time a blast of black smoke escapes the tailpipe, and the engine comes alive. It squeals—the fan belt is loose—but finally settles down, humming as if freshly tuned. He steps out of the car, slaps a plastic ice scraper against the palm of his gloved hand, and begins working the frost off the windshield.

I slink up behind him. He scores a second thick stripe through the white glazing. He taps the blade on the tire's sidewall to dislodge the powdery build-up and is about to strip off some more when I reach in front of him and cover his whole face with my bare hand. I shove my ring and middle fingers deep into his moist nostrils and grit my teeth. Even when he is not facing my direction, the sourness of his breath is overwhelming, as if his sinuses are rotting. It smells like garbage. He grunts, and I cup his chin and shove his mouth closed. He fights, but I contain him. I yank back his cranium, elongating his neck, dig with my fingers until I get hold of the cashmere scarf, slip it off, and drop it on the cement. He pries at my fingers and slugs at my forearm. His legs flail.

I slice clean through the jugular.

Blood spurts onto my sleeve and the frosted concrete before waterfalling down his neck.

He squirms. He kicks like he can't decide if he wants to fight me off or run away.

He gasps, swallows, elbows at me, but makes no contact. He recoils and shoves his leg out, and this throws off my balance, so I twist, keep his feet elevated, and lean my hip up against the back fender of his car to anchor myself. Crimson fluid sprays against the back window, bumper, and the frozen pavement. It drips from the sleeve of his fresh woolen coat. It doesn't take very long for the chi to leach from his muscles. Once he is weak enough, I drop him on the white grass. There he sits, his legs buckled under him. He presses a leather driving glove to his neck, and dark fluid leaks from between his fingers. A gurgle works its way up through his throat. He looks around, as if trying to spot the culprit. Steam rises from the dark puddle growing in front of him.

That's what I saw. All night long. Over and over.

At least eight times that winter, I actually crawled out of bed just after four a.m., slipped on my thermal underwear, boots, and fatigues, and drove to that North Campus neighborhood. I hid my rice grinder there in that patch of darkness just across the street from Gustavo's bourgeois four bedroom with its long driveway and Cold-War era layout. In that frigid air, intent on my NPR, I picked up the skinny-bladed knife, thumbed the stainless steel edge, yanked up my coat sleeve, and to test the sharpness, shaved away arm hair, leaving a postage stamp sized bald patch just below my wrist watch. That tempered steel was so well-honed a rabbi could use it to kill a bull. Through the binoculars, I saw him moving through that front window.

Those mornings I didn't drive out to Gustavo's house, I spent my pre-dawn moments with my imagination going totally psycho-killer. I visualized the slaughter and, sometimes, even felt the cold steel slicing through the stubbled skin of his neck, cutting through muscle and tendons. I felt metal scrape against bone. I obsessed on it, like some crazy man. Night after night after night. For months. Maybe for years. I still think about it now, but no longer see it with the same kind of microscopic detail. As far as I know, that bastard Gustavo never saw my car tucked into the opaque darkness under his neighbor's evergreens.

In the end, I let Gustavo live. For whatever reason, I allowed that demon to go on fouling up perfectly good air. I let him see his children grow up. Yet, there are still nights when my anger and hatred overwhelm me. Sometimes I think I might one day finish the job.

MICA

My cell phone buzzes all spastic against the lamp on my night stand, so I reach from under the covers, grab, and flip it open. I clear my throat and croak this "um, yeah" into the mouthpiece. On the other end some Godzilla is all like "Yeah yourself." I ask who it is, and he gets majorly riled, going on about how he plans to string me up from the nearest telephone pole and flay my hide the next time he sees me, and so like I need to look both ways twice before crossing the street and everything. I ask his name again, and this fires him up even more. He says something like "this is Gordon" or Gordy or some alien name like that. I'm all like "Dude, you tapped in the wrong digits" and everything, and he's all like "I'm gonna stomp your ass out." So I tell him to double his lithium dosage, call 911, and to try to listen only to the nicey-nice voices in his head.

Gordy goes at it, so I like punch the little green button to eighty-six the call and everything, but instead of shutting it down, I somehow put the unit into speaker phone mode, which scares me even more. So I snap the thing closed, and his cussing still pumps out of the back, so I like totally hold down the power button with both thumbs, and the whole front screen stays like all illuminated as the tirade rages on, Gordy all squealing and squawking about how he wants his money, ranting like I just kidnapped his prize pit bull or something. I claw at the back of the unit, find the slot at the bottom, and pry at it with my thumbnail until the polycarbonate backing snaps off. My heart almost pumps out of my chest as I disengage the battery, and it tumbles onto the floor and under the bed. The apparatus goes dead.

I like so know that the dude has the wrong number, but that leaves me all frazzled just the same. I curl up, pull my covers all up over my head and everything, and try to untangle my thoughts, trying to get my heart rate out of scared-rabbit mode.

Just before dawn, I zip the last pocket on my suitcase when this heavy pounding comes from the other side of the front door, loud as shotgun blasts. I am still like massively angsty and everything, and so I slink out over to the picture window, kneel on the couch arm, and stick a finger between two slats of the mini blinds, just in case some South Valley vato drove up to the Heights and is all ready to shank me on my porch. I'm still like totally rankled, thinking that I can actually expect some cholo assassin to be polite enough to knock on my door before he guts me like a fish. Out in the coolness of dawn, this hot air balloon floats over the housetops, this massive tongue of fire blazing up through the pear-shaped envelope as it goes all luminous against the ultramarine sky. Mark stands under the porch light, his lips all puckered like he's whistling or something, his hands shoved deep in the pockets of his cargo shorts. He gazes up, all fascinated by that spectacular and luminescent bubble all floating over the housetops.

Minutes later, I drop my suitcase into the trunk of his Volvo and hang my dress shirt on the handle by the back window. As I'm buckling my seat belt, I'm all telling Mark about the Gordy. This is so totally my first heart-to-heart with Mark and everything. I mean, like we exchanged phone numbers at the comedy club the week before, when we made plans to drive out to Arizona together, but that was like purely utilitarian. So as I situate myself in his sedan, I like know nothing about this guy except that he is this new Albuquerque comedian with some major joo joo—so awesome I'm like all intimidated and everything— and all the other comics think I am so lucky that he chose me to be the emcee for the Tucson show. We drive off, and within a few minutes the guy has me totally at ease.

I got my back against the door as we scoot down Interstate 25, and in like five minutes we like start playing trivia about all the places we pass. Just the other side of the airport you got your town of Los Lunas, a name which I say means "the moons," and he says that since you got your *Los* Lunas—with an O—rather than your *Las* Lunas—with an A—it's gotta mean the name comes from some family named Luna or something. He tells me that some rock & roll pioneer named Bo Diddley once lived there and everything, and I tell him he must be good at history since he's lived through most of it.

Further on down the road, you got your town named Belen, which means "Bethlehem" in the Español, which is something we both know. So we exchange like a million more tidbits. The dude like knows everything.

Then you got your city called Socorro, home of the nerd haven called New Mexico Institute of Mining and Technology. I tell him the city of Socorro means "help," and he says that it was probably named for Our Lady of Perpetual Help, who is like a favorite of Byzantine Catholics, the religion he grew up in, but he always called the church in Albuquerque "Our Lady of Perpetual Hell."

Beyond that, you got your remains of San Marcial, this town that got all washed away in the mondo flood of 1929. He says that God was punishing America for homosexuals, even way back then, and I think he's like all serious until he can't hold it in any longer, and we both lose it. As we banter, he like offers me all the caffination I want, telling me to help myself to the Viennese roast in his Stanley thermos, which is rattling around there in the back seat every time we take a curve. After that he like totally pulls out your tortilla chips, your Fig Newtons, trail mix, pistachios, and clementine oranges, and puts them all directly at my disposal. I offer to help with gas money, but he's like all like no way, dude. Like I'm totally the headliner and everything.

I ask him how many years he's done comedy and everything, and the answer he gives pretty much astounds. He tells me he just started. That he just did his first open-mic like a month before. I say that's totally amazing. That I've been making the Albuquerque amateur comedy rounds for going on four years and just got my first paying gig. I ask him if he has thought about trying to get into one of the Improv clubs or even Pancho Pilot's up in Denver, which seems to be a springboard to the stars and everything. For most of us, it's like totally impossible to get into, I say, but I am sure he could do it.

"Pancho Pilot's?" he says, like he's all trying to remember where it is. "Oh yeah, people tell me I should go there. But I'm not sure that's the path I want."

I don't get it.

"I want to build my career around the Albuquerque area," he says. "I'm just doing the Tucson gig this one time."

A comedy career just working Albuquerque? The dude is like totally talking in riddles.

We push on down the desert highway, past these radical sandstone cliffs, the likes of which I've never seen before, or maybe I just never ever noticed. We shoot up these small mountains and pass all these empty country roads south of the Gila Wilderness in New Mexico's boot heel, out past the Hatch—the chile capital of the world—past the Deming, and onto the Lordsburg, where we stop for more coffee. Once we get back on the road again, Mark's like all sipping from his travel mug and then just like says right out, like he's been cogitating about the whole drama for three hours, that Gordy's phone call was a sign from God. I got like zero clues as to what he means. He says it is some coded message that I needed to focus like a laser beam right in on something—treat it like it's some deep, unsolvable problem, like a Zen koan or something. My first thought is that he's totally punking me. Turns out the joker's like totally serious. That I need to keep at it until I find the way—perhaps the only way—to get the whole thing to unravel.

I'm telling you, the dude like totally talked in riddles.

He goes on, chattering about signs from the universe and everything. Just then my phone buzzes, and no number comes up, and so I flip the unit open, and the Gordy maniac is on the other end, going schizoid all over again about how this is the last time I backstab him and how he plans to totally reduce me to a grease stain. This proceeds on at least two minutes until Mark grabs the phone—like so yanks it out of my hand—and says, like utterly cool and calm: "If you want this guy, you're going to have to come through me. And I'll shove my finger in one of your eye sockets, hook it through the other, then strip your nose bone out of your face."

It's not just what he says but also the way he speaks, man. Like he's got total understanding and intimacy with every bone, muscle, and tendon he mentions. It's enough to leave me wigged out. I mean, you just can't help but get all swept up in his spell and overpowered in the tidal wave of strength that gushes out of him—the conviction, the power, the life force. It totally lives in every word he speaks, the way he annunciates each syllable, the way the sounds seem to come from deep in his gut. At that, Gordy disengages. Mark listens for a second to make sure the connection really stays dead and then snaps the phone shut and hands it over, like he's offering me a stick of gum or something. That's the last I ever hear from that demon Gordy.

After a while, I lay my head between the headrest and the shoulder of the seat, and I like totally tune out.

I have no clue as to how long I sleep. My dream fizzles, and I like return to consciousness as all these crazy noises just like bombard me: the slapping and squeaking of a shredding windshield wiper, the hum of an electric motor, that rhythmic patter of the thick drops against the glass and the metallic roof, and a low and muffled wheezing. I rub my eyes, stretch my neck, and let out this yawn. When I can finally pull the pieces together, I am like totally amazed. It is like I have to blink and blink again just to clear the clouds from my eyes and brain. Even though he stares into that dark and gnarly sky, Mark still wears his sunglasses. He drives up behind an eighteen-wheeler so fast it's like we're going to ram the bumper or at least get caught up in its air pocket and get sucked along the highway. Once we finally pass and Mark glances back to check his blind spot, I catch this shiny thing moving down his cheek. I mean the dude is like totally weeping, like his grandma just died.

So I'm like so wondering what has him so disjointed and everything, and he sticks his finger under the lens of his Ray Bans and then sniffs back some snot. He finds this napkin in the side door pocket, opens it, and lets out this trumpet blast of a nose-blow. He sniffs some more, wipes his lip, and like sniffs again.

He feels my eyes on him and everything, so finally he just says something so soft I gotta make him repeat.

"Your father," he says, then glances my way and then back to the road. "Did you grow up with him?"

I'm all like, "Well, kind of, you know?"

He's all like, "What do you mean 'kind of'?" and so I decide what the hell? Since we've been joking around like long-lost cousins or something. Besides, I am like so at ease it's no big deal to lay my own private melodrama on him.

You see, back when I was a kid, I say, I mowed lawns and chopped weeds for two summers straight, just saving up money for this radical Washburn acoustic twelve-string. The deal was that I would pay for half of it and Dad would pay the rest, including the tax. So like that summer I turned fourteen, Dad and I talk on the phone every night for a week. The plan is that on Thursday he comes for me, and we head down to Gabriel's Vintage Instruments in the South Valley to check out these guitars. After that, the plan goes, we'll stop for pizza and then wind up the night down at Isotopes Park, to take in some minor league baseball and then stay for the fireworks show.

So I'm like all waiting there in grandma's living room all afternoon, sprawled out on the braided rug and all doing crossword puzzles and Sudoku games and everything, just to pass time until he knocks. I'm all secretly hoping he'll come early because I haven't seen the guy since before school let out. Finally, the dude staggers past the front gate like forty-five minutes late, almost trips coming up the porch steps, and smells like rocket fuel. Grandma holds the screen door open and lays into him. She's all like, "You're not taking the boy out when you're all soused like that," and she like won't let me get near him until he gives up his car keys and everything.

So they joust a few rounds and grandma gets all overheated and tells him to leave and that we can try it again next week. Finally, the old man tosses his keys onto the candy dish on the bookshelf, grabs my hand, and like drags me out the door. Even though this monsoon is like swelling out above the Sandia Mountains and threatening to unleash, we walk around the corner to the park down by the schoolyard, and he settles into this rubber swing and crooks his arm around the chain. He tells me he has to go like far, far away, speaking all slow and precise, like I'm mental or something. He goes on, not letting me talk until he sticks a finger inside the flip pack of his Marlboros and fishes out this yellow pin joint, each end twisted all perfect. He has to pat his pockets for like two minutes to find his cigarette lighter, and after he does, he sits there puffing all nonchalant, like he's just gnawing on licorice or something—like totally oblivious that he's committing this felony in public and that a suspicious cop could come and like massively change the course of his life. He looks across the way at the hard lines of the old hospital building and the angled roofs of all those Queen Anne and pueblo style houses. At the wall of olive and poplar trees that look all Gothic because of the thunderstorm moving in and everything. Then he cranks up the Jewish jokes:

Why did the Jewish-American Princess refuse the colostomy? She couldn't find shoes to match the bag.

What do you get when you squeeze a synagogue? Juice.

Have you heard about the new German microwave? Seats twelve.

A cop stops an old Jewish guy on the highway and tells him, "Did you know your wife fell out of your car two miles back?" The geezer says, "Oh, thank God. I thought I was going deaf."

What do you get when you cross a Mexican with a Jew? A janitor who owns the building.

The reefer is all bouncing between his lips and jets of smoke shoot out of his nose as he laughs. He puts a fist to his mouth. He still smells like cheap gin or whatever he's been chugging all day. He holds the joint out between scissored fingers as he like grips the swing chain and laughs until he coughs and more smoke flows out his nose. Then he pinches the very end of the reefer, lays his foot across his lap, and all delicately rakes the ash end against his shoe, makes sure it's out, squeezes open the cigarette pack, and drops in the roach, like he's dropping an olive into a martini or something. He starts telling me about how sometimes manhood demands that you make some hard choices. He dries his eyes with the heel of his palm, all dramatic. Before long he hides his whole face with his hand, plants a toe in the gravel, and pushes himself back and forth. He tells me how, when he was fourteen, his stepfather caught him with this water-damaged copy of *Penthouse* magazine in the shed out back and beat his back and hips with a razor strop while his kid brother looked on. He's like getting totally maudlin and weepy and stuff about how he never wanted to be that kind of a father.

That's when he lays the whole trip on me, the one about him checking into detox and everything.

Three years later, he calls me the week after my birthday, like he's all tore up because he hasn't seen me in years, and he wants to know if

I feel like I'm ready for high school, and I tell him I graduate in a few months. Then, in early May, I get this handwritten, touchy-feely letter about how much he wants to see me. That he's trying like hell to beat it back to Albuquerque before the end of the summer. That's when he so totally fades into oblivion.

I tell Mark that, in his heart of hearts, the old man so thought himself a good and decent person, someone who believed he did his best. I believe it, too. That that was the old man's level best. That's the funny part.

"The other thing I gotta give my old man," I say as I lower the window and release a handful of nut shells into the wind, "is that he loved jokes. Maybe that's why I want to be a comedian."

Mark puts a finger under his nose and sucks back more mucus. He switches to the other lane, and we zip past a motorcycle. Lightning flickers over the southern hills.

"Count yourself as a lucky man," Mark says. "A lucky, lucky man."

I tell you, the cat totally spoke in riddles. I kept thinking that, sooner or later, he might push out an explanation for one or two of them.

EDDIE

The waitress working the comedy show is a Bengali transplant with a name tag reading "Lakshmi," and she has a creosote-black braid, thick as a bowline, hanging over her shoulder. I order a Blanton's single barrel on the rocks with a splash of soda. As with just about everybody else in Española, New Mexico, "soda" translates as "cola," and a few minutes later she delivers a mixture with the golden glow of root beer sans the foamy head. My first impulse is to send it back, to protest the waste of fine liquor, but her thick lips, the top one curved like a cupid's bow, stretch into this smile so radiant it practically sets a glint off her incisor with the "ping" of a percussionist's triangle.

Besides, the cocktail comes just as Mica Pierson finishes his set and Jana Boan, this cute little lesbian with wild green hair who serves as the emcee, introduces me. So all I have time for is to thank Miss New Delhi, smile back, lay two bills on the polished granite, and run up to the stage. It seems that for the next fifty minutes I am doomed to sipping on top-notch bourbon ruined with caramel coloring and high-fructose corn syrup.

You can blame me for the situation, at least up until that point. I came late from my room after an extra-long nap and shower, so I didn't get to the showroom until Jana was on stage, talking about dying her hair green and then spooling out her monologue about how she gets involved in a lesbian wedding. About how the couple has a bridal registry at a hardware store, how she ends up buying them hers and hers towels, and how instead of a first dance they have a softball game. It's a strong chunk of material that would endear her to the crowd just about anywhere else. Then Mica, this big burly guy with geek eyeglasses, goes up after her, and I don't catch much of his set because I am at a table in the back of the lounge, going over the jokes I'd come up with on the ninety-minute drive from Albuquerque and still agonizing about how to fit them into my routine. Composing jokes, that's the easy part. The hard part is remembering them and carving out places where they'll work.

Both Jana and Mica get only get a couple of decent laughs, but I don't tune in enough to be aware of any subtleties, so I really don't know what I am getting into. That's what happens when you come in late and don't get a feel for the crowd.

I do, however, catch Mica doing his "guy stuff" bit, his usual closer. It's this act-out about how he and his buddies get into activities like going hunting for cougars—in downtown Albuquerque on a Saturday night—and how his girlfriend gets mad when he mounts his trophy in the den. It is an inventive—and incredibly visual—piece of stand-up. Usually, it leaves the audience rocking, clapping, and holding their sides as he inserts the microphone into its collar, waves goodbye, thanks the emcee, and exits into the wings. This time he draws the whole thing out, going about two minutes longer than usual, talking about how one of the women was a paranoid, codependent agoraphobic who wouldn't leave her house unless accompanied by somebody she thought was stalking her. About how when he finally found a woman who had been around the block a few times, she turned out to be a Jehovah's Witness.

All the bit elicits this time is a crackle of laughter from the middle of the room and a few titters from the corners.

Finally, Mica plants the mic stand atop the masking tape X on the floor, reinserts the cordless, shakes his head, and stomps down the steps as Jana comes up. He doesn't even wave goodbye.

Jana stands in front of the microphone, the colored stage lights making the spikes of hair running down the middle of her head all the more dramatic. She reads off a napkin, announcing that bottles of Rolling Rock beer are two dollars and well drinks are three. She talks up the next show, which will feature three Amarillo comics. She wads up the paper, sticks it in her pocket, and announces, "Are you ready for your headliner?"

A single "woot-woot" emanates from the darkness, then some tepid cheers. Up front, a dark man in a sleeveless flannel shirt pushes his cowboy hat farther up on his head and slaps his hands together three times, clapping as if he's being sarcastic. He drains the last of his Coors, sets the bottle on the table, and grabs a roll of his belly fat that is as thick as a bread loaf. He jiggles and examines it, as if mystified as to when it got there.

"I said, are you ready for your headliner?"

This time Jana gets a few more hoots and some applause. She proceeds.

"You're gonna love this guy. He's an author, a comedian, a playwright, a scholar of sacred literature—and a spoiler of women. Let's give it up for the professor, Eddie Tafoya."

I go up, and as I extend my hand, Jana ducks behind me and whispers, "Good luck with these trogs." I push the stool aside, plant my setlist on the seat, and my drink on top of that. As I go into my opener, this hefty youngster comes from the back of the room, plodding down the center aisle. She looks no older than twenty-five. She's in a T-shirt that doesn't come far enough down her waist to conceal her stretch marks or muffin top, and she's got a gingersnap-sized tattoo on her shoulder. She strides down like she's making a beeline to center stage, like she's determined to tell me off or cuss me out for abandoning her and our child. She screams: "You dirty son-of-a-bitch! You filthy motherfucker!"

The cowboy up front raises himself up into a respectable position, scratches his head, works a wad of gum, and pushes a clump of graying curls behind his neck. When the girl gets past the first row, she angles out toward the emergency exit, the change in perspective revealing a cell phone pasted to her ear. She struts on, still screaming: "You better hang up those shirts, every last one of them, or you'll be praying for death. Hear me? Praying for death!"

With my opening joke ruined, all I can do is go for the saver:

"Looks like the bus from the trailer park has arrived."

Someone in the back shadows chuckles. A lady with teased and lacquered hair under the Coors sign checks her watch. Her husband drums the top of his cane with his fingertips. I drop back into the opening sequence I planned.

"Give it up for Mica and Jana. I was back there laughing like a dyke at a mullet festival."

A twenty-something in a Dallas Cowboys jersey off to the side gets that one, so I add the tag that usually brings them around.

"But I've been doing lines with the waitresses."

The cowboy up front stands, teeters, unbuckles his belt, and hitches it up a notch. He gives his head a quick shake, as if to clear out the fog. He pulls a roll of bills from his pocket, sways as he wipes the corner of his mouth, unfolds a single, and slides it under the coaster. He sticks a thumb under a strand of curls hanging on the side of his face and sweeps it behind his ear, pauses, and resets his hat. He takes a breath and stumbles up into the darkness, waddling off toward the Texas Hold 'em tables.

Casino shows come with rules all their own. For one thing, the profit doesn't come from the entertainment—unless it's a national icon like Steven Wright or Chris Rock. What the owners want is to get people in to watch the comedy and then lure them to the slot machines and roulette tables. Besides, the crowds tend to be old and unsophisticated: a lot of blue-haired ladies puffing on filterless Camels, dragging around oxygen tanks and diabetic husbands. Real John Birch, Tea Party, urban hick crowds. Unless you really know what you're doing, you can't risk getting into jokes about politics. If you decide to stride into the areas of coitus or oral sex, you can only suggest. Once you reference any sex organ directly, the crowd could turn on you. It's happened to all of us.

Since I contracted for fifty minutes, I have no choice but to keep at it. I reel off another one-liner, and then another. Then another. Just as I get to my next extended bit, the Desi cocktail waitress comes up the aisle with a tray full of bottles of light beer, that sable braid bouncing against her breast and those swollen and unpainted lips framing that electric smile. She gleams at her customers as she leans down and distributes the drinks. Her patrons say they want food but can't decide between the regular or super nachos. Everyone in the room hears the conversation. Bottles clink and she scratches out the order on her pad.

I go on.

"By the way, tonight is lady's night. Not here in the lounge, but meet me in the parking lot—I'll give you a two-for-one."

That gets nothing, so again, the situation demands that I go for making the lemonade. The waitress jots something on her pad, and I point at her.

"Let's have a nice round of applause for Lakshmi. She looks like my second wife. And I've only been married once."

Lakshmi checks the couple at another front table and surveys the room on her way out, oblivious to my punchline. I move into my chunk about working as a college professor, when a voice hidden in the back shadows bellows out: "Tell nigger jokes."

Whoever's yelling has an Oklahoma twang that emphasizes the hard Gs. I adjust the microphone saddle and try to ignore the catcall, but another heckle comes.

"Tell jokes about them goddamn Negros," he says, rolling the R, pronouncing the word as the Spanish word for "blacks."

I go on about how I started out in college studying sacred literature, stole the textbook for my Bible class, read it, and gave it back.

But another interruption drowns out my reveal: "Tell nigger jokes. Tell goddamned jigaboo jokes!"

I take a short sip of bourbon and cola, set the glass down, tug one sleeve of my sport coat and then the other.

"Listen, dude," I call to the opaque blackness. "If you shut up, I'll buy you a drink. Whatta ya having?"

The guy barks back something like how he's drinking a hell of a lot more than I am, so I ask again: "Seriously, what are you having?" He slurs "All night long" and then breaks into this extended bray.

I search the back of the room for the waitress, pretend I see her, and say, "Sweetheart? Let's get this guy a double shot of Kaopectate. That stuff's great for shutting up assholes."

The foursome at a front table chortle. Three people behind them actually clap. I move on into a bit about my being a Latino who looks like a white guy.

"Now, I am supposed to be Latino . . ."

I adjust the whole mic stand, but before I get through the set-up line the swarthy cowboy who sat up front before he left in disgust trudges down the side to the front of the stage, wobbling like one leg is shorter than the other. He stumbles over a wrinkle in the carpet but regains his balance. He totters forward and bumps the table he just vacated, causing the empty to teeter, fall over, and rattle onto the floor. He burps and says, "I tol' you to tell some goddamn jungle bunny jokes."

He takes off his hat, runs a hand over his graying curls, clasps his hair at the back of his head in a ponytail, and lets it go as he tugs the Stetson back into place.

I scan the peripheries for a security guard. The only action anywhere is the bartender in the back lining up of a row of shot glasses. The cowboy sways and wipes his mouth with the back of his hand. I let loose with another joke. He snarls.

"You gunna tell us some goddamn jigaboo stories or am I gunna-hafta to mop that stage with your dumb güero ass?"

I stick one hand in my pocket, and with the other pick my cocktail up off the stool and stage-whisper into the microphone, "This is not the obese, inbred, alcoholic, retarded truck driver part of the show. We can watch you puke later."

"Up yours, vato," he says and wipes his mouth again. "You wanna throw?"

"I want to tell jokes," I say. "Not talk to one."

His cheek juts out, swollen with a wad of chewing gum. A drop of sweat runs down his neck behind a silver crucifix half-hidden in a nest of black-and-gray hairs. He takes off his hat and slaps the crown against his fist.

"Somebody just migh' hafta shut your goddamn pie-hole for you, son."

I pick up the mic stand and slam the base into the floor, just for effect.

"Listen, Hopalong Martinez," I say. "I am working here. Can you see that? When your mother's working, I don't run up on stage, grab her ankles, and drag her out from under the donkey."

The room erupts in laughter, and the steer rustler pulls his chin to one side of his mouth and chews some more. He cocks his head, as if suddenly realizing other people are in the room. His chest puffs up. He scratches his chest and fidgets with his medallion.

"You goddamn, white boy son-of-a-bitch," he says.

I take a longer drink this time and punctuate my gulp with an extended "aaahh." I have their attention.

"Why don't you throw away that Stetson and pull a condom over your head?" I say. "If you're going to act like a dick, you may as well dress like one."

A loud hoot punctuates the swell of laughter. He glances up, then over at the exit sign, and lets the insult sink in. He is the center of the vortex. He pulls his hat on tight and stands with his arms hanging out at his sides, as if he's expecting a gun fight. I stare him down.

"You bastid," he says. "Pinche bastid. You better take that back."

I take another gulp of bourbon and Coke, and as I set the glass down, a beer bottle shatters against the back wall of the stage. A shard of glass clatters and spins by my shoe. The cowboy chews some more, snarls, and spits on the floor.

"I didn't mean to insult your mama," I say. "I am sure that having a donkey's cock shoved in her pussy is a welcome improvement over the horse's ass that came out of it."

He says something I don't get as he plants both hands on the wooden planks and swings his leg up past the wooden lip of the stage. The heel of his boot catches the edge but slips back. He tries to hoist himself again, and just as he does, his elbow buckles, his whole shoulder collapses into the hardwood, and he falls back onto the floor. He struggles to his feet, and as his fat hand grips the lip of the stage and he works to pull himself to a stand, I run to the stairs at the other end, push past the velvet curtain, and open the emergency exit door, fully expecting to set off a bank of sirens. Once out in the parking lot, I bend over, hands on my knees, trying to quell my laughter while staying alert to the sound of approaching boot steps. I take a deep breath and listen. I put a fist to my lips as another chuckle bubbles up.

The parking lot is calm enough. The streetlamps cast a golden sheen on the rows of cars and trucks that stretch out toward the mesa. There is just enough light to make each of the tops look freshly washed. Over the far hills, a three-quarter moon shines through a sheet of clouds, the cottony wisps of fringe glowing silvery white. In the circle drive, at the hotel's entryway, a half-ton pickup idles, the engine eliciting a low rumble. A door slams. The Toyota engine revs and groans. The driver slips the transmission into gear, and the truck rolls off toward the highway. I chortle again and look behind me, and someone coughs. There, under the casino portico, next to the valet parking drop-off, stands a short and slight man with a hand on his hip. He says something I can just make out to someone I can't see, someone either taking luggage into the resort or bringing the stuff out.

He speaks again, and this time the words ring out clearly: "Eddie should be on soon." It is Mark's voice. I am sure of it. I take one last survey, making sure some rabid Okie isn't sneaking up, ready to slice me with a Bowie knife, and I make my way over to the main entrance to greet my best friend. To tell him how he not only missed my whole act but also a floor show teeming with fun, excitement, and threats of violence.

By the time the automatic doors slide open and I enter the lobby, the only person there is a kid in a blue button-up. He stands at his podium and jots something into a log book. I ask him what happened to the man who was just there, and all he can do is lift his head and look nonplussed, as if I just asked about finer points of brain surgery. I explain that twenty seconds before, a short and bald man stood out at the drop-off with a load of suitcases. The kid says he hasn't seen any action since he punched in just before nine thirty.

"Right here," I say. "Right out there in the breezeway. Just a few seconds ago."

He caps his pen and glances off to the side, at the fountain by the front door, and then back at me. He holds both hands out at his side, indicating his confusion, insisting that nobody has come in.

I tell him okay, cross the room, and examine the area: the smoked glass doors, the lobby fountain, the gas fireplace in the far corner, one hallway leading to the gift shop and slot machines, the other to the restaurant and hotel rooms. At the lobby bar, I lean on the imitation granite. The fat bartender points a remote control at a flat-screen television and asks what I'm drinking without looking back at me. I tell him a Blanton's and water, hold the plastic. He asks what I mean as he

66

flips through channels, and I say I don't need a swizzle stick. He finally decides on a basketball game, Celtics and Nets. My drink comes, and I lean on the bar and watch the hallway and wait for Mark to stride out and tell me he's searched all over the joint, that he's disappointed he missed my set. I stay ready to run, just in case the gum-chewing cowboy runs down the corridor foaming at the mouth. I gulp the last of my whiskey, ask for another, drop a ten spot on the hardwood, and I relocate to an overstuffed chair in the middle of the bar, one that gives me full view of the hallways and the main entrance.

The elevator pings and the stainless steel doors part. A hunched old man in a fishing cap and grayed socks up to his calves trudges out, looks up one way and down the other, orienting himself. He points toward the restaurant, as if directing the specter who follows him, and heads off in that direction. I reconsider the person I just saw outside: the body shape, posture, and voice. The sounds and pulsations of his words. I am absolutely sure that was Mark, so I wait a little longer. After the Celtics win, the bartender switches the television to a NASCAR race. I fish the last ice sliver out of my glass, crunch it between my molars, shove myself to a stand, and go see if I can find Mark.

HELEN DENISE

I undo this real little silver and crystal teardrop from its cardboard and hold the cute piece of jewelry up to my earlobe. As I check myself in the mirror mounted on the tent post, a woman bumps me, and then steps directly in front of the display spindle. She doesn't even bother to say "excuse me" or "pardon"—she doesn't say a darned thing. In fact, she acts like I'm not even there, as though our shoulders didn't just collide, as if none of the other people in that canvas booth saw the way she just about knocked me over. She places to her lips this imitation jade cigarette holder—you know, one of those real long thin tubes that were all the rage back in the 1920s—and crosses her arms like she's real hot stuff or something. She wears this bright-pink beret and a pair of red-framed, oversized sunglasses. She pulls her lips to one side and blows a line of smoke my direction and then, that lady, she raps on the display case with the back of a gloved hand, like she's gaveling her court to order. She commences to throw this conniption, demanding that the girl at the other end pay attention.

"Becca? Becca, dear?" she says as she taps the glass. "Over here."

At the other end, the twenty-something named Becca spreads a velvet rectangle on the glass and lays a turquoise necklace atop that, showing it to a pair of tourists. The girl pulls a ballpoint out of the clump of hair on top of her head and with it points out the details of the craftsmanship, the quality of the metal, and the spider markings of the stones.

"Becca, my dear," the woman repeats. "Over here, girl. Over here."

Becca calls back to her without turning her head.

"Just a little sec, Lola. Let me finish here, and then I'll be right over."

Lola crosses her arms and taps her bicep with her two middle fingers. Smoke swirls out her nostrils and from between her lips. She appears to glance out, across the way toward the stage where a musician sets up his snare drum and cymbals, but with her wearing those big, bug-eyed glasses it is impossible to tell exactly just what that woman's looking at.

Lola finishes her cigarette, plucks out the butt, drops it on the wood, and lets it smolder. She perks up again.

"You know Liza Jane?" she says, going on with the conversation with Becca as if some bell just dinged, signaling her turn to talk. "My cousin Liza Jane? She runs this operation, you know? She said some of these beads have flecks of magic. The real magic, not the fake stuff that her husband—who won't even talk to me anymore—tried to sell me last time. Just where'd you put them? I want some. Where are the enchanted beads? I especially need them today."

Becca nods at her customers and excuses herself as she reaches behind her head and pulls out a chopstick from her hair. Curls fall like a veil just above her shoulders.

"As a matter of fact, Lola," Becca says as she gathers her dark hair like a cord, twists it, sets it in back in place, and inserts the stick. "Liza called not five minutes ago. She wanted me to tell you that the ones with enchanted crystals, well, they just didn't come in today. We expect another shipment tomorrow. Or you can check next week at the Westside shop."

Lola sticks her smoker between her lips, plants her hand on her hip, clucks her tongue, and lets out a breathy, "My God." She shakes her head and says, "This always happens. Just when I need them, I can never find them."

She taps her foot, bites on the chewed end of the long tube, and reassesses. She pivots on her heel and steps out into the sunlight, merging with the river of people working their way through the temporary food, jewelry, curiosity stands, and the other canvas-walled shops of the Albuquerque Wine Festival.

I check my watch, replace the set of earrings on its hook, pull my bag strap higher up on my shoulder, and step out into the sunlight to look for Mark.

We arrived at the fiesta grounds out on the north side of town— you know, that big ol' 360-acre city park where they hold the hot air balloon competition every October—just after the gates opened, just as some of the merchants finished setting up their stores, and we had to wait in line only a few minutes for any of the samplings. Over the next couple of hours, the clouds rolled in, the day cooled off, and Mark and I tried the claret, the plum wine, a chocolate port, a cabernet flavored with New Mexico green chile, two tempranillos, some mead, and something called Indian Paintbrush from one of the wineries up in the Sangre de Cristo foothills.

Now, people flood the dirt pathways, going from stand to stand, chatting and laughing as they wait to swirl half ounces of Sangiovese, Riesling, and Merlot around in their teardrop-shaped glasses and pretend they really know a Shiraz from a Zinfandel. It's a real fun time. Parents push strollers, couples hold hands, high schoolers and college students strut around like they own the whole darned world—you know, like kids tend to do. I never attended anything like this before, mostly because I never was much on wine before I met Mark. This big ol' fair, though, is much more than I expected. In addition to the vintners' stations, you got places that sell not just the regular county fair foodstuffs like curly fries, polish sausages, turkey legs, and cotton candy, but you got stands and little wagons serving up Spanish tapas, Argentinean empanadas, spinach crepes, and even vegetarian sushi.

So there I wait, out of the way, in front of an arrangement of round boxes of garlic-flavored goat cheese stacked next to cocktail cups full of broken corn chips—for sampling, you know—and some more of red, green, mango, and tomatillo salsa, the bowls arranged so nice on top of a wooden platform. The place is getting so crowded I have to keep stepping out of the way of people who meander by. The whole time I look east, over the heads, hats, and faces headed my way, and can't help but get a little hungry smelling the greaseburgers grilling in a wagon nearby.

A cute, green-eyed, and unshaven young father walks my way, his toned pectorals showing through his thin, gray V-neck. He scans the crowd, as though trying to find somebody. At his shoulder he holds this darling little boy, an infant not even a year old, who has on a blue sunhat with the brim turned up. The child's eyes find mine and stay on me as they pass. I smile back. The baby pulls three fingers from his mouth, showing the slivers of those bottom teeth just coming in, and as he does a glob of saliva rolls down his arm. He reaches out to me with his wet hand and says something that sounds like "dah!"

How can you help but tingle when a child so young picks you out of the crowd like that?

After another minute or so, I finally catch a speck of off-white bouncing among the heads and faces. It draws nearer, and I am sure that it's Mark's cream-colored, woven fedora. I bought it for him for his birthday just two months before. The whole time I knew him, why, that was his favorite.

But even more telling is that gait.

He just about jangles when he walks—like he's always poised on the brink of some profound discovery. He gets closer, and I wave with just my fingers, and when he spots me his face blooms into a smile big enough to beat the band. He steps between two couples, past a group of teenagers, and maneuvers his way over. When he's just a few feet away, his lips part as though he's just dying to ask me something, but then something stops him in his tracks—something I can't see because three women cross in front of me and block my view. I step around them and what I do see, why, that shocks me to my very core? Lola, that loony lady from the jewelry tent, she has him stopped. She has refreshed her lipstick and smeared the red all past the lip line. She looks up at him and squeezes his wrist. She removes her sunglasses, mumbles something, and reaches up, takes his shades by one of the temples, and lifts them up just so carefully past his eyebrows.

You can't miss it. She has his deep-set eyes, the same freckled cheeks, that same celestial nose.

She puts the sunglasses back in place, brushes his hair from his forehead, traces the contours of his cheekbone with her whole hand, and cups his chin.

"My God," she says as she touches her middle finger to his lip. "My holy God. Good gracious. You look just like him. Exactly like your father. You even walk like him. My holy, holy, God."

72

She puts her fingertips to her breastbone, removes something from the corner of her eye, shakes her head, replaces those big glasses, steps behind him, and darts out toward the park exit like the dogs are after her.

I never ever saw Mark out of sorts before. He never gave anyone so much as hint that he was capable of anything but total equanimity. Yet for a good twenty seconds, there in that crowd, he stands stunned and immovable, as if a Martian just blasted him with a ray gun. His lips part as he searches for words. He appears to grab for something floating around him, like he's trying to explain something to himself. He turns, searches the sea of people, then glances back at me. Finally, he pushes his way through the crowd, lighting out after Lola.

The place is just so jam-packed that it takes another fifteen or twenty minutes for me to catch up. When I finally do, he's under the awning there by the entrance where latecomers are all lined up, waiting to get their complimentary glasses and pink wristbands. More and more people click on through the turnstiles. I step up behind him and grab his finger, just to let him know I'm right there with him, you know? I want so badly to tell him about Lola at the jewelry counter, but that's when I spot the pink beret just the other side of the chain-link. In that dirt lot now packed with cars, Lola hurries down a trail of trampled weeds and loosened soil, out toward the thoroughfare, sucking on the end of that ten-inch cigarette holder. To this very day, I don't know if I did the right thing when I pointed and said, real matter-of-fact like, "Over there. That her?"

Just the other side of the fence, a motorcycle rumbles by and kicks up a big ol' cloud of dust. Mark asks what I mean, and I tell him that Lola's scurrying across that parking lot, walking out toward the city.

He searches for a second and then spots her. At that, he darts over and grabs the wire, hooking his fingers into the loops.

"Hey there!" he yells. "Hey, lady."

She shifts her tote bag to her other hand and turns immediately, as if she felt his eyes on her all along.

"Hey there. Your name. What's your name?"

She calls back that her name is Lola. Mark puts a fist to his mouth, like he's thinking of what to say next.

Then he hollers, "And his name? My father? His name?"

She says "Elroy" or "Eli"—or maybe "Eloy"—but we can't hear because just then a pickup truck with that hip-hop music blasting out its speakers rumbles by. Mark shouts again, asking her to repeat, and as she does another Harley-Davidson thunders past, suffocating the sounds.

That's the last we see of Lola. That poor lady in her skintight jeans, her high black boots, and her fluorescent beret, leaning into that busy street and waiting for a shuttle bus to pass before she crosses the parkway and hastening, almost running, across that field of dry weeds, the plastic cigarette holder swinging out by her side, still wedged in her fingers. That poor, tortured lady, running off to be alone with her demons.

You see, Mama, she raised us Roman Catholic, something that wasn't always so easy in that desert Texas valley where just about everyone we seemed to know—friends, cousins, and even people from the parish—more and more seemed to be migrating over to those born-again Christian churches. At least they were back in the seventies and eighties. Swear to God, my earliest memory, early as I can recall, is of that dear woman leaning and reaching into the back seat of the Plymouth, pulling a bobby pin from her mouth, and affixing a little doily to the top of my head just as Daddy parks the car and we ready ourselves to walk on into that church, looking real prim and proper. Mama demanded Marti and I jump through all the hoops: First Confession and First Holy Communion at the end of second grade, Confirmation the year Marti turned twelve. Marti playing the violin and me playing the gut-string guitar as we both sang "Salve, salve, salve Regina" at the Saint Agnes May Crowning. And Daddy, he went along with it. Guess he had to.

But things happen.

I pretty much had enough of Catholicism by my junior year of high school, and that was about the time I, too, fell into that whole born-again thing. That had me going out to Bible meetings in a Quonset hut out on the south end of town. Every Friday night, for the next seven or eight months, that's where you'd find me. But that changed one night when this tiny little lady in a powder-blue pants suit—she had this little curlicue of bright-gray hair hanging over one eye—came in as a guest preacher. Well, this one night she leads us in prayer. We rise up out of our padded folding chairs, me and the rest of the youth group there at that church they called The Answer. We sing hallelujahs and grab each other's hands and raise them up to the Lord to invoke the spirit of Jesus to descend upon us.

But right then, in the middle of all that, something hits me. I practically feel it, the hard physicality of it, you know? The very idea slaps me, knocks me right in my head. You see, for five months before, we prayed for a nuclear war. All thirty or forty of us in the youth group actually did spend time and energy—both inside and outside of church—imploring God Himself to send ballistic missiles flying both ways across the Atlantic. We were, in fact, praying and singing, giddy with expectation for those explosions and that firestorm that would suck all the oxygen out of the atmosphere, for those radiation clouds that were sure to reduce every person on the planet to a shriveled, skin-covered skeleton.

And they had us all believing that Jesus was going to transport some of the more tender souls away before things got ugly and rotten, while warriors like us would stick around and fight Satan's forces, something just about everybody in the room that night appeared all too ready to commit themselves to. That special guest, she primed us for all this, telling us that just when the best among us were left clinging to that last thread of hope, the earth itself—the whole wide world—would split itself down the middle and turn itself inside-out, just like you do a pomegranate. Then we would know—then everybody in the world, everybody who ever lived would know—that the paradise called the New Jerusalem had been hidden just beneath the Earth's crust all along. And just as sure as anything, the Lord Jesus himself would descend from the clouds, bringing us a thousand years of love and peace.

I guess you could say that I just had that moment of clarity that alcoholics talk about, when they see the trap they built for themselves from a complete outsider's perspective. That night, as I offer Jesus my heart for about the hundredth time, the ridiculousness of the whole Bible thing just comes real clear. Especially the idea that Jesus came to die for our sins. Two days before, I would have thought that those thoughts were nothing less than the product of Satan injecting his lies into my soul. Then, suddenly, I simply can't sit with the whole idea that God created beings so flawed that we could not help but disappoint Him, that He had no choice but to send His only son down to earth to clean up the mess—and save His own creations from His wrath. And the only way Jesus could fix things was to allow His flesh to be shredded and His body nailed up on a tree. I tell you, for a split second, it seemed all so utterly ridiculous I laughed right out loud. I really did. I let go of the hands I was holding, picked up my ski jacket, draped it over my arm, and slipped it on as I walked toward the side door. I pulled my car keys out of my pocket and drove away before that first song finished.

So it is not that long afterward, not really, not even seven years, that I found myself spending most of my free time and half my study time with that dear boy Mark.

That night of the wine festival, after we get back to my casita, Mark sets two canvas sacks full of wine and goat cheese on my kitchen table and pushes the napkin holder and salt and pepper shakers to the side, making room for the cartons of beef and broccoli, Kung Pao chicken, fortune cookies, egg rolls, and fried rice that I'm holding. I take a quilt from the bedroom and spread it out over the braided rug and light five candles and arrange them atop the woodstove and coffee table. And Mark, he finds in the tote bag the bottle of mead we just bought, looks over the label, decides he wants to try some, cuts off the foil wrapping, and twists the corkscrew into the top. The stopper squeaks and pops as he opens it, and we sit ourselves on the blanket before he pours. Just as I finish shoveling chunks of chicken and eggplant onto his plate, he places a Beaujolais glass full of this shimmering something in my hand. He doesn't say anything, but I get a feel for the way he's working real hard to sweep away the memory of Lola's hand on his face.

All these years later, what comes back to me most vividly is not the food or the honey wine, but rather the way that I seemed to be actually standing outside of myself, looking in on the silhouettes of two faces outlined in firelight: the eyelashes, the noses, cheekbones, the curves of our lips. And for some reason—a reason I don't understand—I chose that of all nights to tell him about how deeply entrenched I was in that whole welter of Christianity.

We enjoy our supper enough, mostly talking about the festival and that period in my life. After a while, the candles burn down to nubs, so I put out some more. And then Mark comes in from the back step after shaking out the bed cover and opens another bottle, this one of Black Beauty chocolate dessert wine. He fills my glass and then his own.

He rubs his lip with the tip of his finger and stays real still for a second. Then he decides—you can just see it in his face—that it is time for the come-to-Jesus moment. And he tells me about that one day he decided to become a god.

The whole idea for that Halloween costume, he says, well, that probably came out of either some book report his teacher assigned him, some cartoon, or maybe one of those Classic Comics magazines so popular back when we were kids. Still, for whatever reason, and for weeks, he pretty much insisted on it. And he said so to his parents, his adoptive parents, the folks who raised him since he was two. So all day that Saturday, after church on Sunday, and after school on Monday, he and Mrs. Wladika worked there in the kitchen. With glue, cotton, scissors, and newspapers all spread out across the table, Marie dabbed rubber cement onto cotton balls, pasting them onto this old swimming cap of hers, making it as pretty and full as she could. When it was all done, at least when she thought she had done her best, she took the boy to the back bedroom, went down on one knee, pulled the makeshift wig onto Mark's head, then stood back, looked him over, turned him to the full-length mirror, and asked what he thought.

She called in her husband to have a look. And Yossi, why, he said the get-up looked good but could use just a few more flourishes. The man tugged on some of the tufts, elongating them into wispy little spears, and then glued on more cotton while Marie put the finishing touches on the blue-and-white robe crafted out of bed sheets and safety pins. After supper, Marie whitened Mark's face with pancake makeup. Then Yossi, using a concoction of corn syrup and white flour as a kind of homemade spirit gum, fixed more cotton to the boy's face, giving him extra-bushy eyebrows and a big old beard just full of those wild white curlicues.

That night, Yossi and Mr. Crow, from right next door, escorted Mark and four of his friends around the neighborhood, and after a while the two men decided that there was sure to be better candy in the rich parts of town. So the two adults, they loaded the children into the Dodge station wagon and drove to a neighborhood miles away, to a place where, as Yossi said, "all them highfalutin doctor-types live." There, the kids went from mansion to mansion, walking down these slatestone pathways, past manicured lawns, up to fancy brick porchways with big ol' jack-o-lanterns out in front.

And I could just see them, you know, those two grown men going down the sidewalk, trying to keep control of those five children: a Batman, a vampire, a princess, an elf, and—out in front of the pack—the Zeus. A bunch of kids scurrying up the sidewalks. Children who were every bit as excited by the other costumes they saw that night as they were by the miniature chocolate bars, wax lips, candy corn, peanut butter kisses, and boxes of licorice candy they were collecting.

Once they got to the end of the subdivision, Mark was just so excited that he got away from his father and ran across the boulevard without looking for cars, causing the driver of a Cadillac to slam on his brakes.

The tires screeched, and Yossi screamed out, but the boy seemed not to hear. He glanced at the car, realized what he had just done, and kept running up the curb, across the yard to this apartment complex, this small and square two-story cluster of maybe fifteen or twenty units surrounding a tiny brick and grass courtyard. The eight-year-old slipped behind the line of mailboxes, ducked under the wrought-iron stairwell, and stopped at the first door. Out of breath, he pounded with an open hand and announced "trick or treat," his tiny little-boy voice muffled through all that cotton.

Before the others caught up, the door opened and there, in the glow of the white porch light, holding a ceramic mixing bowl with miniature Tootsie Rolls and grape, cherry, and cinnamon lollipops, appeared this man Mark recognized. The boy studied the slope of the man's forehead, the rise of his nose, eyes that were the same pale green as his own. The man smiled back, offering not so much as a flicker of recognition. The boy held open his pillow case, and as candy dropped in, fragments of memory came back, all these pictures that kept rising like bubbles through the well of his consciousness. Mark knew that crooked jaw, that spot on his neck, and even that Arizona State baseball cap. He recognized the smell of the Old Spice antiperspirant and even his "Jesus Saves" T-shirt with its ripped collar. And all this took him right back to some place he should have forgotten long before—or perhaps never should have remembered in the first place. And standing right there that boy recalled some night long before when, bawling and wailing in the arms of some stranger, he reached out to that man with both hands. He remembered that man walking down a long blue hallway where he pulled open a door, gave one last glance over his shoulder, and disappeared into the darkness.

Mark and I, we don't go to bed until real late that night. Instead, we talk. I curl up to him, and he puts his arm around me. He tells me about those months upon months he spent at the city library and the Bernalillo County Clerk's Office, just paging through old telephone books, scanning city directories with a magnifying glass, and going over microfiche volumes of the *Albuquerque Journal*, the *Albuquerque Tribune*, and the *Albuquerque News*. Of how he collected copies of police reports, hospital records, and census rolls. About how fruit crates in his parents' shed were packed with manila folders just bursting with photocopies. All that going on since the summer before he entered seventh grade, just as soon as his mother would let him ride the city bus all by himself.

Sitting there in the dark, sipping on the sparkling wine, I felt just so sorry for the dear boy—the way he always, at every other moment, seemed so in control, so totally comfortable with the way the world worked. Now there he was, his face outlined in golden candlelight, looking so much the scared and abandoned child. This lost child trying to come to terms with those mysteries that, sooner or later, every adopted child needs to make peace with.

Yet, what haunts me even more, what chills my core to this very day—that picture remains so seared into my memory—is that of Mark standing there, paralyzed, in the middle of that massive wine festival crowd. The dear boy so scared, so vulnerable, his face going so pale as he stands, looking so abandoned, there in that mosaic of hats, bright shirts, sundresses, heads, backpacks, baby strollers, tote bags, and faces.

EDDIE

Mark rotates a five-inch, cigar-shaped bar of glass under a flame that shoots from the nozzle of an acetylene torch. He has the tank mounted on cinder blocks atop his dad's workbench, fixed in place with four nylon bungee cords. The gooseneck sticks right out in front of him, and at the end of the nozzle burns a tongue of blue fire the size of a fountain pen nib, so steady and controlled it appears hewn out of blue and orange acrylic. It doesn't jiggle like the fire on a birthday candle or struck match, its consistency due to the high pressure of the hissing gas.

It is about six thirty on a Saturday night, our last semester of high school, and my brother just dropped me off at the Wladika home. For the last week, Mark and I told our parents repeatedly how badly we wanted go to the local art house to see Akira Kurosawa's film *Dersu Uzala*, and they believe that's what we'll do. Such ploys have yet to fail us. More than likely, we'll get in his Volkswagen Beetle, drive out to the south side of town, and follow dirt trails out to the open fields behind the airport. He'll park the car, set the emergency brake, and crank up the radio. We'll listen to Pink Floyd or the Allman Brothers on eight-track tapes, or maybe progressive rock on the FM station. And we'll get high. That's been the agenda for most Saturday nights since August.

But big changes are coming.

Just that week, I received my acceptance letter from New Mexico Highlands University, a tiny school up in the northeastern corner of the state. Mark got his a month earlier. Since before Thanksgiving, we've talked about going there together, where I'll study sacred literature and Mark will pursue a mechanical engineering degree. We'll be dormmates our first year and rent an apartment together the next.

At least, that's the plan.

When I arrive, his mother calls me in without coming to the door. She insists I try the country chicken and home fries she is about to put away. She tells me Mark has occupied himself all afternoon with God-knows-what, that she never can keep up with that boy, and she points toward the garage.

Gnawing on a chicken leg, I step through the laundry room and down onto the freshly mopped slab, but Mark doesn't acknowledge me right away. Once I drop the bone in the trash can next to him, however, he removes his baseball cap, wipes sweat from his forehead, gives me a nod, and refocuses on the project at hand.

On the table next to him and on top of an orange mechanic's towel, he has laid out six metal tools that look like things lifted from a dentist's tray. Next to them sits a nearly full bottle of Vernors ginger ale and half a glass Coke bottle that has been sliced off cleanly at its waist, just below the petals of the contoured glass. He has that ladyfinger-shaped thing he's molding suspended between two plastic-handled metal prongs as he draws it in and out of the flame to control the temperature. He keeps at it, working and manipulating, meticulously distributing the heat. He concentrates, picks up one of the prods, and works a hole into the side of the bowl.

Finally, I piece together the larger picture. That afternoon, Mark took a diamond-wheeled glass cutter and scored the perimeter of the pop bottle, heated the scratch with the torch, and then rubbed it with ice. It split easily in two pieces, the bottom half now essentially a water glass curved like a woman's torso. Over the course of the next three hours or so, he delicately worked the top half, melting and reducing the glass until it became as pliable as modeling clay.

As I stand there, he reaches up and tightens the valve. The flame flickers, gives one last indigo lick on the brass lip, and disappears. With a pair of wooden-handled tongs, he picks up his artwork and lays it gingerly on a rectangle cut from an asbestos shingle. He tears his cap off his head. His wet and matted hair sticks up like a sheaf of summer wheat. He mops his sweat with another garage rag, proud of his achievement.

"Give it a while," he says, "to cool."

He shakes his head, lets out a long low whistle, and takes a swig of soda.

Finally, he spreads out both thumbs and forefingers on the fireproof tile and turns it, just to give me a better look. In front of me is a shiny, polished hash pipe of translucent green glass, its shaft and bell decorated with the red-and-white swirls of what used to be a painted-on Coca-Cola logo. A finely crafted piece of paraphernalia a movie star might pay a hundred dollars for.

"Happy graduation," Mark says. He rakes his fingers through his damp hair.

Mrs. Wladika was right: you never knew what that guy had in store. The cogs in his head churned constantly, always spinning off into the strangest places. The previous summer, he lay down in the back of his car and had me wrap his wrists and ankles with cotton rope and tie a bandana tight around his mouth. For the next two hours, we drove around Albuquerque and picked up hitchhikers—three of them in all. Mark's explanation: they needed to be reminded of the randomness of the world. Another time, he found a black clerical shirt at the Saint Francis rummage sale and took it home, washed it, starched it, and pressed it. He took an X-Acto knife, sliced up sheet of electro-white construction paper, and inserted it between the two collar tabs.

That night we called the Central Avenue Pizza Hut and ordered two supremes with extra green chile, olives, and pepperoni, and a liter of root beer. Thirty minutes later, Mark strode into the restaurant wearing black slacks, a gray sport coat, and the Roman collar. He slipped past the pimply-faced cook and the apple-cheeked Tweedledum of a night manager. He walked right up to the warming rack, as if he had done exactly that a million times before. He ran a finger down the receipts, found our pies, and pulled out the boxes. He stopped near the door, set the pizzas on a pinball machine, and announced to the employees and the three customers: "The orphans thank you for these. And so does Jesus." He sliced and wiped the air in a full blessing. The dropout of a cook took off his baseball cap and scratched his head. His boss stood there, immobile and silent, her lips parted as she watched Mark push the door handle with his elbow and walk out to the parking lot with almost twenty-five dollars' worth of food her business had to pay for.

Or else, when we wanted beer, Mark slipped on that priest's shirt and we went to the drive-up liquor window. We never got carded.

If he needed to mail me a letter? Mark put my address up in the left-hand corner of the envelope, in the return address slot, and dropped it in the mailbox without a stamp. It worked every time.

The night he gives me the hash pipe, Mark grabs his windbreaker, calls through the two rooms to his mother, informing her that we are off to the art house for a dose of high culture, that he won't be back too late. We climb in his Super Beetle, but instead of driving to the fields south of town, we go east, toward the mountain. We drive for about twenty minutes and then start climbing. We follow the rises and asphalt switchbacks. As we approach the peak, rather than staying on the paved road, Mark slows the car, searches for a tree or rock or some landmark—something I don't see. Then he steers the car between two aged piñon trees, over an uneven patch of shale, and along a path just barely big enough for an all-terrain four-wheeler. Long fingers of blue spruce reach out and brush the windows and roof as the car pushes over another rise. Branches of pine, juniper, and wild sumac etch lines in the paint of the tiny bubble of a car as it bumps, labors, and bounces, the illumination of the headlights looking increasingly feeble against the growing darkness. He turns again, this time between two ponderosa pines, and keeps going. Finally, we emerge onto a rock shelf about forty feet from a three-hundred-foot drop-off and, on the other side of that, the continuing slope of the foothills, and then the illuminated and dusty bowl of the city.

He reaches under his seat, feeling for something, finds it, tucks it in his jacket pocket, and orders me to follow him. Thirty seconds later, he sits cross-legged on a rock ledge, and I lean my back against a small sandstone wall. Mark reaches inside his jacket and takes out a Glad bag with two fingers of sinsemilla, something he bought that afternoon from his hookup in the student ghetto, the neighborhood just south of campus. He holds out an open palm, and I hand him the brand new Coca-Cola pipe.

He pinches out a thick bud and crumbles the leaves into the bowl, then packs it down with the tip of his pinky and drops in some more. He holds it out to me.

"You first," he says. "Your present."

I move over next to him. He flicks the lighter and a spark flies off. He does it again. A long yellow-orange flame wiggles in front of him, and he tips it into the bowl.

I puff until the smoke burns the back of my throat, and I cough. He calls me a lightweight and laughs. I take another toke.

His turn. I invert the lighter and hold it steady. The flame bends and soon the embers glow red-orange as he draws. He holds out the pipe and puts a fist to his mouth.

Mark takes another puff, gets nothing, finds a pine twig on the ground, uses it to repack, and asks for the lighter. He draws up another flame and touches it to the dark hole. This time it catches, and he takes a long and slow inhalation. He releases a cloud of smoke.

After six rounds, we finish the load. Mark taps the glass tube against the pale rock to loosen the ashes and resin.

It does not take very long for the buzz to come. My feet dangle over the white-gray platform, and I lean back on my palms and surrender myself to a swirl of thought. Red lights of a helicopter blink over the Northeast Heights. Perhaps it is a news team reporting on an accident. Perhaps another prisoner escaped from the county jail. Above me spreads the expanse of the velvet sky and the fins of the Milky Way. Off to the north appears what looks like a jet liner, cruising in for landing. A puff of cloud drifts by, and I realize that bead of light is Jupiter in retrograde, dangling out there like a radioactive dot, the constellation of Orion just off to the side. Below, the glowing latticework of the Albuquerque streetlights.

"Guess what I did today."

Mark's words jostle me out of my reverie, bringing me back to the mountainside. I pluck a blade of grass working its way through the crack in the rock. He flicks open the stainless steel lighter cap with a twist of his hand and closes it with his thumb.

"You finally called Miriam," I say, "and begged her forgiveness."

"Nope," he says and taps the bowl with the metal lighter to loosen more residue. "Something far more dramatic."

A lightning bug or some glow-in-the-dark piece of debris appears from the sky, floating and spinning just feet in front of me. I grab at it, and it jumps away. I pluck at it again, and it evades, as if teasing me. It circles in the air, drops, and disappears.

"You converted to Judaism."

"Wrongo," he says. He scrapes the edge of the pipe bowl with the twig. "One more guess," he says. He finds another bud, crushes it, and dribbles the flakes into the reservoir.

"You got me," I say and lean back against the rock, my hands clasped behind my head. Venus—or maybe Mars—pulses like a beacon overhead. "Just tell me."

He puts my pipe to his lips and lights up one more time. His nose and cheeks glow red. He holds in the smoke and passes the pipe and, as he exhales, says, "I enlisted in the Marines. I report to Camp Pendleton, just outside of San Diego, in eleven weeks. Eleven weeks from Tuesday."

"So," I say. I take the lighter from him and flick the flint wheel. A spark flies out. I remain fixated on the illuminated diamond dust of the sky. "That punches a hole in our college plans."

"You can still go," he says.

"I was going because you were. So…" I say, wondering if I am feeling hurt or abandoned. I decide it is not that big of a deal. "Maybe I'll just stay. Go to college here."

"Still thinking about doing that whole 'sacred literature' thing? Whatever the hell that is?"

"Sometimes. Sometimes I want to be a comedian. Maybe I'll just work in my dad's store for a while."

"Religion and comedy? They could work together, you know?"

I laugh, and he laughs. He says he is serious. The pines rustle behind us and go still, but the chill stays with me, and so I pull my jacket closed and tug up my collar. The city sparkles.

"Look at that city," he says. He sticks his hand in his pocket.

"Awful pretty, isn't it?"

"Sometimes I come up here by myself and sit right here on this rock, you know? I imagine that somewhere out there my old man—my real old man—walks through the Winrock Mall or up Central Avenue, maybe down along the river in the South Valley, wondering about me, what kind of guy I became. Then I get to thinking of these things stirring inside me, these urges that just seem built into my biology. That stuff that just comes out of me from God knows where. Stuff I know didn't come from Marie or Yossi Wladika."

"Like making a marijuana pipe out of a soda bottle?"

"Guess so," he says and leans back on his elbows. "I imagine that he still lives out there in that city. Maybe he's this aeronautical engineer or a physicist working down at the labs."

"Maybe an artist. A jazz saxophonist or a poet or something."

"Maybe," he says. "Could be anything, I suppose."

The helicopter makes another sweep along the eastern foothills, the red taillight glowing bright and fading, the lamp on its front searching like an insect's proboscis.

He repositions himself and rotates his head, cracking his neck.

"Then, sometimes," he says, "sometimes I come here to sit in silence. To find the Buddha."

"The Buddha lives in Albuquerque?"

"Shut up," he says as the lights before us reflect off his eyeglass lenses. "Just shut the fuck up."

The wind whistles through the trees behind us. I close my eyes and bite my lip, letting thoughts swirl around me. I am deep in some obscure and profound thought when Mark speaks again. His words jostle me.

"I'm sorry I let you down, dude."

He looks at something far away, at some distant galaxy shining like a speck over the far hills.

"People let each other down," I say. "Ain't that the game?"

"Guess so," he says. "I suppose it's the imperfections that give life its texture."

I don't follow. He explains.

"Think of it this way," he says. "Come Judgment Day, you'll stand before the Almighty. He'll be up there tall, broad-shouldered, and dapper in his designer sunglasses, his Italian suit and tailored shirt. In his pocket, he'll have a starched red handkerchief that perfectly matches his hand-painted Italian tie. Around and behind him shimmers golden light while everyone you ever loved—hell, everyone you ever knew: cousins, uncles, aunts, grade school teachers, your first boss—will watch you from the bleachers. Your aunt will wag a finger. Some lady will smirk in disgust. You'll bow your head, embarrassed by the red chile stains on your freshly pressed shirt and dirt on your jeans. A choir of angels will lay out a Bach oratorio in twelve-part harmony. You'll sniff away a tear and breathe in the stink of your own karma. You'll ask yourself why you weren't kinder, more diligent, and more appreciative—why you didn't work just a little harder to nurture His universe.

"And right there in front of you will stand the Big Guy, checking off your violations. He'll remind you of that time you snuck into the movie theater through the exit. The time the Burger Chef guy gave you back an extra ten-dollar bill and you stuffed the money in your pocket, grabbed your food, and slunk to the outside table. The time you told Tamar you were grounded so you could sneak on over to Joanna's house when her parents weren't home. Those times you snuck out your bedroom window so we could get high.

"You'll stand there, drenched in guilt, remorse, sorrow, and shame. Then you'll raise your eyes—just a little—to Yahweh's shoes, polished like mirrors. Then to that perfect crease in those shimmering silk pants. He'll rattle off the details about that time we siphoned gas out of Coach Nathaniel's truck and the time you stole that six pack from Barnabas's dad's garage. You'll crush another tear and, just as you do, that titan standing in front of you will unbutton his blazer and draw back the flap. That's when it'll come into focus.

"Perhaps the metal teeth won't be spread apart enough to give you a glimpse of the whole shebang, but there will be that little pull tab and enough distance between the tines to offer you a glimpse of his boxer shorts. Underwear with clowns or dachshunds on them or something ridiculous like that. That's right. The Almighty will tower over you, looking so sublime, so awesome, so majestic. Looking so preternaturally polished, so unimaginably cool in those Ray Bans. And his zipper will be open.

"You'll cover your mouth with your hand, and you'll try to squelch it, but eventually, the laugh will leak out. Just this little burst of mirth that'll earn you a few more eons in purgatory. That's when you'll know it."

"That's when I'll know what?"

"You'll know that the perfect always contains at least a fleck or two of the imperfect. And that's the way it should be. The unfolding universe has to be flawed. When it becomes perfect, that's when it stops creating. And that's when you run out of miracles."

"Really?" I ask.

"Really," he says. He balls his hand into a fist, covers it with the other, and puts it to his chin. "That's the way I see it."

He finds a pebble in the dirt, holds it in front of his nose, and fixates on its jagged edges. He pitches it away, and it bounces off the ledge, down into the darkness.

Just after seven, the morning of Monday, June 20, I took my brother's truck, drove from the near North Valley across town to the Wladika home, and parked on the curb. I grabbed Mark's gym bag off the metal chair on the porch and loaded it into the bed of the Chevrolet as Mark hugged his mother, told her not to cry, and embraced her again. Once in the cab, he asked me to make a loop up along Central Avenue and assured me we had time. He didn't say much on the drive. Instead, he tapped his chin with his fingers and stared out the window, as if trying to memorize everything we passed—the missing and broken light bulbs outlining the roaring dragon on the sign above Jimmy's Oriental Cuisine, a place we visited after hours of pot smoking and philosophizing; the Highland Theatre with its ornate, Hollywood Palace-style marquee of paint and incandescent bulbs; the tiny storefront that is the Guild Cinema. He swallowed as he took one last look at the smoked-glass windows of the line of rooms that is the Frontier Restaurant, another hangout; at the college student who rushed across the street against the light, as if daring the oncoming cars to mow him down; at the homeless guy in dreadlocks and dirty army fatigues with a banjo strung across his back; at the Chevy Camaro turning off the avenue into the main entrance to the University of New Mexico campus, the car rumbling on toward the residence halls.

At the station, I sat on the long oak pew, and he stood by the window, looking out at the strip of gravel and cinders, at the idling train. I asked if he was ready for what he had gotten himself into. He said he could handle it. When the train growled and released a blast of steam, he walked outside, and I followed, carrying his bag. An old woman boarded and then her husband. I handed Mark his suitcase, and he stuck out his hand for a handshake, and I threw my arms around him. That was the first time I ever hugged him. He dug his ticket out of the side pocket of the carry-on, walked away, and waved over his shoulder without looking back, like he knew I was still watching. I stood at attention and saluted, just the way my father showed me when I was a boy. The motor revved, a horn sounded, and Mark turned and called back over the noise.

"Good luck with that whole sacred literature thing you got going."

Then he slung the strap over his shoulder, climbed up the steps into the passenger car, handed the conductor the boarding pass, and disappeared down the aisle. I didn't see him for another three years.

One afternoon that September, I entered my parents' house through the back door and dropped my basketball on the recliner in the den. I checked the refrigerator as Mom called from another room that a package came for me, that she put it on the shelf of the china cabinet. In the living room, I picked up a stack of notices leaning against my sister's wedding portrait: the electric bill, a special offer from Ford Motors, and a notice that we might have already won the Publisher's Clearing House Sweepstakes. Leaning against the dime store bowl of plastic fruit was something wrapped in brown paper, its seams sealed with cellophane tape. In angular handwriting and scrawled in the upper left-hand corner, in the return address slot, were my name and address.

Standing there in my gym trunks and a sweat-soaked T-shirt, I worked my finger under the flap, tore through the wrapping, and found a hardback, the cover showing two eagles in silhouette, flapping down for a landing. I balled up the stiff wrapping paper and read the title: *The Community of the Beloved Disciple: The Lives, Loves, and Hates of an Individual Church in New Testament Times*. Scribbled on the first page, in Mark's jagged handwriting, were the words, *I meant it. Good luck with that whole sacred literature thing you got going*. Stuck in the middle pages was a letter giving Mark's news. He graduates from basic training in a week. He earned the master sharpshooter's badge, doesn't know if he can make it home for Christmas, and he just returned from a meeting with his commanding officer. There he learned that he had been chosen for Special Forces training. He ships out to Paris Island, South Carolina, in mid-January, where he'll become an expert in hand-to-hand combat.

I refolded the letter and stuck it between the pages as I walked back to my bedroom. There I pulled off my Adidas high-tops, clicked on the turntable, set the stylus on the second song of an Allman Brothers' album, sat on the bed, and laid the book across my lap. The heavy pounding of the bass guitar vibrated the walls, and that searing guitar lick came in. Soon, two guitars played in perfect unison, creating a wall of sound. It took a few minutes for me to grasp the full reality of the situation. By the time we were one year removed from high school, my five-foot-four-inch, one-hundred-and-sixty-seven-pound best friend would have a body mass index in the low teens, and he would be able to reach down your throat, grab your heart, yank it out, and show it to you before you drop dead.

MICA

At the Crazy Geri's in Tucson, things look morbidly bleak. We have like nine people in the showroom. Two-thirds of a dozen droopy audience members, all spread out and hiding in the corners, like they're roaches or something. I count them at least fourteen times while Barry Bass and I sit there in the back of the room at the comics' table, waiting for Mark to come from the manager's back office.

You got your middle-aged couple off in the corner, your table of college students on the other side, and your old man by himself in the middle, and some more youngsters in the back. We're supposed to play there the next four nights, and the total energy sink that is that showroom has me feeling like I'm all trapped in Kafka's basement or something.

Then, not seven minutes before the lights come down and everything, some ginger-headed oaf in green sweatpants bursts through the double doors, and he's all projecting this big old attitude, like he's daring anyone to cross his path or something. The guy is downright monstrous, like he could be the new linebacker for the Arizona Cardinals. Behind him trails an Italian, Lebanese, or Arab girl who looks like she totally needs a fake ID to get past the front counter. She's this olive-skinned beauty with a thin waist and green-gray eyes set into deep-cut eye sockets. This total princess in a frilly miniskirt and brown curls. After them comes this skinny dude with blond sheaves spilling out from under a sweat-stained Pennzoil baseball cap, super-tight jeans, a wife-beater, leather jacket, and cowboy boots. This guy is all sauntering down the aisle with his thumbs stuck in his front pockets, looking like he just came from some redneck fashion show. He follows his friends down to the front and center table, like it was reserved for them or something.

When you got two or three hundred people in a crowd, everybody's energy feeds off of everybody else's, and the laughter flows in fast and easy. But twelve people, all spread out like that? This is like so Nightmare City.

But, like they say, the show must go on and everything.

After a while the lights dim, the intro music blasts from the corner speakers, my off-stage introduction comes, and I race up the steps, doing my little pointy-elbow dance, just to get energy flowing in the place. The music fades, and the couple up front keep whispering at each other. I tell everybody that they came on a great night, like I almost believe it. Right as I get to my third punchline, the Mediterranean model shoots up out of her chair, like she's all animated by a spring and a timer. She like picks up a glass and splashes beer in the linebacker's face. Her hand slams down all hard on her car keys on the table, and the rattling of the metal against the wood echoes through the club. She clears away this black mascara tear, slings her purse over her arm, tugs her skirt, and hurries like mad up the sloped aisle and out the showroom doors.

Anymore, when I get all thinking about the way the girl popped up so fast and the way her metal chair teetered before toppling over, the way she held her bag with both hands as she raced for the door, it all comes back pretty innocuously. I'm usually all laughing when I tell the story. That night, man, I am still so totally green—I have only been a professional comic for like three minutes or something—that the sudden drama plunges me into deep pain. Once she's gone, I focus on the guy wiping lager off his Arizona State T-shirt.

"Did she just find out about your boyfriend?" is the best ad-lib I can muster.

The behemoth dabs his goatee, scrunches the saturated napkins, drops them into a half-empty water glass, and stares me down, like all daring me to come at him again. I crack another joke, and his lip creases and twitches, and he launches into this slow-motion head shake. So I like fall back into my prepared material.

I go to my next chunk, and in the back of the room, a beer bottle crashes into a trashcan, like completely overpowering my best punchline. By that point I am totally asking myself if this whole comedy thing really is the right career move.

When the night began, the energy in the club was lower than what you'll find in your average methadone clinic, and all the psychodrama pulls it down to gas chamber levels. Barry Bass, the feature act, gets fewer laughs than I do. He finishes his half hour, and so I go up, slide the barstool back into its rightful place there by the mic stand, ask for a big round of applause, and don't even wait for a response. I tell them all about the drink specials and everything and how Thursday night is ladies' night and military people get in free.

Then I introduce Mark. But instead of coming up the steps on the side of the stage the expected way, he enters through the front of the room and just like totally takes his time walking down that center aisle, sauntering all ceremoniously toward me, holding a fifth of Jack

Daniel's in one hand and a rocks glass crammed full of ice in the other. Meanwhile, I stand up there looking like a goof because I don't know what to do. He strides up right in front of me, crouches, and leaps up and lands on both feet on the hardwood, right in front of the mic stand, and an ice cube goes skidding across the stage. He lays the glass onto the wooden seat. He shakes my hand all firm and everything and looks totally steamed, so I just skitter down the steps.

He doesn't say a word, at least not right away, not even "How ya doin' tonight?" or "Let's hear it for Barry and Mica." Nothing. Instead, he stands there all illuminated by the spotlight, looking over the crowd. I mean, the dude just waits there, rolling his sleeve tight against his forearm, and then lets his hands drop to his sides, his body language insisting—*actually demanding*—that everybody in the space train their eyes on him. Finally, he cranks the black cap off the whiskey bottle, drops it onto the stage, and kicks it down onto the main floor. He looks over the room again before taking the bottle by its neck, lifting it, and draining about half of it. He lets out this big "Aaah."

Never saw anything like it. For one thing, the guy practically glows. I mean light, genuine cosmic light practically radiates from the dude's body. But there is even more to it. In fact, it takes me like another like four months to figure out exactly what he is up to that night. How he could take such a low-energy environment and just pump it all full of life with little more than his sheer presence? But once I get it, man, the message comes through clear as a polished glass.

Mark understood, better than anyone, that generating laughter is not just about the jokes. It is about making people empathize with you, feel close to you, and trust you as you totally command their space. It is about making everybody in the room acknowledge that you have the power, as you make them feel part of something so much larger than they know—whether they realize it or not. You gotta make them let go and trust you. If can walk that particular tightrope, they'll jump to catch everything you throw.

So because of the way he works his opening into this all-out ceremony—that, combined with his killer material and stage presence—the crowd totally falls in love with him instantly, just like every crowd does. You see, sharing food or drink, that's like Holy Communion, man, and that's why the whiskey bottle—which, it turns out, was filled with apple juice—is like so vital to his act that night. The dude was creating ritual. He knew how to Cadillac that like nobody's business. Total wizardry.

Once he has everybody's attention for a solid minute, he yanks the microphone out from the stand and, instead of speaking into it, tosses it over his shoulder, and as it clunks on the stage behind him, the mesh screen pops off, rolls toward the steps, and a spark flies out of the mic's neck—like he planned it that way. *And he still hasn't spoken a word.* He leaps down onto the main floor, plants his foot on an empty seat, gives it a shove, and sends the chair sliding over to another table. He stops in front of the old man in the middle, rests his butt on the back of an empty chair, crosses his arms, and leaning there, cranks out his material like he's relaying stories to a bunch of old friends.

After his first chunk, he tells the people on either end to come to the middle, to join the fun. First, the old lady on the other side insists to her husband that they move in, and then one of the youngsters comes and straddles the seat and folds his arms over the backrest. Then the college boys, bringing with them a half-finished order of cheese fries. As he lays out the next set of jokes, Mark picks up a plate off the college boy's table and takes an extra-long potato slice and holds it up and drops it into his mouth. Then—*as he is still chewing*—he hands the platter to the linebacker and tells him to pass it around. After some more stellar one-liners, Mark calls to the waitress and tells her to bring over plates of thermonuclear Buffalo wings and lots of napkins for everybody in the room.

For the next sixty-four minutes, they all sit there, all eleven guests, dipping chicken wings and celery into bleu cheese sauce and wiping their hands on greasy napkins. Everyone in hearing distance, me and Barry included, all totally cackling at Mark's stories about how he was adopted and how he's spent thirty years scouring shopping malls, telephone directories, and flea markets, searching for his father and everything. About how a kid on the playground once called him a bastard. Mark said to him, "How did you know?"

It becomes a party.

Never seen anything like it.

The next night, Thursday, the house is about three-quarters full, and the manager has to call in an extra waiter to help with all the tables. By the time Mark and I arrive at the club from the comics' condo on Friday, the line to get in the place snakes through the alcove of the strip mall, all the way down past the back parking lot. For the second show that night, we not only have standing room only, but the owner pulls Mark into the office and practically begs him to do a midnight performance. Says he'll pay him an extra six hundred.

That second show that Friday, that's the one that blows my mind. By nine thirty, the place is like totally bursting with people. Not only do we have every regular seat filled or spoken for, but they got these metal folding chairs all lined up against the back wall and a couch pulled out of the manager's office and set next to the two steps leading up to the VIP section. All along the back bar and the two far walls, people stand waiting, apparently willing to remain there for the next hundred minutes or so. And sitting there in the second row, next to Mr. American Trailer Trash, sits the same football player who got the face full of Coors two nights before. He wears the same green sweatpants and the gold-on-maroon Sundevils pullover.

The lights go down, the music starts, and green, red, gold, and silver flash all around us. Once the off-stage introduction finishes, I hurry up the steps, do my little dance, and totally swan dive into my material. My first six jokes land hard—two of them before I even get to the punchline. That's when you know it's good. All this tells me that, if I ever had a chance to break out the risky material, this was it, so I go with the jokes I'm still working out. I talk about dating a Native American woman, about how every time I take her out dancing it starts raining. Then, I go with the follow-up.

"During sex she tied me up, spanked me with a riding crop, and yelled, 'I'm going to dominate you like I'm the U.S. government.' Then she kicked me out of my house and sold the mineral rights to Exxon-Mobile."

Everything I throw out, the audience totally swallows whole.

I go on about how my college roommates used to stay up late shooting craps, the six of us crammed in the bathroom and pointing a twelve-gauge at the toilet. A joke from my first open-miker set. Usually, a line like that is hackneyed and totally lame, never getting more than that dead-fish applause. But not this night.

I close my set, give the feature's intro, and float down the steps. I hadn't felt that high since my stoner days.

Barry goes up and slings all this stuff about being gay, about how when he came out his father collapsed into a heap, crying right in the middle of the living room and saying, "Oh my God, how can I afford to buy him a Mini Cooper?" He goes on about how he got back from

101

his holiday vacation in Alaska and his mother tells him that she is so happy that he got to ride on a boat and celebrate at midnight.

"That's not what I said," he says. "What I said was I 'climbed on a fairy.' And I blew a noisemaker."

Gay stuff is totally risky, especially in an ultra-conservative, retirement home paradise like Tucson. But Barry is a hit, and he closes with a joke that I can't imagine ever working again.

"Then I got hired to do comedy at a gay wedding. They ate my shit up—and even liked my comedy."

When he comes off, the air is totally supercharged. I mean, my hair is like practically standing on end, the atmosphere is so totally electrified.

Once I bring up Mark, like everyone is on their feet, like they know him from television or something kooky like that. One of the fraternity brothers balances himself on his chair, pumping his fist in the air. His buddies around him scream and hoot. Mark strides on stage, carrying that same whiskey bottle filled with apple juice. A wave of sound booms in from the back, the cheers gelling into something like a single, deafening, and tactile substance. Mark puts his glass on the stool next to him and then holds a clenched fist in front of him, claiming some kind of victory. He stands at the mic, unscrews the cap of the liquor bottle, and this time tosses it into the crowd, which gets even more cheers. He takes his long swig, again drains about half the bottle, punctuating the long gulp with that dramatic and extended "Aaah." This majorly stokes things. The crowd stays tuned in to his every move, every twitch of his lip, every cant of his eyebrow, like he's totally controlling them with his subtlest movements.

At first, Mark doesn't make a sound. Instead, he stares down this straight-laced, bourgeois gray-hair sitting up front. Mark sticks the bottle on top of the stool, like he's sticking a flag in the dirt or something, and comes down, sits on the edge of the stage, and like totally mimics the guy. This is a tall, uptight, insurance salesman type with greased hair and big old eyeglasses, and Mark is this short little bald guy and looks nothing like him. But just ask anyone there that night, any of the people standing around like they were a bunch of high schoolers watching two freshmen duke it out over a girl. First, Mark imitates the way the guy sits with his elbow on the table. Mr. Modern Middle Class gets all nervous and crosses his legs, and Mark executes the same motion exactly as it happens. This goes on for a good four minutes, as if the two rehearsed the bit for weeks.

The funniest part, though, comes when Mark sucks in his nostrils, pulls down the corners of his mouth, and changes his face so that he looks like the guy's evil twin. Supremely uncanny.

Then Mark goes into material, getting off some of the best jokes ever about how he dated a woman who was three days away from her divorce. They get back to his place and start making out. He goes on.

"The bra comes off. The panties come off. The bustier comes off, and she starts crying, 'I can't do this. I can't do this.' I said, 'Why not?' She said, 'I didn't know you wore those things.'"

He tells how he wonders why they have Braille instructions on the drive-up ATM. How he always wondered why his black girlfriend spent sixty dollars a month at the tanning salon.

The show totally slips into overdrive, careering along at its own momentum, and Mark plays the crowd like he's some master violinist. Just as one laugh peaks, he comes through with another punch. Just as that one subsides, he lays down a tag that gets a monstrous reaction. It's like a high-powered Disneyland ride with surprises popping out of every corner.

Things roll along until a waitress slinks down the front row, bends at the knees in a Bunny Dip, and takes a Coors Lite bottle off the linebacker's table. That's when Mark sees it: the guy has a cell phone leaning against his water glass and pointing right at center stage, a little red light in the corner showing that recording is in progress. Microphone in hand, Mark stops in the middle of his next joke—he doesn't even get through the whole set-up—points at the guy, and says, "Turn that damned thing off." Just like that—*"Turn that damned thing off"*—with that guttural and commanding voice powerful enough to drill a hole right through your skull. The monster stares him down, picks a toothpick off his plate, and sticks it between his greasy lips. He forces a frown, leans back, crosses his arms, and gives his slow and steady head shake.

That awkward moment causes a real hiccup in Mark's momentum and everything, so he doesn't even finish the bit and switches to the next, a chunk about dating a younger woman. He gets the audience back in about five seconds and goes on, building up to his closer. That last joke hits really hard, so hard, in fact, that once again everyone is out of their seats, and the air is thick with hoots, applause, whistles, foot stomps, and screams. Mark resets the microphone, tells the crowd to stick around for the extra late-late show, waves again, and hurries down the steps. He ducks through the green room, out the kitchen door, around the building, and into the breezeway. There, he waits in the shadows, watching the droves of people spilling out from the double smoked-glass doors, some smiling, some laughing, everyone happy.

He doesn't see the jock at first. Rather, he catches the blond hick pulling open that front door and holding it for some lady in a wheelchair and then waiting for an old man coming slow behind her. The redneck eventually adjusts his Pennzoil cap as he steps out to the curb and hooks his thumbs in his belt loops, waiting for his buddy. More people spill out, and seconds later comes that ogre, that six-foot-five, two-hundred-and-ninety-pound meat tower with cabled arm muscles, mouth agape, and muscles bulging out his neck. He takes slow and even strides, his arms out at his sides, like he just finished a sixth set of bench presses, his posture and movements daring anyone to get in his way.

He stands at the curb, tugs at his sweatpants, twirls the toothpick in his mouth, and adjusts his package, like he doesn't care who's looking, like he's got special privilege and totally wants people to see him all touching his junk and everything. He gives the strip mall the once-over, looking for a place to get the night's last beer. He doesn't like what he sees, so he steps down and strides in front of a Cadillac working its way to the exit, past the rows of illuminated taillights and grumbling engines, out toward his Jeep, those beefy arms swinging out by his sides. At his vehicle, he steps on the chrome running board and grabs the door handle. Mark calls out from behind him.

"Hey you," Mark says. The titan halts, wonders if someone could really have the gall to be yelling at him, and turns.

"You. You there," Mark says. "Let me see that phone."

Standing in front of him, Mark holds out his hand. The behemoth looks off to the side, like he can't believe what he hears, like he thinks Mark has mistaken him for someone else.

"Yeah, I'm talking to you," Mark says. "Come on. I'm asking you nicely."

The monster pushes the door closed behind him, spits on the asphalt, checks to see who's looking, and widens his stance. Mark stares him down and keeps his palm out.

"Let me have it," he says. "Come on, man. Please. I'm asking you nicely."

The linebacker looks off to the side and then back again. He smiles.

"Why don't you come get it?" he says and points at the phone with his lips. "It's right there in my pocket. There ya go. I'll even lift it out halfway."

He grasps the unit and works it so that half the face shows. He chews on his toothpick and nods.

"Come on," he says and crosses his arms. "Get it. It's right there."

I barely see the motions. The stride Mark takes is like so totally fluid he looks like, for a split second, he turns into smoke or something. He lunges forward, taking the hard heel of his palm and slamming it up into the Goliath's nose. One short, quick, fluid motion that concentrates every modicum of force into that single and vulnerable spot. Instantly, the giant's body crumples, collapsing in on itself like a flaming milk carton. Then the dude falls to his knees and covers his face with his hands as blood gushes out from between his fingers. He lays his head on the asphalt, his moans rising from deep inside his massive core. That oversized man is rendered all pathetic, groaning and writhing against the painted lines of the parking space as thirty or forty people look on.

Cool as a bubbling spring, like he doesn't know he just busted some guy's face, Mark reaches down, pinches the phone between his thumb and forefinger, and slides it out of the pocket. He flips the thing open, bends it at its hinge, working the metal and plastic until it breaks into two pieces, dropping one half onto the tarmac, letting it bounce in front of the pooling blood and mucus. Then he pries off the back of the other part, pulls out the memory card, and snaps it in two as well.

He turns around, shoulders his way between two onlookers, through the crowd, and back into the side door of the club, ready to start the midnight show.

JACK

My troubles with Gustavo Kaiser begin back when I was a junior at the University of New Mexico. That story's more complicated than Chinese calculus.

Back then, I fancied myself this wicked, badass photographer. If I have natural talent, it's in the visual arts. I understand visual composition and lighting instinctively, like a duck understands swimming. I've known that since the second grade, when during a school field trip to the Albuquerque Zoo I shot something like seven thousand million rolls of film, something that really put Mom's panties in about a hundred square knots. Years later, people said I was some kind of a genius at stand-up comedy. To tell the truth, I'm not naturally funny. I don't think like a Groucho Marx, a Jonathan Winters, or a Richard Pryor. In fact, before I started the whole stand-up thing, people said I was over-the-top serious. I only got into comedy because, back then, my frog-faced counselor suggested it as a way to let all my rabid anger out. After a few years, it really worked. I calmed down a lot.

Nathania, the therapist, recognized that I was smart enough to construct jokes and make them work, that I am pretty much a hotshot with words and everything, and to me, seeing things from a million different points of view comes pretty easily. What can I say? I am usually the most astute person in the room—and that's not always as easy as you might think.

Still, what I loved, what really lit my torch, was finding the right angle, the right lighting, the right moment while peering through that viewfinder, and knowing exactly when to snap the shutter button. Nothing gets me all hot, bothered, and gushy like freezing the motion of a butterfly with the morning sun shining through its wings or catching a border collie in mid-leap the split-second before he bites down on a Frisbee.

I was especially comfortable using longer lenses, getting all these nice tight shots. In fact, the spring of my sophomore year at UNM, Professor Elder handpicked me for an internship at the *Albuquerque Tribune*, one of the local dailies. The next semester, that turned into a paid position. My official title was "lab technician," something that made more sense a million years before when people like me spent hours in the darkroom mixing chemicals, agitating film in canisters, fixing photo paper to the easel of an enlarger, using wooden tongs to fish prints out of the fixing bath, and breathing all this chemical-infused air. By the time I came on the scene, though, everything was all digitized. The only time I ever stepped into a darkroom was when a professor took us through the silver-gelatin print process because she thought, for some nutty reason, it was important we know it.

At the newspaper, I spent half my workday in front of a Macintosh computer, working the Photoshop program, tweaking pictures. The rest of the time I was responsible for things like mugshots. You know, the postage-stamp-sized pictures of faces you see in the paper? And studio shots, where you set up a photo illustration for some soft news story for the Sunday Living Section. Every once in a while, though, when my bosses came in feeling all warm and fuzzy after they just got laid or something, I went on assignment with the other photogs. Later, I even got to take the jobs those real professionals didn't want or couldn't do because of scheduling conflicts.

So, bleeding hearts that they were, the bosses pitched me bones now and then. I got to shoot these boring, low-class affairs, like Class AA football championships and the festival over at Saint George's Greek Orthodox. On the rare occasion when they just wanted me out of their faces, they sent me out to make feature photos: a snowman made with tumbleweeds or the best invention at the mid-school science fair. Crap like that. One time I got a kid with a toilet paper roll affixed to a bike helmet, this strange contraption he made to keep you with a steady supply of tissue when you get the sniffles. The shot ran in the back of the B section. You know, piddly little stuff that meant nothing. I produced shots like the pictures that you see standing by themselves right above the obituaries. I didn't mind. In fact, I thought it was kind of cool because, for one thing, I got my name in the paper on a regular basis. Besides, I could work on my school projects right there in the office and get free coaching from professionals. And I didn't have to wait tables or flip burgers to get through college.

The person I worked best with, the one who taught me more than any of my professors, was this old Jewish guy named Jesse Shepherd, who had these wild black-and-gray eyebrows about ten inches long and the same kind of shoots coming out his nostrils. This guy who had been a fixture in that office since the Mesozoic. A nice, gentle, old guy, who on hot days had body odor that could melt the enamel off a bathroom stall. He and his wife even had me sitting at their Passover Seder a couple of times. He was happy to stay after hours with me, sitting down at the screen and going over the images I brought in, walking me through the subtleties of composition, depth-of-field, histograms, bounce flashes, side lighting, and shutter speed. He showed me how to create a real mood by making miniscule adjustments in tone and contrast. The best part was that any pictures I produced for the newspaper I could use for class assignments and put in my portfolio, even if they didn't get published.

One day I was out in the field, just looking for anything the least bit odd or intriguing, just something to break up the gray space above the weather report. The whole time I was thinking about what Jesse taught me. There is always something interesting to capture on film, the hard part is finding it. So, in that way, the photographer's job is pretty much the same as the comedian's. You take the stuff everybody else glosses over and frame it so that it intrigues and becomes beautiful, so it provides some kind of insight into the human condition. You have to find the right angle, the right exposure. The same way, what separates the good shot from the great shot or the good joke from the great joke is timing. Sometimes it's one five-hundredth of a second.

Life rolled pretty fast back then. My future spread out right in front of me. The journalism faculty tacitly dubbed me their golden boy, and everyone knew it. Other students sought me out for advice and critiques and even looked up to me and told all the newbies that I was the star to hitch their wagons to. I worked late nights in the studio and at my computer putting together my portfolio. I wanted at least seventy shots that knocked people over, photographs that overwhelmed anyone who came near them and thus enhanced my chances of getting a graduate assistantship at some snotty East Coast arts college. And it was happening. My future began to take shape. I was on my way to becoming a world-famous shooter and living out my life in prestige and comfort as an art professor or an artist or something respectable like that.

Well, this one particular Tuesday, I'm over there in University Heights, just south of main campus, around ten thirty, maybe eleven in the morning. There at this park, these kids and this Catholic priest are assembling model rockets, adjusting the fins, and setting them off. The whole dynamic has the magic of your 1940s feel-good movie. The assistant pastor in his cleric's collar, the one awkward, fat kid with the backwards ball cap who keeps clapping, just so bursting with enthusiasm every time a rocket goes up, and the tomboy in oversized glasses, pulling up her sweatpants as she orders the boys around. I put a fresh card and a newly charged battery in my Nikon, step over, and ask them if I can stick around and see what I can get. The cleric says of course, and the kids get excited about having their faces in the paper.

So I work all the angles. I get on top of the concrete picnic table and crank off a few rounds. I lie down on the moist grass and get my jeans all wet just to get an upward look at the faces of these tweens as they study the positioning of the red-and-yellow missile. I climb an elm and brace myself against one of the branches. I think I might have one or two decent shots when I take out my reporter's notebook and write down the correct spellings of the kids' names, thank them for letting me intrude, and tell them that if the picture runs it will be on Saturday or Monday, but I wouldn't count on it.

I turn around to go back to my car, and there in front of me, in the shade of a poplar grove, sits this sanitation worker. He appears about two or three years older than I am. Just this dopey kid, really. He's propped on the back shelf of his garbage truck, and he wears a chambray work shirt, poplin Dickies, and an orange vest, as if he's going for that whole working-class fashion statement, you know?

He bites into a sandwich that looks like it is made of potted meat on white bread or some processed, poisonous crap like that. Something disgusting. He digs in the plastic bag by his thigh and fishes out a tortilla chip flavored with powdered orange carcinogens. Then he takes a long swig from a cold Coors beer and sets the bottle on the metal gate, right there next to him.

Stupid me. I line up the shot and squeeze the shutter button. I hold it down and reel off three exposures. I go down on one knee and crank off two more. I wasn't thinking. I even tell the guy that, although the badge on the lanyard around my neck says I am from the press, that I am just doing it for a college class. He's flattered by the attention and introduces himself as Uriah Baron.

The thing is, I made that into one hell of a good environmental portrait. That's what Elder called shots like that. You know, pictures of people in surroundings that reveal who they are, what they are all about, what they're made of? Every last little tidbit and nuance in the frame worked. The slanting lines of the iron machinery, the dirt on his unshaven jowls, a streak of sunlight illuminating his kinky hair, the line of sweat on his chocolate-colored cheek. The creased lip and the smile that was only on one half of his face. The guy looked so real, so unpretentious, so unapologetic. So totally authentic with the weathered decal of his truck, "M2540," just over his right shoulder. I could already imagine Elder projecting that image up on the Smart Board and circling the sections with a laser pointer and going over how it should be in the national student journalist competition—crazy stuff like that.

Once I get back to the office, Jesse hooks up my camera to the computer and uploads my pictures. He does it right away, like he had nothing else on his plate, like there was nothing to worry about for the next day's edition. He goes directly to the garbage man frames. I mean, the images practically reach out and slap him upside the head. We go over each of the exposures. The angles, the expressions. We run off two or three different prints of one of them to make sure that the tone is right. You see, Jesse was old school. He liked seeing things on paper rather than on the "*teevee* screen," as he called it. He takes me through the steps and points out about a million tidbits. And he's right—as always. Back at the Photoshop table, he slices about an eighth of an inch from the top of the image, and then a sliver on the right, and then tweaks the contrast. In about seven minutes, he totally transforms the portrait so that Uriah Baron radiates. The picture is so damned perfect. Jesse prints out a proof, looks it over, tosses it in the trash can, twiddles some more computer buttons, fiddles with the mouse and more keys. Before I can catch on to everything he does, the Canon photo printer at the end of the room grinds out a full-color, glossy print. My first full-blown masterpiece. So I take it, think about having it framed, and save the image on my flash drive, just so eager to show it off in the junior seminar.

A week later, I am in the Old Town Starbucks coffee house, not doing anything, really. I feel kind of dull because, between work and school, I had been going at it about a million miles an hour for what feels like three thousand years—plus, I got stoned the night before. There, on the table in front of me, lies a copy of that day's *Tribune* that had been gone through about a thousand times. The sections are all out of order, and the broadsheets are all wrinkled and dimpled. There're even brown coffee stains all over the business page. I scan the headlines and subheads of the sports page and, of course, automatically critique the pictures and check the photo credits. I stir some raw sugar into my latte, tap the wooden mixer stick onto the side of the mug, and lay it on a napkin. I check the box scores of the Dodgers-Mets game, lick my finger, and turn the page. There, above the fold of the front page, is my shot of Uriah Baron—replete with smile, deviled ham sandwich, Dorito chip, and beads of condensation on the shoulder of his beer bottle. The photo credit running along the bottom announces it as the work of John David Marison.

So I get in my car, speed back to the newsroom, and hustle past the reporters' desks and layout tables, back to the photo office. Inside, Jesse holds the telephone to his ear with his shoulder, scribbles something down on a yellow legal pad, all serious-like. When he sees me swing open the glass door, he points, commanding me to stop where I stand, and so I do, right there in the doorway. He says into the handset, "Let me check it out. No. I said no. I said I'll check. After the meeting. The man blew his own head off, for Chrissakes." He punches a button on the receiver and tosses the phone on the table. He swivels in his chair, releases a sigh, shakes his head, moves his reading glasses to the top of his head, and rubs his eyes. I let go of the handle, and the door lazes back into place. Something's coming down.

"The city manager got a load of your beer guzzler and went buggy," he says as he jots some notes. He unbuttons his sleeve, yanks it down, and turns up the cuff. "At six fifteen this morning, the old lizard fired your buddy Baron."

He replaces the spectacles, looks up, then back down, and scores a squiggle under the last word he wrote. He underscores again and slaps the felt-tip down on the paper. He undoes the top button of his sweater vest.

"Then Baron went home, took a shower, shaved his head, and loaded up his twelve gauge. His wife found brain and skull fragments all over the tin of their carport."

He clenches his teeth and holds the heel of his thumb against his eye.

"Awe, mercy. Mercy, mercy," he says and rips the top page off the tablet. He shoves himself to a stand, folds the paper in half, and with his thumbnail, rubs a stiff crease into it. He pulls the door open and steps out of the photo office into the newsroom. He shakes his head. I follow.

"Aw, mercy," he says as he rubs his hand over his face. "He left twin daughters and a pregnant wife. Aw, mercy, mercy, mercy."

He tugs on his pants and walks toward the meeting room. I walk alongside, and he fills in the details. That Wednesday morning, Gustavo, the managing editor, comes in at four thirty, and as usual, when he's still the only one there, goes through the reporters' desks, just to see what they're up to. In the photo room trashcan, he finds the copy of the shot of Baron.

"When he gets a chance that afternoon, he hacks into the digital image bank," Jesse says as he stops in front of the copying machine. He puts his hand behind his neck, as if giving himself a massage. He loosens the knot on his tie. "He finds the electronic version of the Baron pic, emails it to the city hall reporter, and orders him to use the truck number to verify Baron's name and identity. When Gustavo gets all the info, he runs the shot on the front page. Listen, I'm due in a budget meeting seven minutes ago, so I'm already on the bossman's hitlist. When I learn more, I'll give you the skinny."

He turns, shakes his head, and walks down the corridor, the unbuttoned sides of his vest swinging at his sides, the folded slip of canary-colored paper tight in his fingers.

"Aw, mercy," he says as he gives me one last check before pulling open the dark glass door of the meeting room.

I survey the office. At the desk in front of me, a copy editor and a page designer discuss how to rearrange the Sunday feature section, one circling a section of copy with a blue pencil, the other pointing at the broadsheet with a felt-tip. Behind them, the police reporter mouths her story to herself, scanning for typos. On the other side, a business writer hurries back to a copy editor who holds out a telephone receiver.

Everything seems just so goddamned normal, as if nobody just died. Like the *Tribune* had nothing to do with Baron's death. This shocks me. The lives of five people—two of them children and one unborn— were ruined because Gustavo somehow decided that embarrassing a garbage man was a good way to move papers. I stand paralyzed in the middle of that office, wondering how I can be part of it.

I rub my forehead with the heel of my palm, stride over to the meeting room. On the other side of the glass sit all the bigshots, talking about the next day's headlines. Along the sides, the seven men and two women the reporters call The Suits—the sports editor, the metro desk editor, assistant desk editors, the copy desk chief, the city editor, and Jesse. At one end of the long table, the editor in chief with his sleeves rolled up and his interlaced fingers covering his mouth, his eyeglasses set near the tip of his nose, and the corners of his lips turned down, as if he's pondering some life-or-death decision. At the other end, closest to the door, elbows on the table and leaning, as if to hear advice coming from the woman in the next chair, sits Gustavo himself.

I throw open the door and step over, reach between two bodies, knocking over someone's soda. I hit Gustavo in the pectorals with the heels of my hands, grabbed fistfuls of his shirt, heave him out of his chair, and push him into the corner. The thud of his body knocks an award certificate loose off the wall. The glass and frame clatter on the carpet. A button pops off his shirt.

All I say is, "You maggot."

His raw breath spills over me as he tries to pry my hands off of him.

I want to say more. My left hand goes to his throat, and I cock my right fist, ready to lay across his chin, but someone catches me from the back. Then there are two people on me. Then more. As they pull me back, I cling to Gustavo's shirt, and the seam rips. I kick and twist, knocking over a chair, and tell whoever holds my shoulders and chest to let me go. Two of the guys drag me away. Before the door swings closed, I lance the air with my finger, right at Gustavo.

"You killed him," I yell. "You killed Baron!"

Gustavo pants in the corner, his glasses askew on his face. He shoves his shirttail into his pants and snarls.

"Whaddoo I care?" he yells back as he straightens his tie. "Whaddoo I care about some city worker grunt? Some jig guzzling cheap beer on city time?"

Ten minutes later, once the meeting ended, I was fired.

The Jews, I believe, were the first to connect breath with spirit. There's all that stuff in Genesis that tells us that God forms the dust of the earth into this golem and huffs the divine breath into it. That holy wind animates Adam. The Romans and the Greeks also understood the intimate connection between air and the soul. I could not help but think of this the first time I met Gustavo, the first time I got close enough for him to breathe on me. His exhalation was downright fetid, like a pile of dead dogs on an August afternoon.

At first, I assumed he had a rotting tooth—or maybe two or three. But that smell was there months later. A year later. Much longer than decaying tooth enamel can last. Every time I spoke with him—which didn't happen much, since he was a hotshot managing editor and I was just a photo slug—I got that putrid blast. You could practically see that dark-green cloud swirling out from between his teeth. Then one night Gustavo slinks into the photogs' room, digs through the wastebasket, and finds what looks like incriminating evidence that some minimum-wage city working dog with a two-digit IQ is having a cold one after slinging trash since before sunrise. He sticks the photo on the front page above the fold, just to stir a little intrigue, to sell a few extra newspapers. Then he suggests the guy is expendable because he is black.

Tell me getting rid of a guy like that wouldn't make the world a better place. I dare you. Hell, I double dare you.

NICHOLS

Is honesty usually the best policy? Sure.

Is that true right now? Probably.

But sometimes you just gotta pull an extra ace out from under the table, make the sign of the cross, and promise yourself you'll make amends down the road.

That's what I tell myself as I roll back my chair and make doubly sure the office door is locked. I uncap a tube of Super Glue and squeeze out a bead thin as a strand of monofilament fishing line around the collar of a fifth of Jack Daniel's bourbon, wipe the excess goo on my pants, reset the white plastic cap, and tighten it as much as it will go. I blow on the new commissure and count to ten. Then I grip the glass shoulder, squeeze the top, and give a hard twist. The new seam comes apart with a mighty crack, as if the bottle just came fresh from the distillery. I toss the cap on the desk, fix a plastic funnel to its mouth, and pour in two inches of tap water from a refilled Evian bottle, then apply another dose of adhesive and reseal. I do the same to the other eleven bottles I have pushed up on the desk next to the dusty computer screen: Seagram's 7, Canadian Club, Jim Beam, Evan Williams, Wild Turkey, Old Grand-

Dad, and Cuervo Gold—you know, the usual suspects. Once I finish, I fill two wooden crates with the liquor, load them one on top of another on a hand truck, and cart them downstairs to the supply room.

At times like this, I feel like I should have stuck it out at the community college and finished that degree in video production.

A few minutes later? I got that same dolly stacked with flats of Pabst Blue Ribbon, Fat Tire, and Marble Red, one of our local brews. I puff on a filterless Camel and squint against the smoke. I prop open the back door with the toe of my boot and maneuver the rubber wheels over the metal threshold and into the back bar, my home for the next twelve hours. Maybe eleven, if we shut down early again. What do I have going right then? A good, solid, lose-lose situation. If we actually make money tonight, that means I have to work until at least midnight and drag myself in fatigued and grumpy the next day. If things stay bad? I come in sleep deprived anyway, since the whole situation has me up worrying.

Out at my battle station, I tend to more menial stuff, tasks normally left to the grunts: running a rack of steins through the dishwasher, stocking the bar cooler, putting out the limes and olives, and filling up the wash and rinse tanks with fresh solutions. I dump five gallons of ice into the front bin and retreat to the kitchen for a refill. Just as I come through the wood-slatted saloon partitions carrying another bucket, who struts in from the main room? Black Tom and that little faggot Firecracker Rael, who plants himself on the stool, right in front of the beer spigots. Tom has a cigarette tucked behind his ear. He lays his forearm on the bar and stays standing, eyes on the dark entryway, as if he expects a loan shark's henchman to come through at any second and break his thumbs.

I crush my cigarette butt in a coffee cup, take the pack from my shirt pocket, shake out another cancer stick, and place it between my lips. I tap my lighter on the bar, sliding my thumb and forefinger down its length, and turn the thing over. Then I do it again. And again. Nervous habit. Once I get tired of waiting for these two to snap to attention, I ask Tom what he's buying, and he stays watching the foyer shadows. After I light up and take the first drag, I rap on the wood with the lighter. Tom finally summons up the good grace not to ignore me. He turns, like he just discovered other people in the room. He rubs the stubble on his chin as he scans the bottles on the top shelf, like he hasn't seen them a million times before. I tell him we're fresh out of Colt 45 malt liquor. He says he wants an Amstel, and I say that's not an option, and so I drop the Bic on the rubber serving mat, slide a coaster in front of him, pop the top off a bottle of Rolling Rock, and flick the metal disc at the trash can. It pings off the plastic liner and rattles on the floor.

Then Firecracker comes out with this protracted "uhhhmm," like I got nothing better to do than listen to his hemming and hawing. I drum the wood with my fingertips, just to suggest that I'm actually working, then take a long and dramatic drag and blow a stream up toward the "No Smoking" sign affixed to the wall above the dartboard.

"Go ahead and take your damned time," I say and point past the cases I just wheeled in. "See those boxes there? They can un-load themselves."

Finally, he claps his hands in front of his face and proclaims he fancies an appletini. I say, "Hallelujah! The oracle speaks." I ask what the hell an appletini is, even though I've cranked out hundreds of them and could whip one up with one arm tied behind my back. Excuse me, but I just don't feel like going through that kind of trouble. Besides, I got work to do. I mean, come on. I haven't even got a chance to get to the window to switch on the open sign. And that little girly-man? He acts like he's all special. He laces his fingers together and rests his chin on top of his hands, like he wants to flirt or something. He goes on about Calvados shaken with Grey Goose vodka and served with a slice of Granny Smith apple and a maraschino cherry. I lean on the counter, my cigarette smoldering between my fingers. I glare. Don't say a word.

"Well, geez," he says in his little girl voice. "You can make one out of apple Schnapps. And you have a bottle of that right there. Right there, under the Drambuie. You see? Right there?"

"What are you?" I say and take another drag. "Some blue-haired old lady at the country club? That's who drinks appletinis."

He raises a finger, as if he wants to make a point, but I cut him off, saying that if he wants a froufrou drink he can ask for it over on East Central Avenue, in that bar where they serve all the other queers. That *I* run a damned sports bar. A man's bar. A bar with cold beer and chicken wings so hot they'll lower your sperm count. On Saturday afternoons, we all gather around the big screen in the main room, turn on a rugby match, and call players pussies as their teeth fly out. You want lime, salt, and a double shot of Patrón Gold tequila? We'll accommodate. Wild Turkey straight up? You've come to the right place. You want something that looks and smells like Kool-Aid with chunks of fruit shish-kabobbed on a toothpick with some Chinese-made umbrella sticking out the top? Forget it. Serving that liquefied candy damages my reputation.

Not two minutes later, Black Tom slams his empty bottle on the bare counter, strings of foam on the inside sliding down the longneck. He pushes it over toward the edge and asks for another. He taps the filter of a fresh Newport on the polished maple top to compact the tobacco and asks if he can use my lighter. I tell him that if he wants to suck a butt he needs to go outside, at least twenty-five feet from the front door. Why? City ordinance. I point to the sign.

"What?" he says. "The rules don't apply to you?"

"I am the rules," I say and plant my coffin nail between my lips, inhale, and turn to grab the stainless steel shaker from the drain board. "It's not real power unless it's arbitrary. Didn't you learn that in school?"

A thread of smoke curls up into my eyes as I shake ice off the scoop into the silver tumbler.

Tom chuckles as he picks up the lighter, snaps up a flame, and cups his hand around it. Before fire touches paper, however, I reach over, grab the menthol, and break it in half. I squish and grind, then open my hand, letting tan, blond, and brown flecks spill from my palm onto the polished wood and waxed concrete. I clap my hands clean.

"Didn't you hear me? We don't allow smoking," I say. I release a white stream toward the ceiling and flick off more ashes. Once I get the vibe that he'll give no static, I slap on the shaker top and agitate. "You got a problem with that? Go to City Hall and talk it over with Mayor Chavez."

I got height, width, and bulk—and I don't mind using them when I need to. I slide a cardboard coaster in front of Firecracker and plant a cocktail glass on top. I affix a coiled strainer atop the metal canister and serve up five ounces of diluted bar vodka and plunk in an onion. No toothpick. No umbrella.

Firecracker wants to know what happened to the vermouth. He stomps the brass footrest and claims that he deserves the same treatment I give other customers. I say I rinsed the glass in vermouth when he wasn't looking. He says he hasn't moved since he ordered and that he watched me the whole time. I say apparently he got distracted because I sure as hell know how to make a simple martini. Hell, I've been doing it since five weeks after I turned twenty-one. I tell him he can come to this side of the bar and sniff the waste sink, if he doesn't believe me. Anyway, I learned that particular trick when I bartended at a comedy club in Indiana in the 1990s. When some guy orders a martini, what he's really saying is "Gimme a big glass of vodka, and disguise it so I don't look like an alcoholic." So forget the Cinzano. It's too damned expensive, anyway. Besides, once I started pouring straight isopropyl, I practically became famous for my martinis.

I disappear to the back and return six minutes later, steering in another dolly load past the flip-up counter gate. This time I bring in more Corona, Blue Moon, Samuel Adams, Rolling Rock, and extra Marble Red. I unload and return in a few minutes with four cases of Budweiser. Don't ask me why we sell so much of that pisswater. A New Mexico thing? Maybe. But then it's also a Minnesota thing. And a Bloomington thing. And a Santa Fe thing. Eight out of ten redneck drunkards everywhere prefer Bud. I should sell that slogan to Anheuser-Busch.

In any event, I drop the first case on the rubber matting and the bottles clank inside. Then I pinch my Dockers at mid-thigh, tug up the legs just a little, and go to my knees. I stick a hand through the slit in the top of the box, rip the cardboard, and arrange lagers and ales in the bottom fridge.

I get halfway through the first flat when Black Tom leans past the counter, grasping the edge so that he cantilevers over. He wants to know when we'll put on another comedy show. I tell him I don't know, maybe after he learns how to come up with a decent punchline. I put the last Marble in its place, fling the empty corrugated behind me toward the doorway, and rip into the next box. Tom keeps at it, telling me that we should do another one. He says that he and Firecracker will pay for the spotlight and sound system rental, charge five dollars at the door, and split what they make. Me? I get to keep what they generate from liquor sales. A clean, slick, and simple business proposition—just like those in years past, when the shows always ended with me getting the shaft. I can't find a place to fit the last three bottles of India Pale Ale, so I invert them and shove them down deep into the ice bin.

Firecracker says something about the shame of me not properly utilizing such a good stage and such a large downtown showroom. I wipe my hands on the bar rag, toss it next to the sink, grab the stainless steel lip, and hoist myself to a stand. I plant both hands on the bar and bring my nose to within an inch of his. I talk into his waxy, over-cosmeticized, little girl face. My goal at that moment? To scare the hell out of him. Watching makeup-laced tears trickling down his cheeks? Thrills me to no end.

"Last time," I say. "Remember last time? Twelve comics. And their girlfriends. Together, what'd you get? Five laughs? After what? Ninety-three minutes? Besides..." I kick the empty Budweiser carton. It careens off the wainscoting and tips on its side. "Besides that, we had twenty-four people in here. Usually, on a night like that, I should sell two, maybe three hundred drinks. A hundred and fifty woulda done the trick. What did we get out? Maybe sixty? Sixty-two? Then all you comics, all you drink is Miller Lite and Budweiser. Why don't you try a drink that costs more than three lousy dollars? Challenge yourself. Besides, you guys destroyed my mic stand—again. That's the third one."

Firecracker tips up his glass, still holding it between his thumb and middle finger and with that little manicured pinky sticking out, then tells me he doesn't remember regular martinis being so good, and he wants another. He reaches to the waitress stand, pinches a napkin out of the plastic holder, and dabs the corners of his mouth.

"How 'bout we do this?" he says. "We guarantee you one hundred dollars. The first twenty five-dollar bills that come through that door, you keep. We get the rest."

These guys must be sniffing glue. One hundred big ones. At a five-spot a head. In a room that holds three hundred people, if we arrange it right. The last three shows? We had thirty-eight people, max. That's counting comics and girlfriends.

"Why don't I just set up a card table out on Central Avenue," I say, "and hand out free shots of Johnny Walker Blue? I'll make more money that way."

I pull the bamboo cutting board from behind the sink spout, wipe it off with my hand, lay it on the bar in front of me, position a Tupperware bowl next to it, find my paring knife, and pluck a ripe lime from its basket. With one even slash, I split it down the middle.

"Think about it," Black Tom says. "We'll bring in Phil Fletcher. He headlines the B-level clubs, like Loco's in Amarillo, Crazy Geri's in Tucson. He's about to break into Pancho Pilot's—and that's a top-notch venue. Wherever Phil goes, he brings in at least twenty fans. They love him. And Firecracker here? He always brings a crowd. Then there's Jack Marison."

I spear another lime in its sweet spot and freeze. "Marison?" I ask.

"Sure," Tom says. "A bit green, but good potential."

"That blond college kid with that storage unit full of one-liners?" I ask.

"That's the one," says Firecracker, all ecstatic, like I just guessed his birthday or something. "That little darling."

126

I point the blade at Black Tom's nose and then over at Firecracker.

"This time the girlfriends gotta pay, just like everybody else," I say. "In fact, the comedians, the performers, they gotta pay, too. I'm tired of being Santa Claus. By the way, I got a sound system. You guys come up with the spotlight and a mic stand. I'm tired of you jackasses tossing perfectly good mic stands around like they're disposable chopsticks or something."

I shove quartered fruits off the bamboo and into the plastic container. I uncap a fifth of bar vodka and refill the homo's glass and then pour two fingers' worth into my coffee cup.

"Aren't you even going to chill it?" he asks. "I mean, shake the vodka up a little with the ice?"

"It's cold enough in here," I tell him.

Black Tom says that Mica, Tafoya, and Jana Boan won't like paying to perform. I suggest that maybe they'll like not performing even better. He scratches his chin with his middle finger and scrunches his lips as he thinks it over. Firecracker watches something in the corner of the room. Finally, Tom slaps the counter and says, "Okay, deal." He sticks out his hand for a handshake. I tap off more ashes and take another drag.

"The deal," I say, "means you bring Marison."

So what do I do first thing Monday? I get on the horn to my Budweiser salesguy and order up two eight-by-three-foot banners with the words "Comedy at Nichols' Silver Dollar" emblazoned diagonally across the beer logo. Big, bright, red and yellow letters. I buy a three-column-inch ad in the back of the *Alibi*, one of those weekly hipster rags the college crowd seems to be so hot on. I telephone a friend of a friend who works up at the FM station, tell him about the show. He says to bring him ten tickets that he can give away during one of those "be-the-ninth-caller" types of promos. Says he's thrilled to do it—if I buy two hundred dollars' worth of radio spots. For that? I max out my credit card.

By that time, I knew the personality of that particular state well enough. New Mexico time runs about ninety minutes behind the rest of the country. At least Albuquerque does. Places like Raton, Española, Gallup, and Artesia? We expect them to enter the twentieth century any day now—never mind it's the twenty-first. The signs and ads announce in bold letters the show starts at eight thirty, but I don't plan on unplugging the juke box until fifteen after nine. That's how it works here in the Land of Entrapment. If you want your dinner guests sitting down by eight, your invitations need to say six thirty. Must be something in that Rio Grande water.

What do you think happens come the big night? You don't need to be Nostradamus to see this one coming.

By ten o'clock, Firecracker has his skinny little ass planted on a barstool in the middle of the stage. He flips his boa over his shoulder, a black feather flies off, and his little girl giggle reverberates across the showroom. He announces that yes, indeed, he is a man. He talks about sipping coffee in the morning wearing nothing but a leopard print thong, and how that gets him kicked out of Dunkin' Donuts. About how his friends call him "Neal" because that's his favorite verb. Then he holds the microphone to his mouth and strokes it like it's a big cock. Like nobody ever thought of that before.

He calls this comedy.

Meanwhile, his oversized boyfriend, still in his poplin jacket and denim shirt, uses the edge of my stage as a goddamned ottoman, his work boots scuffing up the already worn molding. He crosses his arms and tips his chair on its two back legs. I think, if the son-of-a-bitch breaks it, I swear to God, he'll pay for two more. It always mystified me as to why that Jonnie would run around with Firecracker. I mean, the guy doesn't look like a flit. Then he hardly ever makes a sound. How do you know he's laughing? His shoulders bobble, that's how.

In the rear of the room, perched on the high stools, you got this white-haired drunk who came in once before to watch the Pro Bowl, and next to him some haggard-looking troll with sagging wrinkles, close-cropped hair, and an overdone, fluorescent-red curl sticking out the top of her head like a rooster's comb. Maybe she's his mother, his girlfriend, his daughter, or his hook-up for the night. Who the hell knows in this incorporated freak show they call Albuquerque?

Then you got a table of lesbians off to the side, Jana Boan's crowd. One in a shiny vest and a woven fedora and holding her Michelob with both hands. Next to her sits another cutie with an orchid bobby-pinned behind her ear, who keeps smiling like she's fighting off bubbles of abdominal gas. Then, the one I like. She looks like a marathon runner with her auburn ponytail pulled through the back of her baseball cap and delicate nose just the slightest bit retroussé. She stirs her Cosmopolitan and places the swizzle stick between two luscious and plump lips. A forty-something with hazel eyes and just too damned fine and feminine to be a dyke.

That's pretty much my house, the gathering throngs Black Tom and Firecracker promised. Even after I went to the main bar, put the ball game on mute, and announced that everyone in there had free admission to Nichols' Comedy Room, as a customer appreciation thing. Anything to get a few more asses in the seats to try to gin up the mood of the place and tease out some laughter, to create the illusion that people were actually enjoying themselves.

Did Black Tom and Firecracker cause this disaster? Not all of it. Do I blame them? You bet your sweet ass.

Hell, they didn't even bring the mic stand like they were supposed to.

But the real kicker? That comes eleven hours later.

I sit in my bathrobe at my kitchen table and tilt a Winston into an ashtray. I take a swig of coffee to get down my Levatol. I open the *Albuquerque Journal*, and what do I see on the cover of the Metro Section? A picture of Civic Plaza, that concrete downtown courtyard down there by the city offices that covers, what? Almost six acres? Something like that. The place swarms with bodies. Crowded as the Washington Mall during the Martin Luther King speech. You'd think a jetliner carrying the Beatles was landing up the street. Just this sea of heads. People perched on the concrete steps, on the walls of the big water fountain out toward the back. The big wide-angle shot of this massive crowd—I mean, thousands of people—all with their eyes on the stage that glows with spotlights under the neon proscenium.

What do you see lined up there right along its Second Street border?

Delivery vehicles from Pizza Hut, Papa John's, Dion's, Home Run, Domino's, Little Caesars, Pudge Brothers—all these pizza kitchens. A few names I don't recognize. Maybe fifty, maybe sixty delivery vehicles. Hell, maybe a hundred. I mean cars, pickup trucks, vans, and scooters, all lined up like boxcars up Tijeras Avenue, around the corner, and all down Second Street. What's going on in the corner of the shot? Some teenager with her hair up in a bun, walking toward the crowd holding four pie boxes on her outstretched arms, like she's carrying a body to the altar for sacrifice.

What's the hoopla about? A goddamned comedy show, that's what.

Of course, nobody tells Jude Nichols about this particular happening. I gotta read about it in the newspaper. The next day.

I never finished my degree in video production because I wanted to go into business to make money. That's when I bought the Silver Dollar. After years as a surefire income generator, Nichols' Silver Dollar looks like it's tanking. So what do I do? I think outside the box and put on comedy shows and charge my patrons five dollars a pop. Is that reasonable? Hell, yes. What do they get? A mediocre show—if you give clowns like Jana Boan, Mica Pierson, Black Tom, and Firecracker the benefit of the doubt. Then, on the very night we're supposed to put on this major showcase, what does that jerk Mark Wladika do? He stars in this big old comedy extravaganza right there in the heart of the city and doesn't charge a damned cent. Then he gets all these sponsorships so that he can hand out free pizza to boot. How in hell do I compete with that?

HELEN DENISE

Mama stood in the doorway of my bedroom, shaking a dust rag at me. She had half-moon sweat spots at her armpits and her hair wrapped up under a green bandana with a knot at the base of her skull, the two dotted corners of the fabric sticking out like little thumbs.

"You go put that blessed thing right back where you got it, Helen Denise," she said. She planted her fist on her hip with the ends of the shredded cloth all dripping out. "My God. And don't let me catch you with it again."

You see, my sister Marti, she was the tomboy. And the president of the Future Farmers of America. And runner-up at homecoming. Me, I was the bookworm. And what did I do to get Mama so riled? You'll just die when I tell you. You'll simply die.

In the corner of her living room, every darned day I lived in that house, sat Mama's little altar. It was really just a two-tiered coffee table she and Daddy brought with them when we first moved in three months after Marti was born. On its top shelf stood a three-foot high statue of the Sacred Heart of Jesus. You know the one. Jesus looking all serious with two fingers stuck in the air and the other pointing to his exposed heart with all these flames flaring up behind it. A real horrifying picture, if you think about it too long. Throughout my childhood, that hand-painted, plaster of Paris figurine stayed right there in that far end of the room, and Mama only moved its table on Saturdays, when we vacuumed. Over the years, we added to it three rosaries we bought on our trips to Mexico, strings of beads I put around Christ's neck. On one side, Mama had a smaller icon of the same style, this one of the Virgin of Guadalupe. On the other, she kept some other saint, a balding man with white and red robes and a little spike of fire jutting out the top of his head. I never could determine who that one was.

Hidden away on the bottom tier—back there behind four votive candles and pictures of me and Marti as little girls in matching red jumpers and with our bangs cut straight across our foreheads—that's where Mama kept the family Bible. It was big with a thick cover of gold lamé and the second page filled with lines where she inked in all our names and birthdays, including hers and Daddy's.

Well, one day I took the book out, lugged it upstairs, and went through Genesis, Exodus, Leviticus, which I really didn't like, and Ecclesiastes, which I found kind of interesting, but awfully short. The whole thing held my interest enough, though, at least until Mama marched into my bedroom that particular afternoon, yanked the book off my lap, and threw her little conniption.

Maybe I can't really blame her. You see, in all my years living there in Fort Stockton, I simply can't recall a day quite as hot as that one. That was either the summer between seventh and eighth grade or between eighth and ninth. In any case, I was still just this itty-bitty thing. And after Mama yelled at me to clean up the room, slammed the door, and carried the book back to its rightful place, I switched on the radio, and the announcer said that the mercury just climbed past one hundred and seven and showed no signs of coming back down until the next day, when the rainstorms might come in. So I forced open the window and pushed my bed out from the wall so the rush of air from the ceiling fan would blast me right in the face. I still fumed at Mama. How was I supposed to know I was doing anything wrong by reading the Bible? So I sat on the bed, blew my nose, wadded up the Kleenex, and tossed it at the wastebasket. And I fell backwards onto that knitted bedspread, just listening to the whir of the fan motor and watching those curtains flying and snapping with all the air rushing through the room.

I didn't really want to move—or do anything to stir up body heat, not even a smidgen. I locked my fingers behind my head atop that pillow with its case already damp with sweat. Above me, the fan just cranked away, its axle wobbling like the whole contraption couldn't hold itself together another minute. And up there, stuck to one of the blades, was this teeny-tiny cobweb, this little thread that I kept expecting to come loose and float down on my chest or face or something.

After a while, my anger drained out of me, so I closed my eyes for a nap, but the heat kept me from drifting off. Before I knew it, I found myself fixated once again on those wooden slats rotating above me and that little brown-gray fiber rippling like a kite tail. I couldn't keep myself from watching it. I thought about switching the thing off and wiping it with a tissue, but that required just too much work on such a brutal day. After a while, I found myself thinking about all those stories of the preachers and patriarchs I read over the past half week. And I felt myself dropping into deeper and deeper levels of contemplation.

I guess that's just my nature.

Those Old Testament episodes left me a little disappointed. A few of them packed a punch, like the one about El Shaddai, the Lord Almighty, destroying Sodom and Gomorrah or Jacob wrestling an angel until daybreak. But for the most part, I really didn't see the big deal, why these stories got people so worked up, causing folks to start wars and bomb abortion clinics and such. But for whatever reason, one episode in particular, it really dug its nails into me. The one about how God calls Abraham to take his son, Isaac, the boy Abraham and his wife waited decades for, to the top of Mount Moriah and offer him as a burnt sacrifice. That broiling afternoon, as I turned that whole story over and over again in my head, I remained captivated, stuck in the story's webbing, just thinking what those two guys must have gone through. I tell you, the images just about hovered over me until the whole scene practically swallowed me whole.

I saw the two patriarchs in full three dimensions. You got this old man with a beard, sandals, and expensive robe. And he reaches down and takes that little boy, pecks him on the cheek, sets him on his donkey, musses his hair, and tells him he loves him. Then they, along with two servants, go on this three-day trek on up to that holy spot. The little squirt with apple cheeks and dimples under the rolled brim of his Sumerian hat, clutching a wooden toy in his little-boy hands. That kid smiling, so ecstatic to go on a trip with his daddy. At least that's the image I conjure.

Then, once on the mountain, father and son leave the animals and servants and walk up to the peak. They build this platform out of stones, sticks, and branches. Then Abraham, why, he wrestles his youngster down, ties up his ankles and wrists, preparing him for slaughter. He takes his knife and gets ready to gut the child, like he's a trout or something. His dear little boy. I even choke up thinking about what went through that innocent's mind, the horror he must have felt. The way Isaac finds himself strapped onto an altar, unable to move, his mouth tied closed—all this at the hands of the man he trusts the most.

I mean that Isaac, why, he must have gone all hysterical, just struggling to get loose as his father raises that shining blade.

Just as Abraham gets ready to plunge the knife into his child's chest, what happens? Well, the Angel of the Lord sweeps down and stops the old man's wrist in mid-air, telling him not to lay a hand on the dear boy. What really drops my jaw is that Yahweh, why he actually orchestrated the whole thing. The set-up as well as the surprise. Like it was some big joke. You read down to the end of that passage and you practically see the sky opening up, the shaft of golden light coming down, and God raising a finger and calling out from the clouds, "Ah-ha! Gotcha that time!"

What a crazy story. So disturbing. Maybe that's why it always stayed with me, why I thought about it for so long. I guess my life changed in ways I didn't fully appreciate that particular scorching afternoon. You see, by my junior year, that story lead me directly over to Søren Kierkegaard, the Danish existentialist. He went to town on the whole Abraham and Isaac thing in that little book, *Fear and Trembling*. Professor Benavidez, he called that Kierkegaard's masterpiece.

By the time I finished high school, I read all of Kierkegaard's work and started in on Friedrich Nietzsche, a German from a few decades later. Then, once I went to the junior college, my focus changed to Georg Wilhelm Friedrich Hegel and then, the semester after that, to Karl Marx. I swear I must have gone through that *Communist Manifesto* at least seven times that summer, mostly because Professor Ritchman, well, he had me involved in this long and real complicated analysis all about looking at the characters of the movie *The Wizard of Oz* as a Communist fantasy. The Tin Man is the alienated worker, the Scarecrow the country bumpkin, the Cowardly Lion the proletariat who finally works up the nerve to become a Communist, the Wizard as the intellectual, and the Land of Oz as the Communist state. After I came to the University of New Mexico and finished my first semester here, all those phenomenologists—mostly Edmund Husserl and Martin Heidegger—well, they had their hooks dug pretty deep into me.

So I guess it only makes sense that twelve or maybe thirteen years after I first thought about Abraham getting ready to slice open the abdomen of his own child, and after I found myself in Albuquerque and living alone for the first time in my life, that I still couldn't get over that crazy story. Not really.

By that time, I pretty much knew that the lesson of that twenty-second chapter of Genesis wasn't so much about overcoming despair by choosing despair, as Kierkegaard went on so long about, nor was it about blind obedience to God, like Thomas Aquinas claimed back in the thirteenth century. Rather, I determined that the heart of the story belonged not so much to Abraham, God, or even Isaac, but to the angel. That Angel of the Lord, I determined, wasn't so much a supernatural being with flowing, white garments and spreading out his big ol' white wings so much as he was just this momentary flash of insight across Abraham's mind. Something deep inside him—call it an epiphany, call it an explosion of consciousness, call it whatever you want—announced simply, firmly, and directly: "This is downright ridiculous. I won't kill my own child. Period. The era of human sacrifice is over. And this particular revolution begins with me, right now, right here."

So one afternoon after I moved here to Albuquerque, I got my legs tucked under me as I sit on the futon, squeeze lemon juice into a cup of Lady Grey, and I sketch out notes for my honors thesis. I list the main points, jotting them on a legal pad. Right then, I feel the reality of the situation just about smack my cheek. It surprises me as much as it does anyone else. Some overwhelming force directs me to study that New Testament.

I didn't have some conversion experience. Not at all. People always ask about that. To this very day, I hardly consider myself a Christian. I didn't, and still don't, buy that whole business that Jesus died for my sins—or for anyone else's. Christian logic really doesn't hold. God sends Himself to be sacrificed by Himself to save us from Himself. But something about those stories—and not just Abraham and Isaac, but ones like David and Goliath, the wedding at Cana, you know, where Jesus turns the water into wine, and the raising of Lazarus from John's Gospel—why, they certainly plucked some harp string deep inside me, some note that still vibrates. To this day, I can't say exactly why.

So I put down my pen and reach over and feel my mug, just to see how much it has cooled. Just the other side of my window, the lilacs are in bloom, and the new branch of the elm sapling hangs down, heavy with purple-brown buds. My tea practically sizzles because the water's so hot, so I hold the cup on my lap. Then I set the tablet and mug on the coffee table, get up, go to the closet, pull on a pair of hikers and Daddy's black cardigan, and walk out the back, out toward the river. I don't even lock the door.

I follow a dirt path—one of those snaky, skinny little animal trails—down through that cottonwood and willow bosque that lines the Rio Grande. Fresh green shoots of ragweed, cocklebur, and milk thistle sprout from the drying mud, and the water flows in broad and steady milk-chocolate ripples. A ring-neck duck waddles on the bank, shakes, crouches, and takes flight, rising and dipping over a little grove of Russian olives and the teepees of iron and wire put there to fight back any rising river waters that might come along some day. Off to my side, branches rustle and something crushes the bed of leaves and twigs that have been there since October.

I trudge on, passing a big ol' salt cedar, bent like a drainpipe. A breeze kicks up, so with one hand, I hold the sweater tight around me and, with the other, I hold a willow switch. I take little swipes at the new growth, at cottonwood shoots, at ferns, and puffs of grass. I don't do it real hard, but like I'm teasing them or something. I step up an incline, and out from a clump of bushes a dog appears, this tiny, mottled Shar-Pei mix. This cute thing with a short, square snout, and all wrinkled with sagging jowls. She sniffs along the bank and up toward that ribbon of flattened earth. When she gets wind of me, she stops, raises her head, gives me the once-over, and bounds up, welcoming the chance for human contact. I crouch down and offer my palm. And that little thing, she pads forth, stops, hunches down on her front legs like she might want to play, her tail waggling like she's fanning her rump. She decides I'm harmless, licks my finger, darts away, trotting out in front of me, leading me along, her collar tags jingling.

You see, I stopped being a Christian one day back in Fort Stockton when I couldn't stand it anymore and walked out right in the middle of the youth group service. So as I hike along the Rio Grande, I ask myself more than a few questions. I figure that if some deity lives out there somewhere, then that God must be some kind of healing, creative intelligence rather than the damning, cranky old bastard that Genesis, Deuteronomy, and the Book of Revelation say will torture us forever if we don't love Him. I reason that that pool of divine energy must be responsible for not just the moon and the stars, not just for black holes, quasars, and supernovae, but all those endless strings of universes quantum theorists can't seem to shut up about. And that same being, that same force, whatever it was, summoned atoms, molecules, and quarks right out of the great nothingness. It drew this thing called *being* right up out of the cosmic void, all those vibrating strings of energy that make up subatomic particles—so, therefore, all matter. This has to be the spirit who spoke through Catherine of Siena, Simone de Beauvoir, Kierkegaard, Bach, and Virginia Woolf. Right then and right there, it all comes crystal clear.

And I see it. If this is really all true, how could I possibly do wrong by this creator? How could any human action—rape, murder, war, or genocide—be anything more than meaningless?

My mind keeps working. Back when I was a little girl, one of the nuns, why, she screamed at me for reading a book during math class, saying that I need to praise God every minute because He surely could have made some other little girl besides me, so I owe Him. Out on that hike that afternoon, that kind of thinking just strikes me as downright ridiculous. Then the obverse comes into view just as well. The divine spirit loved me so much it chose to manifest itself through me, as me. It created my heart, my soul, my face, and my body as a vehicle for its purposes. So I trudge on, and I come to the conclusion, one I hold quite dear to this day, about this thing we call "sin." That we can lie, cheat, steal, blow each other up, or whatever, and all that stuff, in the great scheme of things, means about as much as a ladybug's sneeze. To think we can somehow offend the creator of all that? Well, that just has to be the height of arrogance.

Something out there that day told me that God can't forgive because God doesn't condemn in the first place.

JACK

Before sunrise, I parked my car in the lot of an abandoned hot dog stand across the street from Barbara Lyon's counseling office, cut the engine, and slid my thumb under the lid of my twenty-ounce cup of Starbucks Italian roast. A droplet that had condensed onto the rim dropped onto my jeans. It surprised me, and I jerked, causing steaming liquid to slosh over onto my lap. I winced and rubbed the coffee into my pants and clicked on the radio, my beloved NPR. On the seat next to me sat a roll of duct tape and, in a polished mahogany case, the six-inch boning knife, which was razor-honed by a professional knifesmith just two days before. I set the coffee in the cup holder, picked up the box, and lifted the top. I inspected the polished steel. The ergonomic handle of tempered walnut, decorated with brass rivets imbedded in the wood. With just two fingers, I lifted it out, appreciated the weight and balance. A product of superior craftsmanship. A damned work of art. In some factory out in the far reaches of Illinois, some workman poured his soul into this, totally unaware of the crazy journey fate had laid out for it.

I touched the honed tip to the skin of a knuckle—applying no pressure—and the flesh parted, releasing a dot of blood.

For six, maybe seven weeks, this is what I did. I threw off my comforter when it was still dark, pulled on my thermal underwear and camping pants, went outside, and warmed up the Toyota. I drove up Central Avenue, down San Mateo Boulevard, over to Lomas, and parked there on the decaying asphalt amid pits of gravel in this parking lot littered with beer cans and Taco Bell Gordita wrappers. I didn't do this every day, and I certainly didn't stay all day long. But I went out regularly. And methodically. The vision that persisted in my imagination was both consistent and vivid. The former Sister Julia is planted in her desk chair, her thin wrists duct taped behind her, her ankles affixed to the chair legs. The woman sweating and weeping.

The first time I actually made it there to scope out Barbara's office, it must have been at maybe five thirty, maybe five forty—before dawn— on a pretty warm February morning. I figured most sane people start their workdays at eight, and some roll into the office about nine or ten. Every once in a while, however, you get some freakazoid who shows up at the office, tanked up on espresso or Red Bull who wants to get things humming before six. So I just wanted to make sure I understood the situation, in case I eventually did muster enough courage to actually settle the score. For some reason, I assumed that the only people working in that converted adobe home were Barbara and, perhaps, some part-time secretary. I never considered how she might share a space with other shrinks or counselors or whatever you call those folks. I never considered that the interior of that office might actually be divided into dinky little cubicles, and that it probably had a break room in the area that back in the 1960s was a nice middle-class couple's kitchen. I wanted a window of opportunity, a time when I could find Lyons—or Sister Julia, or whatever name she went by— alone in that building.

Still, no matter how the scenario assembled itself in my head, the one thing I always imagined was that woman in a chair, her arms and legs rendered immovable. And me there, kneeling in front of her, pointing the razor-honed stainless steel tip right at her voice box. No witnesses. No accessories. No one to spoil the moment.

That first day, I knew I wasn't going to step out of the Toyota. I just wanted to see what options might present themselves. I wasn't even sure I could go through with it. Considering the ten thousand million hours of thought, energy, imagination, work, and late nights I put into killing Gustavo, when it came right down to it, I ended up allowing him to live. So that particular morning, the first day I actually waited for Barbara, I felt pretty safe in my steel cocoon. But I stayed for a long while, parked right across the street, looking through my binoculars, sitting with that fine piece of Chicago Cutlery on my lap.

About a quarter after six, this sea-green Subaru comes down Lomas Boulevard, slows just before the closed liquor store—no turn signal—and makes a left onto Camino Chiva, that residential street where the office sits. The wagon turns and rolls into the driveway, and as it does, the automated porch light flickers and then stays on. The car door squeaks open, and the driver reaches out and drops the last of a cigarette on the pavement, extends a nylon-stockinged leg, and crushes the butt with the sole of her shoe. She gets out, reaches under her jacket, yanks down her skirt, and swings the metal door shut. She appears to be in her late twenties or early thirties. A stylish woman in a wool button-up coat with the belt hanging loose. A real hottie, a total MILF.

She flips her hair back over her shoulder, hair that looks blackish under the amber glow. She adjusts her thick, plastic eyeglass frames. Nice legs. She must work out, even if she does smoke. She has a leather briefcase in one hand, keys in the other, and her purse hangs off her forearm. Her heels click against the brick sidewalk as she disappears behind the wall guarding the porch. Five seconds later, light spills out the Venetian blinds of the front window.

At six forty-nine, a Jeep hardtop approaches from the other direction. That is an area just jam-packed with about a hundred thousand middle-class homes with garages, second cars, backyard swing sets, patios, and sliding glass doors. Total bourgeoiseville. There is even a city park with goal posts back behind those rows of houses where my buddies and I played tackle football. The car is sand-colored or maybe gunmetal gray—it's hard to tell in the dawn—and has an aftermarket luggage rack affixed to its roof. The macho-mobile crawls up the driveway into a special parking slot, designated with a little aluminum sign that I can't see from my angle. It's not a handicapped slot—just reserved. The operator ratchets the gearshift up into park, and the sound of strain leaves the engine. The motor goes silent, and the emergency brake crunches. The driver gathers and arranges materials, pulling stuff together. No hurry.

Then, from behind the fender, a woman appears. She has a canvas satchel—not really a briefcase—slung over her shoulder, and, with two fingers, she holds the handle of what looks like a Tupperware lunch kit, holding it like it's made of French crystal or something super delicate. She stops, points her key fob at the Rubicon. She does it again, and this time the taillights flash and the horn beeps.

She looks like she's a thousand years old. Well, she seems to be in her sixties. Short. No taller than five feet. It sure looks like the former Sister Julia, Order of the Sisters of Charity of Cincinnati. In that cotton skirt that goes past her knees, she looks downright Amish. Once she's on the walkway, I get a clear view. Her hip swings out as if she's limping, just had surgery, or maybe had polio as a child. In any case, that labored walk tells me this is the woman now known as Barbara Lyons, a widow and a counselor with a Ph.D. who specializes in treating depression and weight loss. Over the years, ever since I first thought of ridding the world of that particular snake, I was downright relentless in the way I did my homework. I discovered quickly that after she left the nunnery—or maybe she got kicked out—she went back to her regular name, Barbara Negromonte, then married some twisted soul named Lyons. To me, she is still Sister Julia.

I knew I was crazy. Even then.

The next eight weekdays, I got up, drove the two miles or so over to Midtown, and scoped out the comings and goings at Julia's office, and things moved pretty much on schedule. Each time, the Subaru lady showed up first and carried out the same ritual. She parked in the same slot, opened the car door, dropped the butt and crushed it, and disappeared behind the guarded porchway into the building to switch on the fluorescents and, I assume, the coffee urn.

At ten minutes to seven, more or less, Barbara drove over from the rows of sleepy homes. One day she came at six forty-six and never arrived later than six fifty-four.

I was rock-solid sure that I wouldn't even step out of the Toyota, at least not the first few days. I wasn't sure if anything was going to happen at all, to tell you the truth, not after the whole Gustavo failure. What kind of scared me, however, was that, when it came to Julia, I was more consistent. Perhaps this was because I could, with a dab of imagination, get into Gustavo's head and understand why he did what he did, twisted though it was. With her, I could muster no empathy whatsoever.

Like I said, I did not drive out every day, but I did it three or four—sometimes five—times a week, and it went on for a few months. On those mornings, before heading over to the campus, I drove up Central and down San Mateo, over to where I parked my truck in the lot that used to belong to Griffin's Red Hots. When my cash flow allowed, I stopped at the Starbucks drive-through and treated myself to a twenty-ounce tank of their finest drip blend. Then I waited right behind the abandoned fast food stand with its window sporting the faded cartoon logo of a dancing, anthropomorphized frankfurter and carton of fries. I sipped my coffee, thinking things over, listening to *Morning Edition*, and wondering exactly what kind of horror I was capable of. What it would be like to watch the blood of an ex-nun spreading across an office floor.

By late April, perhaps the first weeks of May, I started going down there in the afternoon. After about the seventh or eighth day, another pattern emerged. Just after five, almost every time, the fashion model with the Subaru came out the front door first, always between eight and twelve minutes after *All Things Considered* began. She tossed her bag into the back seat, got in the car, and backed out—like she actually wanted to get caught in rush-hour traffic. Or maybe she had to get to daycare before they started charging extra. She always looked very official, always primped, with her starched blouses, business suits, and multicolored hair hanging over her shoulders, always with her high heels that matched her purse, and always looking freshly showered. Then out came another woman, someone I didn't see in the mornings. A short, pear-shaped thing with close-cut curls. A real peasant, you know? A dark woman in her fifties. Sometimes in white jeans. Sometimes in a flowered skirt. She climbed into a silver Nissan, backed it out of its slot, and headed off toward the valley.

Finally, at about six oh five, maybe six ten—six thirteen at the latest—out came Sister Mary Beelzebub. Eddie Bauer bag slung over her shoulder, her empty plastic lunchbox clutched like a book at her side. She jabbed the air with her keyless remote and the lights on her sedan flashed and the door locks clicked to attention. Always the last one out.

I decided all I really needed to do was to make an appointment, to conjure up some story about how I keep getting this urge to walk into a lake, to overdose on sleeping pills, or to throw myself off the bridge at the Rio Grande Gorge. I even concocted a fake name for the occasion, although I wasn't sure I could use it, since she probably would ask for about a thousand official documents proving who I was. Then I could finally, after all these goddamned years, come face-to-face with that beast. All I had to do was schedule the last appointment of the day.

Four thirty could work. Five would be better. Five thirty would be perfect.

HELEN DENISE

I scratch a wooden match on the side of the cardboard box, creating a trail of sparks. I do it again, and this time the red-and-white phosphorus head erupts into a tiny yellow-red rosebud. Once the burst calms down, I touch the flame to the wick of a cinnamon-scented candle the size of a juice glass and let it catch. Then I light three jade-colored tapers in pewter candlesticks sitting on the breakfast table in front of me. I walk with two of the candles across the kitchen, over to the living room, where Mark sits on the floor, leaning against the couch. Shadows undulate across the curtains and far wall as I set a candle on the floor. It casts this golden sheen on the curves of his cheek and chin. He concentrates on his bare toes.

The electricity had gone out a few minutes before, and outside the wind moans, a young poplar lashes the back window, the roof shingles shake, and rain whips the roof and skylight. Another gust comes, and the house creaks and the wind whistles, causing the elm in the backyard to convulse, its whole top bending, shaking, and getting stripped of its leaves.

The clouds began collecting over the Sandias just as Mark and I went into the campus gymnasium that afternoon, and the drizzle started when we were working the barbells. Ninety minutes later, by the time we were in his car and coming down the little dirt road back to my cottage, the rain came in slanting sheets. Pellets of hail pocked the puddles in the yards and collected in the roadway, rat-tat-tatting on the car hood and the tin roof. Lightning cracked right over us as Mark jumped out of the car, fumbled with the keys, dropped the ring on the concrete stoop, wiped them on his sweatshirt, and finally got the door open. The plan had been that, once he got it unlocked, I would dash from the car to the kitchen. It really didn't matter, though. We both got soaked.

Once inside, I went straight to the bathroom, took out my contact lenses, and then walked back out, scrubbing my scalp dry with a fresh bath towel. Thunder clapped again, shaking the house. The light over the kitchen table flickered. The house went dark.

I had known Mark for about a month, maybe six weeks, by that time, and I am astounded by how close I feel to him. I mean, I never felt quite this comfortable with Mace the whole time we went out, even though we just about grew up together. Even so, the things I need to confess weigh down on me. Now I ease myself next to him, onto the braided rug, with my back against the couch. I tell him I have Brie cheese in the fridge and fresh pears and Fuji apples, straight from the farmers' market, on the counter. That we can slice them up whenever. He says he'll get them in a minute. That he doesn't feel like getting up. He takes one of the table candles and holds it to a wine bottle so he can read the label and decides that particular vintage and year will do just fine. As I blow a speck of lint off my glasses and wipe them clean, the cork pops and liquid glug-glug-glugs into a wine glass. I inspect the lens, holding it in front of the flame, and wipe it with my T-shirt.

Mark's usual brightness is gone. He appears to bite the inside of his cheek and hasn't looked at me since I sat down. He hands over a half-full glass without looking at me. He tells me not to drink yet, and then braces his palm against the hardwood floor, repositions himself, as if trying to adjust for sore muscles, then takes his glass by the stem. He turns, and luminous threads of condensed light reflect in his green eyes. Our glasses clink. The Zinfandel is as rich and velvety as I ever tasted—oaky, with hints of blackberry and currant. I ask what's bothering him, and he says it's nothing, and he forces a smile and turns back to his feet. I tell him just to say it. He insists it's no big deal. I know something is up, I say, that a million possibilities dance through my head, not one bringing me a dab of comfort. Blurt it out. Let's deal with it, I say. Let's exorcise those demons before things get even more complicated. I get downright aggravated, just wondering if he is married, has herpes, is in love with another woman—or, perhaps, even another man. He chuckles, takes another swallow of wine, sets the glass on the floor, shifts his weight, and says his problem is far more pedestrian.

His new running shoes have left the soles of his feet tender, he says. It wasn't so bad when we ran across the parking lot to the car, or even when he darted through the mud to the back door, but once he changed out of his gym trunks, the burn shot up through his calves so terrible he didn't think he could make it to the living room.

I cup my glass with both hands, drinking the wine like it's hot soup, and I ask just how bad the pain is, and he says it would be impossible to walk even four or five steps. That if the building catches fire, he's in real trouble, so maybe we're lucky we're in the middle of a squall. I tell him to wait where he is and carry one of the candles into the bedroom, over to the closet, and go to the top shelf. When I come back, I have the whole sampler kit with me. Thirty-six half-ounce vials, arranged

150

in this honeycomb of foam padding. I sit next to him and uncap one with a cream-colored top and wave it under his nose and ask what he thinks. He says it is awfully strong. I say essential oils are supposed to be strong. Try this one, I say, and I let him sniff the cardamom. He says he likes it. Then we go through the myrrh, the pine, the honeysuckle, the cinnamon, and the sandalwood.

He asks why I have so many, and I tell him that I sell them. That I started my own little business just after I graduated high school. He says he didn't know I was so enterprising, and I say there are a great many things he doesn't know about me. As I say this, I fold back one cuff of his flannel sleeper pants and then lay his foot across my lap. I tell how, during my second year at the Midland, I helped my professor publish a paper that appeared in the *American Philosophical Review*. How once, when I was a born-again Christian, I participated in a ritual to cure a fellow churchgoer of homosexuality. And it worked, until her girlfriend knocked on her door just crying her eyes out that very night. I tell him how, as a high school junior, I had my full gainer so razor-honed, I took third place in the regional diving championships.

He says that what intrigues him is how I come with so many layers, how I always reveal something new. As he speaks, I uncap a tube of eucalyptus, tilt it, and drip a thread of oil into the gap between his first two toes. I say I'll just bet he's got secrets he won't share. He says he's not a betting man. He asks if selling the oil brings in enough money for me to get by. Oh, God no, I say, this little enterprise is for supplemental income, but that I can move quite a bit of product while working at my other job—words I regret even before they come out. Then I have my scholarship money, I say.

I work the unctuous liquid into the fatty mounds right beneath his toes and go down toward the metatarsal, squeezing the whole foot like

I'm kneading a lump of pizza dough. The problem, I say, is that those shoes are causing the fascia to constrict. That the soles are not wide enough. He needs double Es. Maybe triple Es.

He asks what I mean by "other job."

I take a sip of wine and get oily smears on the bell of the glass. I tell him I don't really want to reveal that much. He says we need to exorcise the demons now, before things get more complicated.

I tell him to brace himself. He says he's braced.

I dig the tips of my fingers into the middle of his feet, at the arch, apply pressure, and hold. He pours me more wine and moans.

So I tell him.

Even though I had scholarship money and everything, I say, once I got to Albuquerque, I still needed a regular income, you know, just to keep up my car payments. Just so I didn't end up out on the street, really, or worse yet, running back home with my tail between my legs. Why, I didn't know anybody who might lend a hand. At first, Daddy hooked me up with a job checking groceries at the Safeway, but that fell through, so I took a job at a call center, trying to get folks to sign up for cable television. There they had me working thirty hours a week and getting home after eleven sometimes, my head full of folks screaming at me about how I ruined their suppers or television shows or whatever. Talk about feeling hated. After about three weeks of that hell, I took off my headset right in the middle of my shift, picked up my purse, and walked out the door, knowing full well my rent was already late. The next day, one of the girls in my existentialism class suggested I get into the whole cocktail-waitressing thing. She said I was right pretty and could do well, and she scribbled down this number for me to call.

Mark finishes his wine, sets the glass on the floor, relaxes against the couch, apparently feeling better. He appears primed for yet another come-to-Jesus moment, so I work his heel and go on.

I guess I should have been creeped out by all of this, but from the instant the guy answered the phone, something felt right. Maybe it was the softness of his voice. And I knew right away what was going on. Long before, I decided what is right or wrong depends upon a whole bunch of factors, not just on what rules, mores, and conventions happen to be in style. What is right in one moment may not be so in the next. That's something I learned from studying the New Testament.

I go on, telling Mark how the very next morning, while I am on my way to campus, I drive over to this office in this little strip center over in the Sawmill District. I'm in a faded denim jacket and matching pants, and I have too much makeup on, I know that. The building is exactly like the man described on the phone: an abandoned hardware store next to three little offices, his second from the end, with no sign on it or anything, just silver numbers on the window. So I double-check the address, pull open the door, and walk through the main room that is just stacked with cartons of papers and books and a whole bunch of other stuff. Other than the twanging voice and the tinny and staticky whine of a pedal steel guitar coming from a radio in the back room, the place looks, and feels, pretty much deserted. I wait, and nobody comes out, so I run a brush through my hair and check my eyeliner. Then I find a stick of gum in my purse, zip up, and pull the strap up on my shoulder. I put the Dentyne in my mouth and wait there with my arms crossed. Nothing happens. So after a few minutes, I call out, "Howdy? Anybody home?" Something stirs in another room, a file cabinet closing or something. So I ask again. Just paper shuffling.

Finally, I poke my head in past the doorway and there, behind the desk, sits this fellow in a thick, close-trimmed, black beard, and hair hanging in his eyes. He doesn't even get up when I walk in, just keeps both elbows planted right there on the old gray desk in front of him.

He wears this coal-black, long-sleeved T-shirt, and the front is just covered with crumbs and big sugar crystals. He says something, and I ask him to repeat, and he asks again, "Please, please, sit, sit" in just the softest, sweetest, little-boy voice I ever did hear. I ask if he's the man named Saul I talked to the day before, and he snaps a sugar cookie in half and holds the larger piece out to me and tells me he just washed his hands. I take it, and as he chews, he brushes some of the crumbs off his chest and slacks, then he sweeps the debris off the front of his desk into his palm and drops it all in the wastebasket. He claps his hands clean, and all this glittery sugar dust falls all over the rug.

He's totally up-front. In fact, the way he speaks, I mean, he comes off so shy, so non-threatening. Just so darned nice. He explains all the rules. I dance three minutes at a time. That I can choose any songs I want. That I do my own choreography. If someone wants a lap dance, they must keep their hands behind them, and every cent they hand over afterward is mine to keep. If someone invites me to the VIP room, whether I go is entirely up to me. At the end of the night, two bouncers escort me out to my car and make doubly sure some creep's not out there, fixing to follow me home.

I tell Mark that there wasn't a whole lot I could do, not in light of everything going on at the time. And it all seemed clear-cut enough. After the first night, I had two hundred and eleven dollars in my purse, besides. I never considered somebody from school might walk in and see me working.

So I go on, telling Mark how I can't say I'm proud of what I do, but I'm not real ashamed of it, either. Good and bad, right and wrong, I tell him, why that stuff changes depending upon the circumstances. Just ask all those folks in the parable of the Good Samaritan or that one about the dishonest steward.

I tell him how, once I started at Bathsheba's, I only worked Tuesdays and Thursdays, some Wednesday nights when Saul found himself in a pinch, and I brought in almost twice as much as I did at the call center. Besides, I was able to get the transmission on my car rebuilt. And that's when I knew I could probably get through the next two years and maybe even through graduate school.

Mark holds his glass up in front of the candle flame, spins the liquid inside, and waits for it to streak down. By this point, I reckon I've gone on too long. I am thankful that his feet hurt so much because otherwise he might leap up and run away screaming. He grabs the bottle and inverts, giving me the last few dribbles.

"So, you're an exotic dancer," he says. "Well, well, well. In a million years . . ." and his voice fades off, like the news is sending him into deep turmoil. Once more he swirls the last of his wine and watches the liquid spider down the glass. He shifts his weight. Finally, he sips, swallows, straightens himself, and says, "Two days ago . . ." and takes another sip, this one longer, and studies the bottom of the glass.

"Two days ago," he says, "my doctor told me I'm sterile."

Water plinks in the drainpipe.

"That's horrible," I say.

"Yup," he says. "If you take a million of my tadpoles, only one of them is going to swim."

He lays his glass down and folds his hands over his stomach.

"How do you feel about that?" I ask.

"How do I feel? How *do* I feel?" he says and taps his chin with the tips of his fingers. "How do *I* feel? I feel that you're a stripper and I'm sterile. And everybody's got something to hide, except for me and my monkey."

He finishes his Zinfandel. I pick two hairs off his talus bone, put that foot down, pick up the other, and start massaging all over again.

"The rain," I say. "It stopped."

"So it did," he says as he rests the back of his head against the couch cushion and closes his eyes. "So it did."

NICHOLS

What do comedians do in their spare time? Probably watch their own videos and whack off. How do I know this? I've been in this business for more than two minutes. Don't believe me? Get to the comedy club about forty minutes before showtime, and sit at the back table, deep in the shadows, where all the jokesters like to congregate—whether or not they plan on getting up on stage that night. Watch them trade one-liners. I'll bet you five dollars that within three minutes they launch into that game I call "My Dick Joke Is Bigger Than Yours." It's a whole lot of fun. For about ninety seconds.

But to hell with all that.

Why did I drop out of community college and open my own business? Why do I put on comedy shows? To make money. It's called "show business," not "show charity." And how do you succeed at business? You think win-win. I excel at that. When it comes to symbiosis, I'm practically a born natural.

So one morning before my place opens, I sit on a stool at the bar, filling in the slots of the waitress schedule with a fresh pencil, and listening to music on my laptop. That day I already spent more than an hour of valuable work time tying myself in knots, wrestling with who could work and when. I swear, sometimes hammering out a simple schedule feels about as complicated as working out a differential equation. Deborah can't work late on Thursdays because she has yoga. Paloma can only work late on weekends because that's when her mother can babysit. Just the day before, Cyn came in whining, begging to get next weekend off because her husband comes home on leave. I pour some Seagram's into my coffee and stir it with a ballpoint, toss the implement on the bar, and rub both hands over my face. Just taking a little breather to get some perspective. I wonder if I can really get by with just one waitress for happy hour on Friday. Probably.

The phone rings. Cyn's mother's number flashes across the caller I.D. screen. I know it's that girl again, checking for the umpteenth time if I need her to work the football game on Saturday. I switch off the ringer. Two seconds later? My cell phone vibrates on the polished oak. Same number.

I tap my teeth with the pencil eraser when the thought comes to me—instantly and fully formed. A goddamned epiphany.

I get to thinking of the words of my favorite philosopher, Miles, from that film *Risky Business*: "Sometimes, you just gotta say, 'What the fuck.' When you say 'What the fuck,' that gives you opportunity. And opportunity? That makes your future."

The phone buzzes again, and I light a Marlboro, get up, and walk down the hallway to the storage closet. The door is unlocked—it shouldn't be—and I step in, tug on the light chain, reach behind one of the patio umbrellas we never use, and wrestle out the canvas bag sitting on a beer keg in the back corner. I flick a daddy longlegs off of it, wipe the dust, unzip the top flap, and take out the high-definition camera I bought way back when I started my third video production class. A piece of equipment we haven't used since we tried putting our wet T-shirt contests up on our website. When we had a website. I hold it up right under the light bulb and punch the power tab. It not only works, but the damned battery still has juice. I think I may just climb out of this little trench I dug myself into after all. I rearrange boxes of baseball caps, beer glasses, and bar rags wrapped in heat-shrunk cellophane. I crush another spider with the ball of my thumb, find the tripod, and lift it out.

I go back to my spot at the drink station, call up Laffs' website, get the phone number, and punch the numbers into my handset. I slap the top of my cigarette pack against the heel of my palm, and three filter ends pop out just as Herman Esau answers in the middle of the first ring, like he expected my call all morning. I put a fresh menthol between my lips and then lay out the details. I ask what he thinks. He pretends to mull it over, and the hesitation tells me, loud and clear, that I hooked him. This is Five Card Draw 101. When the guy across the table can't fill his inside straight, he moves his cards close to his vest. Santa Claus couldn't deliver a better sure-fire tell.

Finally, Esau—the bigshot comedy club owner—comes back on, says something like how he needs to build up the local talent pool any way he can. That nothing builds a comedian's act like consistent review. Audio recording helps a lot. Audio-visual helps a hundred times more. That it sounds like a good, solid, business venture. He thought about doing the same thing last year but just didn't have the time, and that he never knows when he'll be out of town, not with his gigs in Vegas and everything. I tell him I like thinking win-win, and he says he'll only charge me five bucks a night for the electricity I use and, because he likes me, he'll give me a dollar off my first drink.

What a guy.

He tells me he'll be out of town the next Sunday, so I have to deal with his underling. He lays down the rules, in that hardnosed and inimitable Esau style. Come Sunday, I am to record the open-mic show, the amateur show. It starts at five minutes after seven—not three minutes after seven, not six minutes after—and shuts down at eight. Not eight oh two. The first comic for the professional show needs to be on stage by eight thirty-one and needs to get his first laugh by eight thirty-six. Then he asks what kind of camera equipment I have, and I tell him, and he tells me to go ahead and plug a patch cord right into the sound board. I can just drape the line over the four-foot wall of the booth if I fix it in place with duct tape. He'll have Leah, the house manager, leave the front door unlocked. I can show up any time after six.

Three days later, I walk into Laffs right on schedule. I got a camera bag strap slung around my shoulder, and I carry my tripod like it's a tree I just cut down. The only light in the place spills in from the kitchen. Pans and utensils clank and thump on the other side of the swinging aluminum doors. I peek through the little porthole. There stands Leah at the polished stainless steel table with her back to me, wearing her tight red sweatshirt and black jeans. She tears leaves off a head of iceberg lettuce and stabs them one at a time into a grid of salad bowls. She, the manager, is doing menial work. Either someone called in sick or maybe they need to cut back on staff, the same way I do. Behind her the cook scrapes something out of the oven, something black and crusty, reminding me not to order food in that joint.

So I survey the space and go to work. I choose a spot that is out of the way and yet affords a clear shot of the stage. I shake the tripod out of its bag and slide out the first telescoping leg, lock it in place, and make sure it won't slide back in, the way that leg tends to. Once I get that all set up, I go to the sound booth, reach up over the wall—I got to go to my tiptoes—and plug right into Esau's soundboard. I tape the extension cord in place. The last thing I need is some clown like Mica Pierson or Black Tom to come off a bad set, knock back too many shots of tequila, stumble over one of the wires, and send two hundred dollars' worth of equipment crashing to the floor.

Once I get everything set up, I lay out on the two back tables stacks of flyers with my picture, email, phone number, plus a coupon for a drink at my place—buy one IPA and get a second at half price. The handout explains things so perfectly, so clearly, even a goofball like Firecracker can understand it. I record the whole show. If you want your set on DVD, all you have to do is let me know and then hand over ten dollars. I even take checks. Sounds like a bargain to me. For a lousy ten rocks, these bozos can watch themselves on stage and get their jollies. The more astute performers? They'll learn where the jokes hit and where they fell flat. For a few, the pain of seeing themselves panic under the spotlight will be too much to bear, and that dream of headlining at Pancho Pilot's, The Ice Palace, The Comedy Store, or doing *The Tonight Show* can die a quick and humane death.

You see? I always shoot for the win-win.

What does all this mean for me? It means that I can invest, what, sixty-five minutes at the show, max. That's ten minutes setting up, fifty minutes for the performance, and five minutes breaking down. I figure I can put in about an hour on my office computer, sitting there in front of the Final Cut Pro program and splitting up the video into segments and then burning each onto a separate disc. For this? I pocket anywhere between sixty and a hundred and twenty dollars of legal tender. Minus, of course, the fifteen dollars and change for the spindle of blank DVD+Rs, eight dollars for the flyers, and the five spot I got to hand over to Esau. That means I stand to make anywhere between two hundred and twenty and five hundred extra dollars a month. That will make a difference—at least until business at my place picks up or I figure something else out.

I tighten the knob of the camera mount, securing the recorder in place, when one of the kitchen doors opens. Leah shouts something back behind her to the cook about a bag of steak fries in the walk-in and then sticks her little blondie airhead through the opening, fingers her freshwater pearl pendant dangling at her sternum, and smiles that cute, vapid, and over-lipsticked smile of hers. She crooks a finger for me to come talk to her and leads me all the way to the back, where she allows me the privilege of watching her fold table tents announcing some special, upcoming hypnotist show.

What's so important? She tells me that Esau said for me to go ahead and plug right into the sound equipment. Like I'm mental or something. I tell her I already did it, that Esau and I went over the technical stuff on the phone. Then she says I have to move the camera five feet back from where it stands, as close to the back wall as possible, fire marshal regulations. I say whatever. She takes seven minutes to tell me something she could have covered in five seconds with a shout from the doorway. No wonder she makes just over minimum wage.

When I come back to my equipment, there at the little round table, right where the waitresses come through with their orders, sits that dykey Jana Boan with her Mohawk haircut freshly done, tinted orange and electric green just for the occasion, and her ragged spiral notebook propped up against her leg. In the next chair is her skinny little girlfriend, Jamie Jupiter, with the brim of her baseball cap all askew on her head, like she's a newsboy from the 1930s or something. I tell them my plan to provide recordings for the performers, and Jupiter stirs her coffee with a spoon, taps the utensil on the side of the cup, and lays it on the bare table. Boan rips a page from the tablet, wads it up with one hand, and rolls it off her fingers next to the saucer. She writes something else down, strikes it out, then looks up and says she likes the whole idea. She would want to do it if she had a camera. She says that if I keep at it, those comedians who stay with it can actually chart their growth, and that I should probably charge twelve or fifteen bucks a pop instead. I tell her we'll see how the first few rounds go, that I really don't feel like bothering with counting out change during a show. But she has a point.

That first night? Everything comes off without a hitch. Boan, Jupiter, Mica, Firecracker, Black Tom, and a few others pay me right on the spot, and two others say they'll drop by the Silver Dollar during the week.

Once I get back to my place, about eight twenty, I pour myself a shot of V.O., roll the chair in front of my computer, and spark up the Macintosh. I feed the video into the hard drive and get down to business. Things take longer than I expected, mostly because I haven't used the program in more than a year. But just after eleven that night, I slide the last of the empty video discs into the external drive. A few seconds later, the little plastic drawer slides out. I pick up a felt-tip, scrawl "Mica" and the date across the silvery surface, and snap the disc into its jewel case. I calculate: the whole process took three hours and forty-three minutes, give or take. So I pour another drink—this one of Seagram's 7—and punch numbers into the calculator to work up output versus income. The final tabulation? I made sixteen dollars and eighty-four cents an hour.

Not great, but not bad for a first haul with virtually no advertising. I figure the momentum will build. More comedians will catch on, more orders will come in, and I'll become more agile with the equipment. I'll get my video production chops back. I'll order discs in bulk and keep the same digital tape in the camera until it wears out.

How could it miss?

The next Sunday? The enterprise pulls in seventy dollars, and I spend thirteen minutes less at the computer. The time after that? I make an even hundred, minus thirteen dollars for drinks. And the five dollars for Esau's electricity.

But the following week, my fourth night recording, I felt I was standing at the plate, top of the ninth, after my team just went up by two. I waited, ready for the knuckleball, slider, or hanging curve. What did I get? A beanball. And where did I get it? Right in the groin.

That night? I get to Laffs right about six twenty, no later than six twenty-five, before any of the comics arrive. I drop my jacket on a chair and then draw out the telescoping legs of the aluminum tripod and double-check the latch that always gives me trouble and proceed with my usual set-up. I unzip the side pocket, looking for the roll of silver tape, and don't find it. I look in the other pouch. Nothing. I dig out my car keys and trudge back out to the parking lot, to my car, and pop open the trunk. In the side compartment, under half a quart of motor oil and a greasy T-shirt, I find the spare roll. One edge is flattened, and one side has something spilled on it—maybe coffee, maybe Coca-Cola. Who knows? But it'll do the trick.

Back inside, at the table there in the shadows, a few comics chat away, trading war stories. Then they erupt in a burst of laughter, the kind of stuff I learned to tune out. I scrape up a corner of the tape's ragged edge with my thumbnail, strip some off, and nip the side with my teeth to get the rip started. I tear off a section and get ready to secure the wiring when someone taps my shoulder. It's this little bald dweeb who says something so meekly I can only make out a couple of words. I ask him to repeat, and he says something like he doesn't want me to record when he goes up on stage. I ask who the hell he thinks he is. He sticks his hands in his pants pockets, shrugs, and brings his cheek down to his shoulder, as if wiping a tear on his sweater. Then he says it again, this time a little louder.

"Please. I don't want the camera running. Not when I'm on stage."

What do I do? I laugh. I actually let out a big "ha!" right in his chicken-skin-colored face.

I figure I know his type. He'll get up there, say into the mic, "How's everybody doing out there doing tonight?"—that horrible opening line that all the newbies can't resist for some reason—and then go dumbstruck with stage fright right before he crawls home and rinses out his underwear. You see that happen at least five times at any open-mic show. I sever another section of tape.

"Honestly," he says, "I'm not asking you to tear down. I'm simply asking for a little courtesy. Please turn off the camera when I go up on stage. Please. Don't record me."

"Where do you come off, telling me how to run my business?" I say and pull off more tape. "When I want any lip from you, I'll rattle my zipper."

"I'm asking you nicely," he says. He still has both hands deep in his pockets, and he stands there looking shy, like a second grader admitting that he just peed his pants. "Please. Please turn it off. I am asking you nice."

"Listen, girlfriend," I say. Over at the comics' table, Jupiter twists the bill of her cap around, as if shielding out the light. Boan stares into the far corner of the room, thinking of a punchline. "I'll do whatever

I damned well please, when I damned well please. You don't want a recording of your act? Fine. Your loss."

"Honestly," he says. "You can record anybody else. But when I am on that stage, please shut off your camera."

So I plant a hand on my hip, pound the tip of my index finger into his sternum, bend down, and bark in his face like a drill sergeant.

"Look, fucktard," I say. "I don't take orders from anybody, especially little bald, nasally-voiced women like you. You don't want a recording? Fine. Don't buy one. Between now and the time I finish, I want you to just sit down, shut up, and not breathe too much of my air. The last thing we need around here is turds like you stinking up the place."

At that? His hand flies out of that front pocket, up toward my face, and I blink. By the time my eyes reopen, he has his thumb and forefinger digging into my larynx, the back of my skull pressed against the painted cinder block wall, and my left hand twisted up behind me. My work boots practically dangle off the carpet.

He grits his teeth.

"I said," he whispers, "turn the damned thing off. I asked you nicely."

I try to nod but can't move my head.

"If I see that little red light go on when I'm on stage, your proctologist will be doing major surgery to remove that camera stand," he says. He lets me go. "You got that?"

He stands square in front of me. He reaches under his shirt cuff and yanks down one sleeve. Then he straightens the other.

Never before in my life did I feel that kind of force, that kind of sheer power, radiating from a single body.

What did I do? I shut off the camera right before he went on stage.

Who was that guy? Wladika, that's who. The guy who all that summer had the whole of Albuquerque going apeshit. I didn't realize it until Black Tom announced his name, bringing him up to the stage. I saw firsthand how every eye, every ear—every modicum of energy in that room—laser-beamed itself on that little bald man who just about ripped my throat out.

All week long? I seriously considered never going back there, to Albuquerque's only fully-fledged, dedicated comedy club. For one thing, I couldn't handle the embarrassment. For another, I didn't want to face Wladika again. But the next Sunday? I showed up anyway. I popped the trunk of my car, slung the camera bag over one shoulder, heaved the tripod over the other, and walked over to the entrance. And what do I discover? Esau's place lost its lease and shut down for good the previous Wednesday.

What was I thinking at first? It is a damned shame that Albuquerque lost its only stand-up venue.

What did I think next? This was an opportunity. A gap Nichols' Silver Dollar could fill.

EDDIE

Remember when that short, curly-headed Latina rested her feet on the lip of the stage and tipped her chair so far back that she almost fell over? Remember how you zeroed in and made no pretenses about the way you delivered your jokes straight to the rise of the gracilis muscle leading up her skirt? Remember that, Eddie? I couldn't get over how every comedian came up and made a spectacle of it. That night I sat there gripping my chest and just about falling over, watching you guys, the way she reduced all of you to babbling thirteen-year-olds. Even the two women who went on stage that night couldn't help themselves. All of you acting like horny adolescents, peeking through the knothole in the nudist colony's fence. That's when the insight came, flashing across my mind like the blue of summer lightning.

"Do you remember that, Eddie?"

I had pretended I didn't know what Mark went on about. I had pretended I needed to sort through hundreds of memories before I isolated the details of that one clear picture. The truth of the matter, however, was that those images returned all too easily. I still see the woman smiling as she lifts her blended margarita off the waiter's tray, her freshly manicured pinky extended, as if she purposely points it toward the exit sign. One foot rests on the edge of the stage, the cork sole of her shoe hanging loose like a flap. Then she lifts the other leg and lays that one on the wood, pushes her chair back, and rocks.

The night of that particular showcase, nobody except the head-liner—some New York bigshot nobody ever heard of, even though he supposedly starred in three cable television sitcoms—got more than five minutes of stage time. Yet, what I remember most is that girl. Her smooth, almost porcelain-like skin, except for a line of acne dots on one cheek. Her sunglasses on top of her head like a hairband, holding her curls back, as she sat alone at the front table, lifting that elegant leg and planting the toe of her high heel on the stage just as I went into my closer. It was enough to make me lose my bearings. When my last bit clanked and got nothing, I waved goodbye, and reset the microphone.

Then Mica Pierson, who pulled the emcee duty that night, came up the steps to center stage. He whipped up another round of applause for me, set the metal stand behind him. He knelt down in front of the girl, like he was looking through a keyhole, and delivered three of his worst one-liners directly to her crotch. Then he called out to Jana Boan, who was on stage right before I was, and asked her to come up to tell just one more joke. She went up and dished out two of her stillborn bits, straight between the woman's legs. Once she got off, Mica brought up Jana's girlfriend, Jamie Jupiter, this thin-shouldered girl in army fatigues and a sideways baseball cap, who dealt out some of her lamest material. She, too, aimed her one-liners right at the obvious target.

By that point, the quality of the jokes hardly mattered. Besides, the situation warranted improvisation, and everybody, even Bartholomew, the assistant manager, understood that much automatically.

After Jamie came off, Mica called up Phil Fletcher, then Jim Shuter, and Firecracker Rael. Once all the comics got their peek, up to the stage came Bartholomew himself, a guy who never wanted to be a comedian. He didn't even know enough to get the metal stand out of the way, and he just stood there, behind the empty pole, holding the microphone. He adjusted his skullcap and stumbled through a street joke before he left, laughing. The kicker came when Mica introduced Andre, the dishwasher, who was mopping spilled beer from the back steps when he asked about all the fuss. Mica stood under the spotlight, calling out to Andre, telling him that he needed to tell a story on stage, that Bartholomew would surely let him, under the circumstances.

Andre guided his bucket by the metal mop handle, leaned the pole against the curtain—everyone on one side of the room saw it—but it slipped on the fabric, slid down the wall, and clanked against the tiled floor, the mop strands surging out of the brown-gray water. The kid stood in the middle of the stage, smiled widely, raked his fingers through his sweaty hair, and said, "What's the deal with . . .?" and wiped his palm on his shirt. "I mean, what *is* the deal with . . . ?" and ran out of words.

He glanced at the tiled floor and then out to the audience and then back to the stage. He raised his head, and his initial elation drained out, deteriorating into the fear of someone confronting a sea of strange faces, someone who never so much as participated in a sixth grade Thanksgiving pageant. His eyes glistened, his cheeks and forehead went flush, and snot leaked out his nose. He released an anguished breath and his jaw moved, as though he were trying to bite down on his words.

He hovered there, as if balanced on a wave. In the back of the room, someone coughed.

After a few seconds, all Andre could get out was, "I don't know no jokes." His eyes filled with water. "I just wanted to see a beav shot."

From the comics' table in the back came this cacophonous burst, a sustained explosion of laughter that lasted for a full forty seconds, maybe more. A roar of bellowing, hooting, and the sound of a chair tipping over onto the hardwood floor.

"Of course I remember that," I tell Mark. "How could I forget? That's part of the magic. The war stories are every bit as satisfying as those swells of laughter."

Mark and I recalled that moment one night after talking for hours out on his balcony on one sweltering San Francisco night in mid-August. I leaned the chair back on two legs, gripped the iron railing, and steadied myself while trying to process everything that transpired over the previous seven weeks, all those protracted conversations that he roped me into. Before that night, I never thought my mind had the intellectual depth and plasticity of his. As he poured my fifth glass of good bourbon, I was absolutely sure of it.

That was when Mark was staying at a place in Cathedral Hill, a mostly business district of San Francisco, about halfway between Union Square and Japan Town. When the evening began, I carried a dinner plate heaped with wild boar chops, rosemary garlic Parmesan mashed potatoes, and braised asparagus—stuff Mark whipped up in his kitchen after we got home from a Dada exhibition at the San Francisco Museum of Modern Art. Once we sat down, I twisted open a bottle of Francis Ford Coppola Petite Syrah, poured two glasses full, and we toasted to the previous two months and went on about what a joy it had been, about how we would never get a chance like that again.

We sliced into succulent pork, appreciated the hints of basil and hazelnuts. We talked. We drank fine wine. Then we talked some more and brought out the bourbon. I checked my watch again. It was after midnight.

Mark drizzled out the last of a bottle of Bushmills and tossed the top over the iron railing, into the courtyard three stories down. The tin cap bounced on the concrete and lost itself in the unmowed grass. I tipped my chair back again, held to the railing, contemplated his wisdom, and steadied myself. Somewhere below, in one of the first-floor apartments, a light went on, the amber glow spilling through the curtain slit and over the textured lawn, zig-zagging over the landscaping stones. A second later, the yard went dark again.

"Want more ice?" he said.

"Sure," I said.

"Then go get it," he said. "You know where it is."

I laughed. "Maybe I'll have this one neat."

"I have a bottle of Knob Creek somewhere in the kitchen, probably in the cabinet next to the coffee cups," he said.

"What about that Black Maple Hill I brought from Albuquerque?"

"That small batch bourbon? Good stuff."

"Yeah. Go get it."

"You go get it."

"Maybe later," I said.

The plans for this particular get-together began back in May, the very day I signed my divorce papers. That cold, windy, and cloudy afternoon, I walked home from the university feeling pretty low. I stood on the porch, checking my pockets for my keys, and held the screen door open with my toe. When I finally turned the dead bolt and shoved the door with my shoulder, I accidently kicked a baseball-sized box covered in brown paper and delivered sometime that morning. In the living room, I dropped my briefcase on the easy chair and tore the wrapping off the package. The box held a ball of tissue paper, inside of which was a shot glass with an image of the Golden Gate Bridge etched onto it. Curled inside the souvenir was his note:

Congratulations on your return to your natural state: single. Come stay with me in San Francisco for the summer. You've slept on that couch before, so I know your back can stand it. I'll spring for the plane ticket.

> *You're welcome,*
> *Mark*

I had departmental money that I needed to spend, and since I could claim that a trip out there was for research purposes, anything I shelled out I could write off on my taxes. Besides that, I needed time for healing. By all accounts, God wanted me to convalesce on the West Coast.

When God talks, you listen.

I arrived in San Francisco on Saturday, and the next day Mark and I drove out to the Napa Valley for a winetasting tour. The next weekend we hiked through Redwood National Park. Two weeks later we trekked down to Monterey, to Cannery Row, the aquarium, and then to this dive bar called the Trident Room, where we raised glasses of rye to John Steinbeck, even though neither one of us knew which libations the novelist preferred. We knew Hemingway liked mojitos; Fitzgerald, gin; Faulkner, the mint julep and Kentucky sour mash; Bukowski, vodka, cleaning products, astringent, gasoline, and silver polish; Flannery O'Connor, mint tea. We conjectured a socialist like Steinbeck would go for the workingman's drink. We settled on the rye, since neither one of us ever tried it before.

Over the next few weeks, we took in Bizet's *Carmen* at the San Francisco Opera, watched the Giants and the Dodgers go into extra innings at AT&T Park, and got to see a midnight performance of the play *Picasso at the Lapin Agile*, the story of the artist and Albert Einstein running into each other at a Paris bar. We ate dinner at Brazilian, Tanzanian, Ethiopian, Chilean, Estonian, and Nepalese restaurants. We visited jazz clubs on Fisherman's Warf, North Beach, the Mission, Bernal Heights, the Haight, and the East Bay. We saw Jake Johansen at Cobb's Comedy Club on the wharf and Mitch Hedberg at the Punchline down by the Embarcadero. We ferreted out information on, and visited, three smaller stand-up shows—one in a restored movie theater over in Glen Park, another at a Bohemian coffee shop in Pacific Heights, and one in a refurbished warehouse in the Castro.

We did that stuff at night. During the day, I followed pretty much the same routine. I rose before Mark went to work, folded the bed sheets, and turned my bed back into a couch. I dressed, brushed my teeth, and slipped out the door with my briefcase slung over my shoulder. At an espresso shop in the Fillmore, I read and wrote about the subject I'd obsessed on for the previous eight years, the subject to which I devoted a whole chapter of my dissertation: stand-up comedy as sacred literature. Some mornings, I managed to make it down to the Gleeson Library at the University of San Francisco, a twenty-minute walk from the apartment. Other times I settled for the stacks at San Francisco City College.

On seven occasions, I took the Cal Train to Palo Alto to spend the day at the Cecil Green Library on the Stanford campus, seeking out, copying, reading, and notating articles and book chapters about any kind of comedy. Everything from Henri Bergson's *Laughter: An Essay on the Meaning of the Comic*, Sigmund Freud's *Wit and Its*

Relation to the Unconscious, and Robert Provine's *Laughter: A Scientific Investigation*, to transcripts of interviews with comedians like George Carlin, Woody Allen, Richard Pryor, Bill Cosby, and Moms Mabley. I reviewed film clips of television shows, listened to talk show segments, and read reviews. I interviewed small-time producers and comedians.

My last night in town, there I was, drinking and talking and contemplating with my best friend since tenth grade. I swirled whiskey in my glass and looked out over the quiet and empty courtyard. At the potted geranium on the fourth floor window across the way. At the neon glow of downtown radiating from behind the building. And I lost myself in the stuff Mark was saying. It was as if, since our high school days, only two things really changed. Mark took a temporary assignment in San Francisco, and we drank better liquor.

"You know," he said. "I still can't get over all you comedians going apeshit over a little bit of pubic hair, like you'd never seen the stuff before."

"That whole night was ridiculous, I gotta admit."

"It was funny," he said. "But not so much the jokes."

"That hot little mama had to be really dense not to understand what was going on."

"She knew exactly what she was doing." He clasped his hands behind his head and yawned.

"We need more liquor," I said.

"In a minute. Got a question. Did you glean any comic insight out of all that?"

"Other than that chances like that only come once in a lifetime? That what you mean?"

"Helen Denise always found your obtuseness really charming."

"Whatever happened to her?"

"Moved back to Texas, last I heard," he said. "Had a kid."

"I always liked her."

"She liked you, too," he said. "But where were we?"

"That beav shot at Laffs."

"Oh yeah, right. Just so funny. The way that group of 'professionals' homed in on the dark spot between some coed's thighs. That's all you saw, right?"

"That's what everybody saw," I said.

"Before that night, I always suspected something about stand-up, but it sure came through loud and clear then. That girl with her legs spread—she was the surrogate mother, and everyone was competing for her, albeit unwittingly and symbolically. Even the lesbians. It became so obvious right then. The comedian comes up on stage—"

"Which comedian?"

"Any comedian. Listen to me, knucklehead."

"I'm listening. Get the Black Maple Hill."

"In a second. Listen," he said. "The comedian gets up on stage. Once up there, he is higher, I mean because of the stage, he is physically above everyone else. The audience literally must look up to him. Because of the sound system, he has this booming voice. He is in total control of the room. If somebody heckles him or something, he jumps on it, tears the guy a new one. Dishes out this verbal spanking. The comedian is in charge. Do you know what he's doing?"

"Making people laugh. That's what he's supposed to do."

"He's reinforcing the experience of infanthood. Taking us back to a time when each one of us crawled around on the living room rug, to a time when our fathers were in charge of the limited spheres of our lives. When, to us, Dad stood like a giant. When his voice boomed. When he could crush us with a single blow or a single step. When he had complete power over us. If he didn't want you to live, you didn't live. When he controlled access to the mother. That's what makes stand-up so special."

"I don't follow."

"The whole of human experience, you know? Everything about being human," he said. "It's about reconciling ourselves to our parents—usually our fathers. Look at world literature. The *Tao Te Ching* says, 'You must learn to follow the Tao.' And what is the Tao? The 'mother of the ten thousand things.' That's what it says. Look at children's stories. *Peter Pan, One Hundred and One Dalmatians, Pinocchio*—take your pick. Or else the Greek myths: Cronus, Hercules, Poseidon, Demeter. All stories about the quest for reconciliation with a parent. Seven times out of ten, with the father. Adam and Eve get separated from God the Father. That's their punishment for being bad children. Huckleberry Finn runs away from his biological father and to a surrogate parent, the mighty Mississip. Gatsby chooses Dan Cody as his spiritual father and has to go about his father's business. For Captain Ahab, the substitute father is the white whale. Look at our movies: *The Godfather, Finding Nemo, Home Alone, Psycho, Star Wars, E.T. the Extra-Terrestrial*. The list goes on. They're all about characters on quests to reconcile with their parents—biological, surrogate, or otherwise. Even Jesus' last words are about how His father has forsaken Him."

"I thought the subject was comedy."

"Take a second," he said. "Think it over. I'll be back."

He disappeared through the sliding patio door, flicked on the kitchen light as something, some elusive shadow, flapped, fluttered, and dissolved behind the building. Mark returned, plunked three ice cubes into my glass, poured me more whiskey, and topped it off with

177

a dash of purified water. Then he put the bottle down and sat, looking rather regal, his hands hanging off the armrests of oxidizing iron.

"Focus on what I am saying," he says. "Shut off that chatter in the back of your brain for once. I could be handing you the keys to the kingdom."

"Let's go over it again."

"The comedian on stage is the authority figure who undermines authority. The father who sets down the rules and then breaks society's rules. Look at any joke. Look at one of your jokes. How does it go? Something about how you do a lot of work helping students get into nursing?"

"Yes," I say. "I get them pregnant."

"Everything in the set-up line, all those words between 'I do' and 'nursing,' involve you pretending to play by society's rules, doing nothing immoral or dissonant with ordinary, expected, socially acceptable behavior. When you come through with the reveal that you use the girls as sex toys, you shatter all that. You violate simple societal protocol. The audience member hears this, and his brain needs a split second to harmonize these two conflicting scenarios. The natural reaction to that nanosecond of cognitive disorientation? Laughter."

"I don't really do that. Mess with my students, I mean."

"I know that, Einstein. The point is that when you are on stage, you are the substitute father who allows the audience to violate society's rules. At least vicariously. You are the authority figure who undermines authority. When you do that, you know what you have?"

"No. What?"

"Reconciliation with the father."

"Really?"

"If only for a split-second at a time. But it is more direct in stand-up than it is with the novel, the play, the painting, the poem, or the short story because the audience is right there. You talk directly to the individuals. To people who sit right in front of you. That's why a recording of a stand-up show really can't heal the way it's supposed to. In fact, it violates the whole experience. You have to be right there. Face-to-face. That is the pure beauty of the art."

I labored over stand-up, aesthetics, humor, and psychological theory for almost a decade—never as much as I did that summer in San Francisco. Yet Mark managed to cull this one golden insight just from hearing me talk about my work. That and watching a bunch of grown men acting like schoolboys who just stumbled upon their first *Penthouse* centerfold.

"Mark," I say. "You're a bastard, you know that? A goddamned bastard."

"Why do you say that?"

"If you're so brilliant, why don't you give stand-up a whirl?"

"Maybe I will." He lifted his glass to his nose and stared into the distance, over the jagged silhouette of the skyline. "You know," he said, "I might. I just might."

JACK

With the tip of the boning knife, I prick the flesh above the exterior jugular of Barbara Lyons' neck. She winces. A bead of blood grows like a bubble and then collapses, trickles down to her shirt collar, leaving a long stain down the skin. She yelps and groans. When she realizes I will not slice any deeper, she draws a long breath and exhales slowly. Tension leaves her body, and her head drops to her chest like she wants to sleep. She is exhausted from crying.

Somewhere outside, a siren screams, heading our way. I push myself up off my knees. I don't know how many hours have passed since I stepped into the office, but it is past midnight. It's gotta be.

Outside, the wail grows louder.

She sits almost as I imagined her as I lay in my bed every morning for months: her arms behind the backrest, the wrists held together with layers of duct tape. Her ankles are bound, and her middle is strapped to the spine of a rolling desk chair. She rubs her chin on her sweater, maybe to wipe off sweat. Perhaps she has an itch. Dots of perspiration form a mustache on her upper lip, and clumps of her artificially brown hair are stuck together with sweat. She looks as if she wants me to say something, and when I turn her way, she averts her eyes, fixating on the imitation hardwood. She keeps her head down, as if she is intent on a bug crawling across the floor.

I wipe the spot of red off the hardened steel and touch the red dot to my tongue. I walk to the window and bend back the polyester drape. Luminescent red flashes against the façade of the electronics store down the block. The wail of the emergency vehicle grows louder, and the reflected light grows brighter. Headed this way. Finally, from behind the far building, an ambulance appears, siren at full blast, its beacons electrified. It passes, shrieking, speeding up Lomas Boulevard. A few seconds later, all is quiet. An old Chevy rumbles by, and a breeze rustles the elm across the street, releasing a cloud of dime-sized seedlets that flutter down like firework sparks. In the neighbor's yard, a dog sniffs along the grass, following some scent. The beagle cross detects something and stops, raises his head, looks back, decides not to let it worry him, and then trots off toward the alley.

"Just let me go," Babs says. "You can go out the back way. Nobody will see you."

Her voice is raspy and thin. The sudden sound shocks me, and I feel it in my chest. I didn't know I was so fatigued. Her sigh tells me she would rather go home and collapse in bed than see me arrested and charged with false imprisonment. I pound my palm with the walnut handle.

"Right behind the dumpster," she says without opening her eyes. "There's a break in the cinder block wall. You can slip out between the buildings. Nobody will see. You don't even have to cut me loose. I'll figure something out. I promise I won't tell anybody. Honest to God."

"You don't understand," I say. "This is not about getting away with anything. This is bigger than that."

"I know," she says in a voice that is raw, as if her throat is sore. "I know what I did. I don't remember all of it, but I know what I did."

"This is about doing right by God," I say.

"Then just let me go. Do you really want to spend the rest of your life in prison?"

That, indeed, is a good question. I turn from the window and walk back.

"Let me tell you a story," I say. "A sad story. Maybe I told you parts of it, but you don't know the whole thing. I'm sure."

I scoot a chair in front of her.

She raises her cranium, rolls her eyes my direction. They are bloodshot, the irises ringed with gray where the color has drained out over the years, the skin around the sockets sagging and pink. Her head collapses to her chest, as if she is too tired to hold it up anymore. The top of her blouse is translucent with sweat. She sighs. She is tired of being afraid.

"I don't want to hear it," she says as she takes a deep breath. "I really don't."

I grab her hair and yank her head back so she has to look up at me. I let go, wipe my hand on my jeans, straddle the seat before her, and fold my arms across the cushioned backrest, my knife resting in cupped fingers. We lock eyes for a second before she turns away. The fear I wreaked on her hours before is no longer there.

"Why did you do it?" I ask.

"I already told you. I couldn't have children biting each other," she says. She gazes at the fake Persian rug, as if she is trying to move it through telekinesis. "You had to learn."

I bite the nail of my pinky and survey the room: the open folder on the desk, one of her eighty-dollar Parker pens lying on her calendar blotter, the other in its brass sleeve just a few inches way, next to the engraved name plate that reads "Babs." A box of Kleenex, one sticking up like a flag. Atop the credenza next to the window is a strip of madras, and on top of that is a framed snapshot of a gray-haired man in horn-rimmed glasses. Then a University of New Mexico diploma in a cherry-colored sleeve. All of this against a background of ochre walls sponge painted with streaks of muted orange. The baseboards and doorway molding are painted with off-white, shiny enamel. On the far wall hangs a reprint of a painting of the Sandia Mountains at sunset.

"It's a sad story."

She sniffles and stares blankly at the floor. Her chest rises and falls, as if she is bracing herself.

So I tell her.

Not very long ago, a seventh grader hoped to play second base—or maybe even right field—for his middle school baseball team, the San Felipe de Neri Tigers. After four afternoons of tryouts, the coach unhitched the tailgate of his Chevy half ton, slung a U.S. Army duffle bag full of Louisville Sluggers, hardballs, and bases into the bed, and perched himself there on the makeshift bench. He ordered seventeen boys to gather around. He read aloud the names of his team members, the squad for the next eight weeks—ten weeks if they did well in the parochial school tournament. He held a page torn from a spiral notebook in front of him, adjusted his sunglasses, and announced: Junior Martinez, Chas Pike, Eddie Chavez, Lawrence Serna, Jonah Menzies, Reese Hoskie, and so on.

No Jack Marison.

As we dispersed, all Junior could do was slap me on the shoulder and say, "There's next year, man. You'll make it next year." That was the only acknowledgment I got.

I understand that I didn't do well. On that afternoon alone, I missed a line drive, and I could never hit Richard Baca's hanging curve. Still, I thought I did okay, handling pop flies and connecting a few times during batting drills. I even stole a base. The clincher came when Junior slapped a fastball past the pitcher and right at me. If it had been off to the side, I could have just played the bounce. But it shot right at me. I didn't know how to catch it.

Maybe that was the reason. Or maybe Coach Sebastian never liked me. Some people just don't like you for reasons you never know. Sometimes adults just don't like certain children. I guess you can't really blame anybody for that stuff. But coaches, teachers—and especially priests and nuns—well, they should know better. They have a different standard.

But that doesn't really matter. Not in the grand scheme of things. What is important is on that very afternoon, instead of walking home along Rio Grande Boulevard like Mom always insisted, I took a shortcut through a construction site. Today, those four acres are a sprawling city park with picnic tables, rolling grass hills, basketball courts, and even a soccer field. For a long, long time, though, up until it got its facelift the following June, it was just a dirt lot full of ragweed, devil's weeds, plastic Walmart bags, and broken Budweiser bottles. Remember that? Today, it's a nice family picnic area. Parents have their kids' birthday parties there, you know? College students play volleyball there.

That day, I headed home feeling as low as I ever felt. The sun was just dipping behind the bosque. Shards of that spectacular New Mexico light shot through the branches of the budding cottonwoods. The heavy equipment in the field was shut down for the night, and there was a slit in the temporary fencing. Junior and I got through that way the week before. So I figured, what the hell? I could shave five minutes off my walk and have a little more time alone, to mope in private before I had to make an appearance out on the boulevard with all those cars whizzing by. There was nobody there. No one I could see, anyway. Just those big yellow earthmovers. The thought that I might actually be putting myself in any danger never occurred to me. I thought that when Mom told me not to walk that way, she was just being Mom. Overprotective. Doing her job.

I punched the pocket of my glove. I bit my lip and tried to keep from crying because I was so wracked with disappointment—knowing full well I didn't really earn a spot on the team. Knowing I'd probably never be a good baseball player. I kicked a Coca-Cola can, and it went clanking over the dirt. A couple of steps later, I kicked it again. This time it tumbled behind the giant scoop of the bulldozer. I tugged a leather lace on my Rawlings fielder's mitt with my teeth, trying to bring the thick fingers together. Then I tucked my glove under my arm and secured the knot, pulling those leather strings tight. When I looked up, Angel Lucero blocked my path. He stood right there in his super-tight Wranglers, his pie-plate belt buckle, his shit-kicker cowboy boots, his legs spraddled.

He just materialized, like he was beamed down from outer space. Maybe he saw the whole practice session while hiding there behind that John Deere. One second he wasn't there. The next he towered over me with his thumbs hooked in the pockets of his bootcuts and with a wooden match sticking out the side of his mouth.

"Saw you miss that grounder, Marison," he said and twirled the stick and chewed on it some more. "Any pussy coulda handled that trickler. You know why you bobbled it? It's 'cause you're a goddamn faggot. Nothing but a goddamn joto. We gotta cure you."

I smiled, hoping he was joking. I tried stepping around him, and he reached out, grabbed for my T-shirt, and I spun, making a dash for the open lot, but my sneaker caught on something. Maybe a rock. Maybe a depression from one of the fence posts that was removed the week before. Maybe a root or a boulder. I fell into the dust and weeds. Got all these stickers in my right arm and dirt in my mouth. Angel grabbed my ankle and drew me into the shadows. Between the backhoe and the bulldozer, he flipped me over and ground my head into the earth.

"We can't let queers like you go around embarrassing us," he said. A dab of green snot wiggled in the bottom ridge of one nostril. He always looked like he was snarling, you know, because of that extra cuspid growing out the middle of his gum. He lunged to unbuckle my pants and yanked loose the buttons of my 501s. I kicked at him. But he was twice as big. The product of a broken home and three years older. Already a man.

He took my jeans and sprinted across the field, whooping and twirling them over his head like they were a helicopter blade. If only that was all he did. That day I walked home in nothing but a T-shirt and my Batman Underoos. It was just after six, so there was still rush-hour traffic on that busy street. There I was, dodging cars on that crowded thoroughfare. Trying not to look up, in case anybody recognized me. In sneakers, a soiled T-shirt, and torn underwear, with blood caking on the backs of my thighs.

I walked home along the irrigation ditch and snuck in through my bedroom window. It was dark by then. Thank God, Mom had a late class.

"I never did find out what happened to that baseball glove."

Babs appears to be sleeping, so I snap my fingers in front of her face. Her eyes fly open.

"Do you know what it is like, Sister Julia, to feel your rectum being torn open?"

I kneel on the rug in front of her, and once again I hold the tempered steel a hair's breadth away from the rise of her jugular, ready to empty her blood supply.

"Forget about the humiliation," I say. "Forget about that. I am simply talking about the physical pain. No lubricant. No stretching out the sphincter with a finger. Just forcing it with a penis. Do you know how many nerves are down there? Do you know what it is like to writhe on the toilet as ribbons of blood trickle out of you? To be afraid to eat because you are so afraid of the pain that shoots up your back when you defecate? Do you know what it is like to be standing in line in the school cafeteria and feeling stuff leaking out of you and having nuns scream at you to be still?"

Her chin is flat against her chest. She takes a short breath and then inhales deeply. Her chest expands. She releases.

"But there is more to this story," I say.

I go on.

When I got to school the next day—it was warm for early March—I was in just a fleece jacket. I came across the elementary school playground, followed the pathway between the two buildings, out to the gravel, by the big tree where Junior, Leo, Rudy Montoya, and the other sixth graders and I usually waited for the bell. It hurt to walk, and it hurt to sit, so I propped myself against a tree and tried to look natural. Over at the edge of the playground, leaning on the chain-link, there with the other ninth graders, wearing his cowboy hat and holding his thick geography book, Angel Lucero laughed with his friends, baring that extra tooth growing out from his gum. His eyes glommed onto me when I turned the corner. I felt their heat. I avoided looking over. When I finally slipped up and let him catch my eye, his hand went straight to his crotch, and he cupped his junk. He gave me that quick chin lift, the reverse nod. He held his pants. He jiggled his cock and mouthed the words, "Want some more?" His lips stretched into a smile. Behind me, Carolina Zamora laughed. It was a laugh of recognition, of special knowledge. Like she knew the story.

Angel dropped his book, and it clacked on the blacktop. He stepped in my direction. He spread his legs and bellowed, "Hey, Marison. You're a goddamn faggot. Nothing but a goddamn cocksucker. We gotta cure you."

People laughed. Everybody saw him as he strutted toward the gravel. Junior chuckled. Carolina laughed again. Then Rudy, Eddie Chavez, Margaret Dominguez, and the Wilson twins. I was at the center of this swell of guffaws. Within just a couple of seconds, Angel was on top of me again. His shoulder drilled my spine into the rocks, and his free hand tugged at my pant waist.

What did I do, Sister Julia? I sank my teeth deep into his shoulder, right between the neck and the clavicle. I clamped down. He slugged at my groin, and I didn't even feel the pain. Getting punched in the nuts doesn't really hurt the morning after you have your asshole torn open. Out came Mrs. Sanchez, the math teacher, and Sister Regan, that bull-dyke who taught social studies. Remember her? I don't remember how exactly the whole thing broke up. I don't remember everyone involved. Sister Regan dragged me away, and Angel Lucero sat on the gravel, clutching his shoulder. A dark spot grew on his polo shirt. He went home after that. Then to the doctor.

"Sometimes," I say, "sometimes I still feel it." I crush a tear with my middle finger.

Julia sniffs. I lean my head against the wall and close my eyes.

I pound the wall twice with an open hand.

"I got Angel back, you know?" I say. I step over to her desk and tug at the tissue and the whole box comes up. I shake and the Kleenex comes free. "It took me four years. I was in high school by then, but I did it. That's when I was playing summer basketball, so I was in good shape and taller than him by then. I was running down in the far North Valley, just trying to stay fit, you know? I came around a corner by this old, dilapidated adobe hovel where we used to go get high, and there were all these planks and boards with nails lying around. Angel had his Schwinn laid out in front of him and his back against one of the walls with big chunks of plaster missing from the exterior, exposing the mud and straw. As I drew closer, the essential facts became apparent. He had something pinched between his thumb and forefinger and, with his free hand, readjusted whatever it was. In case you can't figure it out, he was smoking a roach, finishing up a joint.

"He released a cloud of blue, his hand hung off his knee, and he didn't see me. He probably couldn't have seen me if I had stood right in front of him and lit a cherry bomb, he was so high. So I snuck behind the wall, and I waited. It didn't take but two or three minutes, and he got up, lifted his bike, and was ready to mount it when I took a two-by-six, stepped over, and busted it across his cheek.

"He didn't scream. He just collapsed to the dirt, clutching his face, rolling around on the ground grunting while blood pumped out of his face. I stepped back, cocked my leg, and took a long, swift, and powerful stride, pegging him square in the balls. All you heard was this muffled 'oomph.' One hand covered his bleeding nose, and the other held his crotch. Then I did it again. And again. And again.

"And I went on with the last three miles of my run.

"Last I hear, Angel is a junkie, wandering around downtown Albuquerque, begging for quarters and arguing with some stuffed rabbit he keeps in his shopping cart. Still limping. I actually saw him, just a few months ago. At least, it looked like him. I stood outside the KiMo Theater downtown, right there at Central and Fifth Street. I recognized that hooked nose, that dark skin. He pulled half a chile dog out of the trash can and picked off a cigarette butt before biting into it. When karma comes knocking, you know.

"But I digress," I say. "This is not about Angel. This is about Babs. The former Sister Julia, Order of the Sisters of Charity of Cincinnati. And oh yes. This is where you come in.

"That morning, the morning after I was raped—that morning I put everything I had into keeping myself from having a cock shoved up my rectum for the second time in thirteen hours, this time with an audience—you waited until everyone else, all the other students, were all lined up and ready to enter the junior high school building. Once they all had full view, you forced me into a desk, asked me if I indeed bit that poor boy, and before I could answer, you reared back and slapped me. With every ounce of strength you had. To this very day, it still haunts me. That hand just came sweeping around, crashing across my cheek. My head snapping on its pivot. That warm spot on my cheek that would turn into a bruise that would last for days. Everyone saw it. Those kids I grew up with. Most of them from my neighborhood. Teresa Anaya shuddered. Someone giggled. Sister Regan crossed her arms and smirked with pure sanctimony. See, her body language said, that's what happens when you have the audacity to believe that you are here for any other reason than to suffer for Jesus.

"You screamed at me that I was from a good home, and that I was lucky that my mother was so good to me. That I should feel sorry for Angel.

"You kept me there. All day long, planted on my ravaged butt. For what? Six hours? Maybe longer? I sat there at that desk, repositioning myself again and again and again, just to ease the agony. Put the weight on one buttock. Then on the other. Sit on the edge of the chair. Put the weight on my feet.

"I was on display. You didn't even let me pee.

"Each time the bell rang, faces streamed by as students changed classrooms. All gawking. This line of faces. Me there with my fist covering the bruise on my cheek, my head down, my feet swinging, tears dripping onto the laminated desk top. Six minutes of hell every time the bell rang and all those students flooded the hallway. Then lunchtime came, and they all ran out of the building, passing me. I felt like an animal, some beast on display. I was your example. Your living proof that God demands suffering.

"When you finally did pull me into your office, I told you I was innocent. You screamed at me, asking me if Jesus started biting people when He was being nailed to the cross. I was hysterical. I told you Angel raped me and was going to do it again.

"Remember what you did when I said that? You stood in front of me and demanded I repeat myself.

"I stared square into your face and said: 'He raped me.'

"At that, you reared back, raised your hand, and this time you backhanded me. An eleven-year-old child, still reeling from a trauma no one should go through. The blow of those knuckles crashing against my cheek.

"Perhaps you thought it was my Christian duty to let myself be this guy's sex toy. You screamed at me, 'Are those your tooth marks on his shoulder? Are those your bite marks on his shoulder?'

"Do you remember that, Sister Julia? Do you remember how I told you he fucked me in my ass? Do you remember how I told you that you could expect me to cut off your tits when we met in hell? Do you remember that?"

She sniffs. Translucent fluid trickles out her nose.

"Don't you have anything to say for yourself?"

She blinks. Her sclera are thick with swollen veins.

"Want to hear the worst part?" I say.

Her breath is shallow and quick. The mucus has found its way along her lip line, leaving a shiny trail. I stand in front of her. I reach down, cup her chin, and jerk her face up.

"I said, do you want to know the worst part?"

Her skin beneath her eyes is moist and red, accentuating the liver spots on the side of her nose.

"You made us come to school that Saturday—me and Angel. You made us clean the junior high as our punishment for fighting on the playground. You lectured us about how you wanted to teach us a lesson. About how God wants us to get along. Then you left us alone, locked in the building. That Saturday morning, in the girls' restroom, Angel fucked me again."

I kept Barbara there another two hours. Maybe three. Finally, I stood in front of her and pointed the knife blade at the tip of her nose.

"I am going to let you go," I said. "I am going to let you continue to breathe, to allow the blood to pump through your arteries. Do you know why?"

She shook her head, crying again, giving me that look of contempt I remember so clearly from my childhood.

"Because if I slice your throat, that's it. You die. You go to hell. This way, you get to spend the next twenty years thinking about it—ten if you are lucky and get ovarian cancer or something. Then, one of these days, you'll find yourself on your deathbed, and you will have to say to yourself, 'I am a horrible person because I gave up a child to be raped.' Until then, you get to think about it from time to time. Let it haunt you."

I sliced through the layers of tape, freed her hands, and slipped out the back door to the break in the wall behind the dumpster. I went back to my apartment, popped open a beer, collapsed on my couch, and waited for policemen to come knocking. For whatever reason, they never showed, which means Babs never reported the incident. Which is the closest she ever came to apologizing. Every once in a while, I find myself in the grip of terror, thinking that something might come of that night. But anymore, these days, I am pretty sure nothing will.

Then there are those late nights when I think I might finish the job.

NICHOLS

Why do my knees hurt?

Because I'm crouching on the cement behind my building, counting off cases of Stella Artois, tapping each box with the pencil eraser, and then checking them all off my list. I got an unlit cigarette, a quarter of it smoked, tucked behind my ear, and I ache to finish it. As Damon, my Budweiser delivery guy, wheels more boxes down the ramp of his truck, I move over to the cases of Bud Lite and make sure everything is present and accounted for. Damon is this kid with flames tattooed on his neck and grommets stuck in his earlobes. First time I saw him, I thought he wanted to run off to Ethiopia and become a Murzu tribesman. I thought maybe schlepping Budweiser was his Plan B. This morning, once again, he comes late, five minutes before it's time to switch on the lights in the main salon, so I am already steamed.

We pile up cases of longnecks there on the ground, when who comes around the corner? Cyn, my de facto bar manager, this tall and thin girl with big hands and this sultry kind of walk, reflecting the years of ballet training she got as a child. I stick the cigarette between my lips—but don't light it—and then work the keys for the front door off my key ring and tell her to bring them right back. She says she wouldn't want to bother me, but that we know how pissy I get whenever we miss a couple of drink sales.

I tell her to return the keys ASAP, pronouncing it like it's a single word.

She turns around, raises her hand, and wiggles her fingers, like she's tickling the air, and says, without looking back at me, that maybe if I got laid every once in a while I wouldn't be so crabby. That's gratitude for you. So I go back to work. Damon rolls down his sleeve and feels for the cuff button. I tell him he's one case short. The dumbass needs to check my invoice and then count all that stuff that he just stacked there on the concrete—and he's gotta do it twice. Like I got nothing better to do but wait.

Excuse me, I say, but I got a business to run.

Once he plops the last carton of IPAs on top of the others, I sign the invoice, tear off the top copy, and hand it over. I wheel the first load through the back door and the kitchen and into the walk-in cooler, Damon following with his stack. He's going on about the Minnesota Vikings and how the night before they ran the wrong play and lost the game. All I hear is static. I just love the way guys making minimum wage think they can coach better than professionals with decades of experience making millions of dollars.

He holds the door open with his elbow and maneuvers the dolly so we can put things in some kind of order, when who pokes her head through the open door? Paloma, this cute thing with a plump and round little ass and thick red curls falling like bead curtains over her shoulders and back. She says she wants to talk to me, and she grips the side of the doorway. There's a white speck of tissue in her hand. She says something as I count the beer cases one last time, but just then the refrigerator motor clicks on. She repeats, blathering on about how it's important. I tell her not to worry. I say that as soon as my alarm buzzes every morning my first order of business is making her life easier, and that I must apologize that my busting my ass to keep my business afloat keeps interfering with her daily schedule.

Once we get the boxes stacked, I tell the girl that I need a count of Coors Light at both the front and back bars. I already have a pretty good idea, but I need to get her to shut up for a second.

Back in my office, I park it in my chair and swivel around to my computer, call up the Wells Fargo bank page, and turn the screen so that a nosy ass like Damon can't see how badly things are going. I check the balance, shake my head, open my book, fill out a check, rip it out, and hand it to him. I'm punching the numbers into my spreadsheet, when who do you think appears there, hovering in the doorway looking all weepy? Good ol' Paloma, that's who. She hands over a frayed scrap of cardboard with the two bottle counts.

Damon gives the girl a two-fingered salute, and she flashes her meek little smile at him, a smile from that coquettish pose she has perfected over the years: head angled down, eyes up. That fool Damon lights up for a nanosecond, entertaining this fantasy that he actually has a chance with her. He pushes his hand truck down the hallway and disappears toward the kitchen. Paloma checks the main bar to see if one of the other girls saw her come in, places her hand flat against the office door, and pushes it closed. She holds down the brass handle to make sure the latch clicks as softly as possible.

Right then, I know I'm in trouble.

Paloma blows her nose again and leaves the snotrag balled up in her fist and stands there like she wants me to invite her to sit down. Me? I take the Camel filter from my ear, tap it on the three-ring binder on top of my desk, and show I don't care. Never mind that I'd hump her in a minute. I mean, who wouldn't? Every guy who steps in the bar more than twice falls in love with that sweet young thing.

Paloma? She's got a problem. And a classic one at that. She grew up in this small town in Northern New Mexico, the only child of a single mother. Last she heard, her father was serving time for attempted murder—or maybe it was murder one. Who knows? Who cares? Hardly matters. Her senior year of high school comes, and guess what. You got it. She turns up pregnant. Now, four years later, the girl's still got plenty of fire, you know? She works on that bachelor's degree in studio art, taking about four classes a semester—one or two during the summer—and lives with the three-year-old in this one-bedroom south of campus. Her mother comes down most weekends to help with the little boy and the housekeeping and all that, to give Paloma time to work on her masterpieces. Do I have doubts about that girl's future? A few. You gotta be extra special to make it as an artist these days. If I were her, I wouldn't pin my hopes on taking New York or Zurich by storm any time soon.

Can Paloma go places? Absolutely. Smart. Ambitious. Totally devoted to her child and her education. Just not to her job, and therein lies the rub. Sometimes I can actually get her ass into second gear when it comes to carting drinks over to the tables, polishing the silverware, or sweeping up. When I was forced to put her behind the bar during happy hour, I had to stop everything every forty-five minutes to help her catch up. When it's her turn to close, you plan on staying an extra half hour.

So Paloma finally drags over a chair, sits, and proceeds to fuss with her ball of napkins. She spreads one of the things out, covers the two ends of her index fingers with it, and digs them into her nostrils to clear out any lingering debris. She sees me check the clock behind her, and then I take a deep sigh and drum my fingers on the desktop. But she's still not ready to talk. I find a book of matches in my top drawer, bend over one with my thumb, scratch up a flame, and relight. I shake the matchbook until the fire goes out, toss the book back in its slot, shove the drawer closed, and turn back to my computer. I fill in a couple of blocks on the spreadsheet and let her think things over. I study the screen, and I tell her that whatever she needs to say she needs to say quick because at any second Cyn will come through the door squawking about how someone needs to work the back bar.

Paloma holds the knuckle of her index finger under her nose, glances over at my poster of the St. Pauli Girl holding six foaming beer mugs and displaying this magical cleavage, then across the room to the wads of paper on the floor around the wastebasket, to the stacked cardboard boxes holding Fat Tire gimme caps, Red Bull T-shirts, Coors Beer coasters, and Jack Daniel's party poppers left over from New Year's, then back over to me, and finally to a coffee mug crammed with cigarette butts. She crumples the napkins again and rolls them in her palm, like she's making a ball out of modeling clay.

She looks up, forces a smile, and then studies that thing in her hand again.

"I need more hours," she says. Just like that. Like the whole thing is that simple.

"You can't have 'em," I say and cup a hand to my mouth like I'm shouting to someone in line and yell, "Next!" I swivel back to the computer.

"But you—you don't understand," she says. "You just don't understand."

"No," I say and take a puff and keep the cancer stick between my lips so that it bounces when I talk—for emphasis, you know. Curlicues of smoke float up between us. "*You* don't understand. I make the schedule. If you work, you get paid. If you don't, you get fired."

198

I tap ashes into a cup.

Her sob story? Three days before, the university daycare phoned her right in the middle of her drawing class, telling her that little Matthias, that's her kid, just broke out in red blotches all over his arms and back. So she has to leave class and run him over to Urgent Care and sit with him all afternoon, and then she ends up coming in two hours late the next night, just as the football game ends, and spends the next hour after that begging me to let her leave early. At the pediatrician's the next Monday, nurses, physician's assistants, and doctors poke and prod the little guy, and three hours later they have the tyke so traumatized that he wails like an air-raid siren every time she steps out of his sight. That night—another football night—she leaves me short-handed.

It turns out the kid has asthma—so severe that the little guy's gotta see a specialist, and that will just about break Paloma's budget. Like she's the only person in the world with financial troubles. As she speaks, her eyes get flooded and red all over again, and she sits there with her bare knees together, and she's looking like a pathetic and hopeless school girl as she goes on and on about how she has to drop her Western Civilization class, and how going down to part-time at the university doesn't only mean she'll lose her scholarship but also that she'll have to delay her graduation another semester, maybe a year. That means more time on food stamps.

Just about then, someone pushes the door open. Cyn pokes her head in, gets a load of Paloma's streaking mascara, and clucks her tongue in my direction. She says she just ran out of Hefeweizen, and someone needs to change out the keg. Who does she mean by "someone"? Yours truly, that's who. She works here three years and still can't do simple stuff like that.

I take one last puff and snuff the butt out, grab my keys off my desk, and tell Paloma I'll think it over but that right now she has to make sure we have enough clean martini glasses and beer schooners to make it through another happy hour.

Like that will be a problem.

Just after three that afternoon, I lean against the beer cooler and trim my fingernails with the scissors of my penknife. Paloma stands at one of the tables in the far corner, drawing out the logo for Blue Moon witbier on one of the blackboards. She pulls a blue stick of chalk out of her apron pocket and then fills in a patch of color, holds up the sign, assesses her artwork, lays it back on the table, and goes at it with some yellow. She hums to herself and keeps drawing, and I wonder why none of the regulars have come in yet. Paloma hasn't said anything to me—not even "coming behind you" or "excuse me"—since our little tête-à-tête that morning. I clip off a splinter of dry skin next to a cuticle, check if I got all of it, and see if I can bite off what's left.

Just then, an eighteen-wheeler rumbles by on the avenue, and the whole building shakes like we're in an earthquake. The light above me flickers, like I got a loose connection up there. It winks again, goes dark for a few seconds, and then comes back on. That's when it hits me. I turn and punch the "No Sale" button on the cash register, and the whole thing lets out a loud "chih-ching" that just about echoes through the room as the cash drawer shoots out. I grab a handful of quarters out of the change dish and slap them on the counter.

"Hey, Paloma girl. Hey, sweetie," I call over. "Put some music on. Let's inject a little life into this joint."

Seconds later, the gorgeous redhead stands there in her black skirt with the bow of her apron accenting the sculpted curve of her back, that tiny waist that sits just over the rise of her buttocks. She has one of those elegant hands spread out against the red-and-pink fluorescent lights of the juke box. She presses the arrow on top of the machine, and one metal page slaps onto another. She pushes the arrow again, and another page falls. She appears to be thinking hard, searching for something special. She bites her fingertip, punches the button again, reads the fine print, and keeps looking.

Finally, she turns to me, reaches behind her, pulls loose her apron ties, slips the whole thing over her head, and tosses it on a freshly wiped two-topper.

"Step out here," she says. "Just for a couple secs."

I ask her what she thinks she's doing, and before she answers, I tell her I don't dance. She clasps my right hand, puts my other hand on her waist, and says that anyone who can walk can dance. The machine snaps, whirs, and sighs. Then comes the olive-oil voice of Dean Martin crooning "That's Amore."

The girl says the dance is simple enough, and she guides me through the motions. Take a step forward with the right, bring the left foot up beside it, but don't put it all the way down. Instead, bring it out to the side, plant it, and put the right foot next to it. Repeat the process in reverse. Do it all over again.

"Count," she says with her head down and her eyes up. "You can count, can't you?"

"I can count," I say. My feet look like Frankenstein monster boots next to her Barbie-doll flats.

"No need to look at your feet," she says. "They're still there."

We step together, and I catch the tip of her shoe with the toe of mine.

The Rat-Packer croons on. I step forward. I slide. I put all my weight on my right foot. I step back. Paloma whispers, "One, two, three. One, two, three. One, two, three . . . ." Her breath brushes my ear. We move in three-beat pulses around the room, skating past tables and chairs over toward the bar.

We step. We slide. We make half turns. She spins. She tells me not to look at my feet. I look at my feet. Finally, the song ends, and we stop, standing face-to-face in front of the waitress station. She touches her lip with the tip of her finger, cocks her head, and bats her eyes. She smiles.

"Told you," she says. "Your feet are still there."

"Back to work," I say. "Hang that sign." As the words come out, the machine whirs and clicks, and the sounds of rapid mandolin strums start up again, then the orchestrated voices, and then Dean Martin. She leads me into yet another box step, saying with breathy whispers, "Step, glide, step, feet together. Step, glide, step, feet together. One, two, three. One, two, three. One, two, three."

Twenty-one minutes—and six more installments of "That's Amore" later—and I almost got it. In the last round, I only step on her toes once. That time, as the song winds down, she steps back from me, still holding both my hands, then steps forward, and turns so that my chest is flat up against her back and my arms wrap around her. We end—on the beat—standing face to face. Then, right in front of me are those thick, pink lips, the bottom one with a regal crease right down its center. I smell her herbal soap. My chest aches. So do my loins.

"Maybe," I say. "Just maybe, I can give you Friday happy hours. The girls seem to like those. Maybe. But no promises."

The thin white crescent of her incisors appears beneath her upper lip.

"But you understand," I say, "the Silver Dollar is going belly up. We got maybe a month. Six weeks tops."

"I know," she says as I hold her hand above her head, and she pivots and then turns back. "Cyn told me."

Just then Cyn herself calls through the hallway, asking if I know how to make a Singapore sling. I am relieved to know that we got some action in the front. I tell her I'll be out there in a second. That if you don't measure the Cointreau just right, you mess it up. Meanwhile, Paloma stands between two tables, folding the collar of her shirt around her apron straps.

"You know," she says, "you should go out with a splash. Seems only right."

In the darkness of the hallway leading to the other bar, I stop. I look over my shoulder. Paloma picks up the chalkboard. She glances over.

A voice inside my skull whispers, *Sometimes you gotta say, "What the fuck."*

In the seven seconds it takes me to go to the front and find a decent bottle of cherry brandy, I start planning Nichols' Last Show.

EDDIE

Mark pinches the top of the trashcan liner at each of its corners, and a breeze ripples the ultralight plastic. Twenty six-gauge piano wires dangle from the hem, holding in place a cup he fashioned in about seven seconds by molding layers of aluminum foil. Into the center of that reservoir, I placed a cotton ball and then squirted in three inches of camp stove gas. Now, I kneel on the wet grass and click the trigger on the campfire lighter. Sparks fly out the slits above its handle. I try again, and this time a long blue-and-orange flame hovers over the tip of the chrome-colored nozzle. It wiggles, bends, and flutters, flickers out for a second, and then reappears. I study the glowing and inverted teardrop, the luminescent blue inside the layers of bright orange. Mark tells me to just light the damned thing. I do as he says, and immediately a foot-long tongue shoots up through the transparent sheeting, and Mark jumps back like he's been goosed. I laugh out loud. He chuckles, regathers himself, and tells me to hurry. The fire in the little gondola regulates itself, and the bag swells with hot air, and a yellow-orange glow washes over Mark's jeans, jacket, cheeks, forehead, and then grows brighter. Now it is fluorescent neon orange with pinkish highlights. At least, I believe it is.

It is a Saturday night in early November, about a month before finals, and the winter cold has yet to settle in. Mark needs one more full semester before he graduates. My best guess is that I lack three credits before I can declare myself a junior. But I might change my major back to sacred literature.

Over the course of the previous two hours, Mark and I tore dozens and dozens of fifteen-gallon plastic bags off the rolls he stole from the janitor's closet in the science building the week before. We laid the translucent sacks out flat over the grassy hills, near the gravel walking paths, and on the other side of the bridge of heavy timber, everywhere we could in that area surrounding the duck pond in the middle of the University of New Mexico's main campus. We worked our way around, from bag to bag, attaching the wires and makeshift aluminum cups. Now the plan is that we will launch, one at a time, a hundred and fifty or more of the miniature, homemade hot air balloons.

This venture began in my apartment almost three hours before when Mark slapped a cassette tape into the stereo on my bookshelf and cranked up Joaquin Rodrigo's *Concierto de Aranjuez*. The music poured out as he arranged in our backpacks the rolls of plastic, spools of wire, two boxes of aluminum foil, cotton balls, and two quarts of the fuel in plastic bottles. Meanwhile, just a few feet away, I dug through the cabinet under the sink and pulled out the Osterizer blender my grandmother gave me when I first moved out of my parents' house. I washed out the dust, moth carcasses, and spider legs, dried it with a clump of paper towels, set the carafe on its base, dumped in two cans of Minute Maid orange juice, filled the rest with cold water, and fired it up. Once the mixture was good and frothy, I added six desiccated caps and stalks of psilocybe semilanceata, magic mushrooms purchased that very morning from a U.S. Marine reservist who sits next to me in physics class.

As the palpitations from the French horn and guitar strums filled my efficiency apartment, the blender ground away, chopping the fungus into bits that looked like large flecks of black pepper swimming in the yolk-colored liquid, some of the bits sticking to the sides of the glass. When the concoction got a good dull orange-green, I poured out even portions into two plastic tumblers and handed one to Mark. By that time, the warm strums of the adagio wafted through the room, followed by Christopher Parkening's minor scale run. Mark and I toasted to the stars, the heavens, the ordered universe, and the great souls who came before us—the Platos, the Saint Teresas, the Leonardos, and the DesCarteses. To Mozart, John Lennon, the Marx Brothers, Søren Kierkegaard, Mary Magdalene, and Albert Einstein. And, of course, to Rodrigo and Parkening. I drained my portion in one long pull. Juice trickled out the corner of my mouth, and I wiped it with my dishrag. Mark took a long swallow, gave a smile and a nod, and then polished his off.

He handed me a backpack, slipped the strap of his over his shoulder, and I followed him out the door, through the back gate, through the twilight, and down Central Avenue, our packs heavy with the supplies.

Out on the main drag, I told Mark that the things would not fly. He said that if I wanted to lay down a bet, he would surely take it. As long as the thickness of the plastic did not exceed six microns, we were good. I asked what a micron was, and he started explaining, cleared his throat, looked for cars, told me not to worry about it, and dashed out to the median. I followed and asked why we were doing this. He said that I didn't have to help him, but he knew very well I had nothing going that weekend anyway, so I may as well join in the fun. He was going to do it, one way or another. We ran across the street, out to the campus.

So now we are just about ready for the first launch. He holds the bag in place, and I fall back on my thighs. The reflections of the flame condense into streaks on the round lenses of his eyeglasses. He concentrates.

I still have no clue as to his motive.

When he is sure the craft will fly, Mark releases one hand and then the other, and the pouch of hot air rises like an innocent spirit in front of us. It latches onto a breeze we can hardly feel and lifts itself over the fountain courtyard in front of Zimmerman Library, past the bare branch of a fruitless mulberry extended like a witch's claw, up toward the overhead lamp illuminating the brick mall in front of the Arts and Sciences building. It pauses and rocks, threatening to tip over. After a second or two, it steadies itself and appears downright sentient, as though contemplating its course. Finally, the glowing bag meanders southward, drifting off to explore the skies above the Student Ghetto, the sports stadiums, Albuquerque International Airport, and the open desert surrounding Isleta Pueblo.

Mark's eyes are slits. At first, by the way he stands with his hands on his hips and his head cocked, he appears zoned out, even unconscious, as though he's sleeping standing up. Then it becomes clear that his eyes are trained on the floating bead of light, and he places a hand against his chest, containing his pride. The bag floats toward the neon lights of Central Avenue.

There is something regal about the way he stands. He scratches his cheek, and as he folds his arms at his chest, a blue light, razor thin and dull at first but growing brighter, outlines his body. He looks as though he should be attired in a white beard and long robe. His eyes grow narrow once more, and he rocks on his heels and keeps smiling, telling me that we need to move on to the next one. That we have a lot of work to do over the next couple of hours. So we step over to another bag and repeat the ignition process. Mark holds its corners, and I light the little translucent cotton ball of a fuse. A puff of smoke dances up through the cloudy plastic membrane, and after a few seconds, the whole thing drifts off. This time, however, as it rises past the tree, a gust disturbs the contraption, turning it on its side. The fire eats through the film, and the plastic shrivels up almost instantly. It drops like a dead bird onto the brick courtyard where the incendiary spills and flares, diminishes, and goes dark.

Mark laughs. I say this could get dangerous. He says of course it could. But it won't.

"I wish I had your confidence," I say.

"Everybody does," he says.

We launch another craft. Then another. And another.

After more than an hour, countless miniature, makeshift hot air balloons drift over the city. What strikes me is that all of them appear to have their own personalities, their own individual mindsets, and I somehow feel a special intimacy with each. One moves swiftly, even enthusiastically. The next is sluggish and looks shy, as if it is scared to get too far off the ground. Another one hurries ahead of the others, trying to lead the pack.

Behind me, spread out against the slope of the grassy incline, lie six other patches of plastic that look grayish-white in the darkness. They await our attention.

I ask Mark how many we've set off. He says he doesn't know, but that there were supposed to be fifty bags in each roll. That we had four rolls, but he doesn't know if all were full, and that the bags spread out on the other side of the pond are all we have left. So he calculates. We already launched at least a hundred and thirty, but some have since exhausted themselves. Who knows where their remnants have fallen?

"But look up," he says, "look around you."

He points past the trees and buildings to the open sky.

A crescent moon hangs in the eastern sky, illuminating patches of snow in the creases of the Sandias. A jet liner approaches the airport, its landing light pulsating. Closer to us, over a line of trees out by North Campus, nine of the lanterns hover near the power lines, arranging themselves in three undulating waves, one balloon just below another. All of them are evenly spaced, like quarter notes on a treble clef. Off to the south, a few more cluster together, as if working as a team. Everywhere above us, it seems, are these tiny little bubbles of iridescence, each carrying little bits of fire to different parts of the city.

"Let's finish," Mark says, "and I'll buy you a burrito."

I follow him across the bridge, out toward the open grass.

The next one we release fails to gain much altitude. It struggles to lift itself higher than twenty or thirty feet. It rises, dips, floats up, and snags itself on the point of an extended elm branch, which punctures the plastic. The bag deflates, the foil cup tips, and a stream of fiery liquid pours onto the earth beneath it.

"Wow," Mark says. "That was a close one."

"Shouldn't we go put it out?" I say as I flip up the plastic cap of the can of lighter fluid.

"It's out."

"How do you know?"

"You don't see any flames, do you?" he says as he turns away, going out toward the grassy slope.

"You never know."

"I know."

So we do another. I hold the bag, and Mark clicks the lighter and gets sparks, but no flame. It might be out of butane, Mark says. Slap it against your palm, I say. What good will that do? I don't know, I say. That's what Dad used to do with his Zippo.

Finally, Mark summons up a pea-sized speck of fire on the end of the torch, and he points it right into the middle of the little gondola. After a second or two, the grayish-white mass sizzles, then catches fire. The flame grows but, for some reason, stays weak, burning not nearly as brightly as any of the others. Eventually, the air inside the bag heats up, the plastic expands, and I wait, letting the envelope build up a little strength. Mark freezes, whips his head around, as if he hears someone sneaking up on us. He looks through the branches of the clump of evergreens behind us, out toward the circle drive leading up to the bus stop shelter and the jogging path.

"What was that?" I ask.

He says it's nothing but thinks that maybe the university police might not be too happy with what we're doing out in the middle of campus. He thought he heard something, but it must be the hallucinogens. They tend to put you in that state.

When the bag looks ready, Mark tells me to let go. The thing floats away, but only about five or six feet off the ground. As though it is skating, it zig-zags across the grass to the red brick courtyard, floating, falling, and then rising again, as if, at any second, it hopes to crash and put itself out of its misery.

It gains some altitude as it approaches a stuccoed wall and lifts itself right into the extended branch of a silver cedar. The balloon struggles to get free, but the limb snags the plastic, causing the warm air to spill out. The bag shrinks, the fuel spills down the trunk, and a flame shoots up through the branches. Mark clutches his chest, then his stomach, fighting silent paroxysms. The golden fire licks the side of the tree. Mark's hands go out at his side as he tacitly asks what we should do. I shrug. My chest quakes. I am scared. I am laughing. Just then, the brittle *chunk* of a slamming car door echoes off the building in front of us. Through the branches of the fir trees, we see it. There on the circle drive, in the fire lane, red-and-blue lights rotate atop a university patrolman's cruiser.

Mark's eyes flare. Flashes flicker through the evergreen branches and across the walls of the humanities building. He checks behind again, just to see if the officer is coming our way. The cop calls out, and I take off, sprinting across the courtyard toward the dormitories. The policeman yells again, something I can't quite make out. As I round the curve toward the education building, Mark passes me, racing down a cement path between a lecture hall and the counseling annex. He turns down a concrete drive, toward a loading dock, where he hoists himself up over the cinder block wall, his feet kicking as he fights and drags himself up and rolls over, disappearing behind it. I chase him but can't get over on the first try, so I have to go back a few steps and get another running start. I leap, grab, and struggle, clinging and scrabbling with all my might, but finally get over. I collapse onto the dirt. I pull myself to my feet. Blood trickles down my arm. I take off again.

When I see him again, Mark stands on the white line of the four-lane boulevard, waiting for a city bus to pass. Finally, he dashes across the avenue, out to a line of homes, and becomes a shadow slinking through the dark alleyway, running out toward the Disciples of Christ Church.

When I finally catch up with him, I am out of breath, and he stands on a grassy mound just across the way from the stained glass door. He bends over, clutching his abdomen and panting.

"Oh, God, it's just you," he says.

He falls to his knees, his torso still quaking with laughter. Directly overhead, suspended, almost stationary, hangs one of our sky lanterns, as if caught between opposing breezes, its internal glow just barely visible. I slow my breath, listening for footsteps. Somewhere behind us, an air compressor kicks on. A block away, on the main drag, a car screeches to a halt. Someone blasts a horn.

Mark gasps, says he thinks we're in the clear. He flops down on the lawn, rolls over on his side, his arms crossed against his chest. He covers his face again to quell the spasms.

My heart slows, and Mark composes himself. He digs his fingertips into the soft earth, places the back of his hand against his forehead, and lets out another whoop. He apologizes for leaving me for the authorities and then convulses again.

"You don't have to outrun the lion," he says, "as long as you're not the slowest runner in the hunting party."

I hold my forehead and wonder if I am going to jail. I fall to my knees and bend forward. I stick my whole face in the grass.

A few seconds—maybe a few minutes—later, I open my eyes. High above me, one of the sky lanterns dangles like a beacon. Mark chortles as he pushes himself up and slaps grass blades and poplar leaves off his jeans. The blue halo that surrounded him an hour or so before is there again, this time more radiant.

"What are you looking at?" he asks.

"Nothing," I say. "Just nothing."

"That was fun."

"Wasn't it?"

He extends a hand and pulls me to my feet. I brush dirt off my butt and thighs, and we walk through the shadows of those Victorian homes and cross the street, going out toward the lights of Central Avenue.

"Should we go home?"

"Let's get a burrito," he says. "But stick to the shadows, just in case."

He ducks into an alley between two houses. The sounds of a Gregorian chant pour out a bedroom window.

"God," he says. "Must be after two."

I check my watch. It is ten thirty-seven.

"I gotta get back home," he says. "Helen Denise is probably wondering what happened to me."

"She's not working tonight?"

"She got off at midnight."

"You know, I always liked her."

"She likes you, too."

We walk back toward the restaurant, and I sling my arm around his neck and pull him tight against me. I tell him how much I treasure his friendship. He pats my forearm and tells me he feels the same way, but I need to let go before we get picked up for soliciting. We turn the corner, onto the avenue, and an Albuquerque cop car shoots by us, the driver activating warning lights but not the siren. Then the blaring and roaring of a fire engine, and for a second something flickers in my conscience, some deep fear that somewhere a home is burning because of us. He tells me not to worry, that the wind was blowing the other way.

I ask him why we went through all that, why he was so hell-bent on setting off all those sky lanterns. He says that he first did the calculations for the miniature flying bags when he was in the fourth grade, working everything out on a Big Chief tablet. He always thought that kind of activity was something a father should do with his son. He said he knew it was crazy, but that he could never let go of it. But he always imagined that if his father—his real father—still lived in Albuquerque, he might just look up into the sky, see one of the lanterns, and think the same thing.

"You're right," I say. "That's crazy."

Even though I have a paper due Wednesday, I sleep in the next day. I get up around one in the afternoon and am still groggy. I bump into my kitchen table, knock over a juice cup, and mop up most of the mess with newspapers. As I wait for the coffee to perk, I open the refrigerator, reach under the lip of a grease-pocked box, and remove a two-day-old wedge of pepperoni and green chile pizza. I tell myself I have to get started on my Taoism paper. Seven minutes later, I sort through my hamper for clothes I might need for the week, stuff the socks, underwear, and T-shirts into a tall kitchen bag, put the stuff into a laundry basket, and walk out the door to the laundromat a few blocks away.

There, I punch the ball of my thumb through the perforated flap of a detergent box and tear open the cardboard as the washer fills up. I sprinkle the powder into the gushing water, and as I shut the washer lid, a guy with a graying ponytail backs his way through the door and gives me the once-over. He wears a leather jacket with zippers along its sleeves and lapels and side pockets. He takes off his glasses, wipes one eye with the back of his hand, stares me down, and puts them back. My first thought is that he's mistaking me for someone. I crumple my garbage bag and toss it in the cracked plastic basket.

He commandeers the washer two spaces down, on the other side, and as he shoves clothing into the tank he glances my way, wanting to say something. He sprays some prewash fluid on the front of a work shirt and looks over again. He pulls his tinted spectacles farther down his nose and peers over the lenses. His lips part, revealing the edges of graying teeth. He says something in a gravelly whisper, and I ask him to repeat.

"Your luminescent egg," he says, "it's glowing."

"My what?"

"Strands of fibers forming your aura. They're shining real bright, you know?"

"No," I say. "I didn't know."

He smiles a gap-tooth grin, punches his load down into the suds, and lets the metal top slam down.

"Maybe it's the company you keep," he says.

I think it over. Finally, I say, "Must be."

"Gotta be," he says. He takes a rolled up magazine from his back pocket and steps over to the plastic chairs by the window, checks out the street as a police patrol car switches lanes and shoots up Central Avenue. The siren squeals and dies away.

He sits down, grabs his ankle, and props his foot on his knee, exposing goat head burrs and bits of mud in the Vibram sole. He opens his issue of *Time*, finds the place where he left off, and begins to read. After a few seconds, he lifts his head, raises a finger like he is going to say something, changes his mind, and goes back to his article.

NICHOLS

I ease my Chevy past the façade of Nichols' Silver Dollar, and what do I see? You know that "open" sign with the Pabst Blue Ribbon logo hanging over it? Gray as a Seattle sky. Why? Because Cyn forgot to turn it on again. Why is Nichols' Silver Dollar empty half the time? Missteps like that. So I drive through the alley to the back lot, park, stretch over and punch down the lock on the passenger door, pick up the manila folder off the seat, and straighten out the stack of papers inside. I get out and walk through the alley and go in the front door—something I never do—thinking how I probably won't miss that dank, dark entryway or that concrete floor that never looks clean. Once inside, I reach behind the shutter and tug the little chain. The gizmo blinks, flickers, and, after a second or two, glows sapphire and neon pink.

At the main bar, some guy in a crew cut, sideburns, and creases welded into his Wrangler ropers brushes something off his pearl-button shirt and leans on the counter next to one of the barstools there by the beer lines. He runs the bottom of his boot on the brass footrest, like he's scraping off mud or something. The way he stares at Cyn's D cups? He has all the subtlety of a bloodhound staring at a T-bone. You'd think he'd notice her ring.

Does my bar manager even notice what's going on? Of course not. She licks her finger and turns a page in the bar book. As I pass she calls out something about needing to know how to make a sloe gin fizz. I tell her the bottle of sloe gin has been there so long it's probably vinegar by now. She should take it home and make salad dressing. She says she really needs help, and I tell her that when she gets a chance she needs to round up Paloma, Deborah, and that kid Timothy who works the back bar, and meet me in the office. She wants to know if the news is good or bad because the suspense is killing her, and I tell her to thank God for unemployment insurance. I close my office door behind me, work on the schedule a little more, and wait to see if, this time, my lieutenant can round up three people in under twenty minutes.

It only takes about fifteen minutes—which makes no sense to me since we only have like four customers in the place—but eventually Timothy walks in, tugging on his belt like he hasn't finished dressing. He slogs his way to the back and just about knocks over a barstool— something that should be out front propping up some customer's ass. He makes his way to the back, and I tell him to pull his pants up. He perches himself on top of an empty beer keg, crosses his arms, leans in the corner, and closes his eyes like he's napping. Then Paloma comes in and pulls over the plastic chair right in front of me, sits down, smiles, and then directs all her attention to a sliver or blister in the ball of her little finger. I tap my pencil on my open hand and wait. Like I got nothing better to do.

After a few minutes, someone raps on the hollow wood with a knuckle. Suddenly Cyn gets this bug that she has to knock to come in. Deborah comes in right after. The youngster plants herself on the high stool, pops her gum, gives the room the once-over, and then with her birdie finger pecks at her cell phone, like the message she's sending just can't wait. Cyn leans in the doorway, and I have to tell her to step inside and make sure the door closes tight. I don't want any of the customers to hear what's going on. She asks "What customers?" and Timothy, who still has his eyes closed, snorts through his nose like she's so damned amusing. As I wait for the energy to settle, Cyn tells me three people just walked in—two guys and a woman—and I ask if she's serious. She says yes, right there, and points. I tell her they can wait. I say that I already told her to shut that door tight.

I toss the pencil on my desk. I rock and my chair squeaks, and I brush back my hair with both hands, cover my face for a second, and then relax, now with both paws hanging off the arm rests. Paloma inspects her finger.

"Smell that stink?" I say.

Deborah snaps her gum and sneaks a look at her phone. She closes it and lays it in her lap with her hand on top, like she doesn't want me to see it. Timothy's eyes open, and he cocks his head, like he's listening for an approaching train.

"That, my friends," I say, "is the odor of a dead business. For three damned years, we meant something special around here. Nichols' Silver Dollar? It was *the* place to come and watch University of New Mexico football and basketball games, *Monday Night Football*, and catch an occasional comedy show. For three full years. Too bad we've been open for seven."

I explain.

"If you're gonna weep," I say, "weep now. I just came from my lawyer's office, where I signed the papers. Come the last hour, the last minute, the last second of the first day of the month, Nichols' Silver Dollar goes belly up, kaput, defunct. It gets launched into the ether or rolled into the tomb. Unless, of course, I win the lottery. Yes, friends, the fat lady stands out in the green room, gargling on lemon juice. The good news? You full-timers get to keep your health insurance for an extra two months and are eligible for unemployment compensation. Besides that, we are going to have one last comedy show. I already contacted the Anheuser-Busch people, and the signs are being printed up as we speak. We're billing it as 'Nichols' Last Show.' Black Tom, Firecracker Rael, and a few others say they are down with it. The headliner? I want that kid Marison from Denver. The guy's going straight to the top."

Deborah blows a pink bubble. Cyn covers her mouth. At first I think she's hiding a gasp. Turns out it's a yawn.

There in the corner under the three-year-old calendar featuring Bud Girls, Timothy shifts his shoulders, trying to get more comfortable. He appears to be studying one of the ceiling beams. He pulls off his baseball cap and speaks up with all the enthusiasm of a stoned tenth grader waking up during a civics lecture.

"Marison's okay," he says, "but you know, you really should get that Mark dude. You know, Wladika?"

Deborah's bubble pops, and she tears the coating off her cheek, inspects it, and puts the gum back in her mouth. Cyn bites her lip. She sticks a hand in her apron pocket and says that the hipster is right. If we are going to have one last bender, we should really go for it. What's the worst that can happen? Mark is the best this city has ever seen. We need to get him before he goes national and starts demanding ten grand a show.

What's my first thought? That Wladika is the son-of-a-bitch who threw me up against the wall in Laffs, just about ripped out my voice box, and made me look like a fool in front of half the comedians in town. I pick up the pencil, drum it on the edge of my desk. The faces of my four employees loom in front of me, like over-inflated balloons.

Deborah chews her cud. Paloma wiggles her butt on the plastic chair, tugs her skirt to the middle of her thigh, and her finger goes up to her lip, like she's in deep thought or something. Cyn crosses her arms and listens for what's going on in the main salon. Timothy takes off his ball cap, smooths back his hair, puts the thing on backwards, and resumes his slouch.

"So, what's it gonna be?" he says.

Paloma gives a quick glance to Cyn, who shrugs. The redhead turns those big eyes back to me, flicks a ribbon of curly hair over her shoulder, and says, "You know, sometimes you just gotta say, 'What the fuck.'"

The clock in the back ticks. A chortle burbles up from Timothy's chest and leaks out. Then comes another. Deborah shields her eyes and her chest shakes. Cyn puts a fist to her mouth and lets out one big ol' long horse laugh. Everybody breaks up—even me—and the walls just about vibrate with the noise. I haven't heard that much mirth coming from this place since the Celtics won the championship.

"Yes," Cyn says as she slaps her sternum and tries to contain herself. "When you say, 'What the fuck,' that gives you opportunity."

They all say it together, since they've obviously heard it a million times, "And opportunity makes your future."

Then they crack up all over again. You'd think I just gave them all raises.

I rub my forehead and then turn to my top drawer to yank a fresh pack of Newports out of my desk. I tap the top against the wood, scratch at the cellophane, and peel off the plastic ribbon. I shove the drawer closed and ask, "Okay, okay, okay. Just how do I get a hold of this guy?"

Timothy finally comes to life. His arms go out to his sides, and he stretches, like he just woke from a nap. He says, "Just call any of the comics in town—Firecracker, Mica, Jana Boan, any of them—and they'll give you his number. What, you stupid?"

Once the sting of the kid's comment cools a little and we settle up a few more details for the coming week, I sweep them all out, back to their battle stations, and tell Paloma to make sure the office door latches behind her and that I am not to be disturbed for two or three hours or until I emerge from the office, whichever comes first, because I gotta track down this Wladika guy.

Back at my desk, I light a coffin nail, dump yesterday's Evan Williams out of my coffee mug and into the waste basket, reach under my desk, feel for the fifth, fish it out, and uncap it. I pour in a fresh dose, give a toast to my mother up in heaven, and shoot it back. Then I dig through a stack of worn business cards, find Mica's phone number, and give him a call.

Three minutes later? I wait for Wladika to fire up his laptop, to check his schedule, and come back on the line. All he says is that yeah, he can do it, and that he wants Mica to emcee the show. There is no ceremony, no humor, no personality in the way he says it. Downright stoic. He says we have a deal, and I hang up. I lean back. My chair squeaks. I'm surprised because that was so damned simple. Then it hits me. We never even discussed his fee.

I end up putting in two, maybe three hundred dollars' worth of advertising. If that much. The Budweiser people send us two five-by-fifteen vinyl signs that we suspend over the top shelf in the main bar, and then Cyn and Timothy staple the second one to the fascia outside so that no one trolling along Central Avenue can miss it. I also order

up twenty two-foot-by-two-foot plastic jobbers on wire braces, these
little vinyl signs from Kinko's print shop that Paloma and I plant at a
few choice freeway exits. All they say is:

COMEDY SHOW
NICHOLS' SILVER DOLLAR
7 O'CLOCK
MAY 1st

Then along the bottom, up one side, across the top, and down the
other, they got our address.

So the big day comes, and what do you think happens? First of all, I
feel totally relieved. I start the morning at my house loading up a bunch
of old shirts and ragged pairs of jeans into corrugated beer boxes,
thinking that soon I can run them over to the Saint Vincent de Paul. At
least I won't have to worry about Timothy or Cyn helping themselves
to the till anymore. I drive over to the bar just before five and come
in the back way, fully intending to hit the back banquet room and see
if Timothy set up the P.A. system the way I told him to. I come out of
the kitchen, and as I push open the door, it smacks some Poindexter
square in the elbow, causing beer to slosh onto his hand. I tell him
"Excuse me" as he shakes off the liquid, and I realize the place is thick
with bodies, and the air crackles with energy. A chorus of laughter
breaks out at one of the front tables, nearly shaking our foundation.

The Silver Dollar is about as crowded as the state fair midway on
opening night, and I have to step sideways and slither between bodies,
tap people on the shoulder, and guide some lady to the side just so
that I can get over to the bar. There, Cyn moves at full speed, tilting a

schooner under the amber ale spout and yelling something at Paloma about how we need another bottle of Seagram's from the back. I have to ask four different people to step aside just so I can lift up the wooden gate and get some beer glasses out of the dishwasher rack to help Cyn catch up. She asks where I've been. We have a line of folks six deep standing there at the bar, some who have been waiting more than half an hour just to put in their drink orders.

Cyn shoves a pint glass under a nozzle and pours Irish stout and says that the place is getting near capacity, and that if the Fire Marshall comes we're going to be in trouble. I say what's he going to do, shut us down?

By six thirty, I'm standing at the entrance to the back bar, collecting tickets. People are packed into that showroom, and when we run out of space, I stop a guy in a sweater vest and tell him that's all there is. He rolls his eyes, lifts his hand as if trying to stop me from talking, and he says, "Awe, come on, dude. You can do one more. Just one more." I tell him I already let in three people who begged for "just one more." He tells me he's been waiting out in the bar for at least two hours. So I tell him we're doing another show at nine thirty, that we just added it, never mind that I just decided that's what needed to happen.

We have upwards of three hundred and thirteen people in the showroom alone, bodies packed in, perched on banquet chairs, folding chairs along the side, people standing up against both walls.

And the show itself? A total hit.

The opener, Mica Pierson, just kills it. Every joke rocks the place so that I find myself worrying the room might cave in. He ends with a bang—I don't even remember the joke—and brings up Jana Boan. So I work my way to the other side of the room. There I find Tafoya and ask him for Wladika, and he says he just took his greyhound—

that's vodka and grapefruit juice—and slipped out the back because everyone who came in kept lavishing all this attention on him, and they weren't watching the show. I duck out through the kitchen. Outside, Mark stands on the loading dock, absorbing the peace of the evening, stirring his cocktail with his finger. He sucks off the juice and stares up at the quarter moon. An SUV—a Grand Vitara or something—comes up the alley and enters the parking lot.

Out on the side of the building, a Hyundai is scrunched right up against the gas meter. On the other side of that, you got one of those microscopic Smart Cars, looking like it just rolled out of some toy box. I'm not out there for thirty seconds, and four more carfuls come to join in the fun. I tell Mark that word sure is spreading fast for the nine thirty show, and he says he didn't know we had a nine thirty show. He asks who I got headlining. I tell him I'll pay him double—even triple, if that's what it takes.

EDDIE

As the applause fades, I lay my list of new jokes, scrawled on a cocktail napkin, atop a wooden barstool and plant my pint of red ale on top of that. I grab the mic stand and adjust so that the foam ball screen sits right below my chin and tighten the nut. I hold the metal pole with both hands, lean forward, toward the audience of two hundred and thirty Tucsonans here at Crazy Geri's Comedy Club.

"My name is Eduardo Miguel Jose Lluvias Altamirano y Tafoya," I say.

Titters leak out from the crowd, and I fix the angle of the orbital. In the front row, a Nubian-looking woman with glowing cheeks and a string of pearls over her Harvard University sweatshirt lays a bill on a tray held by this large and pony-tailed waitress making the rounds with Jell-O shots. The patron smiles up at the server, lays her bejeweled fingers across the girl's forearm, and tells her to keep the change. She turns back to me.

I go on.

"This freaks people out. People don't think I'm Mexicano because I have light skin and car insurance."

This sets off the first eruption.

"That's a joke. I don't have car insurance."

And I have their attention.

"I am glad you folks are laughing. I just told that joke up in this little town called Española, New Mexico, where I was doing a benefit for Libya and Somalia, these two strippers from Santa Fe. I'm out there, trying desperately to look Mexicano. I got a cowboy hat, turquoise cowboy boots, big old silver belt buckle…"

The crowd as a whole sits in rapt attention, poised atop something as delicate as a soap bubble. I hit the reveal.

"…and a pregnant girlfriend."

The room falls silent for a nanosecond until there is some inaudible snap, the click of a trigger, the feeling of something like two-by-fours knocking together. I don't hear it, but I feel it. Everybody does. It sets off a detonation of laughter. The black woman's lips spread, her teeth show, and her eyes close. She spreads those long fingers and holds her necklace in place as her chest shakes. I don't hear her laughing, but I feel it. I got her. She loves me like a father. If only for the next twenty-eight minutes or so.

The laughter crests and the ebb begins. I strike again.

"I am from the great city of Albuquerque, New Mexico. From a part of town that is very poor and very Catholic. Once a year we get together to baptize the pit bulls."

This sets off another blast, so I keep going.

"We had a drive-by shooting in my neighborhood last summer. The little old lady who lives three doors down was on the evening news saying, 'A y, Dios mio. I can't believe it. I can't believe I missed.'"

Seventy-five seconds into my set and I have a tight grip on these people. I can take them anywhere. I proceed.

"It was hard growing up there because I was so different from everyone else. My parents could vote. One time during recess, three kids corner me on the playground and start calling me 'gringo.' And I wasn't doin' nothin' to nobody. Just sitting there under a tree, minding my own business, playing with my dolls. These badasses throw me up against the fence, start beating me up. Finally, the leader recognizes me and yells out, so her sisters stop hitting me. I run home crying. My mom says, 'It's okay, 'jito. It's okay. You don't have to teach there anymore.'"

The jokes flow—naturally, organically, rhythmically—as if orchestrated by some ethereal composer. Each pulsation, each morpheme, each caesura, each accented syllable adds to the momentum. I move easily from premise to set-up, set-up to punch, punch to tag. I shape and mold each word, each beat, each reveal. Material I know so well. Jokes and deliveries I have worked and reworked, shaped and polished for so long, some for as long as eight years. Material that has become part of my being. I intuitively insert the inflections, pauses, emphases, and the new jokes, adding bits of punctuation with the subtlemost gesticulations and facial movements. I hit another punchline. The audience and I merge.

For a moment—just a moment—there is no performer, no audience, no subject, no object, no existence outside of Crazy Geri's Comedy Club. The rest of the cosmos has dissolved.

I check my watch and take a sip of red ale as laughter subsides. I go on.

"I went to Mass last Christmas. I should know better because, you know, the holy water burns. And as I'm walking to the parking lot, some guy peeks over the bushes and whispers, 'Hey, dude. Wanna buy a joint?' And so I'm thinking—*I'm thinking*—as he's counting back my change, this guy was just in church. I say, 'This don't feel right, Father Martinez.' He tells me it's okay because proceeds are going to charity. And I'm thinking, Charity? She works with Libya and Somalia.'"

I tell them I have been taking Omega MP3s, fatty acids I download from the internet, and about my crush on Amazon Annie, that tall and curvy waitress. I tell them I got her phone number because I just went through her purse. I tell them that I have a degree in sacred literature because I once wanted to become a Jesuit, thinking that the long black cassock would drive the chicks wild. I tell them about my son, about how he is a sophomore in high school, and how with cell phones, Facebook, and Twitter, I worry that someday he just might find me. This brings another burst, an eruption that is clear, raucous, and sustained.

"I am only joking. My kid's out in the car. Amazing what a little chloroform can do when you need a break."

Somewhere in there, something, some spirit, commands my body, my mind, and my vocal chords. As the phantasm takes full possession, I feel as though I stand outside my skin, hearing myself perform, surprised as anyone by a joke that speaks itself into being.

"I take that kid everywhere. He blows into my ignition interlock."

More laughter. I sip some ale.

My set goes on for another twenty-one and a half minutes, and I only get through about one-third of the material I planned. I check my watch, realize I've gone past my time, and I move into my closing bit, a sequence about how I come from an Irish-Mexican family.

"That's right. Irish-Mexican. We're green-beaners, lepricanos, unemployed cops, whatever you want to call us. One night someone told us to go green, so we went out and beat up a Protestant."

The very molecules of the air in that room crackle with life, releasing energy all their own.

"But according to census forms, I am supposed to be Hispanic. I don't even know what the word 'Hispanic' means. People tell me that it means you can trace your relatives all the way back to Spain. I'm thinking, most nights, my relatives can't trace their way back through the parking lot. They're not getting back to Spain unless they can take the back roads and avoid all the DUI check points."

People laugh, clap, cheer, and hoot. I tell the crowd they have been terrific—and actually mean it this time—and that I am Eddie Tafoya. I flash them the peace sign and tell them that the best way to support the troops is to bring them back alive. I turn, and next to me on the stage stands Jamie Jupiter, the emcee, who has appeared, almost magically, in her black-and-white suspenders and high-top basketball shoes, adjusting her knitted newsboy cap, and smiling her crooked smile. I hug her, tell her she's lovely, and exit down the stage steps. The Nubian princess stops clapping, sticks her thumb and forefinger in her mouth, and lets out a whistle. She is tall with close-cropped hair, ochre highlights glowing on her coffee-colored cheeks, and those full, plum-colored lips.

The ovation continues. I come down the steps and make my way along the shadowed wall. Some guy in a Boston Celtics basketball jersey stands, nodding and slapping his palms together. He holds out his open hand, as if he's a cop stopping traffic. I draw my arm back, reach out, and lunge into a high-five. Behind him stands another guy, waiting for his turn, and our palms smack together, releasing a loud and brittle snap. Then a small dark-skinned woman wants her hand slap, and so does a fat kid in a sleeveless flannel shirt. And some big guy. Then his lady. Then somebody else.

And there, in the middle of the crowd, packed between walls of patrons in the overfilled showroom, stands this man I swear is Mark. That is his face and upper body hidden deep in that mosaic of people. Those are his shoulders, his freckled cheeks, his glasses, his bald head, the blunt point of his nose. He is out of his chair, clapping, the motion beginning in his shoulders and biceps, rippling through his arms, culminating in quick and energetic bursts as his hands fly apart and come back together and fly apart again. I strut down the side aisle, and someone slaps me on the shoulder. The extolment keeps up, and I get another back pat, and then another, and I give another high five, and someone belts out a whistle, and Mark's hands bang together again and again as I lock eyes on him. A light beam reflects off his watch crystal and hits me square in the eye. He points at me.

The applause washes over me, and I pause and point back at him, then to the back of the room, indicating that I want him to meet me back there, at the main entryway. He pushes his chair aside, steps forward, looks one way and then the other, but the crowd is too thick. He can't make his way out. Standing, trapped in that forest of people, he shrugs. I mouth the words, as best I can, slowly, over pronouncing. *Back there*, I say silently while jutting my finger toward the door. *Back there. Meet me back there after the show.*

He nods, certain of what I am talking about. He applauds. His head bobs—assuring me he understands—and he slaps his palms together. And Amazon Annie steps between us, that tall and thick girl, holding another full tray of Jell-O shots in single-ounce plastic cups, and I lean to get a better look, to make sure it is him, and I lose him through the crowd.

Fifty-one minutes later, Phil Fletcher ends his set with a bang, a story about how his father taught him how to play baseball. The act-out takes a good four minutes, and the crowd stays with him every second. He ends by telling how the old man told him to "stop the ball with your body," but was really saying, "let it hit you in the face." Once the laughter dies out, he waves, says that he, Jamie, and I will be in Tucson through Sunday, and as he finishes, Jamie strides up the steps, sticks her thumbs under her suspenders, and lets the elastic snap against her torso. She tells the crowd that Barry Bass, from right there in Tucson, will be there beginning on Wednesday, and that Thursday night is ladies' night. She says she hopes they had a great time and to drive safely. Before the house lights go up, I get up from the comic's table, slink along the back wall toward the exit, ahead of the crowd, and take my place just the other side of the curtain there in the lobby, ready to greet people as they exit, ready to find Mark. The room goes bright, and the music plays, and people are out of their chairs, making their ways toward the exit, talking, smiling, still giddy.

I wonder what Mark is doing in Southern Arizona, why he never told me he was in the area, and how I cannot wait to see him. I want so badly to tell him that I am thrilled that he was there on this night, the night I finally found the Buddha. I cannot wait to go out to a late dinner and, on the way back to the comics' condo, grab a bottle of Blanton's Special Reserve. We can sit out by the pool drinking good bourbon, talking until three or four in the morning. Like we did in college.

There in the back, I lean against the wall and tell Phil he had his best set yet. The patrons file by. The kid with greased hair, who so badly wanted his high-five as I came off stage. His buddy, a tall twenty-something with bad posture. A youngster, who adjusts his baseball cap and then reaches in front of his friend, tacitly requesting a handshake—first from me, then from Phil. I ask them if they enjoyed the show. More people flow by. The black woman who had me so enchanted.

A white-haired man with thick, horned-rim glasses and a plaid suit coat, and his wife with her shawl draped over her arm. A vato in a football jersey with the brim of his cap poking out, straight and stiff as a diving platform, and trailing behind him, his tiny girlfriend with shaved eyebrows and super-tight, white denim shorts. I ask if they're from New Mexico. He gives me a knuckle-bump, and she extends her hand, hesitates, and looks to him for permission. He sticks an unlit cigarette between his lips and nods. The girl and I tap fists.

More people. A short, Jewish-looking guy with graying hair flaring out past his shoulders, and another man with a pot belly, thinning brown hair, and sideburns to the middle of his jaw. He winks at me and walks on without saying anything. A thirty-something wife with a turquoise purse matching her belt and high heels. Two of her girlfriends follow.

I shake hands with an ancient cowboy and his daughter and tell them to come back. I say I'll be back in town in about six months. More people pass, and Phil tells me we rocked the place. Then two stragglers, women in their sixties, exit the showroom toward the smoked-glass doors and tell me, for whatever reason, they're heading down to the sushi restaurant at the other end of the strip center. Out on the sidewalk, a blonde lights a cigarette, talks to people she met there that night, and looks over the lot, probably waiting for her husband to drive the car over. I check my watch, and Phil tells me he's meeting friends downtown for beer and eightball, but he's going to smoke a joint first, and I should join them later. I say I'm meeting an old friend. He says he'll see me tomorrow night, and I peek past the curtain. There, in the shadows of the showroom, Amazon Annie loads a platter, dirty silverware, and crumpled napkins onto her tray. Behind her, a coworker squirts cleanser on a table and wipes it, and the bartender sweeps in front of the stage.

When the place is empty, I dig into my jacket pocket for my car keys and step out through the kitchen into the back parking lot. I drive back to the apartment complex, call Phil Fletcher, and hang up before he answers, just to see if my cell phone is working. I sit in the car for a few minutes, wondering what happened to Mark.

NICHOLS

What do I got spilling out of my pants pockets?

I got tens, twenties, ones, even a few Franklins and Grants mixed in there. So I step back and twist the thumb lock on the doorknob and stack the bills in six piles: ones, fives, tens, twenties, fifties, and hundreds. The walls shake with an explosion of laughter from the other room.

I bite my lip. In front of me, right there between the empty beer bottles and a coffee cup stuffed with cigarette butts, sit all these stacks of cash. When was the last time I saw so much green? Probably never.

Another burst comes through the walls, then applause, a blast so fierce it threatens to shatter the studs and drywall. Mark is still at it. Another thunderous explosion follows, sending vibrations strong enough to shake debris off the ceiling, and the light above my desk swings and flickers like a subway just rattled by. My watch says it is after three, and my gut reminds me that Nichols' Silver Dollar isn't running on *borrowed* time. Every minute, every second—hell, every nanosecond—we serve drinks we're living on *stolen* time. Yet, just yards away, Cyn, Deborah, Paloma, and Timothy still slog out beers and line up cocktails on trays. And Wladika? His voice rises up over the din as he holds the audience in the palm of his hand. I finally gotta admit it. The guy's got some real mojo.

We—by that I mean me, the staff, the patrons, and even the comics—all prepared for Nichols' Silver Dollar to be cast into the dumpster of history after we closed at one thirty. But all day long, people poured through those doors, waited outside, and called the front bar and my office. Even comics came by, practically begging to be part of the show, compensation be damned. After we sold out the second show, we had enough people clamoring, willing to stick around for a third and a fourth, never mind that our serving liquor after two a.m. meant we could all end up in jail, each of us saddled with a fifty thousand dollar fine. And the comics, the ones scheduled to go up on stage? Mark, Jana, Jamie, Mica, Black Tom, and Firecracker? They insisted on extra shows. They all felt it just as much as I did. Mark created a damned tidal wave, and they felt they could ride it to fame and fortune. Everyone was willing, practically insisting, on working for free. All this went on despite the reality that your average, ordinary, run-of-the-mill, garden-variety cop might, at any moment, walk in, shut the place down, put me in shackles, and haul me off, then do the same with Deborah, Paloma, and especially Cyn and Timothy, since they actually poured the liquor. It still could happen. If it doesn't—and it looks like it won't—I swear I'll drop to my knees and thank the cosmic forces for allowing me to thread the needle this one time.

In truth, I suppose, we threaded a whole box of needles.

Go figure.

I had customers hanging out in the sports bar from about three in the afternoon, hooting it up like it was their first fraternity party, laying down cash for watered-down drinks. Twelve hours later, the merriment rages on.

So I count all the cash, fire up the computer, tally up the ticket sales from the three shows, add in the bills right there in front of me, punch in what I need to pay the help, and lean back, rub my chin, recheck the figures. I set aside a grand for Mark. Two hundred and fifty for each of four shows? Sounds like a good night's work to me.

I turn back to my spreadsheet, highlight the column of figures, and command the program to sum things up, to make the final pronouncement. I can't believe what the digits tell me. So I recalculate. Then I do it again, just for good measure.

Seven number crunchings later, I remove my glasses and hold my head in my hand. Rub my eyebrows, forehead, and eyes. I ask myself if the cocktail I am high on—fatigue mixed with excitement mixed with eight shots of Crown Royal—has me hallucinating. I verify the totals once more. My watch tells me it is three fifty-three. Applause and laughter shake the building, and I tremble with genuine fear.

Come about four fifteen, four twenty, something like that, I push open the door to the showroom. Cyn herds six twenty-something chicks out the back door, tells them to take the backroads home—like that will do any good. Paloma wipes off a table and shoves a chair back in place. With the hand broom, Timothy brushes the molding around the edge of the stage. I ask for Mark, and the gingerhead says he and Tafoya walked out about ten minutes before. I ask if he said anything about his pay, and Paloma says he just wrapped his arm around her shoulder, kissed her forehead, thanked her for a fun evening, shoved a fifty in her apron pocket, and walked out the back door, his car keys jangling, Eddie jogging out after him.

I help Cyn and Timothy with the clean-up, then count both tills. Take a quick inventory. Then, just after eight a.m., I call my lawyer, who tells me to make it quick. He says his wife and girls just got in the car. They're headed to church. I tell him what happened, and he orders me to wait and puts down the receiver. Two minutes later, he comes back on, says he'll be by in fifteen. He needs all the bank account info, income tallies, ticket sales records, and accurate counts of the cash on hand. We need to go over everything step by step. He'll bring his copy of the bankruptcy documents.

And what do you think happened? Just after noon, I sign another packet of papers. Nichols' Silver Dollar? Suddenly, it's got new life.

HELEN DENISE

I pulled up the shade just as the skinny nurse slipped the blood pressure cuff off Daddy's arm, coiled up the tubes, and packed it all away. She patted his hand, this petite girl with a beak of a nose, the very tip moving whenever she spoke. She smiled that crooked smile of hers and told him she'd be right back with a pan and a washcloth to give him his sponge bath—as if his mind could even register anything by that point. I mean, the man hadn't so much as swallowed water in more than three whole days. I slid the stuffed chair to the side of the bed, opened my book, crossed my leg, and instinctively, automatically, reached over and put my hand on top of his. I ached just so badly to tell him we had a new family member on the way.

Out in the hallway, the nurse chatted with her shift supervisor, this lady who sounded like she was from Brooklyn or New Jersey or someplace out East. They went silent just as something down the hall beeped, the signal ringing out clear and sustained, echoing down the corridor. As if he had waited for that cue all afternoon, Daddy curled his fingers under my palm and rubbed circles into my skin with his thumb. His eyes, for the first time in more than three weeks, why, they opened real wide.

And just for that little sliver of a second, he was Daddy again. That same person who sat on the porch pouring homebrew and bragging to his brother-in-law and Father Nico about how well I was doing in college. He blinked and looked like he actually recognized me. The corner of his mouth twitched, like he wanted to smile.

And he slipped away.

For a second there, I fell into this little eddy of denial. As one part of me wanted not to believe it, another part told me I should tell the nurse and that maybe she could do something—wheel in a crash cart, maybe give him a shot or something. Still another part of me asked what purpose it would serve to keep the dear man alive any longer. So I clasped his rough hand in both of mine, pressed it against my cheek, felt that wedding ring, so thin and misshapen after all those years. I touched the pulse point right there in front of his ear. After maybe three, maybe five, maybe ten minutes—I don't know how long—I put his arm back across his tummy.

I dried my eyes with my sleeve, straightened my sweater, dug two quarters out of my purse, and walked out into the hallway to report what happened. The skinny nurse stood out by her station, humming and scribbling notes on a chart clipped to a board. When she flipped over the page, I just said it, the best way I knew how, my words stripped of all emotion.

"You know my daddy in B-23? Why, I think he just died." I managed a little smile, and she squeezed my hand but didn't say anything. Then I turned and walked down to the pay phone in the hallway to call Marti. For a good long time, I knew darned good and well that this day was coming. I went to bed that night just so upset, feeling so bad about Daddy and everything. And I wondered, for the first time in years, really, what to do with my life.

You see, three years before, Mark and I planned on moving from Albuquerque to Boulder so both of us could finish up our master's degrees. We made all the arrangements. The university out there offered Mark a fellowship and even offered us a good deal if we chose to live in married student housing, although we hadn't made up our minds just yet. I got an assistantship and was supposed to teach two classes in the fall. In June, we drove up I-25 to spend the weekend there in that hippie town thirty miles the other side of Denver, to see if we'd like it. Then, at the end of the summer, we went up to look at apartments, and this time we actually took boxes of books and winter clothes to a storage unit, to make the whole transition a little smoother, you know?

We never ever talked about marriage, not outright anyway. We never did mention so much as a service, a ring, or a honeymoon. We did, though, talk as if each of us expected to stick it out for the long haul. I mean, we pretty much worked those fantasies into our conversations, like we both understood automatically that the universe shoved us together for reasons we could never really wrap our minds around. We both wanted to come back to Albuquerque, sooner or later, maybe to settle in Huning Highland, right there in his old neighborhood, with all those Queen Anne style two stories, or maybe get a place in Nob Hill, the trendy and expensive district east of the university. I told him I always liked the look and feel of the ancient adobe homes down by the Rio Grande. He said that when you get too close to that cottonwood bosque, then you gotta put up with rats. I told him I lived just a hop, skip, and a jump away from those muddy waters for two years and never did see a problem. He said then we would have to get a cat or a dachshund or something. Maybe we could name it Harpo.

That kind of stuff.

Well, anyway, it just so happens that not two days before we were to move out of our house there by the university—we already had the living room stacked with boxes, and we were sleeping on a futon mattress on the floor because the frame and box springs were packed up in the U-Haul—Marti called. She told me how Dr. Lukes met with her that afternoon to say that Daddy probably wouldn't be around too much longer. That he reckoned we had another four months, if things went well. So that night, lying there in the dark and listening to the cicadas buzzing in the trees, I curled under Mark's arm and lay my leg across his thighs. Right on the other side of the window, the glowing speck of Mars shone through the leafy branches of the Siberian elms, and Mark and I talked it over. Oh, we went back and forth, pretending to explore the options. But that was all just ritual. Both of us knew there wasn't much choice. Marti, by that time, she had her own family to look after, so the responsibility fell on me.

Two days later, Mark kissed me goodbye as tiny drops pecked at the tin roof of the carport. I started up my Honda, backed out, waved through the window, and drove on south, back to Fort Stockton, just crying my eyes out.

Oh, we tried to keep it alive. He came down to visit three times—I reckon four times, really. Once the following Christmas, a few months later for spring break, and then for three weeks during the summer. After that, I didn't see him again for almost two years, not until that January right before Daddy died. Mark dropped me a card telling me that he was doing this presentation at a conference there in El Paso. And how he would just love to get together.

The universe, you know? It works in funny ways. And I guess all this would have been so much different if Daddy didn't take so long to die. I know that must sound so cold-hearted. Of course, I didn't want him to die. But sometimes I got awful angry—with Daddy, with God, with my situation. Even with Mark. I mean, to put everything on hold like I did. To wake up in the morning with my arms wrapped around two pillows, pretending I was cuddling my man? All these years later, I still don't regret taking care of Daddy. But sometimes I just look back and wonder how things would have played out, you know, if he let himself go just a little bit earlier.

I mean, the Daddy I knew, that man I grew up with, he was this lumberjack of a guy. Big chest, broad shoulders, forearms thick as fence posts. But then, in those final months, almost every day, no matter how much I fed him, he withered just a little more. By his last days in the hospital, the ridge of his radius bone showed under his skin any time he lifted his fork or flung out his hand in gesticulation. His speech got slurred, he got a big sore under his cheek, and he grew more and more desiccated until he looked like one of those wasp husks I vacuum off the window sill.

Then, to add to that, I spent so much of my day watching bad television reruns and worse game shows. I gained twelve pounds and actually had to work to keep myself from getting too wrapped up in local news stories. Who embezzled what from the county assessor's office. Why the chief administrator at the Head Start program got fired for unspecified reasons. Why the Pecos County Sheriff Deputy's son got arrested for driving drunk and then went off scot-free. Small town news, why, I reckon it never changes. And that stuff just numbs your brain after a while. Oh, I still read my Heidegger, Plato, Saint Augustine, and my Karen Armstrong, still went for runs, and still took my walks, and Marti drove down once or twice a week. But I really couldn't stay away from that house very long. Something always called me back. Rabbit and mushroom stew in the crock pot, a shot to administer, laundry to fold, an estate lawyer to meet with. Besides, I didn't want to leave the poor guy alone for very long—just in case, you know?

Then, to make matters worse, one morning someone knocked on the back door, and that totally shocked me. I pushed aside the curtains, and smiling there from the other side of the glass was this handsome, dark-eyed black man I just didn't recognize. My first thought was that he was the meter reader reporting something wrong with the gas line. After a few seconds, the pieces fit themselves together. It was Mace. His shoulders filled out since I last saw him, his hair had thinned, and he shaved his Fu Manchu. Now, when he smiled, that single dimple really caught your attention. He was handsome as ever and didn't look quite like the farm boy I fell so hard for back in eleventh grade. The whole thing surprised me. Not just the way he showed up, but the way seeing an old friend, someone I knew since I was eight, made me feel. The way it showed me that Fort Stockton produced me, shaped me, and molded me in ways I forgot about during my years in Albuquerque.

And that wasn't so bad. Not really.

He sat at the kitchen table, and I poured him a tall glass of mint green tea, sweetened with honey from the neighbor's hive. Once I realized he wanted to stay, I put him to work chopping fresh garlic with a razor blade. He rolled up his flannel sleeves and yanked up the cuffs of his undershirt and looked so cute there at Mama's table, trying so desperately to get those big hands to make those teeny-tiny cuts. As the high-carbon steel rat-tat-tatted on Mama's old oak cutting board, he told me that after his father died he used the inheritance to buy the A-1 Mini Storage, how that and his little girl occupied his time, how the work was easy, how the money came in steady, and how he got to work out at Gold's Gym four times a week. After we finished the supper dishes, we split a bottle of Daddy's homebrew, and we stayed laughing and talking at the kitchen table until after eleven.

Then, a week later, he came back. That afternoon, while the sage was in bloom and the taint of polecat spray wafted in from over the hill, we sat out on the porch. Me on the swing and Mace on Daddy's rocker. He opened a paper grocery sack and took out this rolled up thing that looked like it was maybe a baguette or a Roman candle all wrapped up in blue gauze and laid it out right there on the TV tray. Turns out, it was two big ol' kitchen towels, and tucked away inside of them, why, he had two champagne flutes. He wiped the lint out of one and set it down right there on the wicker table. Then he got this big ol' grin, a smile wide enough to show off that big lonely dimple. He twisted the top off a mason jar and filled my glass with this golden brown concoction that looked like weak orange pekoe tea.

"Smell it," he said, looking all serious.

I scrunched up my faced and turned away. "It smells just God-awful," I said.

"Go ahead. Give it a taste," he said. "It ain't so bad."

I sniffed at it again. Awfully sweet.

"You trying to pull a fast one again?" I said.

"I call it the Perfect Marriage," he said.

"Now just what's this Perfect Marriage supposed to be?"

"What do you think? Jack and ginger."

Not quite Mark's wine.

Having company, having someone to talk to face-to-face, why that sure did feel nice. He asked what I studied in college, and I told him about my work on post-modern theory, Paul Tillich, and Christian existentialism. He wrinkled his brow and crossed his eyes, like he was overwhelmed, and glanced over at the morning glories sprouting out by the chain-link fence. He laughed, saying that, over the years, I'd just become more like the Helen Denise he always knew. I hadn't changed, not much, he said. Except maybe I just got intenser. He actually said "intenser."

Well, to make a long story short, my phone calls to Boulder got further and further apart. For one thing, they were just so darned expensive. And after that first year, the cards and letters from Mark, those dropped off too. Then, the week after Daddy was admitted, I woke up in the bedroom in Mace's trailer, his thick arm around my shoulder. I knew right then and there I'd made a mistake. But still, when that cold May morning came, it was Mace who put on his leather jacket and bolo tie and went down to Flowers Etc. and loaded the arrangements into the back of his pickup truck to haul them over to Saint Agnes. And it was Mace who handed me tissues at the gravesite. And it was his arm I held to so tight when Father Nico gave that final blessing. And it was Mace who put a rose right there on top of Daddy's coffin.

I guess you can study all the post-modernism and phenomenology you want, but that sure does little to help you when fate and reality just collapse in on themselves and you get caught up in the folds. Why, I weathered Mama's passing, and then Daddy's a few years later. And for days after that, I just about cried my eyes out, wishing so bad I could sit down with either one of them for just a few more minutes. Just to share a root beer float and talk about the apples on sale at the Piggly Wiggly, or the way our neighbor, Old Naomi Weeks, finally learned how to walk again after her drunk driving accident.

But sometime in there, something got to me. I mean really got to me, like nothing else ever in my life. I mean, something told me in no uncertain terms that out there, out in the vast universe, there was this mysterious something—call it spirit, call it God, call it the Cosmic Forces if you want to—perhaps no real name can do it justice. I mean, as I cried at Daddy's rosary that night before we buried him, as Marti and I stood there in that receiving line, bawling like little school girls and laughing and dabbing our eyes and hugging friends and cousins—talking to some of Daddy's friends we never even met before—I felt my very soul swirl away, like it just got so caught up in the flow of things and lost its shape and definitions. I mean, it was like my soul floated up to the rafters, and I was looking down on the whole ceremony. And for just a second there, I felt a spark. This little electric blip that let me know I was connected to something so much larger than I could ever imagine.

Profound as that experience was, I didn't see it in all its fullness until years later.

You see, Marti, she was a pretty bad Catholic, especially if you count her exploits the two years she waited tables in El Paso. That all changed, though, when she got married and had her son, Dion. So for that first anniversary of Daddy's passing, she paid for a memorial Mass there at Saint Agnes. My aunt Mary Beth came in from Odessa, and so did some of Daddy's friends from the grocery store. And of course Marti, her husband, and their two kids. So that afternoon, I sat in the second pew, right in front of the statue of the Blessed Virgin Mary in her white gown and a blue shawl draped around her shoulders, her arms spread in greeting. That very statue I knelt in front of so many times when I was a schoolgirl. Only this time, I had my eight-month-old child on my lap. My tiny little Jack, this energetic, straw-haired boy, with his pale-green eyes and celestial nose. Why, the boy wasn't even walking yet, and he was already getting into everything. I mean everything.

Just as Mass starts, he grabs one of the missalettes and crumples one of the pages. Then he lets loose with all these nonsense syllables—looking me square in the face, like he's speaking in tongues or something. Then he holds the book out, like he's offering me a gift, and I rock him and hold him against my shoulder and pat his back. Then as the priest prepares the gifts and we all kneel for the consecration, Jack goes at it again, looking me straight in the eye, so serious, like he has something so important to tell me, and he lets loose with more of his glossolalia. And just as I put down the kneeler, Little Jack lets out this big old yell, just this loud "Auuugh," you know, like kids sometimes do? He didn't cry or anything. He just made that random noise. I put my free hand to my mouth and stifled a chuckle.

The Mass, it was short, only about forty minutes or so. But nice enough. We had a whole year to heal, and so we did what you do in those situations. We teared up, we prayed, we thought about Daddy, and took Holy Communion—typical stuff, you know? And Father Nico, right before the final blessing, he was nice enough to talk about Daddy, his life, what he and Mama meant to the parish and everything. Then afterwards, we all went down to the K-Bob's, that steakhouse with the salad bar over on Dickinson Boulevard there on the west side of town. We took up a whole table in the back, you know, eleven or twelve of us, including Jack and me. There, Father Nico, he had us all laughing, going on about playing poker with the boys. How it took Daddy six or seven years to figure out that the priest whistled "Ave Maria" whenever he was bluffing.

What I didn't—what I couldn't—know then about that particular afternoon, well, that took me more than three more years to figure out. And when I did, I swear, it just about shot a flaming spear, over and over again, right through my heart, every time I thought about it. I swear to almighty God.

Jack and I already moved back to Albuquerque by then. And the boy, he was just about four, certainly not much older than that. One day we walked down to this little park around the block from our home, a place he just loved to go to. I spun him around the little merry-go-round, and we rubbed the slide with wax paper to make it more slippery, just like Marti and I used to do when we played at the elementary school yard. I asked Jack if he wanted an ice cream cone from the Dairy Queen, and he got thrilled. I held out my hand, and he took hold of my finger, and we walked across the wet grass. Just the cutest little boy with these big old denim overalls with the cuffs rolled up and sneakers with little cartoon dragons printed on the sides. And we were there on the sidewalk, waiting for a car to pass so we could cross the street, when he tugged so hard on my hand and said, "Looky, Mommy. Looky." Just like that. He crouched there with one foot on the grass, his new shoe already stained, the fluorescent-yellow lace already coming loose.

And he lifted something up for me to see. Pinched between his thumb and finger was this curved little twig, just about eight inches long. I didn't know what the big deal was, so he waggled the stick in front of me, just so excited.

"Looky, Mommy," he said. "Just looky. A 'J.' Now we just need an 'A,' a 'C,' and a 'K.'"

I just had no idea the tyke knew his alphabet, let alone that he could spell his name.

He gripped my finger, and as we crossed the street, he studied that stick like it contained all the mysteries of the universe. He turned it one way, then the other, and was just so intent on it he tripped when we got to the sidewalk, and I had to pull him up and brush the dirt off his pant legs. At the walk-up window, we ordered two chocolate dips and then sat outside at the iron table. Jack tore off a chunk of the chocolate coating and held it up to the sun, apparently fascinated by the way it kept its shape. My little boy, looking just so darned cute, with dark brown smudges and white streaks all across his cheeks, ice cream dripping from his chin onto his new T-shirt, those little lips and teeth tearing into the treat.

I wiped his mouth with a napkin and couldn't help but just brim with pride. I told him that my daddy would have just adored him, would have just loved teaching him how to build a birdhouse or put together a box kite. I told him that my only regret in life was that he never got to see his Grampa Jake. Little Jack, why, he tilted the cone and a dollop dripped through the latticework of the table top, down onto the clean denim. He scraped it up with his finger and put it in his mouth. He furrowed his brow.

"I did," he said. "I did. I saw Grampa Jake. At the church. A long, long time ago. I saw Grampa Jake. I remember."

I told him, why, that was just nonsense since Daddy died four months before he was born. But Jack insisted he saw his grampa. He described Daddy in his black cardigan. He remembered the man's glasses.

"At the church," he said. "A long, long time ago." And he bit off a glob of ice cream.

As we walked back home through the park, I remembered how I took that boy to church but once in his life. The best I could reason was that the whole point of the anniversary Mass was to recall Daddy's presence. And we were all there—Marti, the uncles, aunts, and friends we hadn't seen in so many years, not to mention Father Nico. And it hits me that Daddy had to be right there, too. At least in spirit. I mean, that was the whole point, wasn't it? But it took a child, someone who had not yet been corrupted by the whole silliness of empiricism, to recognize what really went on. After all my time away from religion—any faith, really—on that day something came real clear to me. We had maybe ten or twelve people there at St. Agnes for the explicit purpose of recalling the spirit of Mr. John Jacob Marison. So what happens when you got five or six hundred people coming together to summon the presence of God?

Lest ye become like the little children, you know?

JACK

I downshift into fourth gear, just to give my Toyota a little boost as I climb a hill. I click on my turn signal, swing the car out to the left lane, and pass this tractor-trailer rig hauling liquid nitrogen or some other noxious solution westward, to regions unknown. We speed along U.S. 34, a couple of hours from the Colorado border. About a million miles back, I walked up to the front desk of this roach motel where this Pawnee-looking goofball with a braid held by a silver barrette told me he had four rooms left but couldn't rent me one because he expected six bikers to swarm in at any second. I told that swarthy genius how only sketchy folks check into a hotel after two a.m. and, besides, wouldn't he prefer the bird in the hand? The guy scratched his nose with his pen top, shrugged, and said "boss's orders," and I told him that he shouldn't let his boyfriend push him around like that. He didn't get the joke.

As I turned to leave, the ice machine discharged another load. I shoved open the glass door, stopped, looked back, and said that if he didn't like the way American capitalism works he should go back to where he came from. And besides, his coffee was burning.

What a dope.

Once in my car, I reached into the back seat and fished out a can of ginger ale floating around in tepid water and popped it open. I cranked the engine, pressed the accelerator, and let out the clutch too fast. My new tires kicked up a cloud of dust and sprayed gravel and small chunks of asphalt all over the untended parking lot. I waited at the curbless highway for an eighteen-wheeler to thunder by, headed eastward with its elongated cistern full of fossil fuel, arsenic-tainted milk, or some other poison. Once it passed, I shot out onto the empty road, down this highway through the thin and dry air of the cloudy and moonless night. Across that Martian landscape of South Central Nebraska, a place that makes hick towns like Mora, New Mexico, look downright metropolitan.

Although I've eaten nothing since the two polyester burritos I bought at a truck stop back about ten thousand hours ago, I know that, right now, my first order of business needs to be getting some kind of stimulant flowing through my veins. I'd prefer illegal, but legal will do, although I don't know where I could possibly get it. The warm can of soda pop in my cup holder just isn't doing the trick. I hope, sooner or later, to come across a Circle K, a 7-Eleven, an Allsup's, a truck stop, or any one of those independently-owned convenience stores that sells thousand-year-old Twinkies and twenty-seven-dollar loaves of Wonder Bread. All my situation really requires is twelve to sixteen ounces of your standard acidic sludge, your Folgers or Farmer Brothers toxic mess, mellowed with aspartame-laden artificial cream and sugar, something sure to eat away my stomach lining, deteriorate my nervous system, and keep me semi-alert for the next few hours.

About half an hour down the road, maybe a little more, I find this place called Caesar's Phillips 66 with its road sign flashing, a big "open" sign illuminated in the front window, and its interior lights blazing. I park, step out, and try the door, but it won't budge. Inside of it you have Hostess Snowballs, Ho Hos, and Devil Cremes on frontmost display, right there by the aisle stand filled with hanging bags of beef jerky and shelves crammed with pumpkin seeds, sunflower seeds, chili-seasoned peanuts, corn nuts, beer nuts, potato and tortilla chips. Over the cash register recess, right there above the lottery ticket numbers and shelves of cigarette cartons, a bare fluorescent tubal light flickers, like it wants to go out for good. But no signs of human life.

So I get back into my rice grinder, fire her up, crank up the John Coltrane playing on the stereo, and labor onward.

Before long, I catch up to the liquid transport as it chugs up a hill, the convex back of its reservoir looking like a face—a broad, bland, and bleak circular face with two worn spots exactly where the eyes might be. A detachable ladder rattles across the back, and at the top, on either side, are two triangular metal scaffolds sticking out, like a fringe of bright orange hair. I suppose that metal is there so that the drones down at the oil refinery can climb up and balance themselves as they do their hose hook-ups.

My fatigue settles in again, and so I tap the steering wheel to the beat of this modal jazz CD Mom gave me last time I was in Albuquerque. I take another swallow of soda that by now is just too warm and flat to offer anything valuable. My eyelids droop, and my head drops to my shoulder, but I catch myself and give my whole noggin a wild shake. I switch my headlights off and then on again, just to make sure they still work. I punch a button on a door panel, and the back window descends about six inches, the air rushing through the cabin as I try to figure out how to stay awake on this Godforsaken, third-world road that even the coyotes, prairie dogs, and jack rabbits have abandoned for more exciting vistas. My eyes close, and I jerk myself back to consciousness.

Minutes later, I nod off again and startle myself awake. I lower the driver's window, just to energize the air rush.

The precariousness of the situation calls for more aggressive tuneage, so I switch the stereo from CD mode to FM, tap the scan button, and let the exploration of the airwaves begin. For ten seconds at a time, I get a sampling of the most popular stuff American radio has to offer, sounds that surely signal the downfall of the Western World: the twanging of some country-boy malcontent; the ranting of a Christian chiliastic; the tittering of some pop-tart's love ballad that comes off so sweet and sentimental it threatens to send me into an insulin coma. Eventually, though, the dial finds the throbbing of a bass guitar and the spiraling and swirling notes lifting from the top strings of a Fender Stratocaster. Then Clapton, his voice as smooth as thirty-year-old scotch, eases into some song about a bluesman selling his soul to the devil, and it takes me away.

Miles later, I drift off once more, and this time I catch myself just as the car veers off to the right, rattling on the hash marks etched into the shoulder. I tug the wheel, straighten out, steady myself, point toward Denver, and press the accelerator.

I never did learn to like these fifteen-hour drives, but I had plenty of warning that things might pan out like this.

About twenty-seven hours earlier, I got back to my hotel and collapsed onto the bed just before one o'clock after having four beers and two shots with the other comedians. About two seconds later, when I opened my eyes again, the glow from the parking lot streetlamp shone over the curtain ridge right into my face, like I was being interrogated by Nazis or something. I couldn't sleep because of it, so I dug one of my T-shirts out of my suitcase, bunched it up, and wedged it in the space between the window frame and the metal rod, hoping just to blot out some of that shine. But like five seconds after I got back in bed, the T-shirt came loose, and the light rays just about punched me right in the face again. Usually when I run into situations like this in one of these fleatrap motels, I can just scoot the bed a few feet in one direction and problem solved. This time, though, they had the whole damned platform bolted to the floor and wall, as if those Hindu transplants downstairs thought I might actually fold up the mattress and box springs and stash them in my gym bag.

What a bunch of dopes.

So I scrounged around in the dark, found another shirt—the clean one I had planned to wear on the drive to Denver I would begin in a few hours—rolled it with the other one, and stuffed them between the curtain rod and window frame. That held, for about five-point-two seconds this time. So I pulled the sheet over my head and turned away from the window. Over the course of the next five or six hours, however long it was, every time I straightened out or flung the covers away from my face to get a little air, the beam from that two-million-watt light bulb just the other side of the window stabbed me in the eyes.

Then, come about six or seven o'clock in the morning—the room was already bright with morning light—I flipped back the covers, and my thigh looked like a goddamned connect-the-dots puzzle with about two thousand pinpricks from bedbugs or fleas or some other vermin breeding in the bedclothes. That's all I needed. To get Lyme disease, bubonic plague, or some chronic skin rash just because some new arrival from some third-world ghetto buys a hotel and can't lay down a few dollars to disinfect his five-thousand-year-old mattress.

Keep in mind that that particular circle of hell I stayed in that night, Saint Cloud, Minnesota, is crammed full of fraternity boys, gun nuts, and paranoid survivalist Christians—not an easy crowd for my first real headlining gig. Besides, it was my sixth town in eight nights. Since I had left Denver the week before, I played Cheyenne and Caspar, Wyoming, North Platte, Nebraska, and LaCrosse, Wisconsin. I crossed the Mississippi, all the way to Dickinson, North Dakota, before finding my way back to South Central Minnesota. Today's plan involved getting back to my apartment in that Denver suburb, sleeping for most of two and a half days, finding time to get the Toyota's oil changed, and then setting out for Tucson for a week-long stint as the feature act at Crazy Geri's Comedy Club.

So why do I put myself through all this?

Well, that's a long story.

Ever since I moved to the Denver area, I did everything I could to advance my career as a stand-up comedian and get to a place every comedian in New Mexico, Texas, Wyoming, Arizona, and Colorado wanted to be: a regular at Pancho Pilot's there in downtown. I moved into town on a Wednesday, arriving in Aurora, about half an hour west of the city's core, and checked into the Super 8, the place I would make my home for the next five days. By eight fifteen that night, I stood on the stage at Wits End, this B club out in Westminster, kicking out the seven one-liners I wrote in the car on the drive up from Albuquerque. Two of them hit pretty hard, three of them did so-so, and two just fell flat.

Still, that morsel of success left me stoked, especially considering the whole situation had me frightened, nervous, fatigued, and out of my element. Besides, my audience that night, like those of ninety-nine percent of the open-mic shows, included mostly other comics and their entourages, half of them drunken girlfriends.

But I kept at it. Within six months, offers for paying gigs came in pretty steadily. Usually, they involved one-nighters in dinky-assed bars in small Colorado towns like Montrose, Pueblo, and Greely, or the Denver suburbs like Broomfield and Littleton. After a year, though, I made the rounds pretty damned steadily and secured feature gigs in Wyoming, Iowa, North and South Dakota, and Arizona. I got booked in all these piddly-assed New Mexico towns like Raton, Farmington, and Las Vegas, hitting each two or three times a year. I even worked as far away as Amarillo, Tucson, and, of course, Albuquerque and its satellites, Podunk places like Rio Rancho, Los Lunas, Las Cruces, Tucumcari, Truth or Consequences, and Socorro.

When the schedule allowed, I hit the amateur, open-mic shows at Pancho Pilot's, just to keep my name on the radar over there. The more I worked, the more I made a name for myself, the more momentum I gained, and the tighter and more forceful my act got. Within fourteen and half months of my uprooting from Albuquerque's North Valley, I had built up enough steam to quit my job waiting tables at the Olive Garden and support myself with the comedy alone. Half the time, promoters, bookers, club owners, and other comedians called me, practically begging me to come out to play their particular Palookavilles. I didn't need to hustle for bookings nearly as much and could concentrate on developing material.

I paid rent, bought groceries, and had a lot of fun. Perhaps even more important, however, the success and the constant exposure to laughter meant that, for the first time since seventh grade, I was happy.

And I got so much more comfortable performing. I had two hours, maybe even a hundred and fifty minutes, of rock-solid stuff. I learned how to handle hecklers, how to grab the audience as soon as I stepped on stage, and how, if I lost them, to get them back. People say doing comedy is the hardest job ever, but you learn the tricks.

Then, just a couple of weeks before I headed out for the mini-tour of the Midwest, I was just standing there in the back of Pancho Pilot's, not doing anything really. I leaned against the wall and sipped a ginger ale, waiting for my buddy Phil Fletcher to get on stage and do his five minutes so we can hit another show on the other side of town. Part of me was really jazzed because when we walked into this place I swore to myself that I was only doing totally fresh stuff, jokes I had written over the last few days. Once I got on that stage, I let loose about how I kept going to the gym, how my body was ripped like a pair of old jeans, and how I had just spent ninety-three minutes on the stair-stepper— because I couldn't get the damned thing turned on. I told about how I had girlfriends coming out of the woodwork, and sometimes I felt bad that I nailed them in there. I even told a story about how I dated an older woman, this lady in her forties, who wore grannie panties that came up to the waist.

"Those things used to gross me out," I said. "But watching her get out of them? My dick got harder than a Navajo spelling test."

What can I say? I was a hit.

So I was standing there under the spotlight, just soaking up the laughter. I assumed I'd done like three, maybe four minutes. That's what it felt like. I let loose with another punchline, and as everyone's laughing, I check my watch. It turned out I'd been up there for eight, twice my allotted time. How time flies, you know? I finished up with a one-liner and hurried off, fully believing that the owner and manager are back there in the shadows fuming. Going over your time— especially at an upscale joint like Pancho's—gives the managers just one more reason to go psycho on you and write you off forever.

So leaning there against the back wall, I watched the crowd. Didn't even pay attention to the jokes. That's when Schulman, this dweeb of an assistant manager, who's all stooped over and looks like he weighs about thirty-seven pounds, comes on over and tells me Harrod, the owner, wants to see me. Of course, I was like a thousand percent sure the honcho's going to ream me out for going so long. So the weasel, all pissed-off looking, walked me up the stairs, down a hallway, rapped on the door, flung it open, and left. Inside, Harrod's all intent on this television monitor showing what's happening on stage. My first thought was that if he comes at me I'll just tell him he can eat my shorts. I'd say I didn't get the light at the proper time, and it's Schulman's fault. But I caught myself and determined I really needed to play it cool. I'd worked too damned hard and too damned long to break into his regular line-up.

Harrod said, "Just a sec, just a short sec," like he didn't even care who just walked in. He's this tall, thin guy with a pencil-thin mustache that I am sure he dyes with shoe polish about every four hours. He had on a loose sweater, ironed jeans, and polished, pointy-toed cowboy boots. He kept watching the comedian on his monitor and put his hand to his mouth, like he just burped or something. After a few seconds, he glanced over and his eyes go wide, like he just recognized his old friend or something. He didn't ask me to sit down. He lanced the air with his finger, like he's trying to stall until he thinks of the right word. I told him I was sorry I went over my time.

He didn't seem to understand, then came back with, "Oh, that. Oh, that. Don't you go worrying about that. I told them to keep you up there a little longer."

He held out an open hand like he was carrying a tray in front of him. He smiled.

"Ya see," he said, "I need comedians like you. Fresh. Original. I don't need these sex jokes and jokes about airplanes and traveling and just breaking up with the girlfriend. Tired of all that, ya see?"

It turns out that he wanted to put me in the feature rotation, which means that, with any luck, I'd soon be opening for some of the biggest marquee players in the business: Louis C.K., Steven Wright, Jake Johansen, Brian Regan, Paula Poundstone, or Chris Rock. Who knows where things could take off from there?

"Truth is, ya see," he said. "Don't have a spot for you. Not just yet. Right now we're reworking the schedule, ya see? But when I get one, Schulman'll give you a call. Make sure he can reach you. I need people I can count on. If I can't count on you, it doesn't really matter how much firepower you got, you're not playing at Pancho Pilot's. I need comics I can depend on, ya see?"

I told him I lived right there in Denver, so that shouldn't be a problem.

He told me that he runs a classy joint, that he wanted me in a coat and tie. I told him I didn't have a coat and tie. He told me to run down to the mall and fix myself up. He assured me the investment will pay off.

We shook hands, and I left that office thinking that my big break is on its way. All I gotta do is wait. And upgrade my wardrobe.

Now, as I jet along on that dark highway behind the Tonka Toy of a truck, I remind myself of all this. I race up another hill, and my chin drops to my chest. I snap myself awake, and I blink, and I keep an eye on the white convex tank back. I blink again, and the truck takes a bump in the road, and the ladder shudders. The loose aluminum shakes again, and then the rig hits another bump. I fixate on the shadows between the rungs, and the striated tubes become something like orthodontic braces on eighteen-inch teeth. I fight to keep my eyelids open, and as

I stare ahead, the two triangles at the top become the fringe of bright orange hair, waving in the breeze. My head drops again.

When I reopen, before me is a clown face, twelve feet across, its bulbous cheeks accenting the broad smile, the sinister and laughing eyes wide and taunting, staring me down. I shake my head, rub my eyes, and the face fades, becoming the back of the bowser once more. I drive on, and the ladder again morphs itself into a tin grin, the face returns, and the mouth opens and discharges a laugh. A deep, guttural, elongated, and merciless cackle. I pound my forehead with the heel of my palm until that thing in front of me becomes a liquid transport once more. Seconds later, the face of evil is back teasing me, braying, as if making fun of my fatigue. My chin falls to my chest.

All goes dark.

I lift my head off the steering wheel and open my eyes. My car sits on the soft sand of a hillside with a cloud of dust curling and dissipating before the headlights. I kill the engine. I step out, inspect the area. I rub my eyes. My thighs and chest throb with adrenaline. The passenger-side tire sits at the lip of an eighty-foot drop, an incline of maybe fifty degrees, and for a split second the scenario appears before me: the Toyota veering off the road, down the incline, gaining speed as it falls, tumbling over on its roof with me inside. My breath leaves me, gushing out in one big whoosh. I fall to my knees, there on the sand, and try to breathe regularly again, contemplating how I came within inches and seconds of landing smack dab in the middle of a gully full of rocks and weeds with five hundred tons of Japanese metal on top of me. I ask myself what the hell I think I am doing with my life.

Once I catch my breath, I yank down my zipper, pull out my dong, and wiz off the slope, the stream arcing down and splashing a pile of rocks. I shake off, pack the thing back in its nest, reenter the vehicle, slam the door, and fire it up. It takes a while to get the thing out of the sand. I have to jut ahead, ram the gear shift into reverse, step on the gas, and repeat the process. When I do finally get rolling down the road again, I find a tiny ranch road, turn off it, drive to the side, and kill the engine. I remove the passenger seat cover to use as a blanket, shove aside the cooler and Taco Bell wrappers, and curl up in the back. I sleep for three hours, maybe a little longer. I wake just as the sun peeks over the horizon. I take what is left of the ginger ale, drizzle some of it on my toothbrush, and squeeze a little Colgate on top of it. I brush, rinse with the high-fructose corn syrup solution, start the car, and drive back out to the highway.

The rest of the way, until I finally drag myself up the two flights of stairs to my apartment at about six thirty, I have a long talk with myself.

I wonder if the whole comedy thing is worth the trouble. I pay six hundred dollars a month for a studio apartment that I use maybe, just maybe, eight days a month. My life is simply too unstable to support consistent relationships, so that leaves the prospect of a girlfriend pretty much out of the question. Too often I find myself drinking way too much tequila, too much beer, and smoking way too much pot— sometimes before the show, but almost always after. Then there are those nights when the headliner offers me cocaine. I decide it's time to go easier on myself. I will only work paying feature and headlining gigs in Denver, Tucson, Amarillo, and Albuquerque—places I can drive to in half a day—and cancel all the rest. I don't care who gets pissed off. Then, over the coming months, I will finally put together my photography portfolio and finish my bachelor's degree. I'll apply at the University of Denver, the University of Colorado up in Boulder, and Colorado State in Fort Collins. Maybe even the University of New Mexico.

I figure that if any one of those places accepts me, I can probably squeeze by on student loans and the money I make headlining. Then, when Harrod finally calls and puts me in the permanent rotation over there at Pancho Pilot's, I can go off whatever direction that takes me.

I simply cannot kill myself like this anymore.

NICHOLS

Most mornings? The bleating of the clock radio scratched deep into my core. Lying there in the dark, I covered my head with my hands as the dehydration and fuzzy brain—the result of too much whiskey the night before—compounded the agony.

Once I mustered enough energy to lift myself up and swing my legs over the side of the bed? I just sat in my shorts with my elbows on my knees. There I stayed, looking down at the threadbare carpet, as though it were an abyss opening up before me. I saw my face reflected in the ripples as black as used motor oil. I imagined what would happen if things continued on the established course. Losing the Silver Dollar meant losing the house, and that would ruin my credit pretty much forever. Chances were that never again could I drive a nice car or live in a place I could call my own. Just to stay alive? I would have to beg some kid with a trust fund and a fresh MBA diploma for a job. For the privilege of earning minimum wage plus tips for slogging cheap lager and cheaper bourbon over to ignorant old bikers or, worse yet, toothless old truckers.

Some mornings, I perched there on that mattress, staring at that floor for four or five minutes. Other times? Ten or fifteen. Maybe twenty or thirty. Who the hell knows?

I went through this every day. For months. For years, really. By the end of it all, I was already seven house payments behind. My insurance guy? The one who used to be my golf partner? First he cut me some slack, letting me pay a week late here, two or three weeks late there. Eventually? He cancelled the policy on my car, then the one on the house, and finally, the one on the bar. Then he stopped talking to me.

Morning after morning, as I sat there prodding myself into being courageous for just another day, more horror scenes played themselves out before me. I saw myself moving into a one-bedroom there in the War Zone, over in the Southeast Heights, out where all the tweakers, winos, junkies, and marijuanos feel most at home, for whatever reason. I saw myself walking out to my car, late for work as usual, knotting my necktie. Then, just as I get to my numbered parking space, some methhead stumbles across the street and asks for ride to the Allsup's, McDonald's, or some food pantry. Wherever those folks go.

Had I been in this situation before? You bet your sweet ass.

I saw it happening all over again. I saw myself coming home at two thirty in the morning, exhausted, my feet aching. I saw myself collapsing on the couch and having another snort or two—just to decompress. I saw myself slurping Ramen noodles out of an aluminum pan and watching infomercials about the Shamwow!, this superabsorbent towel; the Abdomizer, a machine guaranteed to give you six-pack abs in two weeks; and the Slap Chop, whatever the hell that thing is. Doing all that for another six or seven years, maybe longer. Suffering and hoping against hope that I could one day pull together enough scratch to buy another chance in the batter's box. Or maybe even starting over in some other line of work. At my age.

Where was I? Hanging on the lip of disaster, digging my fingernails into the cliff's edge, trying to keep from falling a long, long way down.

Then what happens? Mark shows up.

What does he do? He churns out four of the best performances in the history of stand-up comedy, stuff that was as good as anything I ever saw live, on television, or on video. Doesn't charge me a cent. By doing so, he waves his magic wand and transforms Nichols' Silver Dollar into this little gold mine. Not only that, but he creates this wind tunnel that sucks all of us along and makes all the Albuquerque comics—every last one of them—ten times better than they ever hoped they could be. I mean, suddenly I am thinking that these guys I couldn't stand to watch just a few months before, people like Black Tom, Mica Pierson, Jana Boan—even Firecracker Rael—bloom with real *Tonight Show* potential.

So two weeks after Mark's show, because I have some real capital to work with, I put up another night of showcases, this one with Jana Boan and Jamie Jupiter co-headlining. I figure this'll bring in all the lesbos. And why not? Their money's just as good as anyone else's.

Those shows? They're not the stellar performances Mark turned in, but still pretty damned good. And the showroom? Packed to the rafters. I could have sold mezzanine seats. That night? After we get the place cleared out and swept, once the chairs are stacked on the tables so that Timothy can come through with a mop in the morning, Cyn plops down the zippered canvas bag of cash for me to drop off at the bank on the way home. So I scoot a barstool in front of the bank of beer taps. Pour three fingers of Johnnie Walker Black into my coffee cup. I hoist myself up and sit. I rub my eyes. There I am: numbed, fatigued, relieved, scared, sleep-deprived, and drunk—with whiskey and gratitude. I'm still unable to fully process what just happened. For the first time in my life? I sit atop a mountain of cash.

All this momentum? It won't last forever. Twenty-seven years of working in the trenches tells me that. So the task before me? To harness all that energy. To direct it, to steer it, to orchestrate all the sources so that they flow together, so they enhance each other. What am I thinking? Albuquerque's time has come. The best way to make things happen? Tape a television show right there in that space, in that converted banquet room. That's a no-brainer.

So Monday I come in the back door just after six a.m., my bones still buzzing from everything that happened the last few weeks, everything that's still happening, and everything that might happen. I throw on the lights and right away catch the spots and streaks caked into the sheen on the floor, stuff that tells me, once again, Timothy didn't sweep thoroughly before he mopped. Stuff like that? Brings you back to reality. I unlock my office, fire up the laptop, and lug it over to my spot there by the waitress station where I like to work. I rinse out my coffee mug with a shot from the soda gun and pour myself four fingers of Crown Royal. I figure I can work there, at least until Cyn drags over the first bucket of ice and dumps it into the stainless steel bin.

So I go at it for four, maybe five hours. I check out websites, list phone numbers and emails, make phone calls, and chase dead ends. Just before noon, some clanking and shuffling comes from the kitchen—noise that tells me that my crew chief came in five minutes late this time, ten minutes earlier than I expected. As I leave a message on some distant voicemail, Cyn comes out of the kitchen, holding a rack full of fresh pint glasses. She's got two braids sticking out the sides of her head, like she woke that morning hell-bent on looking like a parody of the farmer's daughter—with shiny, blue-black hair. I give her a double-take but don't tell her she looks ridiculous. I tell her she needs to sweep the corners and under the bar, and then give the whole floor the once-over with a mop to take care of Timothy's sloppy job. I tell her that I need to concentrate. I'll be in my office if anybody needs me. And nobody better need me unless some madman runs in with an ax and starts hacking the joint to pieces.

What am I so laser-focused on? I'm calling up agents, comedians, bar owners, lawyers—anyone I can think of—trying to figure out how to a get a television special taped right there at Nichols' Silver Dollar.

That's my routine for the next fifteen, twenty days—Saturdays and Sundays included. Checking websites, calling agents, calling television stations.

Then one day it's like two fifteen, maybe two thirty in the afternoon. My blood sugar takes this plunge, and my mind is mush. I rock in my chair and yawn. The remnant of a Camel filter smolders in the ash tray. My phone buzzes, and I take a gulp of Maker's Mark. I don't have the energy to answer. All these false starts and broken promises for return calls have eaten away at my enthusiasm. The phone sings again, and this time I pick it up, check the number, and activate. On the other end? Some raspy-voiced guy going on about how he works for TVOntario, some midmarket station out of Toronto. The guy coughs, yells instructions to one of his underlings, comes back to me, and asks about Wladika. I tell him about Marison. He wants to know about Wladika. I tell him Marison has the whole package: boyish good looks, great stage presence, killer material, youthful vivaciousness, and a wild mind. That he's headed for the big time.

He asks about Wladika.

After about twenty, twenty-five minutes? I reach up, switch on my reading lamp, and fish a legal pad out of my desk drawer. We hammer out details for a deal. In two weeks, Marison will take the stage, and over the course of two nights, I record three sets. I will take the best moments from each and splice them together into an hour-long set and ship the finished disc off to Canada. If the Ontario bigshot likes what he sees—which he will—and if the video production meets his standards, he'll edit it down to forty-one minutes and run it as an hour-long special, leaving time for commercials and station identification. Marison and I get fifteen hundred dollars to split, plus three percent of the revenue from commercials for me to distribute however I see fit. If the show flies like we both think it will? Then we film shows featuring Mica, Fletcher, Boan, and Jupiter—with anyone I choose to anoint.

Just as I am about to hang up, he's gotta add the stickler. He wants me to record Wladika—at least on audio—to play on their radio show. I tell him Mark won't let himself be recorded. He says there's some big money to be made, that I need to dangle that particular carrot in front of the boy. I insist the guy won't go for it. He says of course he will, if I pony up enough jack. I tell him Wladika's an odd duck. He tells me to give it a try. I tell him that Wladika is scheduled to play the Silver Dollar the next month. Just to get him off the phone, I tell him I'll test the waters.

Just think of what this could do for Albuquerque, he says. A rising tide lifts all boats and all that tripe.

So I figure that sometimes you just gotta throw your hands in the air and say, "What the fuck," you know?

Then that geriatric Canuck tells me he'll have his secretary email the paperwork by the end of business that day or maybe first thing in the morning. He says I have a week to get the documents signed and faxed back. The line goes dead, and so I replace the receiver in its saddle and rock in my chair. I light another Camel. As I shake out the match, pieces of a new scenario fall into place right before my eyes. Marison becomes a major fixture on the American comedy landscape, and I manage his career. I select his gigs, negotiate his contracts, shield him from the corporate parasites, and eventually get him on *The Tonight Show*. In a year or two or three or four? I retire. To a mansion in the Sandia foothills. A place with a hot tub and a wine cellar. I get to liberate myself from hostile drunks, whiny waitresses, flaky bartenders, unreliable distributors, brain-dead truckers, late nights, and Central Avenue's street trolls. For all eternity.

Suddenly, this big, ripe pomegranate dangles in front of me. I get to pluck it off the tree, but I gotta pluck it the right way and at the right time. All this means that, with my new windfall, I have to build a control booth there in the back of the club. Then use what's left to invest in three new high-definition cameras, two high-powered box speakers that I can put up right on the stage, a new bank of stage lights, a sound mixing board, a Macintosh supercomputer with a high-capacity hard drive, and a two or three person production crew. That afternoon I even go online and order up this super-sturdy, two hundred and thirty dollar microphone stand. This indestructible piece of alloy that is heavy, shiny, and rock-solid, with a weighted iron base. Something Neanderthals like Black Tom and Mica Pierson can't destroy too easily.

Shelling out the cash for the renovation? That's the only logical choice, even if it means putting off other things that desperately need taking care of. Stuff like a new deep fryer. Like ripping out and replacing the bar lighting and the ancient stage lights. Like paying my insurance. Not to mention getting my house out of foreclosure.

What's another three weeks living in full-tilt-crisis mode?

Besides, I know that Marison has the goods. With a little wisdom, a little luck—and if I play my cards the right way—he'll be the next sit-com phenom. The kid had a genuine, honest-to-God shot at stardom. Deep in my soul, I know it might be his only one. If I wait another month, the opportunity might not be there.

Sometimes all you get is one shot.

JACK

After the audition, I leave my name and number with the long-hair at the front table, go down the stairs, push open the door, and walk out to the brick mall of uptown Albuquerque, looking for Phil Fletcher, who was three slots ahead of me. My phone buzzes in my pocket, and I think it's him. I lift my sunglasses, take a look, and don't recognize the number. The guy on the other end asks if I am Jack Marison, but before I can answer, he says his name is Nichols. He says he gave me his card when we met at Laffs about ten thousand years before. He says he thinks I'm just about the best comedian the city's got going. I stop in front of this vegan food store called The Raw Deal, and I tell him I moved to Denver about a million years ago, so his facts are off. He says he has some guy from a Canadian radio and television station all fired up about the local scene, and that he wants me to headline his showcase.

I know about Nichols. Every comic within a million mile radius of downtown Albuquerque is familiar with that slug. Jana Boan claims that Nichols once paid her in eggrolls. She told me he promised her two hundred dollars for thirty minutes, and when they ended up with only four audience members, all he would do was cover the price of the appetizers she ordered. But I decide to hear what he has to say, just in case the Angel Gabriel appeared to him and infused him with wisdom. You never know.

So just before three that afternoon, I swing open the heavy door and walk into that dark downtown armpit of a bar. In front of the waitress station sits this guy with his gut spilling out over his pants and looking all sad and stooped over. He shoves a pill in his mouth and gulps something out of a stained Disneyland coffee mug, swallows, and grimaces, revealing a dark spot where an incisor used to be. He jots calculations on a notepad and punches numbers into a computer. He wipes his lips with his hand, but they stay wet anyway. He sees me, and he gets all excited, like I'm the Second Coming.

He tells me to sit down and asks if I want anything, so I say I'll take a Coors. He says a classy guy like me can do better than Colorado pisswater, so he hustles out to the back cooler and fetches me a Sheaf Stout, this bottle of Australian mud so thick and bitter I practically have to chew it. I call it the espresso of bottled beer and say that if he wants me to consume that kind of muck he'll have to provide the knife and fork, so I can carve off a corner and place it between cheek and gum. He just about doubles over with forced laughter.

What a dope.

I didn't trust the guy right away. After about half an hour, though, I loosen up, figuring, you know, what the hell did I have to lose? I should have known right then and there.

The long and short of it is that some guy from Winnipeg or Montreal or someplace Up North wants Nichols to film a showcase over three nights. The plan: Jupiter and Firecracker do ten minutes each, just to prime the crowd. Then I come up and do an hour. Then we break for thirty minutes before we reassemble and do the exact same show. The next night, I show up in the same clothes and go through another run. Then, on that Sunday, we do it again, just to make sure. Nichols will have four cameras rolling the whole time. Over the following two weeks or so after that, we get together and pick out the best bits of each, make it look like a single outing, and even sweeten the laugh track when we need to. I tell him that won't be necessary.

Then, if Mr. Bigshot Canadian likes what he sees, he takes three copies of the DVDs to his corporate office or wherever and shows them to his overlords. If it passes muster, they do two things. First, they play eight, nine, or ten minute segments taken directly from the Albuquerque show. If the response is good, they run the hour-long version.

I figure that if I do this, I'll have a legitimate TV credit, and the worst that can happen is that my fee for headlining goes up by a thousand dollars a gig, and I become a regular B-club headliner and A-club feature. At best, I become an international comedy star.

Nichols says he wants to do this the last three days of July. He says that the camera crew is ready, and the equipment has been rented, and the people at TVOntario are up against a deadline.

I take a long slow sip of toxic sludge and hold it in my mouth, just to give myself a little more time. I rub my upper lip, thinking things over. It looks like a good solid step in the right direction, and when opportunity knocks and all that. We shake on it.

The next day, I'm in my car, shooting up Interstate 25 to do a one-nighter in Casper, Wyoming, and getting kind of excited about the television show—*my* television show. I reach behind the passenger seat, into the ice chest in the back, and fish out a cola.

I head toward Raton Pass, right there on the interstate a few miles south of the state line, when I catch red sparkling in my rearview mirror. I slow the vehicle and groan. Behind me, the lights on a state police car go all spastic, headlights flashing, cherry tops flickering, like they're trying to give me a seizure. I ease the Toyota to the shoulder, but before I can set the parking brake, the trooper shoots by, on his way to some real emergency. As adrenaline seeps into my muscles, I catch something buzzing in the compartment. My automatic thought is that something is wrong with the car's engine—again. I wait for an eighteen-wheeler to pass, then shoot out to the roadway and switch on the cruise control when the vibration comes again. Then I get it. It's just my cell phone buzzing against the pennies and nickels in the ashtray. I flip open my phone without checking the number.

On the other end is Schulman, that hunchback manager from Pancho Pilot's. He clears his throat and says they've got a slot for me. I tell him that's terrific, and I ask when. Wouldn't you know it? He says the last week in July. I tell him I can't, that I'm filming my television special that weekend. I repeat "*my* television special," just to be an asshole. Besides, I say, I haven't bought a suit yet, and it looks like I don't need to. He says "okay" and hangs up without saying goodbye. I drive on, thinking I really didn't need Pancho Pilot's after all.

Like I said, what a dope.

MICA

So Jamie Jupiter totally has her hands all balled up inside the sleeves of her tattered G.I. Joe jacket. She stands, all shivering and everything, there in the corner of the brick recess, next to the glass door of a lawyer's office. After she got off work, that wacked girl came all the way downtown on her motor scooter, like she thought it would be all warm and sunny by then. Like she expected the monsoons would all magically evaporate or something. Like she never noticed that it had already been raining on and off for two days and the streets were still all shiny with puddles and everything.

About an hour earlier, Phil Fletcher and I met Jamie here, outside Nichols' Silver Dollar, and took our places pretty close to the double doors. Now, the line snakes along in front of that biker bar I won't go into, a coffee and pastry shop, an Irish pub, and a few other various and sundry places here in the downtown. Jamie holds her sleeves to her mouth, and I swear they cover three-quarters of her face. She says something I can't make out through the muffling, and so I point at my ear and lean in, and she asks again if I see any sign of Jana. I step out in the middle of the sidewalk and look eastward, toward the train tracks, at that blue-grey curtain of clouds that shreds itself over the Sandia Mountains.

Here on this cold summer evening, you got all these puddles all over the Fourth Street Mall, with lines of neon reflecting on the water surface and everything. The place like totally crawls with people, something you don't usually see on a Thursday night. Heading my way, looking all official and everything, is this lean black lawyer. At least, I guess she's a counselor or a businesswoman or something because she struts my way looking way serious with those sparkling earrings and pressed collar—and not looking the least bit cold. She has all her raincoat buttons undone and a pink and orange scarf flapping at her breast, dangling there just for decoration. She carries a heavy bag that looks like it's full of gold or something, like she's late to a business meeting that is just too damned important to be put off until Friday. Behind her, this swarthy guy in a graying ski jacket and a soiled baseball cap pushes a shopping cart massively crammed with all kinds of junk, including wads of foil, beer bottles, tearing plastic grocery bags, and even a soiled velveteen rabbit. He waddles up to a trash bin and fishes out a Pepsi can, wipes the top, and shoves it into the heap.

Down on Fourth Street, on the other side of the lines of cars, Albuquerque's Rapid Ride bus chugs across the way, wheezes, stops, and the doors open, dumping out even more bodies. I search through the mess, examine the street corners and an alleyway over by Lindy's Diner. That's when Jana appears way in the distance, all intent on what she carries—this cardboard tray with four cups lodged in it, with steam escaping through tiny holes in the lids. I tell Jamie not to worry. The woman she cannot live without for two seconds just came down the sidewalk and is on the other side of the street, leaning out over the curb and waiting for a line of motorcycles to cruise by before she crosses. Jamie calls me a jerk, tells me she can live without Jana but not without her vanilla mocha latte. I shiver there in my denim jacket while Jana takes her sweet time. The guy in line next to me, some oversized construction-worker type in with his sleeves rolled tight against his tattooed arms, tells me that Albuquerque summers are not supposed to be so cold. I tell him that maybe he should have worn something besides just a T-shirt when he saw purple clouds barreling over the mountains. He rolls his eyes, turns his gargantuan back to me, and huffs out loud, like I just insulted him or something.

I let a few seconds pass, and once his mood evens out and everything, I try to break the tension by asking him what we were thinking when we got into the line a full seventy minutes before the doors opened and everything. He tugs the bill of his cap, shoves his hands in his pockets, and turns, looking up the street like he's expecting someone. After a second, his whole demeanor softens, and he asks if I ever had the pleasure of seeing Wladika perform before.

"Yuppers," I say. "The man like doles out the most ingenious hilarity I ever saw."

I tell him how I'm a comedian, and how Wladika hand-picked me to emcee a Tucson show, and how that was my first professional spot. I say that even when he's not performing, Wladika hooks me up with all kinds of gigs. He even put me and three friends on the guest list for tonight.

When Jana gets close enough, I hustle over to her ask which cup's mine, and as I work it out of its slot, she tells me to calm down. It's not so cold that I have to get all freaked out and everything. I tell her that she's lucky to be born hot-blooded. I say that once we get inside, I'll need to sit in front of the hand dryer in the washroom and point the nozzle at my chest for about thirty minutes, just to work off that chill.

I never expected August to be so cold. She tells me to look around. People are wandering the streets in shorts and sneakers. I tell her I don't care. I am still totally freezing and everything.

I hold my paper cup with both hands and take a sip when Phil raps me on the elbow. At first, I think it's an accident. So I take another hit of cocoa and look out across the long line of people snaking all the way down past the KiMo Theatre, the Irish pub, and around the corner. Phil leans in and whispers something to me that I can't quite make out, and so I tell him it can wait. This might be the last time we get to see Wladika before he escalates to national status. He says it again, and the sounds jumble around in my brain before taking on some semblance of cohesion. Boan and Jupiter, he tells me, will hold our places. Besides, we're pretty much guaranteed radical seats up front, anyway. We have at least another ten minutes before the doors open, another half an hour before the show starts, and another twenty minutes after that before Mark takes the stage.

I turn away, but he taps my shoulder, waves me on, tells me to follow him. I do, and he excuses himself, stepping between some guy in a sport coat and his wife, who's wearing this red and turquoise shawl. We go down the wet sidewalk, duck behind the building, down into an alley. He looks over his shoulder before he steps behind a dumpster by this brick wall where we can tuck ourselves away, out of any passerby's view. He lifts the flap of his shirt pocket and produces this joint that is stuffed so tight and rolled so fat it looks like it could give birth at any second.

"Know what this is?" he whispers as he looks out to the street and then leans in toward me. "This is a massive dosage of Sour Diesel, government grade marijuana, some of the most explosive shit ever produced—by amateurs, professionals, the U.S. government, or Stanford grad students."

I ask where he got it, and he says that's the good thing about working the road with national acts. I must look totally catatonic or something because then he's like, "Well? Want some?"

I am like all, "Totally, dude."

An ambulance siren wails down Central Av, brown water pours off the roof spout, and a junkie stumbles by, screaming that he'll kick someone's ass. I wait, all rubbing my shoulders and shivering. Phil looks for cops, turns his back to the breeze, puts the doobie between his lips, strikes up a flame, and cups it with his hand. He takes the first long and healthy hit, presses a knuckle to his mouth, and holds the joint out to me. He scopes out the street action once more.

After four rounds, I swear I am zig-zagging through the ionosphere. I blink, and Phil just about goes all wavy and fuzzy. Acid churns in my stomach, and I get all woozy and everything so that I have to lean in the corner just to stay upright. The guy draws close, says something to me that I don't understand. I laugh and he laughs. We each have another hit. Again, Phil says something I can't quite get. So I nod anyway, giggle some more, and we go back around the building, through this maze of bodies, where we work our way through the crowd and finally find Jana and Jamie just as the doors open.

At the main showroom, the hostess leads us down to the front table, but I have to keep my eyes pasted on Jamie's back just so I don't get lost walking down the carpeted aisle. I can barely feel the tips of my fingers or my feet hitting the floor as I walk. I choke back more laughter and try to look straight. I swear, I have never been so tripping in all my life.

NICHOLS

What did I do? I hanged myself, that's what.

Just as Barry Bass got to his closing bit, I slipped into the control booth, a little Dewar's White Label with a dash of Drambuie in my cup. What they call a rusty nail. There I am, nestled between those walls, staring up at this sound board and then back down to the dark screen of the Macintosh computer that could easily—when activated—preserve every nuance of sound coming from the showroom and the strength and duration of each burst of laughter picked up by three microphones.

All I have to do is reach over, flip a little switch, and suddenly everything—Mark's jokes, as well as the laughter of three hundred and nineteen happy guests—gets preserved as a digital audio file. If I set my mug there on the shelf, right in front of the recorder, in exactly the right spot? It blocks the light that announces to the whole damned room that a recording is in progress. Who'll know the difference?

What will that do? Two things. First, it provides me with a high-quality—and very marketable—recording of Mark's act. Second, it buys me time. It means I can send a sample to the people over at TVOntario, to keep those guys quiet for a while. Then I can sit down with Wladika, get Canada on conference call, and we can double-team him. Show him in cold, hard figures the kind of money we're poised to pull in. I can spell out in precise terms how, over the course of a year or so, we could both become millionaires. How do I know I can reason with him? Because every man has his price. There's no drug more powerful than greed. History tells us that.

The obvious next step? I position the mug so that it blocks that little magenta light, if and when it should ever get illuminated. Then, just as the applause dies, Black Tom bounds up to the stage to reannounce the drink specials. And I'm thinking, *Sometimes you just gotta say "What the fuck."* Don't ask me what possessed me to do what I did.

I reach down and press the switch.

Diodes blink. The computer screen glows, and the lights on the graphic equalizer jump into action.

And we are recording.

Up on the stage, Black Tom says that Pabst bottles are two-fifty, well drinks are three, pints of Marble Red Ale are four, and forgets to mention kamikazes are three-fifty. He asks the crowd if they are ready for the headliner, and the place erupts in hoots, applause, cheers, and whistles. He asks again, and this time the walls and floor shudder so violently the lights actually go out for a split second. From where I stand there in the back of the room, the stage is blocked by this forest of dark bodies. A line of youngsters stands, whooping it up, clapping, screaming, and cawing. One guy actually stands on his chair, pumping his fist. Under normal circumstances? I'd get in his face, yell at him to keep his damned feet off my furniture. Tonight? I let it go.

Mark removes the microphone from its saddle, puts my new mic stand behind him, scoots the barstool to his side, and tells everyone to settle down.

Right by my side? My cup sits exactly where it is supposed to be, the red bud of a light shooting directly into it, like it's boring a hole through the ceramic. A new vision dances through my head: the cover of Wladika's one and only comedy CD, his face in silhouette emblazoned on the front. I'm thinking an honest-to-goodness, high-quality recording of the work of the best comedian since Richard Pryor.

Then the whole damned downtown complex shakes with all the laughter pouring out of that room.

Things swim along just fine. Mark says he comes from a dysfunctional family. He tells us that his first pet was a tequila worm. He talks about how his kid sister has three children—from five different fathers. How last Christmas his mom comes up to him and says, "Do you care if my boyfriend spends the night?" and he tells her, "I don't, but Dad's gonna be pissed." How one Christmas Eve his nephew, an eighth grader, was falling down drunk, and the kid should know better because he's twenty-seven years old. He hits us with another and then another and then another. Soon, the spasms shooting through my whole upper body have me pretty much incapacitated, doubled over, laughing and coughing at the same time. Then what do I do? That's right. I instinctively reach over, take hold of the cup, and gulp some of that high-class swill. Mark sees the light immediately.

That's when he goes batshit crazy.

MICA

After his first set of jokes, Mark takes a long pull off his pint of milk stout, sets the glass on the stool right next to him, lets the laughter subside, then goes headlong into a bit about being adopted. Ever since he came on stage like seven minutes before, he has totally owned every nanosecond of the performance. He tells about how one day he walked into the house without closing the door, and his mother is all like, "What, were you born in a barn?" And he was all like, "Actually, it was behind a dumpster."

He tells how his parents never sang "Happy Birthday" when they brought him his cake. It was always "How Much is That White Kid in the Window?" He goes into the act-out, and Jana leans against my shoulder and laughs so forcefully she practically shakes the concrete floor. Mark launches into another set-up line, but before he gets to the punch, he goes stiff as a mannequin.

I am still loopy from Phil's genetically engineered weed and expect another of Mark's robot routines. The room falls dead silent with anticipation. Mark looks to the back corner of the room, over by the control booth, and his lips part. He cocks his head, and his whole arm goes limp, his hand just hanging there by his thigh, squeezing the microphone. He fixates on something behind us, and half the audience even finds that funny. He bites his lip and balls up his fist, and a vein bulges in his neck. He shakes his head, his eyes locked on something in the back.

Jana looks back, searching through the crowd, wondering what Mark finds so arresting. He taps his finger on the shaft of the mic. He grits his teeth. He growls. People laugh. With one swift and mighty blow, he slaps his beer glass off the stool, and it explodes against the brick, the crash echoing like a rifle shot. Shards rattle on the stage, and lines of foam run down the wall. He stands with a hand on his hip, his back to the audience. He whips the microphone away, against the back of the stage. The electronic head slams into the masonry and cracks open, the black screen popping off and a spark flying out from the loose wires, its plastic cone bouncing and rolling into the puddle of beer where it releases another spark and zap, the snap echoing through the room. The lights flicker, and the speakers crackle.

A wave of laughter works its way through the crowd, as though everyone totally wants to believe this is part of the show and everything. There's another bang and a flash before the back lights blink. There stands Mark, a dark figure towering over us. From the depths of his abdomen comes this bellow, this cry. Some sound, some groaning that totally gurgles up through him. It is something primeval and monstrous, this resonant and guttural trembling that begins deep inside him, rises through his torso, and bursts out as a reverberating and commanding roar, as if he's expelling a demon.

He picks up the barstool and holds it by its foot over his head, shaking it like he's leading the charge with a musket. He bares his teeth and screams. He bellows. There he is, with the golden glow of the center spotlight illuminating only the top of his shoulder, the edge of

285

his ear, the vein in his forearm. He roars. Something I can't quite make out. The sounds emanate from deep within his body, sounds that are not real, not human, something unlike I have ever heard.

He rears back, holding the stool's foot with one hand. He swings it upward like a hammer, the whole body reaching and extending, powerful and brutal. The round edge of the hard wooden seat crashing into the center spotlight, sending glass over the front tables. The taut muscles of his body releasing like an iron spring as he pounds the wooden stool into the spotlight, striking again at the fixture of glass and metal. He holds the chair with both hands and pounds again. Flakes of glass, tin, and plastic spray over the front tables, fragments cascading over some woman who covers her head with her hands, over the man who tries to shield her with his body. Someone turns away, shoves himself away from his table. The lights blink again, and the room goes dark.

It is as if some evil spirit has snuck in like smoke through the air vents. There is a carnation burst of sparks on the stage, like a pyrotechnic explosion, and the room is black again. Then, in the dim amber glow of the floor lights, Mark stands at the edge of the stage. He growls. This towering and shadowed presence with lights scintillating behind him, scattered light rays illuminating the round edge of his head, the bulge of his forearm. Then there he is, looming over us, emitting those guttural, resonant, and reverberating sounds. Screaming and holding the microphone stand over his head like it's a log he's hurling off a cliff.

"Get out!" he yells. "Get outta here! Everybody!"

He holds the chrome pole with both hands, swinging it as though it's a broadsword or a baseball bat or something. The iron base crashes through the black metal screen of the speaker, tearing through the cardboard cone. Mark strikes at it again, this time punching a hole through the wooden casing. The cumbersome oak box teeters on its base, pivots, balances on its corner for a second, then tumbles onto the stage, falls end-over-end onto the main floor, crashes, and splits at its seams.

Someone, some shadow, moves up the aisle, toward the back. Another person follows him, then someone else. Then it is a whole torrent of bodies—fraternity boys and young women, guys in cowboy hats, a young man pulling his girlfriend up the aisle, and three gray-haired women—all these people scampering, pushing each other, rushing toward the door, stumbling. Scared. A man falls, rolls out of the way, and scrambles back to his feet. Mark beats at the speaker with the mic stand. Again and again, reducing the box and equipment to splinters and loose wires alive with electrical sparks. Then something, some spirit, some benevolent specter, lifts me out of my chair, to my feet, and it pulls me down the aisle. Then another crash as the ghost pulls me along. I take one last look back behind. There is Mark in silhouette, there at the other end of the stage. With both hands and a thrust of his whole body, he shoves the other speaker box over. It falls off its pedestal, teetering on the stairs, tipping over, falling to the floor. The box cracks open. Smoke issues from its innards.

"Get out of here!" the voice booms, it echoes. "I said get out!"

Using the bent mic stand like sledge hammer, he pounds into the electronic mess. He pulls the alloy pole free and yells again for everyone to get out. Then he is on the main floor, swinging the weapon in wide circles, as though he's clearing a path through jungle brush, herding people toward the door.

"Get out!" he says. "Get the hell out!"

He kicks at a table, one loaded with beer bottles, glasses, and plates of chicken wings and French fries, and it spins across the cement floor and crashes into the wall, the hamburger bun and red onions splashing up, the platter rattling against the wall. Food platters and liquor skid across the painted concrete. He bends at the knees, grips the edge of a large table, and whips it over. He turns over another. He raises the mic stand, threatening.

"Get out," Mark growls. "I said get out."

He takes a solid oak table, this unit made for eight people, and with one swift, fluid, and deft motion, slams it against the wall, the metal base banging and echoing. Its solid wooden top careens against the cinder block, its corner cracking and splintering, the screws in the metal base tearing themselves from the wood. Another beer glass crashes and disintegrates against the masonry. Tendrils of liquid trail down the brick.

"Get out," Mark says. "I said get the hell out."

I stumble, fall, but catch myself. Something crashes behind me. The air smells like burning electrical casing. I merge with the crowd, tripping out toward the aisle, finding Jamie Jupiter's back through blackness and smoky air. Phil grips my shirt, trying to follow me because he is still every bit as high as I am. Jana guides us, leading us along through the mass of people, toward the exit. I feel along the wainscoting, and someone, something, pushes me forward. It is the crowd, that single and sentient entity that is this fusion of people, moving me, absorbing me, propelling me toward the exit.

"Get out," Mark says from far behind me. "Everyone get the hell out."

Then I am panting in that moist August night. I lean against the brick and cover my eyes with my hands. A breeze cools my face and neck. Pounding shakes the walls of the club. More screams. Something crashes, something shatters, and glass breaks. Another hammer blow rattles the concrete. My head still spins, the space around me undulates, and I close my eyes. My stomach churns, and gasses and acids bubble up through my esophagus, and I brace a shoulder against something solid, I don't know what, to steady myself and lean over. My stomach tightens, like I am going to retch. I look up. There we are, outside. Two or three hundred of us. Maybe more. Scores of people milling around the open glass doors. People spilling off the sidewalk, out into the street, between the parked cars. All those shocked faces. Those scared people. Nobody knowing what to think. Then there are arms on my shoulder. It is Phil, who pushes me, leads me, steers me back to our concrete recess, to the storefront, to the dark glass door of a lawyer's office. I hold my head.

There, I close my eyes, place a hand flat against the wall, and try to regain my balance. I am still tripping so damned hard.

The next time I look up, the police have arrived. Out on the sidewalk in front of the club's entrance, an officer, a petite blonde, commands some unshaven youngster in a V-neck to stand back, at least three feet from the yellow caution tape that's been put up. One moment the sergeant is with the crowd, holding up her hand, shouting that they need to disperse. When I look again, she's talking to Jude Nichols, the club owner, who squeezes his forehead as his cheeks redden again. She's this five-foot-nothing sergeant with her hair pulled tight and tucked up under her cap. I rub my eyes and try to see straight, just for a second. Over on the other side, by the glass office door, Jana whimpers, and Jamie cups the girl's face with both hands and stares straight in her eyes, whispers something, and wipes something off Jana's cheek. Jana covers her face with her hand and cries into Jamie's shirt.

When I turn back around, there, standing in front of me, is that officer, that blonde sergeant, with her shiny badge, her gun strapped to her side, handcuffs hanging off her belt. She looks over the crowd, then back to me. A siren moans in the distance, and she searches my face for evidence of something, as if she wonders what I've been up to. More pounding comes from inside Nichols' place, and when she turns back to me, she lifts a finger, ready to point, as if accusing me of something. I'm all like, "Whoa, there, girl." I am like totally positive she can smell the marijuana on my shirt and everything. I'm all like, "Mark Wladika? Like I hardly know the dude." And she's all like everybody says the two of you are like totally friends and everything, and I take off my glasses and rub my face with both hands and try not to breathe in her direction. I'm all like, "Nopers, man. I just like met the guy once. We just came for the show. Like I hardly even know the outpatient."

FIRECRACKER

Absolutely, positively, totally, categorically, one hundred percent, thoroughly, comprehensively, God-awful. I swear to Mother Quan Yin Herself. I've seen happier faces in abortion clinics. I really have. Watching my grandparents have sex couldn't be more nauseating. In fact, I would have preferred that. Actually preferred that.

Most people there didn't see it. I'll tell you that right now. Mark walked on that stage looking regal as ever. Absolutely elegant. His spine straight, motions so graceful and ever so fluid—that signature lilt in his step—taking the stage the way one is supposed to take it. One thing I learned from that man is that when you begin a comedy show you have to, you absolutely must, take control of the room. It is incumbent upon you to become Princess Grace, striding into the ball and leaving a trail of glitter in your wake. So that people have no choice but to look at you, to be hypnotized by your very presence, your every motion, no matter how microscopic. That's absolutely essential. Confidence—even feigned confidence—needs to exude out of every pore. Absolutely every pore.

That night, Mark went up, took the microphone out of its saddle, and put the pole on the side of the stage, out of the way. As he stepped to the center, under the spotlight, I saw it. Just that little flick of the wrist that sent this longitudinal wave along that black line, that little ripple along the cord, all the way down to where it plugs into the stage.

That just *soooo* set my internal alarms pinging. It absolutely did.

With anyone else, it would not have mattered. Comics do that sort of thing all the time, especially the newcomers. With Mark, however, that was like a major, gigantic, enormous, monstrous, and colossal faux pas. Everything I saw him do for the previous two and a half or three years—however long it was—was just perfect. Picture perfect. He was Vermeer, getting every stroke just right. He was Mozart, following the right note with the right chord with the right blast of orchestration. Mark engineered every modicum and nuance of his performance. Every set-up, every punchline, every tag, every pause and facial expression—everything was razor-honed, absolutely impeccable. So playing with the cord like that? Well, that just announced to me that something was off-kilter. Something, somewhere, was just off. Like four planets were in retrograde.

Then he came unhinged. Absolutely lost his bearings. Right there in front of God and everybody. Just popped his cork. Like nothing I've ever seen. Ever. I swear to Gaia. Totally, absolutely unglued. Just went all Charles Manson as we all watched.

Oh, it took me a while to put all the pieces together. Really. But once this little Firecracker could make sense of it all, I swear, the picture just got uglier than an old fat man in wet whitey-tighties. Early that week, we recorded three of Jack's shows, and we all went there to be part of the performance for this high-quality video that Nichols planned on sending off to some television show in Ottawa or Constantinople or Timbuktu or wherever. We—and by "we" I mean all the comics—were all thinking the same thing. If Mark didn't want to catch the eyes of the comedy gods and make us all famous, that precious Wonderboy Jack Marison most certainly would. No doubt about it. We counted on it. Absolutely counted on it. Every last one of us.

So that night, Barry Bass has this remarkable set. As good as I've ever seen him. He says goodbye to the crowd, and the emcee comes up and says something about the drink specials—about Marble Red and Pabst Blue Ribbon and kamikazes, something like that—and that some guy out of Phoenix headlines there at the end of the month. Fine, right? Well, anyway, Mark walks up on stage and goes into his opener. Something about how he was marching in the Gay Pride Parade and hit on a lesbian and she slugged him back. That gets a fabulous laugh. Absolute hysterics. Then a few minutes later, right in the middle of a bit, he freezes. Goes stiff. I thought the Fairy Godmother tapped him with her wand. He looks at something there in the back of the room.

That's when he slaps his beer glass off his stool and hurls the microphone against the wall. The lights flicker and, immediately, the room is swathed in darkness. Actual inky, palpable darkness. Then the stage lights flicker. Then, oh darling. Mark had transformed into the love child of Goliath and the Incredible Hulk. I swear to Shiva. I absolutely do. That monster just picks up the mic stand and swings it like a war club. He crashes it into a speaker. I have to cover my mouth and eyes, I am so shocked. Really, that's what I did. Someone screams. Mark yells. That's when Jonnie—even my big bruiser Jonnie Boy—gets totally horrified and flings me out of my seat and shoves me toward the door. I cover my eyes, and I'm crying, and when I open them again people are running up the aisle, like we were tear-gassed.

Well, next thing I know, the street and sidewalk out on Central Avenue are just carpeted with people. Through the thick walls and the doorway come the crashing and the echoing sounds of glass breaking and metal clanking.

I don't know how long we stood out there with people yelling and people crying and patrol cars squealing down Central Avenue. I swear, I couldn't stop weeping until after the ambulance crew drove up. I absolutely could not help myself.

What a mess. What a total, comprehensive, utter, absolute, un-qualified, unequivocal, God-awful, saturated mess.

HELEN DENISE

I did what I do every morning. I put the water on for tea, sat down in the breakfast nook, rolled the rubber band off that morning's *Albuquerque Journal*, and spread the newspaper out on the table. I found my reading glasses, scanned the headlines, and checked my horoscope—for fun, you know? When the kettle whistled, I filled my pot, letting my green tea steep, and sat down again, still in that terrycloth robe Jack got me for Christmas just that year. I sat there in my little corner by the window, where I like to watch the first sunrays of morning come peeking through the cottonwoods and reflecting in the puddles there in the backyard. How I do love watching the blue-and-orange ribbons just spilling all across the grass like that.

I folded over the last page of the A section and laid it against the vase of dried cattails. Then a photo caught my eye. I had to look twice and read through the caption four times for all the stuff in front of me to actually make any sense.

Mark's mugshot stared back at me from above the fold of the metro section, and something kicked deep in my gut, you know? Oh, I knew Mark came back to town. How couldn't I? After all that went on for almost three years? I mean, Albuquerque buzzed about the dear boy and the way he lit up the Duke City with his comedy. I even almost got all caught up in that madness myself. One time I even walked into that downtown bar—that place he used to perform—and bought two tickets to one of his shows. When the big night came, though, I just couldn't do it. I didn't know if Mark wanted to see me, especially if he had some special gal with him. And I wasn't sure if I wanted to see him. So I gave the tickets to Jack. And Jack, why, he gave them to a friend.

The news article told about how Mark tore apart Nichols' bar. How he ran everybody out of the place and caused twenty, maybe thirty thousand dollars' worth of damage in just a few minutes. What I didn't know about Mark's little tantrum that night is that, when he smashed the cameras, soundboard, and lighting panel in the sound booth, he also destroyed the video recorder that held three shows Jack just put together to send off to this Canadian television network.

I called Eddie from my office, trying to find out if he knew what happened, and Eddie, well, he offered to meet me for supper and tell me everything he knew. So that night we sat outside at this little French restaurant in Nob Hill. He told me about how he heard that Mark threatened the officers with the microphone stand, hurled the computer at them. That it took four policemen to wrestle him to the floor. And they cuffed him right there, with shattered bits of glass from the light bulbs and computer screen, the cords hanging off the electronic equipment, and bits of masonry and drywall all around him. Eddie wasn't sure what happened to set Mark off. I guess nobody really could be.

I burned with rage for months after that. How I hated Mark. For more than a year, really.

By the next October, though, a new thought settled in, and I knew exactly where it came from. It was as if, long ago, back during those college days, Mark planted this tiny little seed deep in my psyche. And it grew, sprouted, and bloomed—actually took on a life of its own. After a while, it was as if some angel whispered things in my ear, telling me that if I could have just another five-minute conversation with the dear boy, that I could understand the whole thing completely. Not just the way Mark tore up Nichol's bar, but everything that happened since that first tutoring session in the Frontier restaurant. And I just knew that if Mark understood what he did to Jack, why, he would find a way to put things right. I'm just so sure of that.

Then, I could forgive him.

And maybe, just maybe, he could forgive me.

You see, I never told Mark he had a son, and I never told Jack that Mark was his father. I didn't know what to tell Jack if he pressed the issue. But he never did.

But Mark. You see, Mark, he was a saint. Perhaps not in the way most people think of saints, but he was a saint just the same. But look at any saint. Peter, the rock upon whom Jesus built his church? Why, he was a coward, a braggart, a deceiver, a blowhard. James and John, the sons of Zebedee, why, Jesus called them "Sons of Thunder" because they were just so darned emotional. Saint Paul wrote to his followers saying, "What a wretched man I am." And his self-contempt just intensified after that famous conversion on the road to Damascus. Teresa of Avila had all these schizophrenic episodes. From time to time, the dear girl seemed totally detached from reality, seeing things that simply weren't there. Joan of Arc heard voices, just like she was some crazy derelict begging for quarters under some neon payday loan sign out there on Central Avenue. Augustine was a thief and a womanizer. Martin Luther King, why, he plagiarized part of his dissertation, and, like Gandhi, he slept with all these women, even after he was married. And just look at Siddhartha Gautama, the Buddha. A deadbeat daddy, by golly.

Even Jesus, I suppose, He was a little off, too. He was more than willing to go to this horrible death and to send other people to horrible deaths—to let Peter be crucified upside down and to let John be boiled in oil—all for the sake of something called "The Kingdom of God." And nobody even seemed to know what the heck he was talking about.

That's when it hit me. Maybe that's the real message of the Bible. That we're all just so deeply flawed that we have no choice but to depend on each other. That our failings are just part of our perfection.

Well, over the course of those few months—maybe even years, really—I just grew into this new kind of understanding. Mark getting on stage all those times like he did wasn't just about making people laugh and being true to himself, although that was certainly a big part of it. I mean, Mark had to be true to himself. That's the way he was wired. But after a while it came clear to me that Mark truly believed that, one day, something special might just happen. His father would walk into the showroom and be struck dumb the second Mark spoke from the stage. And Mark, he felt right down to the core of his being that if that happened, the man would be so overwhelmed that he would have no choice but to come and introduce himself. Perhaps even stroke his face the way Lola did that time at the Albuquerque Wine Festival. Of course, the odds against it were astronomical.

But Mark always believed in the unbelievable. That was his demon.

Saints, they're always so deeply flawed. Always. And Mark, why, he was no different.

JACK

The Neanderthal at table thirteen pounds on the polished oak with an open hand, causing the forks to rattle and water to slosh over the lip of one of the glasses. He goes all mental because he waited twenty minutes for his food, and when it came, one of his egg yolks was broken and cooked through solid. Like that would kill him. The guy's all unshaven with gray stubble, and his mouth gets all twisted, like he consciously cultivates that whole "creepy alcoholic" look. So I'm all apologetic, and I tell him I'll get the cook to fix it right up, but the inbred says to forget it, to just forget it. At that, he whips his napkin on the table, slides out of the booth, and orders his stringy-haired cadaver of a wife to follow him.

What a dope.

Since I have the platter of huevos rancheros in my hand already, I figure I'll just carry it to the back and maybe that will allow our lethargic busboy to get this table cleared a little faster. As I get to the kitchen, however, Aris—this big Greek guy about a thousand years older than the rest of us—yells something over at the dishwasher and flings open the swinging door with a flick of his forearm. The aluminum panel smacks me square on the knuckle, kicks up the plate right against my chest. Red chile sauce, refried pinto beans, fried potatoes, melted cheese, and one gelatinous yoke drip down my shirt and apron, so hot it just about singes off my chest hairs right through my shirt.

Aris stands in front of me, his mouth all hanging open, the guy too stunned to deal out the apology. All I say is "goddamnit" or something like that. I let the platter drop to the tile and rattle like a coin, and I walk down to the break room, leaving the mess on the floor for him to clean up. There I take off my apron, crumple it, and use it to mop the goop off my chest, stomach, and groinal area. When I get myself as clean as I can, I ball up the black sailcloth and slam it into the trash can. I consider, for about a millionth of second, grabbing a fresh apron out of the supply closet and hustling back to the floor. But I imagine myself serving runny eggs to another slurring barhound, this one complaining about cold coffee, dirty silverware, or undercooked home fries. So instead, I tear my jacket off its hanger. The springy wire rattles on the rack as I push open the metal back door and step out onto the concrete delivery dock. I figure that for the next five or ten minutes the customers in my station can just wait. Or the boss can get somebody else to deliver them their nitrate and trans-fat-laden grease bombs.

The night is peaceful enough, thank God. It is warm for Denver in October, but it is still cool enough that the air, perfumed with a scent of decaying elm and maple leaves, calms me down a little. Over on Colfax Avenue, cars whiz by about five hundred miles an hour. I figure they carry mostly drunks, since the bars are just closing. Up near the stop light, an old Chevy creaks along the shoulder at about two miles an hour, its hazard lights going all schizoid. Its driver cranks the engine, which groans, whines, releases this hoarsy squeal, and gives up. Whoever is at the wheel waits a few seconds before giving it another go. Once again, the engine summons up everything it's got. Still not enough.

A breeze kicks up, and I scratch my head. The back door sweeps open just as my phone beeps and buzzes somewhere deep in the folded fleece on my lap. I figure if the boss woman comes out all ragging me again, I'll tell her that this is my third double shift in four nights, and if she's got a problem with me taking a break, she can just send me packing. That will leave her in the lurch for the rest of the night and probably all of Sunday. I figure I got a little protection from her wrath.

So I don't even look. Instead, I flip open the handset and check the messages that came in over the last couple of hours. The first is from Mica Pierson, who this week is doing his first feature spot at the Tempe Improv. He tells me he's headlining Minot, North Dakota, in three weeks, and that the guy who was featuring for him just canceled. The gig pays three hundred dollars for four nights, plus a room, drinks, and meals, and I can have it if I want it. I text back, telling him that of course I want it, but I have to see if I can get the time off, and that it'll take me a couple of days to get back on the boss's good side.

As I finish punching in the letters, I realize that right in front of me stands Aris, that nine-thousand-pound circus strongman who just minutes before made my already bad night about ten thousand times worse. He has shiny, black, wavy hair and a big old cleft in that monstrous chin. He wraps one of those gigantic hands around the painted iron railing in front of me, and he looks all sensitive-like. He brushes his hair from his eyes and gives me this meek, sideways nod. I ask what he wants before I turn back to my handset and press the "send" button.

"I just gotta say, I really wanna say," the oaf says and points—with his chin—at the brown and yellow stains on the front of my shirt. "It's just that we were out of juice glasses, and that new dishwasher guy was supposed to find some for me. I shoulda been looking where I was going, if you wanna know the truth."

I wave him off. "This is an old shirt, anyway," I say. "I think I got it from the Salvation Army Thrift Store about a million years ago."

That's a lie. I scroll through my text bank.

I ask Aris what's going on inside Grace's Big Fifty Diner. He says it looks like the rush is over.

The next message, this one from Jana Boan, does little to help my spirits. She tells me she just secured a spot at the Comedy Store in Los Angeles. Then, either wittingly or not, she twists the dagger.

> Heard Wladika just played The Ice House up in Pasadena. Barry Bass saw the poster when he featured there. Under the name Marcus Williams or something. Said it sure looked like him.

I peck in a response, and just as I send it on its way, Aris says something about it being such a beautiful night, especially since it is so close to Halloween. That it looks like the storm missed us. Then, trying to be all conversational, asks what I am doing out here.

"Nothing," I say. Then words flow out of their own volition, as if they chose to speak themselves. "Just fantasizing about stabbing some dude in his amygdala."

I chuckle.

The gentle giant's eyes narrow. He does not understand. I tell him to forget it. I unzip the side pocket of my North Face fleece and fish out my hash pipe, one I found in an old chest of drawers my mother's friend gave me. It's a well-crafted number, fashioned out of green Coca-Cola glass, with red-and-white paint swirls worked into the translucence, and looks like it is a thousand years old. Out of the other pocket I dig out a prescription pill bottle about half full of some decent medium-grade. I crumble the leaves into the bowl, pack it down with the tip of my little finger, and ask Aris if he has a lighter. He finds a book of matches in his apron pocket and holds it out. I take it, tear off one, scratch up a flame, and light up. I take a long, slow toke and exhale a stream of blue smoke. Aris looks down at me, all serious. Like he's judging me.

"Oh, where are my manners?" I say. "Want some?"

He glances at the painted metal door and then down the street, as if worried the cops are watching. Then down to the main street where two guys push the inert Chevy toward the parking lot of Grace's Big Fifty.

"Guess so," he says. "Been a while."

"Like riding a bicycle," I say. "Once you learn how, you know?"

My telephone shakes, illuminates, and lets loose with another *boo-boop*. I flip it open. This message is from Firecracker Rael, who is headlining Crazy Geri's in Tucson.

> Black Tom said that someone looking like Wladika
> headlined the El Paso club last week of Sept.—thought
> you'd wanna know. Love ya, Gorgeous. Cheers!

Aris coughs and I tell him to take it easy, not to take the smoke in too fast. He covers his whole mouth with one of those infielder's mitts he has for hands and, with the other, holds the pipe out to me. I take it, reignite, and indulge in another long, slow drag. From somewhere over the city comes the beating of helicopter blades. Aris looks over his shoulder, toward the sound.

The words spill out of my mouth. "You ever think about killing somebody? I mean, you ever think about just wiping somebody from the face of existence?"

That goon rakes his fingers through his hair, trying to get a stubborn hook of a curl away from his eye. He doesn't quite know what to make of this, either. So I go on.

"I mean, you ever wonder what it would be like just to extinguish someone. To consciously blot someone right out of time and space. To make him a memory?"

The Greek scratches his chin. He glances over at the stoplight way up on Colfax. It changes to green. He shakes his head. At first, I think this is his answer. Then I get it. He doesn't understand the question. So I go on.

"I am not talking about the violence it would take to do that. I am talking about just causing someone to no longer be, you know? Just blotting him out forever."

I take a hit and hand over the hash pipe, which looks like a toy in his cigar-sized fingers. He scrunches up his face, and at first I think it's because the herb is too strong. It turns out, though, that he still has no clue as to what I'm saying.

"Forget it," I say.

He sucks in some smoke, this time taking care to be more prudent.

Out on the main drag, a Mazda races by, the driver revving the engine and cutting to the near lane. His buddy, in some kind of expensive coupe, chases after.

Things quiet right before Aris pipes up.

"To tell you the truth," he says and looks down the street and then up toward downtown, where the police aircraft comes into view, its taillight blinking and the searchlight beam at its nose scouring the hills for some particularly elusive criminal. "When I was fifteen, out in Chicago, this tough guy called Lionel—actually, one of my homeboys—gets it in his head that I'm getting too high and mighty. Decides to bring me down a notch. So one night I walk home from working at the pizza parlor, through the park. I come around a line of trees, pass in front of a stone bench and brick restroom booths, and there, waiting in ambush, are Lionel and one of his henchmen. Five minutes later, I got Lionel by his ponytail, and I'm ramming his bloody forehead into a stone wall. So, yeah. Right then, right there. Not only thought about killing, I thought I done it. Not ten minutes later, I'm in the back of a police car thinking I'm gonna be in prison, dying of old age. God's honest truth."

"So what came of it?"

"Old Lionel? He recovered. He always swore up and down he was gonna get me back, but never did nothing. Became some fancy accountant down in Saint Louis. Me? That little episode cost me fourteen months in juvy. Once I got out, Dad sent me down here to live with my aunt."

"That's a brutal story," I say.

"I was young and dopey," he says. "Full of something to prove. Didn't even know what it was." He folds his hands on the iron railing and rests his chin on them. "But while I was doing time, my cellmate starts telling me about the dharma. Has me reading about the Buddhist sutras. Has me sitting, doing the conscious breathing thing, twice a day. I'm not nearly the powder keg I used to be."

The rat-a-tat-tat of the helicopter blades gets closer, that mechanical insect floating over the trees, the searchlight on its front checking every nook, cranny, and shadow.

"So," he says, laying open his oversized hand, asking for the pipe. "Gimme the truth. Who ya thinking of eighty-sixing?"

"It's a long story," I say and pull my leg up to my chest. "But when I find him, well. And I will find him. I don't care if it takes ten thousand years. Well, let's just say that I hope you write me letters when I'm rotting there on death row."

Aris smiles, breaks into a chuckle. He studies my face and realizes I mean what I say. He goes silent and cocks his head again. He runs his hand through his hair and searches over the trees for that police aircraft, which has disappeared somewhere behind us.

"Whoa-kay," he says and tugs down his apron, straightening it. "Maybe we should go back in and tackle these last ninety minutes." He runs his fingers through his hair. The incorrigible curl falls back over his eye. "Whattaya say?" He extends his softball bat of an arm. Pulls me to a stand. I tell him that I have eye drops and cinnamon gum in my car. We should at least pretend we have the courtesy to hide the evidence. I say I'll need a second before I go back in.

Walking back across the parking lot, I open my phone and punch in a message to Mica, telling him I'll take the Minot gig. The old crow can fire me if she wants.

Two minutes later, there in that narrow passage between the coffee station and the silverware stand, I take a second to enjoy my buzz as I shake out a fresh apron and look over the clientele. Some surfer boy in a V-neck, leaning in, giving his sales pitch to some hot redhead who tells him she needs to get home. At the booth behind them, a Navajo-looking woman sits, and her fat chin jiggles with laughter. She seems so totally amused by her date, a blond guy with a crew cut. Behind them sit three guys in white shirts and thin black neckties, Latter Day Saints or Jehovah's Witnesses or something, with a tattered Bible—or maybe a Book of Mormon—at the edge of their table. Guys who are definitely up past their bedtime. Next to them, a bunch of high school kids in T-shirts, and across the way, a man in his seventies spears a triangle of a sausage patty with his fork and sits in silence, as if he's run out of things to say to the blue-haired woman sitting across from him. Once more I study the body shapes, the facial expressions, the mannerisms of everybody around me, making absolutely sure that not one of them is Wladika.

I know I'll stay on the lookout for as long as it takes. But, one of these days, I am going to be walking through an airport, waiting at a train terminal, sitting at a bar, checking into a motel, or working the road, and I am going to look over.

And next to me will be that bastard.

EDDIE

Mystery makes up ninety-six percent of the universe.

The other four percent is made up of atoms and molecules, things you can see and touch. Our best scientists refer to the mysterious substance as "dark energy" and "dark matter" because all they know about it is that it has mass and, for some reason, won't interact with light. Even if you rolled a clump of it in your palm, you couldn't see it. Yet, without it, galaxies would fly apart like confetti shot out of a cannon.

Mark Wladika told me this that night we built a campfire in my backyard. As we talked, he laid a thin elm branch across his lap, inspected the V at one end, lifted out the blade of his penknife, and whittled one of the ends into a point. He tilted the branch toward the fire, inspected the cuts, and then worked the other tip until it had two sharp prongs.

He talked on, saying that astrophysicists see this dark stuff as the glue that keeps galaxies and star clusters in order.

"To mystics, however," he said, "the mysterious substance is the webwork of creation, the bands of cosmic energy that, like the force of empty space that holds the electron in orbit around an atomic nucleus, suggest to them that a loving, healing, and creative intelligence thrives at the center of it all. It is emptiness alive with spirit. Call it the breath of God, for lack of a better term."

To him, Mark said, it is the field of Pure Potentiality, that endless pool of the rawest of raw materials. The stuff that gives volume and expanse to our values, perceptions, thoughts, actions, ideas, and, consequently, the material world.

"There are only two real miracles in all of history," he said. "The first is that there is something rather than nothing. That anything even exists at all. The second is individual human consciousness."

At that, he reached into the plastic tub on the bench between us, fished a hot dog out of the ice water, and shoved the naked points into the pink meat. He set his forearms on his knees and held the stick over the fire, and his face blazed with reflected orange light. I took a bottle of red ale from the ice bucket behind me and pried off the cap.

"Tell me," he said, "that these two great marvels are not part of the same divine ordination. That they were not meant to work together. It is the job of humans to think, to imagine, to create, to generate these things called ideas, and to fashion these thoughts into the substance of life. When we do that, the universe becomes more conscious of itself. It does so through us. So you'd better think big thoughts."

He went on. Is that stuff, that dark matter and dark energy, the Tao, that force which Lao-Tzu referred to as the "Mother of the Ten Thousand Things"? Was it out of this field that Yahweh first summoned the earth and stars with that initial proclamation "Let there be light"? Is it the Word that, according to John's gospel, was in the Beginning?

"Just asking," he said.

He held the hot dog up to his face, lifted his glasses over his eyebrows, and inspected the end. He pinched a piece of ash off the skin and wiped it on his jeans.

Over against the Sandia Mountains, a jetliner drifted along the slant of the eastern sky, the red speck of a landing light growing dim and then brightening again, the aircraft floating by so slowly, looking as though the pilot were in no particular hurry. Soot collected in streaks on the underside of the frankfurter.

"At the very least," he said, "isn't this a potent metaphor? I mean, just think about it. God speaks. With the simple pronouncement 'Let there be light,' the divine draws the molecular world into creation, an action that Adam echoes when he names the flora and fauna of Eden, when he identifies all of those objects that surround him. God summons the universe into the light of existence, pulls it out of the darkness of the cosmic void, into the light of Being. Adam continues the act, actually imitates the process, calling the objects of his world into the illumination of consciousness by the simple act of pointing and naming. Nothing exists until you can name it, you know? What do they say, that language is the house of Being?

"Go ahead, Eddie," he said. "Tell me what you think of all this."

I took a long swig. Something in one of the burning piñon logs popped, and sparks scattered on the dirt and lay there like luminescent bits of sand. I poked the center of the inferno with a metal andiron, turning over a log and holding it in place. A flame crawled up its side.

I shook my head. "I don't know," I said.

Mark went on.

"Just think about what happened with the Wright Brothers. Did the ability for human flight exist before they summoned it into existence?

310

Of course it did. It had to. That ability lay dormant in this Field of Pure Potentiality for all those millennia before two bicycle mechanics teased out the ideas and brought to the equation the wherewithal to work those imaginings out in wood, fabric, and metal. To fashion something the rest of us could see and touch. In exactly the same way, the notes of Beethoven's *Ninth Symphony*, the words of Shakespeare's *Macbeth*, the capability to send documents thousands of miles through the air from one computer to another, to send a rocket to Saturn—all that stuff hid in the ether until someone with enough talent, tenacity, and perspicacity could summon it, translate it into something empirical. That's the way it is with every idea you ever had, with every joke you ever told, every lecture on the Gospel of John that you ever gave, every word you ever wrote. That's the way it is. So please, hand me an ale."

I fished around in the ice for another bottle, popped off the top, and handed it to him. I tossed the cap into the flames.

We talked out by that fire for another four hours, until at least three in the morning. As he spoke, a speck of light appeared in the sky above us. A shooting star streaking, arcing, and finally disappearing over the western hills.

That was our last real conversation.

That final lesson, that last bit of wisdom he bestowed, has stayed with me this whole time. It is as though it hovers over my shoulder constantly, always glowing in the very recent past, always like I just heard it for the first time a few days prior—never mind that he said it just before he disappeared so long ago.

These days, I can only believe that it is out of that very substance, that dark matter, that Mark told me about that night that I have drawn my own residence, a pueblo-style home in Northwest Albuquerque, in a neighborhood not very far from either the Rio Grande or my childhood home. This 2,233-square-foot adobe built in 1959 is rather simple. A master bedroom, a living room where I read and sometimes write, a guest bedroom that, more often than not these days, we reserve for my stepson, who visits us from Denver two or three times a year. On the other side, a study that doesn't get as much use as it should. The residence is tasteful but hardly extravagant. As you enter, a chest-high vase filled with dried flowers sits by the front door. The entryway is painted soft brown, the color of mocha ice cream. Then, the colors draw you in even deeper. The next wall you see, that of the hallway that leads you into the living room, shimmers like a ripe eggplant. The far wall, over by the French doors, is the color of avocado flesh. Visitors instantly feel welcome and comfortable here. They seldom understand why.

Nothing like a woman's touch.

It is Tuesday night, and the clock on the microwave tells me it is just after eleven. I open the cabinet over the stove island and remove a bottle, uncork, pour myself a shot of Black Maple Hill over a single ice cube, add a splash of water from the filtering pitcher, pick my book off the counter, and head back to the living room. There, in my chair, I cross one leg over the other and rest the book against my knee. The cover is tattered, torn pieces now held together with yellowed strips of cellophane tape. I read the inscription written in jagged cursive, the ink so faded that some of the letters are gone completely:

I meant it. Good luck with that whole sacred literature thing you got going.

Tonight, I intend to go over, for about the eightieth time, a passage that always fascinates me:

In the beginning was the Word, and the Word was with God, and the Word was God. He was in the beginning with God. All things came into being through him, and without him not one thing came into being. What has come into being in him was life, and the life was the light of all the people. The light shines in the darkness, and the darkness did not overcome it.

Before I switch on the reading lamp, however, I sit in silence, wondering what my best friend might be doing at that moment. I wonder if he ever returned to San Francisco, and if he ever found his father. I lay the book in my lap and raise the glass under my nose.

I take another sip of bourbon, and the hum of a six-cylinder engine approaches. The car turns the corner, and headlamps shoot light through the curtain sheers, sending daisy-shaped shadows stretching and contorting across the near wall, sliding and bending past the corner before they fade. Then, once more, the room is dark.

I switch on the light and read. A minute or so later, something crunches the gravel in the driveway, and a car engine idles and goes quiet just the other side of the picture window. The short and violent *klernk* of a slammed car door follows, and so I turn off the lamp, step over to the window, push aside the curtain, and look out, my index finger in my book, holding my place.

Out in the driveway, Mark stands with his hands in his pockets, his lips puckered in a silent whistle as he surveys the area, our house, the neighbor's yard, and the cat slinking along the five-foot adobe wall on the other side of the street. His paunch is a little bigger, his shirt a little looser than I remember. He looks over the snaking cracks in the buckled pads of the concrete sidewalk, the smashed weeds working their way through the asphalt. I laugh to myself and turn, ready to go into the bedroom and announce that we have a visitor. I check again, just to make sure.

It is not what I thought.

The driver actually remains in the car. Whoever it is switches off his dome light, looks over his shoulder, waits for a truck to rumble past, and backs the car out of the driveway, going back the way he came.

Just some dark-haired kid who got lost and needed to check directions on his smart phone. I wonder why I keep imagining such crazy things.

So I go back to my chair to finish my whiskey in the dark. I cannot help but see my best friend exactly the way he looked that night during our senior year of high school when he fashioned the hash pipe of the Coca-Cola bottle. The way he leaned toward the blue flame shooting out the nozzle of an acetylene torch mounted onto his father's workbench. The way sweat matted the hair on the side of his head as he concentrated on the indentation he bore into the elastic and molten glass. I sip my bourbon and let out a single chuckle, when a voice from the other side of the room pricks the bubble of my reverie.

"You fixin' on stayin' out here all night long?"

The voice is soft, crystalline, smooth. Very Texan. Helen Denise, in one of my cotton T-shirts worn so thin it reveals the point of her nipple and the rise and darkness of her areola, leans against the bookshelf, her hand gripping the thick mahogany, her cheek against the polished wood, as if she's enjoying its coolness. A shoot of strawberry-blonde hair hangs over her eye. She tucks it behind her ear.

She covers a yawn with the back of her hand and says, "You don't seem to be doing too much readin."

That lithe little body. She steps over and reaches, takes my hand with both of hers, pulls me out of the chair to a stand, and leads me down the hallway.

No, it wasn't Mark. Not this time, either. I really don't know why I keep imagining such crazy things. Still, I know that—one of these days—he's going to show up.

ABOUT THE AUTHOR

Eddie Tafoya grew up scurrying like a beetle through the dust, streetgrime, alleyways, and lavender dawns of Albuquerque's Old Town, Downtown, and Uptown. Educated in Albuquerque's parochial schools, the University of New Mexico, and Binghamton University, he has made a lifetime study of things comical, biblical, philosophical, verbal, and mystical. Since 1996, he has been a fixture in the Department of English and Philosophy at New Mexico Highlands University, where he teaches classes in creative writing, the New Testament as revolutionary literature, and stand-up comedy as literature. He lectures around the Southwest on the history, theory, and impact of American comedy and, when time allows, works as a stand-up comedian, a venture that has taken him to various venues from Wisconsin to Arizona and to feature spots on television shows like *The After After Party with Steven Michael Quezada* and *The Duke City Comedy League*. He also appears in Sean Saul's 2012 documentary, *Alone Up There: A Journey to Understand Stand-up Comedy*.

His other books include *The Legacy of the Wisecrack: Stand-up Comedy as the Great American Literary Form* and *Icons of African American Comedy*. He lives, writes, and teaches in Las Vegas, New Mexico.

www.ingramcontent.com/pod-product-compliance
Lightning Source LLC
Chambersburg PA
CBHW050551260626
47157CB00002B/517